THE CRIMSON SHIELD

GALLOW
THE CRIMSON
SHIELD

NATHAN HAWKE

The right of Nathan Hawke to be identified as the author
of this work has been asserted by him in accordance with the
Copyright, Designs and Patents Act 1988.

First published in Great Britain in 2013
by Gollancz
An imprint of the Orion Publishing Group
Orion House, 5 Upper St Martin's Lane, London WC2H 9EA
An Hachette UK Company

This edition published in Great Britain in 2013 by Gollancz

1 3 5 7 9 10 8 6 4 2

A CIP catalogue record for this book
is available from the British Library

ISBN 978 0 575 11508 8

Typeset by Deltatype Ltd, Birkenhead, Merseyside

Printed and bound by CPI Group (UK) Ltd, Croydon, CR0 4YY

The Orion Publishing Group's policy is to use papers
that are natural, renewable and recyclable products and
made from wood grown in sustainable forests. The logging
and manufacturing processes are expected to conform to the
environmental regulations of the country of origin.

www.orionbooks.co.uk

Also by Nathan Hawke

Gallow: The Crimson Shield
Gallow: Cold Redemption
Gallow: The Last Bastion

Honour has not to be won, it must only not be lost

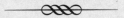

The Vathen rode slowly through the ruins of the village. There was little left. Burned-out huts, not much else. They stopped at the edge, at what had once been a forge, and one of them dismounted and poked through the rubble. Whatever had been done here, it had been a while ago.

'The forkbeards call themselves men of fate.' She said it without much feeling one way or the other, as if noting that the clouds had turned a little darker and perhaps more rain was on the way.

'This is a Marroc village,' said one of the others with a voice that was keen to push on.

'Yes,' said the first. 'But a forkbeard lived here once. They called him Gallow. Gallow the Foxbeard.'

SCREAMBREAKER

1

THE VATHEN

Beside him Sarvic turned to run. A Vathan spear reached for him. Gallow chopped it away; and then he was slipping back and the whole line was falling apart and the Vathen were pressing forward, pushed by the ranks behind them, stumbling over the bodies of the fallen.

For a moment the dead slowed them. Gallow turned and threw himself away from the Vathan shields. The earth under his feet was slick, ground to mud by the press of boots and watered with blood and sweat. A spear point hit him in the back like a kick from a horse. He staggered and slipped but kept on running as fast as he could. If the blow had pierced his mail he'd find out soon enough. The rest of the Marroc were scattering, fleeing down the back of the hill with the roars of the Vathen right behind. Javelots and stones rained around him but he didn't look back. Didn't dare, not yet.

He slowed for a moment to tuck his axe into his belt and scoop up a discarded spear. The Vathen had horsemen and a man with a spear could face a horse; and when at last he did snatch a glance over his shoulder, there they were, cresting the hill. They'd scythe through the fleeing Marroc and not one in ten would reach the safety of the trees because they were running in panic, not turning to face their enemy as they should. He'd seen all this before. The Vathen were good with their horses.

Sarvic was pelting empty-handed down the hill ahead of

him. They'd never met before today and had no reason to be friends, but they'd stood together in the wall of shields and they'd both survived. Gallow caught him as the first Vathan rider drew back an arm to throw his javelot. He hurled himself at Sarvic's legs, tumbling them both down the slope of the hill. Gallow rolled away, turned and rose to a crouch behind his shield. Other men had dropped theirs as they ran but that was folly.

The javelot hit his shield and almost knocked him over. Another rider galloped towards them. At the last moment Gallow raised his spear. The Vathan saw it too late. The point caught him in the belly and the other end wedged into the dirt and the rider flew out of his saddle, screaming, the spear driven right through him before the shaft snapped clean in two. Gallow wrenched the javelot from his shield. He forced another into Sarvic's hand. There were plenty to be had. 'Running won't help you.'

More Vathen poured over the hill. Another galloped past and hurled his javelot, rattling Gallow's shield. Gallow searched around, wild-eyed and frantic for any shelter. Further down the hill a knot of Marroc had held their nerve long enough to make a circle of spears. He raced towards them now, dragging Sarvic with him as the horsemen charged past. The shields opened to let him in and closed around him. He was a part of it without even thinking.

'Wall and spears!' *Valaric?* A fierce hope came with having men beside him again, shields locked together, even if they were nothing but a handful.

Another wave of Vathan horse swarmed past. The Marroc crouched in their circle, spears out like a hedgehog, poking over their shields. The horsemen thundered on. There were easier prey to catch but they threw their javelots anyway as they passed. The Marroc beside Gallow screamed and pitched forward.

'You taught us this, Gallow, you Lhosir bastard,' Valaric

swore. 'Curse these stunted hedge-born runts! Keep your shields high and your spears up and keep together, damn you!'

The Vathan foot soldiers were charging now, roaring and whooping. As the last riders passed, the circle of Marroc broke and sprinted for the woods. The air was hot and thick. Sweat trickled into Gallow's eyes. The grass on the hill had been trampled flat and now gleamed bright in the sun. Bodies littered the ground close to the trees, scattered like armfuls of broken dolls where the Vathan horse had caught the Marroc rout. Hundreds of them pinned to the earth with javelots sticking up from their backs. There were Lhosir bodies too among the Marroc. Valaric pointed at one and laughed. 'Not so invincible, eh?'

They reached the shadows of the wood and paused, gasping. Behind them the battlefield spread up the hill, dead men strewn in careless abandon. Crows already circled, waiting for the Vathen to finish so they could get on with some looting of their own. The moans and cries of the dying mixed with the shouts and hurrahs of the victors. Before long the dead would be stripped bare and the Vathen would move on.

'Got to keep moving,' Gallow said.

'Shut your hole, forkbeard! They won't follow us here.' Valaric picked up his shield. He kicked a couple of Marroc who'd crouched against trees to catch their breath, glared at Sarvic and headed off again at a run. 'A pox on you!' he said as Gallow fell in step beside him. 'They'll move right on to Fedderhun and quick. They don't care about us.'

But they still ran, a hard steady pace along whatever game trails they could find, putting as much distance as they could between them and the Vathen. Valaric only slowed when they ran out into a meadow surrounded by trees and by then they must have been a couple of miles from the battle. Far enough. The Marroc were gasping and soaked in sweat but they weren't dead. There wouldn't be many who'd stood in the shield wall on Lostring Hill who could say that.

The grass was up to their knees and filled with spring flowers and the air was alive with a heady scent. 'Should be good enough,' Valaric muttered. 'We rest here for a bit then.' He threw a snarl at Gallow. 'This is the end of us now, forkbeard. After here it's each to his own way, and you're not welcome any more.'

'Will you go to Fedderhun, Valaric?'

Valaric snorted. 'There's no walls. What's the point? Fedderhun's a fishing town. The Vathen will either burn it or they won't and nothing you or I can do will change that. If your Lhosir prince wants a fight with the Vathen, I'll be seeing to it that it's not me and mine whose lives get crushed between you. I'll be with my family.'

There wasn't much to say to that. Old wounds were best left be. Gallow's own children weren't so many miles away either. And Arda; and they'd be safe if the Vathen went on to Fedderhun. He touched a hand to his chest and to the locket that hung on a chain around his neck, warm against his skin, buried beneath leather and mail. He could have been with them now, not here in a wood and stinking of sweat and blood. 'I'm one of you now,' he said, as much to himself as to Valaric.

Valaric snorted. 'You're never that, forkbeard.'

Gallow set down his spear and his shield and took off his helm, letting the air dry the sweat from his skin. 'It's still your land, Valaric.'

But Valaric shook his head. 'Not any more.'

2

VALARIC

'Not any more.' Valaric spat. Four hundred men. King Yurlak had sent four hundred forkbeards to fight ten thousand Vathen, and no one, not even a crazy forkbeard, was that terrible. The fools on the hill were always going to break. He'd seen that from the moment he'd seen the Vathen and how many they were – and it grated, thinking that if every man standing on the top of Lostring Hill this morning had been a Lhosir forkbeard then they just might have held the line, even outnumbered as they were, and maybe it *would* have been the Vathen who'd broken and fled. Maybe. Because Yurlak hadn't just sent four hundred men. He'd sent the Screambreaker, the Widowmaker, the Nightmare of the North, and the Widowmaker had called the Marroc to arms and Valaric had been stupid enough to believe in him because a dozen years ago Valaric had been on the wrong end of the Widowmaker and his forkbeards four times, one after the other, and each time the Marroc had had the numbers and Valaric had been certain that the Widowmaker couldn't possibly win, and each time he had. A man, he reckoned, ought to learn from a thing like that.

Out of the shadows of the trees a Vathan rider stepped into the clearing. Valaric froze for a moment but the rider was slumped in his saddle. He had blood all over him and he was clearly dead. Half his face was missing.

'Well, well. An unwanted horse. Now there's a blessing.' He grinned at the other Marroc around him. He'd picked

11

them carefully, the ones who'd fight hard and long and keep their wits. Torvic, the three Jonnics, Davic, all men who'd fought the forkbeards years ago and lived, even towards the end when the forkbeards had hired Vathan mercenaries with their plundered gold and sent them in after the Marroc lines broke. The Marroc were used to running away by then, but not from horses. Thousands of men dead. And here he was not ten years later: same forkbeards, same Vathen, only now the forkbeards claimed they were his friends. Valaric was having none of it.

The other Marroc were on their feet now. They were all thinking the same thing. All of them except the forkbeard Gallow, who'd keep quiet if he had any sense. Valaric got to the horse first. He took the reins and hauled the dead Vathan out of the saddle.

'So let's see what we've got, lads.' He left the body to the others and started going through the saddlebags. Food and water they'd share since none of them carried any. A rare piece of good fortune. Someone else's horse and saddle were fine things to carry away from a battle even after a victory. They'd have to divide it somehow. Needed a care that did. He'd seen men kill each other over spoils like this, men who'd fought side by side only hours before.

'There are more.' Gallow was pointing off into the trees on the other side of the clearing.

Valaric growled. He let go of the horse and slipped his sword into his hand and picked up his shield where he'd left it in the grass. 'Men? Or just horses?'

'Horses.'

Horses was more like it. But still ... He looked around the other Marroc. They all had a greedy look to them, but nervous too. 'Right. You lot stay here. Keep on the edge of the trees. Shields and spears ready in case. Me and the fork-beard, we'll go see what's there.' He took a long hard look at Gallow. He was tall – certainly compared to a Marroc, and maybe even tall among his own kind – and broad. His muscles might be hidden beneath mail and thick leather, but the man had been a soldier for years and worked in a forge before and after, and there was no such thing as a weak-armed smith. His face was strong-boned and weathered. Valaric supposed there'd be some who'd say it was handsome if it hadn't been for the scar running across one cheek and the dent in his nose that went with it. He didn't have the forked beard of a Lhosir any more, but Valaric's eyes saw it anyway. *Demon-beards.* Thick black hair that didn't mark him as anything much one way or the other, but eyes of the palest blue like mountain glaciers. Lhosir eyes, cold and pitiless and deadly. Valaric cocked his head. 'You man for that?'

Gallow didn't blink, just nodded, which made Valaric want to hit him. They stood face to face. Gallow looked down at him. Those ice-filled eyes *were* piercing, but Valaric didn't see the things he was looking for there. Forkbeards were merciless, filled with hate and rage – that's how they'd been on the battlefield – but Gallow's eyes were just sad and weary. They had a longing to them.

'You can go back to your own kind after this,' he said shortly and brushed past on into the trees, eyes alert for the horses Gallow had seen. He picked up two of them straight away, two more Vathan ones, riderless this time. Probably they'd followed the first. If there were more, so much the better.

'I have a family, Valaric,' said Gallow. 'A wife and an old man and two young sons and a daughter. Those are my people now, and yes, I'll go back to them. I don't know these Vathen but they'll head west for Andhun. If that falls then who knows what they'll do? Maybe they're set on making new kings and cities and will leave my village alone. Or maybe they're the sort to swarm across the country with their horses and their swords, with burning torches, sweeping everything before them until nothing is left.'

'Two young sons and a daughter, eh?' Valaric couldn't keep the bitterness out of his voice. 'Sounds like you've been busy since you finished raping and murdering and settled to the business of breaking our backs for the pleasure of your king.'

Gallow didn't answer. Didn't care, most likely, and the thought flashed through Valaric's head to kill him right there and then while the two of them were alone. None of the others would think any less of him for doing it. They'd all lost something when the forkbeards had come across the sea in their sharp-faced boats. He had no idea why Gallow had stayed. Married a local girl, a smith's daughter, and that alone was enough for Valaric to hate him. *Our land, not yours.* Nine years ago that was, when everyone had hated the forkbeards and everything they stood for; but over those years the world had slowly changed. Everyone in these parts had come to hear of the forkbeard who hadn't gone home. Maybe he even had friends now, but for Valaric time had healed nothing. Gallow wasn't welcome. None of them were.

'There.'

Among the trees in the shade Valaric saw the shapes of more horses. A dozen maybe, one for each of them to ride and a few spare. Good coin if they could get to a place where they could sell them. Changed things, that did. Not so much chance of a squabble over the spoils. The battle was going to give him a decent purse after all – which wasn't why he'd come to fight it, but a man still had to live.

Gallow pressed ahead through the trees to the horses, his hand staying close to his axe. He moved quickly but with cautious feet. Valaric let him go ahead while he tied up the first two animals and then ran after him. Couldn't let a forkbeard take the best of the pickings, but by then Gallow had stopped. When Valaric caught up, he saw why.

'Modris!' Cursing the old god's name was the only thing left to do.

There were bodies everywhere. More horses too, a lot of them with their Vathan riders still slumped on their backs. The bodies on the ground were mostly forkbeards. Valaric took it all in and nodded to the dead. He pointed through the trees, roughly back towards the battlefield. 'Forkbeards were riding through the forest. The Vathen got ahead of them. They encircled them and took your friends from the front and from behind.'

Gallow nodded. 'The Lhosir made a stand rather than run. They dismounted because that's how we like to fight. Like you, with our feet on the earth. The trees made that work for them. No one ever thought of running. Not our way.'

'The Vathen stayed in their saddles. Maybe that wasn't so clever of them.' There were a lot more dead Vathen than forkbeards. One of them had an arrow sticking out of his chest. Valaric saw it and frowned: the forkbeards almost never used bows in battle. Arrows were for hunting or for cowards, but someone had used one here. For once not losing had mattered more than how they fought.

'They were protecting something,' he whispered.

Gallow was staring around the corpses of his own people. He nodded. 'These were the Screambreaker's men.' He walked slowly among them, axe drawn, eyes darting back and forth among the shadows.

'A pretty sight. Forkbeards and Vathen killing each other. My heart soars.' Valaric didn't feel it though, not here. He'd told himself that he and Gallow were enemies from the moment they'd met, reminded himself that one day they might face each other in a different way, iron and steel edges drawn to the death. He hadn't bothered much about that though, because they both had to live through the Vathen first for that to ever happen, and Valaric had

15

been in enough battles to know when victory lay with the enemy. The Marroc were mostly too stupid and too fresh to fighting to see it, but the forkbeards must have known too, yet they'd faced the enemy anyway. They'd stood and held their shields and their spears and roared their cries of battle. 'Is he here then, your general?'

Gallow crouched beside a man with blood all over his face. He nodded. 'Yes, Valaric, he is.' He stood up. He still had his axe, and the way he was looking made Valaric wonder if that day when they'd face each other wasn't so far off after all. 'He's still alive.' Gallow's eyes were right for a forkbeard now. Merciless. Valaric took a step back. He let his hand sit on the hilt of his own sword. The Nightmare of the North. The man who'd led the forkbeards back and forth across his land and stained it black with ash and red with blood. Whoever killed the Widowmaker would be a hero among the Marroc, his name sung through the ages. And here he was, helpless, and there was only one forkbeard left standing in Valaric's way.

Gallow met his eye. 'Now what?'

Valaric couldn't draw his sword. Simply couldn't. Not that Gallow scared him, although it would be a hard fight, that was for sure. Or he could have called the other Marroc and told them what he'd found, because no forkbeard ever born was strong enough to face nine against one. But he didn't do that either. The honest truth was that the Nightmare of the North hadn't done half the things people said he had. What he *had* done was stand with two thousand Marroc against the Vathen in a battle he must have known he couldn't win. He'd done that today. Valaric turned away. 'They say things about you, Gallow.'

'I'm sure they do.'

'Tavern talk, now and then. They say you're good to your word. That you work hard. Decent, they say, for a forkbeard. Always with the same words at the end: *for a forkbeard.* Which is good. Doesn't serve a man to forget who his enemies are. Why did you fight beside me and not with your own people, eh? Would have been safer, after all. Likely as not they were the last to break.' The words were bitter. *Bloody forkbeards.*

'You're my people now, Valaric.'

Valaric spat in disgust. 'No, we're not. A forkbeard is a forkbeard. Shaving your face changes nothing.' He stared at Gallow and found he couldn't meet the Lhosir's eyes any more. They were the eyes of a man who would stand without flinching against all nine of his Marroc if he had to because it would never occur to him to do anything else. Valaric shook his head. 'I tell you, I got so sick of running away from you lot. Must be a first for you.'

'Selleuk's Bridge, Marroc.'

'Selleuk's Bridge?' Valaric bellowed out a laugh. 'I missed that. Beat you good, eh?'

'That you did.' Gallow's hand still rested on the head of his axe.

Valaric turned and started to walk away. 'I've done my fighting for today. Best you be on your way. You take more than your share of these horses and we'll come after you like the howling hordes of hell. Go. And be quick about it.'

3

DEAD WEIGHT

Gallow saw to the horses first. Two of them, one for him and one for the Screambreaker. That was fair. A man took what he needed and no more when times were hard. He chose Lhosir mounts over the Vathan ones. Stamina over speed. He couldn't see he'd be needing to win any races today but it was a long ride home and there wouldn't be any stopping while the sun was up.

He grimaced as he lifted the general across his shoulders. The Marroc called him the Widowmaker and the Nightmare of the North. To the Lhosir he was Corvin Screambreaker. He was a heavy man, full of muscle, but old enough to have a belly as well, and nearly ten years of peace had done him no favours there. In his armour he was almost too much; but for all Gallow knew, the Screambreaker was already knocking at the Maker-Devourer's cauldron, and a Lhosir died in his armour if he could, dressed for battle with his spear in one hand and his shield in the other. That was a good death, one the Maker-Devourer would add to his brew. Once Gallow had the Screambreaker on the back of his horse he strapped a shield to the old warrior's arm and wrapped his limp fingers around a knife and tied it fast with a leather thong ripped from a dead Vathan's saddle. A sword would have been better, but swords were heavy. Chances were it would fall out and be lost and then the Screambreaker would have nothing. A knife was at least something. The Maker-Devourer would understand that.

The Marroc were still back in the clearing. He ought to lay out the other Lhosir dead and speak them out, tell the Maker-Devourer of their names and their deeds, but he couldn't. He didn't know them. He put swords and knives into empty hands, knowing full well that the Marroc would simply loot them again as soon as he was gone. With the Screambreaker's horse tethered to his own, he whispered a prayer to the sky and the earth, mounted and rode away.By the time he was free of the woods, the sun was sinking towards the distant mountains of the south. Varyxhun was up there somewhere, up in the hills, surrounded by its mighty trees and guarding what had once been a pass through the mountains to Cimmer and the Holy Aulian Empire, but that was an old path. Nothing but the odd shadewalker had come from the empire for more than fifty years now, while the castle overlooking Varyxhun itself was said to be haunted, full of the vengeful spirits of the last Marroc to hold out against the Screambreaker. It was said to be the home of a sleeping water-dragon too, but the Vathen wouldn't bother with it, dragon or not. They'd stay north and move along the coast to Andhun. If Valaric and the other Marroc wanted a fight, that's where it would be. *I'll be with my family*, Valaric had said, but Valaric's family were six wooden grave markers in a field near a village by the coast, far away to the west, and had been for years. Everyone knew that.

He watched the sun finish creeping its way behind the distant horizon. As the stars came out, he stopped and eased Corvin to the ground and gently took away his shield. He let the horses cool and took them to water; when he was done with that he searched their saddlebags for food for both of them and blankets for Corvin. The Screambreaker's breathing was fast and shallow, but at least he was still alive. Gallow forced one of his eyes open. It was rolled back so far that all Gallow could see was white. He made a fire, forced some water into the old man and ate from what he'd found on the stolen horses.

'If you die on me I'll make a pyre if I can. I'll miss a few things when I speak you out, I reckon. Forgive me. The sky knows there's enough that I do know.' He took the Screambreaker's hand and held it in his own. *Talk to a troubled spirit. Helps it to remember who it is.* Some witch had told him that, not long after he'd crossed the sea. 'They say you were a farmer once, no better than anyone else. The old ones who knew you before. Thanni Thunderhammer. Jyrdas One-Eye. Kaddaf the Roarer. Lanjis Halfborn. We listened to all their stories. You were one of them, and you were their god too. Even then people knew you because of what you'd done, not because of a name you carried when you were born. "That a man should somehow be better than his brothers simply because his father was rich? A Marroc nonsense. Lhosir will never stomach it." You said that. Do you remember? I think we'd been talking about Medrin.' He let the Screambreaker's hand go and poked at the fire. 'Things were changing even before I crossed the sea. Some of these Marroc ideas were taking root and a dozen and more winters have passed since then. Was it all different when you went back? Is that why you sailed again? Or was it simply too hard to resist? One last glorious stand. A battle you couldn't possibly win. A hero's death for a hero's life.'

He shifted the Screambreaker closer to the fire and settled down on the other side, gazing up at the stars. 'We weren't all that far from here when we last parted. Andhun opened its gates to us, do you remember? You gave your word not to plunder it. We honoured that. By then we just wanted to go home, to get back across the sea and eat proper food again. Drink water that tasted of mountain ice and marry some big-boned woman who'd bear us lots of sons and sleep in a longhouse with all our kin and not in those stinking Marroc huts. That sort of thing. We talked about it all the time in those last weeks. Was it all there waiting for you just as we remembered it? It must have gone well enough for you and the others, what with bringing old Yurlak home and every ship laden with loot and plunder. But I can't say it's been too bad here.'

The Screambreaker moaned and shifted, still wandering the Herenian Marches where the lost spirits of those neither alive nor dead were cursed to dwell, spirits like the Aulian shadewalkers. Gallow patted his hand. 'I wasn't going to stay. I was as eager as the rest of you. But then Yurlak fell ill and everyone was sure he was going to die before you reached home and Medrin would be king in his place. I'm not so fond of Medrin. So I got to thinking that maybe I'd stay and I watched you all go, ship by ship. You took Yurlak back across the sea so he could die in his own house and among his own people, only then he went and didn't die after all. If I'd still been in Andhun, I'd have come home when I heard but, as you see, I never did. I left. Back to the mountains and the giant trees of Varyxhun. I was going to cross the Aulian Way. Go south, to lands we can hardly name, but on my way I found a forge and an old smith who needed a strong arm to work it, and one of his three dead sons had left a wife behind him and a girl he likely never saw. It was us who left her a widow, us who took the old man's sons, so I won't say they were happy with having a forkbeard around the place. But it felt good to be making things again. I wonder if you can understand that.' He took a deep breath and touched his hand to his chest, to the place where the locket lay next to his skin. 'I took a lock of her hair while she was sleeping. A little luck to carry into battle. I know what you'd say about that, old man. Laugh and scoff and tell me I was daft in the head, tell me that a man's fate is written for him before he's born. But here we are, so perhaps it worked, in its way. No one would have her, see, because she was another man's wife and she came with another man's child to feed when both men and food were scarce, and she was … Screambreaker, you'll understand if you meet her. The Marroc prefer their women a little more docile.' He rose and looked up at the stars. 'A fine woman, Screambreaker. We have two sons of our own now, and another daughter. You'll like her if you last long enough to see her. Fierce and speaks her mind as often as she likes and doesn't give a rat's arse what anyone else thinks. She won't like *you*, sorry to say. Not one bit. Arda. That's her name.'

He lay down beside the fire and pulled his cloak over himself. 'Maker-Devourer watch over you, old man. Don't get yourself lost in the Marches. And don't tell Arda about the hair. I'd never hear the end of it.'

Gallow closed his eyes. The Screambreaker was mumbling to himself. He hadn't heard a word.

4

THE ARDSHAN

Gulsukh Ardshan's horse shifted beneath him, impatient to move. From where he sat, the battlefield looked as though the Weeping God had reached down from the sky and picked the Marroc legion up to the clouds, shaken them fiercely and let them go, scattering them to fall as they may. The light was fading but he still watched from where the Marroc line had stood and looked down the gentle slope of the hillside. His riders swarmed over the dead, the dark litter of mangled shapes that had once been proud Marroc men. Looting mostly, but it served a purpose. His horsemen needed their javelots, those that could be thrown again. There were spears and axes and shields and helms and perhaps even a few swords and pieces of mail for the soldiers of the Weeping Giant, the ones who fought on foot. And, too, he was looking for someone.

In the failing light a dozen riders emerged from the trees at the bottom of the hill. Their horses looked tired, Gulsukh thought. They trotted closer up the slope and he saw that one of them had a body slung over his saddle. Watching them weave their way in and out of the piles of naked corpses and the fires that were just being lit, he felt a hungry thrill of hope, but it died as they approached. The lead horseman stopped in front of him, clenched his fist across his chest and bowed his head.

'And what did you find, Krenda Bashar?' Gulsukh peered at the body. A Lhosir, yes, but from a distance there was no telling who, other than it wasn't the man he was looking for.

The bashar kept his head bowed. He spoke loudly and quickly and a little too abruptly. 'Ardshan! Beymar Bashar is dead. We followed his trail. He caught up with the Lhosir and tried to take them but he was beaten. The men with him were killed. Most of the Lhosir too.'

'But not the Widowmaker.' The ardshan turned away. Failure was in the bashar's voice.

'The Widowmaker wasn't there, Ardshan. But ...' Krenda Bashar looked up with a furrowed brow. 'Ardshan, I would like to pursue this further. The tracks are unclear but the Lhosir bodies were left where they fell. Whatever happened, too few survived to take their dead with them. I ... I think the Widowmaker may have been killed too, and the last of his men took the body with them. They must have been in a hurry.'

Gulsukh shrugged. 'It means nothing without his body.'

'And so I beg your leave to pursue. Ardshan, the Lhosir don't leave their dead, not like this. At the very least they would lay out the bodies and leave weapons in their hands. There were no weapons at all. Further ...' Krenda's frown deepened. 'There is this.' He turned and led over the horse with the dead body across its back, bringing it close so that Gulsukh could see the dead Lhosir's face. 'Lanjis ...'

'Lanjis Halfborn.' The ardshan stared at a face he hadn't seen for ten years.

'We found him. Lying dead as he fell. The Widowmaker would not have left him so if he was alive to do otherwise.'

Gulsukh nodded. 'They were like brothers.'

'We found a handful of horses but most were gone. The trail leads inland. We followed it a short way. They weren't heading for Fedderhun.'

The ardshan closed his eyes. Even one last Lhosir would have laid out their fallen, and they surely wouldn't have have left one like Lanjis Halfborn behind, even dead. They must have had a very good reason to leave in haste and he could only think of one. To take the Widowmaker out of danger.

Krenda coughed. 'I think we weren't the first to find the Lhosir. Some of the Marroc fled through the same woods. They would have followed the same trails. It would explain the looting.'

The ardshan opened his eyes. 'Marroc aid the Widowmaker? I doubt *that*.'

'They'd most likely kill him. Or ransom him, Ardshan, and even his body would be worth a great deal. Perhaps they know that. Or perhaps they simply took him to strip him later, in a quieter safer place.'

'Yes.' Gulsukh smiled and nodded. 'Yes, and even dead they might do that. Then go and follow and see if you can find them, and make sure that every Marroc knows there's a price on the Widowmaker's head, dead or alive. Take some silver to show them. That should make them happy to see you.'

Krenda Bashar nodded. They might have talked more, but Gulsukh's son, Moonjal Bashar, was riding up the hill at a gallop now. The ardshan rolled his eyes. Krenda bowed. 'The Weeping Giant calls again?'

The ardshan nodded. 'Doubtless to debate when we shall press on to Fedderhun. Go. Perhaps while you're looking you could save us all some bother, Bashar. You could probably seize Fedderhun yourself while the Weeping Giant muses.'

5

FORKBEARD

The sun rose. Gallow shook the dew off his blanket and fetched water up from the nearby stream. He pissed on the last smoking remnants of his fire and checked to see if the Screambreaker had died in the night; but the old man was still breathing so he sat and ate breakfast and waited. The sky was a cold blue but the late spring sun was already warm on his skin and chasing away the chill of the night. The sun would have to be enough. Out here on the open downs the smoke of a fire would be seen for miles and the Vathen he remembered had been a restless people. Always with their horses and they liked to roam.

'My helm, man! My helm!' The cry jerked Gallow away from burying the traces of their camp. The Screambreaker was sitting up and staring blankly at the sky, one hand on his head. He looked at Gallow. 'Who are you? What have you done with my helm?'

Gallow took his own off the ground and offered it but the Screambreaker threw it away. 'That's not my helm. Where's my helm? Where is it?'

'Fell off your head when someone whacked you one, I'd say. Wasn't anywhere near when I found you. Probably some Marroc has it now. Glad you're awake.' Gallow rummaged among the saddlebags and pulled out a piece of dirty cloth, something used for polishing saddle leathers by the looks of it. It would have to do. He dipped it in water and crouched in front of Corvin. 'You've got blood all over you.

I'm going to wash it off. Should have done that last night.' Except last night it had been dark and he'd half thought the Screambreaker wouldn't live to see the morning.

He leaned forward but Corvin lunged and pushed him away. 'Get off me!'

'Suit yourself.' Gallow squeezed the water out of the cloth and hung it over his saddle. 'There's a horse there. It's yours now.'

The Screambreaker didn't move. He lay where he was, panting with his head twisted to one side. 'You're not a Vathan. You're not Marroc either. I don't know you. Who are you?'

'I was with you at Vanhun.' Gallow stood up. 'Most of the times afterwards as well, for that matter, until you went back across the sea. Gallow. No particular reason you'd remember me.'

'Gallow?' The old man wrinkled up his face. 'Where are the Vathen? This isn't Fedderhun! Where's the sea? The Marroc won't last the first charge! Where are they? They need their spirit!'

Gallow pointed to the rise behind them. 'See that hill? Good view from up there. I'm going to go and have a look and see if anyone's following us. Doubt it, but you never know. You led us against the Vathen yesterday, Screambreaker. The battle's been and gone. The Marroc held the first charge but it was never going to last. The second one broke them. You don't remember, do you? Thump round the head can do that.' He walked away, leaving the general to gather his thoughts, to sort his memories and get up off the ground and maybe come up and look too, but Corvin did none of those things. When Gallow came back the Screambreaker was asleep again, snoring loudly. Gallow lifted him up and flopped him into his saddle. 'There's smoke a way to the north. Probably not Vathen on our tracks but best be on our way.' Corvin didn't wake. The wound on his head was oozing again. At least the old man still knew who he was.

They rode through gentle hills down into the sweep of the Fedder valley and forded the river. The shape of the land grew more familiar. Gallow started to see places he knew – a lone tree here, the crook of a stream there, a particular hilltop – until early in the afternoon he looked down on the little Marroc village that had been his home for the last nine years. He left the horses beside Shepherd's Tree, a tall old broadleaf that stood on its own at the top of the hill where Vennic the shepherd watched his flock. There was no sign of Vennic today, nor of his sheep. There was no one in the village either, no fire lit in the forge, not even any animals, no clucking and snuffling of chickens and pigs wandering free. He walked back to Shepherd's Tree and climbed into the lower branches and peered out across the hills but there was no sign of anyone for miles. *Strange.* Something had made the villagers run but there was no trace of it now.

Corvin was still asleep as Gallow led the horses round to the forge yard. There were no stables in Middislet but Nadric had his workshop, one side open to the sky, big enough to tie up two horses and keep them at least half out of sight. He hauled the Screambreaker down and laid him on the hard earth and set to work on the old man's armour, one piece at a time, laying each carefully out beside the horses. A man could hardly lie in his sickbed all dressed up in mail and leather, not unless he had one foot already in the Herenian Marches and his eyes already set on the Maker-Devourer's cauldron. He smiled to himself. Nadric would rub his hands with glee if he ever saw all this metalwork. 'Better come out from wherever you're hiding then, eh?' He loosened the buckles on Corvin's leather undercoat and slowly eased him out of it. When that was done he lifted the general over his shoulder as gently as he could and carried him into the house, into the tiny night room where he and Arda slept. It was just a corner close to the hearth fire with curtains of rough-spun wool hanging around it to separate it from the rest of the house, but it would do. In the gloom with the curtains closed no one would see the Screambreaker as long as he was quiet. He set the old man down on the bed of straw and furs, shook him and offered him water.

'Do you remember it now?' Gallow asked him. 'The battle?'

The Screambreaker looked off into the distance, right through the walls and far off beyond. 'The Marroc broke. I remember that. Afterwards there wasn't much to be done. A few hundred of us would never turn away so many Vathen.' His eyes narrowed. 'Who are you?'

'Gallow, old man. I told you that already.'

'You're no Marroc. So who are you, Gallow?' He rolled the name around his mouth, frowning, savouring it as though in some lost corner of his memory maybe it meant something.

'I came from across the sea. I'm one of you. I'm Lhosir.'

'No, you're not.' Corvin stared and Gallow knew exactly where he was looking. At the bare shaven skin where Gallow's forked and braided beard should have been.

'Yes, I am, old man. I cut it off.'

The Screambreaker didn't say anything. A Lhosir cut his beard because he was ashamed, or else someone cut it for him because he was a coward or a liar or a thief. A Lhosir without his braided forked beard wasn't a Lhosir at all. He was a ghost to be ignored and shunned. Until it grew back he didn't exist.

Gallow shrugged. He fetched a blanket and covered the general. 'I have to see to the horses. I'll come back when that's done.'

'Where's my mail?' Corvin didn't turn to look at him but spoke to the wall.

'Cared for and out of sight.'

'I want it here. My sword too. And my shield.'

Gallow hesitated. 'I'll bring you your blade, Scream-breaker.' He could hardly deny a man his sword. 'The rest is best hidden away. There are Vathen roaming the land.'

'I'll not hide from them!'

Gallow brought the Screambreaker his sword and his shield too and then returned to the horses, ignoring the complaints that followed him. The horses had been worked hard and they needed some kindness. He lifted off their saddles and bridles and set to work grooming them; when that was done, since he had no hay or feed for them, he turned them loose in the fields. They were Lhosir horses so they wouldn't go far. Then he went back to the workshop and set about cleaning the general's armour and then his own, wiping every piece with an oily rag and hanging them in the shadows at the back of the workshop among Nadric's old tools, the broken ones that he never got around to fixing but couldn't bring himself to throw away. He hung up his axe and then took both swords and cleaned those too, hiding them under a pile of sacking. The Vathan javelot he propped up in the darkest corner of all. Then, stripped to the waist now, he started on the saddles, cleaning the leather and polishing it. He'd never had a horse so he didn't know what he was supposed to do with all the bits and pieces that came with one, but he knew about caring for leather. Spit and polish and a bit of beeswax, although that was usually something Arda tended to.

When he was done with the saddles he wrapped them in sackcloth and hid them at the back of the workshop. They were clearly Lhosir-made and too decorated to be from anything but a rich man's horse, and too big to properly hide too. He wondered about burying them, but the Screambreaker's beard would give him away if any Vathen came by, and if they didn't then only Nadric would see them where they were, tucked away in the shadows of the forge.

The sun was still high. The village was empty, but if

something had spooked them then Gallow knew where they'd be. They'd be up on the edge of the Crackmarsh, hiding in the waterlogged caves that riddled the hills. A couple of hours on foot, but on a horse he could easily be there and back before dark. He'd look for them tomorrow, he decided, if the Screambreaker was up to the journey, but for now it was useful to have the place to himself. He wondered what had scared them away.

With the swords and mail and the animals cared for, Gallow walked to the well and drew a bucket of water. He threw a few handfuls of it over himself and carried the rest back to the workshop. Nadric always kept a few rags about the place – he was forever on the lookout for shirts that were so worn and torn that they couldn't be patched and repaired. Gallow took one and went back to Corvin. One way or another that wound was getting cleaned, even if he had to punch the old man out to do it.

The thought made him laugh. Punching out the Screambreaker. How many people had tried that all those years ago? A lot, and he couldn't remember any that had succeeded. 'I need to—'

He stopped. The curtains were drawn back. The Screambreaker was sitting up, propped against the wall. He had his sword in his lap and the blankets around his feet and he was staring across the house. He didn't move or even look at him as Gallow came in. Gallow followed the Screambreaker's eyes. The village wasn't as empty as he'd thought. The Screambreaker screwed up his nose. 'I don't think this Marroc likes me,' he said, and Gallow couldn't have stopped himself from smiling even if he'd wanted to.

'Well I did tell you she wouldn't.'

6

ARDA

Vennic had been keeping watch up in the Shepherd's Tree. As much as anything it was something for him to do, but then he'd come running back late in the morning and said there were riders coming. The villagers had sighed and rolled their eyes. They knew what to do: take everything that mattered and hide, let the soldiers come through and be on their way, and then start again once they were gone. The forkbeards had taught them that. Burned-down houses could be built again. People and animals, they were what mattered, and so the men and women of Middislet had run out into the fields and called everyone back and gathered the animals that could be gathered and scattered the rest. The Vathen would come and go, and for most of them life would go on.

But not for all. The forge and Nadric's workshop weren't things you could simply pack up into sacks and throw over your shoulder and carry or herd up to the Crackmarsh. Without them Nadric had no living, and Arda had four children to care for and her man was off to war. Again. It made her furious because it was always *her*. Why did *she* have to suffer the most?

'I'm not having it,' she told Nadric. 'They come here, they'll burn us down over my dead body.'

Which, Nadric pleaded, was almost surely what would happen, but Arda was done with wars and fighting and running away. She took a knife and shut herself in the cellar, and nothing Nadric could say would make her come out. If Vennic was right and a band of soldiers came by then she'd plead with them. The forkbeards admired courage like that, didn't they? Maybe the Vathen would too. So in the end Nadric gave up and took the children away to hide in the Crackmarsh caves with everyone else and left her.

For a long time she sat in the quiet and in the dark and all alone. Trouble with that was it gave her time to wonder. What if the Vathen were different? What if they didn't care? Twice she got up, ready to climb out of the cellar and head after the rest of the village, and twice she stopped herself. Maybe the Vathen, the forkbeards or whoever it was that Vennic had seen had passed on by. Or maybe the riders were actually a herd of deer or simply figments of his imagination. There was no real telling with Vennic. That was what she was thinking – that Vennic was an idiot and there was nothing at all coming their way from the hills – when she heard the first noises above.

Footsteps. No voices. She froze, crouched in a corner, a lot less sure of herself than when she'd argued with Nadric. Vathen? She sniffed the air for smoke. *And if it is, what are you going to do?* She looked at the knife clutched tight in her fingers. *Stupid woman. What were you thinking?*

The footsteps came and went. For a while there was quiet. She was about to slip out of the cellar to see what was happening when they came back again, heavier this time, above her head through the wooden floor. They stopped by the night room and there was some quiet talking and then one set of footsteps left and everything fell still again. It certainly didn't *sound* like a gang of rapacious soldiers burning and looting and smashing everything in sight. More the patient unhurried paces of someone going quietly about their business. Whatever that was in *her* house.

Someone had slipped back from the Crackmarsh! Was that it? A thief? So when the footsteps didn't come straight back she opened the cellar door and crept up and pulled back the curtain from the night room. And there right in front of her was a forkbeard she'd never seen before, lying on her bed for all the world as though he was asleep. She let out a yelp and he lurched blindly awake, sat up, grabbed a sword and then swayed sideways as though he was drunk. She held her knife at him, arm stretched out, backing away, afraid for a moment but only until she saw that the forkbeard's face was covered with old dried blood, that his beard was matted with it. As soon as she saw his weakness, her fear turned to anger. A forkbeard in her house!

'Get out!' she hissed. She took a step forward and waved the knife at him. He shuffled back against the wall. He still had his sword in his hand but he looked so weak she doubted he could even lift it.

'Who are you?' His words were slurred and heavy with that savage forkbeard accent. She held out her knife as though he was a snake. He didn't look as though he could even stand. She had no idea what to do.

The yard door opened. Gallow! The relief was like a sudden dive into a river. The forkbeard kept looking at her. 'I don't think this Marroc likes me,' he said.

'Well, I did tell you she wouldn't. Hello, Arda.' He was grinning, the clothead! He had no idea what he'd done to her. Relief turned quickly to a flare of anger. She was scared, and Gallow didn't look surprised at all by the half-dead man lying on his furs. 'What's this?' she yelled at him and jabbed her knife at the forkbeard. 'What's this in my house? In my *bed*?'

Gallow sat down beside the wounded man with a bucket of water in one hand and a rag in the other. 'I need to clean that wound,' he said. 'You have to lie down, old man.' He was ignoring her in that deliberate *not-now* way he did sometimes. She ground her teeth in frustration. It made her so furious!

The forkbeard didn't move. He didn't look at Gallow at

all, just glared at her. Arda hissed: 'Get him out of my house or I swear I'll stab you both!'

Gallow looked up. 'Where is everyone?'

'Where do you think they are, you sack-headed oaf? Hiding up at the Crackmarsh of course! Vennic saw horsemen in the hills, coming this way.'

'Horsemen in the hills?' Gallow wrinkled his nose.

'Vathen? Forkbeards? Who knows? Does it matter?' She scowled. 'Maybe he saw a cloud with a strange shape that frightened him!' She looked away and snorted. Vennic. Useless fool.

'Well there are no horsemen, I'm sure of that.' Gallow reached towards the wounded man but the forkbeard pushed him away.

'Get him out of here!' Gallow was trying to ignore her, and by Modris she wasn't going to have it. She brandished the knife at him now instead. '*Get him out of my house!*'

'Be quiet, woman.'

'Don't you *quiet woman* me, you tree stump!'

The forkbeard's head swayed from side to side. He groaned. 'Give me back my horse and I'll be gone. I spurn your hospitality, clean-skin.' To Arda he looked ready to drop dead at any moment. And he was welcome to do just that, as long as he did it outside.

Gallow shook his head. 'Don't be stupid, old man. You'll be lucky if you get to the edge of the village.'

Arda folded her arms. 'You heard him. He doesn't even *want* to stay. So, we're all done here now and he can go.'

She watched as the man she'd married took a deep breath. He sat back and looked at her at last. Properly, eye to eye like he should have done in the first place. 'Wife, he's a soldier! I found him like this after the battle, beside his horse. I could hardly leave him to die.'

'He's a forkbeard! And we've got children to feed.' She spat on the straw at the wounded man's feet.

'You mean I should have taken his horse and come back on my own?' His eyes narrowed and grew suddenly cold. 'I'm a forkbeard too, or had you forgotten?'

He had what she thought of as his fighting face on now, the one where he stopped listening. She didn't care. She'd been looking for a fight from the moment Vennic had come running into the village. 'Forgotten? Tch!' She might have thrown something at him, but at that moment the forkbeard's head slumped onto his chest and his eyes slowly closed. Arda peered at him. 'So is he dead now?'

'No.'

'Pity. Why are you back here so soon?' She winced at the anger in her own voice. Not anger that he was back, far from it, but at the way he'd come, at the fright he'd given her. At ... at ... She looked at the furs where the two of them lay together at night, at the battered old forkbeard lying there instead. 'Is it over then?'

Gallow's face fell. He shook his head. 'We broke and ran. The Vathen will come.'

A thrill ran through her along with the inevitable dread of war. *Forkbeards, beaten!* 'So much for your great Widowmaker then.' She spat out his name. 'Murdering bastard. I hope the Vathen slaughtered him.'

Gallow glanced at the wounded man. He was asleep now. 'Where are the children?'

'Where do you think? Nadric took them into the hills.' Her grip on the knife eased. A part of her would always hate Gallow simply for being from across the sea, but she'd dealt with that part and told it to shut up often enough to know how. It was better to have him than not, that was the long and the short of it. Better that he was back than dead. 'You're such a thistlefinger! The Vathen are coming? What if they come here? What if they find *that*?' She pointed at the forkbeard again. 'Do you *want* to see your children killed in front of you?'

His eyes flashed. The children were the chink in his armour, but they were the chink in hers too. Made him hard to hate even on her bad days. 'The Vathen won't come this way,' he said.

She stuck her chin out at him. 'Did you stop to ask while you were busy running away from them, then?'

'They've gone to Fedderhun.'

'Really? Vennic was in the Shepherd's Tree. *He* said there were riders coming. That's why we left. You forkbeards taught us that.'

Gallow cocked his head at her. 'But *you* didn't leave.' She caught a smile flicker across his face and frowned even more deeply. Later, when they were making up again, he'd tell her how he liked her spirit. How it reminded him of home. Every time he said that she punched him. Hard, but he kept on saying it anyway. She pointed her knife at the sleeping forkbeard. 'I don't want him here.'

'He'll go when he can ride again.'

She threw back her head in disbelief. 'You're going to let him keep his horse?'

'It's *his* horse.'

Arda threw the knife she was holding hard into the floor in disgust. It struck the wood and stuck, quivering. Right there was the thing between them that would never go away. Family first. 'You cloth-mouthed scarecrow! There's four children to be fed here. Hungry ones, and it won't be the Vathen that feed them. Soldiers only take, whoever they follow.' She'd lived it once. Never again. 'You'd get silver for a horse in Andhun, even an old nag. In Tarkhun too.' She shook her head. 'You're still one of them. You just pretend you're not because they wouldn't have you any more.' Now she was being nasty. His fault. He drove her to it.

Gallow looked away. They both knew she was right, though: the other forkbeards wouldn't even look at him, not with his bare face. He'd done that for her, years ago when she'd thought it would change him, but of course it hadn't changed anything at all. 'I ran away,' he said, 'with a band of Marroc who were as brave as anyone else. We found horses in the woods with dead men sitting on their backs. This one was alive. We shared the horses between us. I have another.'

'You got two?' Her eyes flashed. 'Where are they?'

'Out in the fields.' Gallow shook his head. 'There are no riders in the hills, Arda. I came that way myself. Vennic probably saw the two of us in the distance and panicked. You know what he's like.' He must have seen the uncertainty in her face. Yes, she did know what Vennic was like, the whole village knew. He looked away. 'Someone should go to the Crackmarsh and bring the others back.'

'Someone should get those horses brought into the yard before they're eaten by wolves!'

Gallow cocked his head at the man asleep on their furs. 'His wound should be cleaned and stitched closed in the way of the Aulians.'

'And are *you* going to tend to him?' Arda let out a scornful laugh. 'Yes, and I should let you! A fine way that would be to help him on to the Marches. Might as well just use that knife on him.' She sighed. She didn't want this other man here but she didn't want him dying under her roof either. A lot of bad luck that was, and she certainly wasn't going to open his throat in her own house, however much a part of her would have liked that. 'Fine then. Since you say he must stay then let him get well or die quickly. When Nadric comes back we'll see. Until then at least let someone who won't stitch his eyes shut tend to him. I'll do it. Go and get those horses and keep them safe!'

They looked at one another. It was hard to be angry with Gallow for long. He'd never been cruel or unjust, he just didn't *think*, that was all. Flesh and blood, children and household, all that came before anything else, and if it hadn't been that way for her then she would never have married him, never even taken him into her home. 'I won't cut his throat,' she snapped. 'Much as I'd like to.'

He gave her a hard look. She threw up her hands in disgust. 'I swear by Modris and by Merethin's ghost! Happy?' Merethin had been Nadric's son and had fathered Jelira, her oldest. The forkbeards had killed him. She hadn't thought much of him before he'd gone off to war and had roundly cursed his name ever since, but she always held him up to Gallow whenever she was angry. She scowled. For being from across the sea, that was what it came to. That's what he'd done wrong. Nothing else.

Gallow nodded. He put a hand on her shoulder and squeezed. He could be kind when he wanted to be, and kindness was something she secretly craved. She didn't flinch away. 'I'm sorry I scared you.'

'I wasn't *scared*, you idiot! Modris and Ballor! Will you get on and do what needs to be done!' Scared? Maybe she had been, but she'd die before she'd admit it to a forkbeard, even him. When he'd cut his beard, perhaps he'd thought it would mellow the hardness she wore like armour, just like she thought it might change him, but it didn't change either of them. It wasn't fair. She knew that. But it wasn't fair to see a husband and a brother killed and a home burned by the forkbeards either. The only time she let him see any other side of her was at night. Women had their urges as much as men.

He squeezed again and then let her be when she almost kicked him away from her. 'Stupid man!' Ah, Modris! If he'd seen how she'd squirmed inside when he'd told her he was going to fight the Vathen ... The thought of losing him, that *had* scared her, and it had turned out to be a far deeper fear than she'd thought it would be. She'd never admit it though, just as she'd never admit she was pleased to see him back. It all turned to anger instead.

'Off with you!' She shooed him out of the house and then

went to look for her bone needles and some thread. She wouldn't be too careful, stitching this unwanted forkbeard back together. It would hurt and he'd have a scar. Both would please her, but she'd keep her promise. He wouldn't die.

7

NIOINGR

Gallow saddled one of the horses and rode it out to the Crackmarsh. In spring when the streams ran fast off the mountains and the Isset was deep and strong the Crackmarsh was fifty miles of water meadow criss-crossed with swamp paths and pocked with smooth bare boulders and little hillocks crowned by stands of stunted trees, a thousand tiny islands breaching the shallow water like the backs of petrified whales. Later in the year it dried out to a huge flat swathe of soft boggy soil between the litter of giant stones and the tufts of trees. Fine growing land if it hadn't been for the ghuldogs.

Around its eastern edge rose a line of low hills scattered with crags and thick groves of trees, guiding the Isset and the Crackmarsh westward out of the Varyxhun valley and the pass that led to the old Aulian Way across the mountains. There were caves here, lots of them. Whispers told stories that the deeper ones ran right across to the mountains, but the deeper ones were always flooded so no one really knew. Gallow found the rest of the villagers there, as Arda had said and he had guessed, bored and fractious and already arguing among themselves about whether they should go back. None of them was pleased to see him. Even Nadric was barely civil. Old wounds had opened with the coming of the Vathen.

It was almost dark by the time he got back to the forge. Arda had finished with Corvin. Her face was furious.

'You said he was a soldier.'

'He is.'

'I saw his sword. He's not just *a* soldier.'

He could have lied. Men picked up whatever they could find after a battle, after all, but sooner or later she'd find out. The old man would tell her if she ever asked. He shrugged. Better to hear it from him. 'He's Corvin Screambreaker.'

Arda hissed at him, bearing her teeth. 'The Widowmaker himself? Are you mad? You bring the Widowmaker into *my* house?'

'I bring a man who is hurt, woman!' For a moment he almost lost his temper. Arda was good at that. 'Should I leave him to die?'

'The Nightmare of the North? Yes, you surely should! If I'd known who he was before I stitched his eye … Get him out of here!'

'When he's well enough to travel on his own.'

'No! Now! What if the Vathen come?'

'I told you, woman! The Vathen have moved on Fedderhun. And why would they come here? Unless someone told them of a very good reason.'

'Don't you *woman* me, foxborn!' She leaned into him, red with rage. 'Never mind the Vathen then – what if anyone else finds out who you've got here? The rest of the village. They'll burn the place down around us!'

He met her gaze, eye to eye. 'Then you'd best not tell them.'

She stormed away out to the workshop and Nadric. In a while Nadric would come inside and tell Gallow that the Screambreaker had to go, and Gallow would say no, and then they'd argue and drink and drink and argue, and eventually Nadric would give in, just like he always did, and Arda would storm away and disappear into the fields just like *she* always did when they argued and she lost, and then she'd come back in the middle of the night and tear the furs off him and they'd make love like dragons. For a moment, after they were done, he'd see the gentleness that was buried so very deep inside her. But only for a moment. He touched a finger to the locket under his shirt. Maker-Devourer, what scorn she'd pour on him for *that* if she knew! 'He stays until he's well,' he called after her.

At the open door little Feya and Tathic peered up at him with their big child eyes. Pursic was probably out in the yard crawling in the mud. Jelira would be watching Nadric in the workshop. Gallow smiled at them and knelt down. 'Listen to me, little ones. When boys grow to be men they may carry swords or they may not, but every man and every woman carries their own heartsong. It's not a thing you win in battles. It's a thing you're born with and you must always listen to it. It will tell you what is right and what is wrong. You must look after it too, because if you don't then one day it might go away, and when it goes it won't come back. More men lose their heartsongs in their own home than lose it in a wall of shields.'

They kept staring, too young to understand. Gallow took their hands, one in each of his. 'There's a stranger here, in the night room. A man who helped me fight. He was very brave but now he's hurt. He'll stay until he's well. You must leave him alone and you mustn't tell anyone that he's here. He'll be gone soon.'

Tathic nodded, his face serious. Feya smiled and yawned and reached out to pull Gallow's nose.

'Do only boys have heartsongs?' asked Tathic. 'Jel says girls have heartsongs too, but they don't, do they?'

'Oh they very much do, little man. Everyone has a heartsong. Boys and girls, men and women, Marroc and Lhosir.'

'Does Ma have a heartsong?'

'Of course she does. Do you not hear it? It's the strongest heartsong in our house.'

'See!' Feya pushed Tathic. 'I do have har-sow!' She

scampered behind Gallow to hide. Gallow ruffled her hair and shooed them back into the yard to chase each other in the twilight. When they were gone he drew back the curtains to see what Arda had done to Corvin. The Screambreaker was sitting up against the wall. His face was ashen but his eyes were clear. He had a gash over his temple and around his forehead as long as a finger and swollen up like an egg. Blood oozed from it. Arda's stitching hadn't been kind.

'She said I was cut to the bone.'

'You were lucky to live.'

'Where am I?'

Gallow sat down beside him. 'You're in the house of Nadric the Smith in Middislet. About three days' walk inland from Fedderhun.'

Corvin closed his eyes. He took a deep breath and moaned. 'Marroc.'

'Yes.' The pain must have been bad for Corvin to let it show. 'No one outside this house knows you're here. Best it stays that way. The Marroc still curse the name Screambreaker.'

'I thank you for your hospitality.' The words were forced between his lips, empty of feeling. 'Send your wife to me. I will thank her to her face even if she spits at my feet. In the morning I'll take my horse and be gone.'

'To where, Screambreaker? Fedderhun is surely fallen and Andhun is a week's ride across unfamiliar country along paths you won't remember. You'll not get any help from any Marroc, not looking as you do. You'll die before you get there. You're feverish already.'

The Screambreaker snarled. 'Who are you to tell me what to do, no-beard? I'll be gone in the morning and that's the end of the matter, and if I die before Andhun then that's my fate and the Maker-Devourer will have me. I'll not lie here like some invalid in the bed of a downy-cheeked *nioingr*.'

The blood rushed to Gallow's face. If he'd had a knife he

might have pulled it. As it was, he grabbed Corvin's head in his hands and forced him to meet his eye. 'I didn't save your life to kill you here, but your tongue will not travel with you to Andhun unless it learns some manners. You're in my house, under my roof. I followed you into battle for years. I've fled from the enemy twice and twice alone. At Selleuk's Bridge and now from the Vathen, and so you'll take those words and swallow them!'

The Screambreaker met his eyes and bared his teeth. 'I will eat them when you show me your beard, clean-skin. I still remember some of those who never came back across the sea. *Nioingr*, all of them.'

'I didn't stay because of any shame, Screambreaker.'

'Then why?'

Corvin didn't flinch from him. Gallow let go. 'Because Yurlak was sick, that's why. We all thought he'd die. Medrin would have followed him, and I'll not serve a king I've seen turn and run while his friends stood fast.'

The last words earned him a glare. 'You call the king's son a coward?'

Gallow shrugged. 'It was fourteen summers ago that I crossed the sea. The Medrin I left behind, yes, I call him a coward. Perhaps he's changed. He must have a beard now.'

'Long and fine, unlike yours.'

'If you say it's so then I shall believe you.'

'What you believe is nothing to me, clean-skin. Send your wife so I may thank her for her attentions. I *will* be gone in the morning.'

Gallow rose and left. Outside the door Arda took his arm and pulled him away across the yard and into the workshop where Nadric was sitting by his anvil.

'We've decided.' She looked him in the eye. 'We'll ransom him.'

Nadric nodded slowly. Gallow shook his head. 'No.'

'Yes!' Arda hissed. 'He's nothing but grief and another

45

hungry mouth, and we can barely feed the ones we have. What happens if anyone finds him here? The Vathen will kill us all and burn our homes. They'll burn the whole village! If any of the others find out he's here, *they* will go to the Vathen. *They* will be rewarded and *we* will be killed. There's no other way that makes sense. We sell him to the Vathen. It's decided.'

'No.' Gallow looked at them both. 'If you do this then I'll burn our home myself with both of you inside it. He means to leave in the morning. No one will know he's here and he'll be gone before any Vathan could get here. Think on how *that* will seem. No. He'll leave us a fine horse and the spoils it carries to keep us fed and we'll have done what was right. Let that be enough.'

'Your Prince Medrin is in Andhun,' said Nadric. He tried, when Gallow and Arda set against one another, to be the voice of reason, always a thankless task. 'Could we not ransom him there instead?'

Arda spat. 'Why, when we could give him to the Vathen and he could get what he deserves?'

Gallow turned away. In their eyes he'd brought an enemy into their house. He understood that. They were Marroc, and Corvin was the Screambreaker from across the sea who'd led armies against their people and conquered their king in the name of his own. What they thought hardly mattered though. The Screambreaker had said he would be gone, and so he would, and that would be that and he'd either reach Andhun alive or he wouldn't.

They slept in the main part of the house that night, leaving the Screambreaker the night room with the curtains closed around him. In the early hours before the dawn he woke them all with a scream, wild with fever. He was not gone in the morning, nor the one after, nor the one after that. Each night Gallow thought he would die. Each day Arda prayed for it, and yet she tended to him as she would have tended to her own children, even as he denied her and his heart kept beating. As far as Gallow could see, no one said a word of it outside his walls. The Marroc of Middislet looked at him just as they always did. With disdain, a sneer and a little fear.

8

VIDRIC

The Vathen gathered around the dying Marroc. There wasn't much left of him. Just a bloodied sack of flesh and bones hung from the branches of a tree by his wrists and ankles. They'd tortured him, beating and flaying him with bundles of wiry sticks. They'd been doing it for hours. The sticks were vicious, splitting the skin like whips as often as not.

'He's done.' Gosomon threw his bundle away. 'He's got nothing more to say.'

The rest of them nodded. The air among them changed. Hostility ebbed and a question grew in its place. Eyes shifted from the dying Marroc to Krenda Bashar. *And?*

'The Screambreaker isn't with them.' Krenda Bashar nodded to himself. Nodded to the gods who'd dealt him this pot of shit. He grabbed the dying Marroc by the hair and pulled up his head. 'There was a Lhosir with you when you fled the battle. You found a clearing and the remnants of a skirmish.' The Marroc had had a gold-handled Lhosir knife tucked into his belt when they'd taken him. Krenda waved it under his face. 'You found Beymar Bashar's ride, all of them dead, and plenty of dead forkbeards too. You had a fine old time looting the bodies. Afterwards the Lhosir who was with you suddenly wasn't there any more. You have no idea whether he took a horse. You have no idea if he took anyone with him. You have no idea whether he found another forkbeard alive or took away one of the dead. You don't even know who he was except his name. Gallow. You have no idea where he went or why. Am I missing anything? Oh, and this all happened two whole days ago, so by now he could be pissing *anywhere!*' He didn't wait for the Marroc to answer. With a sudden jab, he stabbed the Lhosir knife into the Marroc's neck and let him bleed out. 'Mollar and Feyrk!' he cursed. 'Gosomon, take your ride and go after the rest of these Marroc. Maybe one of the others knows more. Find where this Lhosir went and who he is.' *Andhun, surely. Where else?* 'If he's gone to ground, it'll be in the Crackmarsh. That's about a day's ride straight south. Huge mess of a place. Mostly under water this time of year. You can't miss it, but if he's hiding in there and you somehow manage to find him then I'll have you made the next ardshan.'

Gosomon snorted as Krenda Bashar climbed back into his saddle. 'Going back to Fedderhun are you, Bashar? Back to your woman? A couple of soft nights while *we* sleep in the mud?'

Krenda Bashar's face turned sour. 'I'll join you again in a few days, Gosomon. Gulsukh won't like it, but if the Screambreaker is on his way to Andhun then maybe he can get there first if he moves fast. He'd want to know that. But find him for me, Gosomon. Make me look less stupid that I am, eh? I tell you what – you find him, you can have Mirrahj for your own wife, if she doesn't knock you out first, and I'll take a woman who's still got a use to her – how about that? Oh, and if you pass any Marroc, have the sense to ask.' He patted the little bag of silver hanging from his saddle. 'Show them a little of something that shines.'

He kicked his horse into a canter and turned for Fedderhun.

9

THE FESTIVAL OF SHIEFA

Vathen or no, Fenaric the carter and his sons headed off for Fedderhun as they did every year before Shieftane. The whole of Middislet came out to watch them go, clapping their hands at their bravery or else shaking their heads at such foolishness. Gallow thought they were stupid, so of course Arda thought they were brave and pointedly went out to tell them so before they left. A week later they were back, alive and well. They even had what they'd gone looking for, barrels of Fedderhun beer. Fenaric drew up his cart in the middle of the village and stopped and waited while everyone gathered around him.

'Well they haven't burned it down!' He sat calmly on the back of his wagon, used to being the centre of attention.

'There's Vathen everywhere!' His sons were more wide-eyed. 'They look so strange. Short and faces the colour of Harnshun clay and eyes as dark as a forkbeard's soul.'

'Hundreds of them! Thousands!'

'There's people running away too. The roads are full of them.'

Fenaric patted the barrels and nodded sagely. 'Aye. But these Vathen prefer their own brews over good Fedderhun beer and they haven't gone burning anything down, not yet. There's a few folk keeping on—'

He wasn't allowed to finish. 'They're marching on Andhun!'

'They're eating all the food and—'

'That's where the real fight's going to be.'

'I heard the Sword of the Weeping God is coming! Out from the swamps far to the east. They're bringing the red curse back!'

Fenaric looked from side to side, drawing his audience in. 'They do say that, yes.' He looked sombre.

Later on Gallow passed the news to Corvin. The fever had broken but it had left the Screambreaker as weak as a child. 'Another two or three days and you'll be strong enough to ride. I'll go with you to Andhun.'

'No need, bare-face. I'll leave tonight.'

He said that every day, when he was conscious enough to say anything at all. Gallow shrugged. For once he might actually mean it. 'Then I'll leave your horse saddled for you, because you won't be managing that without help and tonight you *will* be on your own. It's the festival of Shiefa. Fenaric has brought ale back from Fedderhun. You'd stand a better chance if you waited a few days more. I'm sure you know it. But ...' He paused. 'If you don't want to be seen then tonight is a good night for slipping away.'

The Screambreaker's brow furrowed. 'Ale back from Fedderhun, did you say? Your carter must be an unusually brave man. Are you sure it's not horse piss?'

'The Vathen never had much taste for Marroc beer. They ferment milk, don't they?'

'They do. Sour stuff.' The furrows on his brow wouldn't leave. He let out a long sigh and shook his head. 'If I were you I might ask him how he paid the Vathen. I think I *will* leave tonight.' The Screambreaker spat. 'Shiefa? Some Marroc god?'

'The lady of the summer rains.'

Corvin shook his head. 'You have a god for everything. I never understood the need for so many. The Maker-Devourer is enough for me.'

'It's their way.' Gallow gave the Screambreaker a long

look. 'They'll be celebrating tonight. If your heartsong says you have to go, I'll make it easy for you. No food, no water, no shelter, no help, riding into a battle from the wrong side, all of those will be trials enough. The house and the road will both be empty tonight. Everyone should be in the big barn. Wait until dark and no one will see you, or if they do then they'll be too drunk to be sure you're not a ghost. For what my words are worth, I ask you to wait. I'd come with you to guide you there. I know this country better than you, and if Andhun falls then Yurlak will need you.'

The Screambreaker roared, 'Maker-Devourer! Andhun has walls and the sea! It won't fall to a horde of bloody Vathan horse lovers no matter how many of them there are!' He turned away with nothing more to say. Gallow went out to Nadric's workshop and finished off a few simple jobs that the old man was working on. Better to let Nadric get himself ready. The Marroc grudgingly let Gallow into the big barn to drink ale with them these days, as long as he kept to the shadows and didn't bother anyone, but they certainly didn't want him dressing up and dancing and singing like he was one of them. So he stayed in the workshop, pottering from one thing to another until after dark, when everyone else was gone and Arda would be dancing with the village men and Nadric would be swaying back and forth with a happy ale-smile on his face and the children would be asleep in a corner with the other little ones. Perhaps Jelira might still be awake this year, yawning as though she was out to catch flies.

Before the forge fire died he lit a torch and took it into the fields, calling the two Lhosir ponies. The old general wouldn't have the patience to stay. *Lhosir pride over simple sense.* Arda's words those, said about him, and when she'd said them he hadn't understood; but now he did and they made him laugh because they were sometimes so true. In the workshop he saddled a pony ready to go. He filled a couple of skins from the well and put cheese and some bread and some eggs into the saddlebags. Arda would see they were gone straight away and they'd have another fight, but the Screambreaker was a guest under his roof and a Lhosir never sent away a guest without at least a first meal for the journey. He took down the Screambreaker's armour and laid it out piece by piece beside the horse. Last of all he left his own helm. The Screambreaker would leave a proud warrior. If the Vathen weren't heading south with torches to burn Marroc villages then he had no need of the helm for himself. He was a smith now, a father, living as a Marroc even if he wasn't. He could let Arda have that much. Peace.

He left the fire to die and walked slowly to the big barn and the bonfire outside. Music and singing and dancing filled the night. He kept to the shadows around the edges, avoiding the other villagers as best he could. They tolerated him – just barely – throughout most of the year, but festival days were bad and today would be worse. They'd be drunk tonight and ugly. A good few had once lost kin to a sword or a spear from across the sea and the Vathen were making them remember all over again. He waved a cup at Fenaric and took an ale from him. The carter seemed to dislike him less than the rest, perhaps because he travelled and saw Lhosir traders now and then in Andhun and sometimes even in Fedderhun, or perhaps because he and his sons hadn't been born in the village and he was something of an outsider himself. Or maybe none of those things. Maybe he simply hid it better.

'Might be better if you go home early tonight,' murmured Fenaric. Gallow thought he was right, but he stayed for a drink because Marroc ale was a pleasure and one of the few things that no Lhosir could reasonably say was done better across the sea. He waved his cup at Fenaric again. Drink always brought out the sea in him. He saw more clearly now: he *had* spent too long living among the Marroc. The

Screambreaker would go tonight because that's what any Lhosir worth his beard would do. And he'd go alone, because Gallow would stay here. Because this was where he belonged. And it would be a shame, he thought, not to share a last toast with the Screambreaker after all the years they'd fought side by side.

He held the cup carefully in front of him as he walked out of the big barn. Share a few memories and a few mouthfuls of Marroc ale with the old warrior. Have their own little festival and then help him onto his horse and watch him go. Better for everyone that way. And besides, a man couldn't bring a stranger into his house and call him a friend without sharing his bread and ale.

As he reached the yard a horse snickered somewhere behind him. Lit up by the embers from the forge, a shadow flitted across the back yard. Gallow chuckled. The Screambreaker moved quickly for an old man emerging from the grip of a fever. Maybe he wasn't as weak as he'd seemed.

The Screambreaker's horse was where he'd left it. The other Lhosir horse was standing beside it. Gallow froze. Then the horse he'd heard behind him wasn't one of his. And that shadow *had* moved too quickly.

Maker-Devourer! He burst into life, dropping Fenaric's cup and racing for the workshop, low and quiet and glued to the shadows. To where he kept his sword hidden. Men creeping about his house? Someone who'd somehow found out about the Screambreaker? Who? The whole village was up in the barn! Who was missing?

He took up an axe instead of his sword and snatched his helm, still lying on the ground beside Corvin's armour. For a half-second he hesitated, wondering whether to take his shield. A Lhosir always fought with his shield, even though it was a cumbersome and clumsy thing inside a house. He cursed himself as he reached out and grabbed it.

A man came out the back door and began to cross the

yard. From the shadows of the workshop Gallow blinked and shook his head. He could see the man clearly in the moonlight and this was no villager. This was a Vathan soldier. A rider!

The Vathan stopped in the middle of the yard. Gallow readied his axe. Two more came out, dragging the Screambreaker between them. The fever made his struggles feeble and turned his curses into groans, but he was fighting them as best he could. Gallow watched them go, waited until they turned away and had their backs to him, and then he charged, his heavy footfalls lost beneath the raucous songs from the barn. He crashed into the soldier on Corvin's left, shield rammed into the man's back, sprawling both him and the Screambreaker forward. Gallow swung his axe at the other Vathan's neck just beneath the line of his helm. The blade hit hard and bit into the mail draped from the back of the bassinet, twisting in Gallow's hand, almost wrenching itself out of his grasp before he jerked it free. The soldier let out a startled grunt. Gallow stumbled over the Vathan he'd sent sprawling to the ground, fell, landed on top of him, straddled his back, pinned him, took his axe in both hands and brought it down as hard as he could into the back of the man's head. The Vathan helm split open and the soldier's brains spilled over Gallow's hands. The other one lurched towards him, sword drawn, staggering from side to side, blood running down his shoulders. Gallow jumped up, casting his eyes around for the last of the three and not finding him. The lurching soldier walked straight into Corvin, prone on the grass, and stumbled. His movements were jerky and full of twitches. Gallow scooped up his shield, let out a roar and swung, whirling the axe, but the soldier didn't move, didn't even seem to see it coming. The axe shattered the Vathan's jaw and left the bottom half of his face a ruin of pulpy flesh and fractured bone. Blood poured down his hauberk. He sank to his knees and pitched forward, face first.

'Get up, you sickly dog!' swore Gallow at Corvin. 'Get up and take his sword!'

An arrow struck his shield. A stroke of luck that he'd lifted it to look down at the Screambreaker. Gallow let out a bellow and ran at the last Vathan, but the rider was already on his horse and galloped into the dark and was gone. At least the Screambreaker was getting to his feet.

'Let him get away, did you?' Gallow ignored him. He sat on his haunches for a while, trying to think. The old man's breathing was hard and he dragged his feet, but at least he had *some* strength. 'They'll be back,' he said.

Gallow stared at him. 'They knew you. Didn't they?'

The Screambreaker gave him a sour look. 'Of course. They knew before they came, bare-skin.'

'Then this village is dead.' Gallow glanced back at the horse and the armour he'd laid out on the ground. 'The mare's all ready for you. I have to go back to the barn.'

'Why?'

'Because I have to warn the Marroc. The Vathen knew who you were. One of them got away. So they'll come back, and when they find you're gone they'll burn my village and kill everyone here. Would you, the Widowmaker, have let this pass?'

The Screambreaker thought. 'No,' he said. 'But they brought this on themselves, no-beard.'

'I would spare my wife and my children.'

The old man shrugged. 'One of them has spoken out of turn. One of them told the carter.'

'The carter?'

'I told you to ask him how he paid the Vathen for his ale. And for his life.' The Screambreaker shook his head. 'I've dealt with these horse-lovers before. I know how they are. Your kinsmen have made their own fate now, bare-skin.'

'They've made yours and mine too.'

The Screambreaker shrugged, indifferent. 'I was going to

leave in the night anyway. *My* fate isn't changed at all.'

'Yes, it is. You were going to leave alone. You would have left a small trail that would be hard to find. Now, when the Vathen come, the tracks will be those of two Lhosir, more if I can make it seem that way, and the trail *I* will leave will be so glaring that even the blind couldn't miss it.'

The Screambreaker looked at him for a long time. 'You think you'll spare these Marroc who betrayed you by drawing the Vathen away? They'll simply split their numbers.'

'But if I don't try then there's no hope.'

Corvin kept staring. He started to laugh and then nodded. 'Then I have a proposition for you, clean-skin. I'll leave your trail. Go back to your Marroc. They might actually need you now. Which is more than I do.'

10

FENARIC

Gallow was gone from the festival for a long time. Fenaric drank his own pale ale and grew pleasantly drunk, relieved that the big forkbeard had found something else to do. He should really stay away from these festivals – they weren't his place and no one wanted him. What he should really do was go home, back across the sea.

He fidgeted, unable to relax. Gallow made him nervous tonight more than most nights. He couldn't settle. He looked over the empty space of the big barn to where Arda was dancing with Nadric since she had no husband to join her and he had no wife. It was a shame, and he wished it could have been him with her tonight, but it couldn't. It was a shame she hadn't been patient eight years ago. Others would have taken her, even with another man's child to feed. She hadn't had to lie with a forkbeard, but now that she had, no Marroc would touch her when Gallow finally left her. Four children, and three of them half-breeds? Even Vennic had more sense. Yes, a shame.

I'd have taken you with a child from another man. It wasn't as though Merethin had been a thief or a layabout or had simply run away. He'd gone bravely to fight the forkbeards and he'd died on their spears with other decent men. There was no shame in that. *You should have waited for me.* But Fenaric had been languishing in a forest full of outlaws a hundred miles away and they'd never heard of King Tane's death or the fall of Varyxhun and Andhun or that the fighting was done with until six months after Yurlak and the Screambreaker had gone back across the sea. It was almost a year before he'd come through Middislet again, and for all that time he'd had no idea that Merethin was dead. He'd seen Arda and he'd smiled and waved and she'd smiled back, and it was only later he realised she was married to the forkbeard now, and he was, again, too late. He glowered at Nadric. He had pushed her into it. Nadric, who was getting old and needed someone who knew his way around a forge.

Well now maybe he was going to be short-handed again.

The music faltered and stopped as two soldiers rode into the barn. For a moment Fenaric was confused. The soldiers weren't Vathen from Fedderhun. Both wore mail hauberks and carried burning brands taken from the fire outside. The first one didn't have a helm but he had the terrible forked beard and a brutal scar from his eye to his ear. The second one was Gallow.

'Fenaric!' Gallow pushed through the barn. The dancing petered out; drunken villagers staggered away from Gallow's horse. Fenaric looked for somewhere to run but he was stuck in a corner beside his own cart and his barrels of beer. Gallow levelled his sword. 'You! You sent the Vathen to my house!'

'No!' Fenaric tried to shake his head but he couldn't. Couldn't even move.

'Who else, Fenaric? You went to Fedderhun; you came back. The Vathen came back with you. Did you show them which house it was? Brave of them to wait until dark.'

'No! No, I didn't!' Fenaric backed into the corner. He cringed as Gallow advanced.

'Yes, you did. Someone told you he was there. Someone sent you. How did you know?'

Fenaric glanced at Nadric. He shook his head and fell to his knees and clasped his hands, begging. 'Modris have mercy!' He should have known better. Never cross a fork-beard. His bladder suddenly felt very full.

'I did it,' said Arda. She stood proud in the middle of the barn, pushing past the others to stand across from Gallow, hands on her hips. 'I told him to do it.'

The look on Gallow's face was murderous. 'Why, wife? Why would you do that?'

'I told you I didn't want that man in my house. I said that many times and you never listened.' She pointed at Corvin and turned to the Marroc around her. 'Do you know who this is? This is the Widowmaker, the Nightmare of the North. In *my* house.' She rounded on Gallow. 'You said he'd be gone in the morning. And he wasn't. So yes, when Fenaric went to Fedderhun I told him to bring the Vathen, that I had a forkbeard from Lostring Hill in my house if they wanted him. I never said who, and I told no one else. Bluntly, I thought he'd be dead by the time they came and that would have been fine for all of us.'

Gallow turned on Fenaric. 'Did they pay you?' Fenaric shook his head but he couldn't help looking at the barrels of ale. 'If they did then that's blood money, and you give whatever they gave you to Arda and let it hang around her like a curse.' He backed his horse away and looked at them all. 'Do you know what you've done?'

'*You* brought him here!' snapped Arda. Sometimes she was the only one of the Marroc who wasn't afraid of him.

'I came from fighting the Vathen with a soldier who was hurt, defending our land!' roared Gallow. 'Does it matter who he was?'

Arda matched him, thunder for thunder. 'Yes! When it's the Widowmaker, yes, it does!'

Fenaric stared at Corvin. 'I didn't know who it was.' *Oh Modris. The Nightmare of the North! He'll kill every one of us.* Gallow's eyes were on him, hard and narrow. 'I swear! I didn't know!'

'And that makes it somehow better? That you betrayed a man without even knowing his name?' Gallow snarled and growled and turned his horse. 'Listen well, Marroc!' he cried. 'The Vathen have come to Middislet. You did that, not I. Now two of their soldiers are dead. That? *I* did that. And Fenaric, you may not have told them who was in my house, but someone did. The Vathen know that the Screambreaker was here and more will come. Go! Hide in the Crackmarsh! Stay there this time and don't wait for Vennic to see ghosts up in the hills – they *will* come. If they burn your homes, let that be all you lose. You're fools, all of you.' He jumped off his horse, grabbed Fenaric and dragged him towards Arda. 'Screambreaker, if anyone leaves the barn before I come back, kill them!'

The forkbeard nodded. He looked distant, as though he was barely listening. His eyes were half closed behind the curve of his helm. Fenaric whimpered as Gallow hauled him along. *Modris, but he's strong!*

Arda looked at Corvin in disgust. 'He's half de—'

Gallow slapped her before she could finish, hard enough to knock her down. Fenaric tried to pull away, certain now that Gallow meant to kill them both as soon as they were outside, but he couldn't break free. He knew, because Arda had told him, that Gallow had never struck her in all the years they'd been married.

Gallow didn't break stride. He tossed his torch among the cringing Marroc and bent down as Arda started to rise. He grabbed her arm with his free hand and dragged them both out of the barn like a pair of naughty children, walked them past the bonfire, threw Fenaric to the ground and drew his sword.

'No!' Arda at last sounded scared. Fenaric couldn't find his voice.

Gallow pointed his sword at Fenaric's face. 'Now listen to me. I'll leave with the Screambreaker tonight. I'll take the Vathan horses and everything they had. There'll be no sign they were here but that won't save you. How far away were they, Fenaric? Closer than Fedderhun?' Fenaric shook his head. 'Then you have two days, perhaps three. Arda, for once in your bloody-minded life, listen and do what I say: Fenaric will take you south in his wagon. You'll take the children with you. You'll go to Varyxhun. There are two horses tethered beside the workshop. They're Lhosir horses. Take them.' He ground his teeth, staring at Arda. 'Take everything you can from the forge. Take Nadric and his tools. You and Nadric can ride the horses. Fenaric will take the children and whatever from the forge that can't be replaced in his cart. The Widowmaker thanks you for your hospitality.' He threw a purse at her feet and shook his head. 'Why, woman? Why couldn't you simply do as you were told for once?'

Arda stared up at Gallow with burning eyes. 'He's half-dead. How do you think he'll stop anyone from leaving the barn?'

'He won't need to. They won't dare to try. You told them who he was and that'll be enough. You'll wait for me in Varyxhun. Keep my sons safe. I'll deal with you when I return.' His glare fell on Fenaric and his sword touched the skin of the carter's throat. Fenaric scrabbled away but the sword point simply followed until he gave up and wept. 'I'll not kill now you, carter, because Arda has need of you, but let it be clear in your mind – that's all that saves you. I've seen the way you look at her. You'll take her to Varyxhun. You'll do whatever you must to look after her and her children, all of them. When I return, and I will, I'll judge you by how well you've done this. And if you run from me, Fenaric, or if you touch her, I'll hunt you. I'll find you and I will sever your ribs from your spine and pull out your lungs like wings and sprinkle salt on you as you die.'

Fenaric gagged. The way the forkbeards had hung King

Tane's huscarls along the roads to Sithhun after Tane was driven to the mountains.

'Do you understand, Fenaric?'

He nodded, weeping with fear. Arda spat at Gallow's feet. '*Now* you care about your family? Now, when it's too late?'

'Stay here if you'd see what *your* caring has done!'

She turned from him. 'Go! Take your Widowmaker. Don't bother coming back!'

Gallow fixed her with icy eyes. 'My sons will need a mother a few years longer. Be thankful for that.'

'You never changed, did you? Cut your beard and pretended to be meek, but the forkbeard was always there.'

He nodded. 'Yes, Arda. As well you know. And neither of us would have had it any other way.' For a long moment Gallow stared at her. The look on his face was a strange one, impossible to read. His hand strayed to his chest as if touching his heart. Then he turned back to the barn. 'When the Screambreaker and I are gone, go and be with our children. They'll wonder what's happening. They'll be afraid. And if you must tell them anything at all, be sure it's the truth. All of it.'

He left. Fenaric watched him go. 'I'm sorry ...'

She hissed at him and glared. 'So was it Nadric who told you, was it?'

He nodded hopelessly. 'He said ... I thought ... Why did you say it was you?'

She rolled her eyes at him and shook her head. 'Pull yourself together and be a man, Fenaric. Go and get your cart ready.'

He lay still, too weak to move. When he finally found his strength again, he lifted his head in time to see the shadow-shapes of two horsemen vanishing into the night. Arda got up and left him there, and the look on her face was every bit as sharp as Gallow's sword.

11

THE CRACKMARSH

Years of living among the Marroc put the words on Gallow's tongue: *You did well in the barn.* He bit them back. Sitting on a horse while Gallow put the fear of the Maker-Devourer into Arda and that idiot of a carter? Nothing for a Lhosir to feel proud about, no matter how hurt he was.

'Since you're not about to die, I suppose you might stay on that horse as far as Andhun,' he said instead.

'I don't want you riding with me, clean-skin.' The Screambreaker's words were weak, his voice at the end of its strength. 'You want to leave a trail for the Vathen to follow, you do that. I'll make one too. I'll make my own.'

'You'll have to speak louder,' said Gallow.

'You heard.'

Gallow sniffed the night air. The trail towards the Crackmarsh was easy enough to follow in the moonlight. He still carried a burning branch from the festival fire and he'd walked the path a dozen times. 'I think I must have taken a blow to the head in the battle too. Hearing's been here and there ever since. You'll have to shout to be sure I don't misunderstand you. Probably not a good idea in the middle of the night.'

'Go away! I do not want you with me,' growled Corvin. It wasn't exactly a shout.

'I think,' said Gallow, as if he hadn't heard, 'that if I were to go back, I might just kill my wife.'

'Do you need me to do it for you, bare-face? For a betrayal like that I'd hang my own brother. You should have dragged her by the hair back into that barn and whipped her to death in front of the rest of them!'

'Your brother's at the bottom of the sea, Screambreaker, and when he was alive, I think most of us were surprised with each day that passed when one of you still hadn't killed the other. The Marroc aren't like us.' He wouldn't kill Arda, not for trying her best to look after what was hers. Couldn't. But Fenaric was a different matter. Fenaric he wanted to hurt. Badly. His blood was up, his axe had tasted the enemy and that's what Fenaric had made himself: the enemy. 'Maker-Devourer. I have two sons by Arda and a daughter. They're too young to ride with us.'

'Good. Then go back and watch over them and leave me be.'

'No, better I ride with you, Screambreaker. I'll save my rage for cracking Vathan skulls, not Marroc ones. You can show me the road to Andhun, which I might not find were I alone, and remind me why I should grow my beard again. And I'll return your generosity by hunting food and water for you.' If he put it like that and made it sound like somehow the Screambreaker was the one guiding them and not the other way round then maybe Corvin would at least shut up about being left to manage on his own.

'That woman took your beard. Is she why you stayed in Andhun?'

'Not at first.'

'But she's why you never came back.' The Screambreaker screwed up his face. 'I've seen how you look at her. And how she looks at you. Women like that make men weak. You forget who you are.'

'You're wrong, Screambreaker. I've not forgotten. I chose to be something else.' They rode in silence after that. Gallow watched Corvin's shoulders start to sag and then the Screambreaker slumped in his saddle. They were only a few miles from Middislet but the Marroc wouldn't start for the Crackmarsh until dawn and probably not for hours afterwards. Gallow reined in his horse. 'It's been a long night and I don't trust these Vathan beasts not to trip and throw me. I'll stop here and make my camp. I have food and water if you choose to join me.' He half expected Corvin to refuse, to insist on riding on alone until he fell off his horse, but the Screambreaker didn't answer. When Gallow stopped, Corvin's horse stopped too. The old man was asleep. Gallow lifted him down and got a fire going. It had been a long night.

He rose again at dawn. The fire was down to embers but they were enough to light some kindling and start a new one. He roused Corvin with warm water and soft bread and the smell of roasting meat. 'Breakfast, Screambreaker. Make the most of it. We won't eat like this again until Andhun. I've got food for another day and then we'll be foraging in the Crackmarsh. You'll not get another fire either, not with Vathen on our trail.'

'Go home, Gallow.' That was all he said, but he didn't spit out the water or throw Gallow's food away. Arda would howl about the meat, the only piece of it they'd had for weeks. She wouldn't have forgotten when he found her again in Varyxhun either, but they'd be doing well if that was the worst they had to scream about by then.

'We'll be at the edge of the Crackmarsh long before the sun peaks,' he said as they rode. 'We'll head west when we reach it. Once the sun is high we'll rest a while. We'll make it as obvious as we can which way we went. Maybe the Vathen will be too eager for our blood to stop and hunt for a handful of Marroc.'

The Screambreaker laughed. 'Shall we scare away the wolves and the bears and the bandits for them? Perhaps the foxes and the badgers too? Their teeth are sharp, after all, and their claws can leave a nasty scratch.'

Gallow ignored the scorn in the Screambreaker's words. 'Outlaws might lurk in its fringes, but the Crackmarsh is no place for food and shelter. The wolves and the bears know that and yes, the foxes and the badgers too. The only things that hunt there are the ghuldogs. You can try to scare *them* away if you like. Likely as not they'll come for us.'

They rode hard through the morning; when they stopped, Corvin didn't so much climb off his horse as fall. The Screambreaker waved Gallow away, made angry noises and then fell asleep. While he snored, Gallow wandered the edge of the woods and the broken stones alone. The Marroc would go to the closer caves a few hours east of here, but if the Vathen came in any numbers then caves and trees wouldn't save them. He'd left a trail that anyone could find so far. Later he'd take that trail into the Crackmarsh. They'd disappear – almost impossible not to in the marsh – but the Vathen would know by then exactly where they were going. Andhun. He had a two-day start, at least, given how long it would take for the Vathen to find reinforcements. Easy enough.

'Why did you face them in the field, Screambreaker?' he asked when the Screambreaker was awake again. 'Why make your stand on Lostring Hill? They were five times our numbers, maybe ten.'

'More than ten,' Corvin said. 'But Fedderhun has no walls, bare-beard. The battle would have destroyed the town and the Vathen would have won all the same.'

'They're only Marroc. Isn't that what you used to say?'

'I did, and there's little enough glory in hiding behind Marroc soldiers on the battlefield, never mind their women too.'

'Little enough glory in riding your enemy down from the back of a horse or slaughtering them with arrows from far away,' muttered Gallow, 'but the Nightmare of the North did both in his time.'

'The Marroc got too good at running.' The Screambreaker spat. 'They wouldn't face us any more. As soon as a man runs, he's no longer a man. Makes him the same as an animal and there's neither honour nor dishonour in killing an animal, it's simply a chore. A bear or a boar, they're a different matter, but they won't run if you fight them one against one and don't hide behind an army of spears and shields.' He turned away. 'Yurlak kept falling ill. See how his strength came back when he returned across the sea to his home? These Marroc sapped the life out of him. The fighting had to end. We needed to go home.' A thin smile settled on his lips. 'Andhun will be different. Andhun has walls and even the Marroc can fight if you give them a wall to hide behind. Varyxhun showed us that. The Vathen won't get past Andhun. We'll smash them in the field and the Marroc will hold the walls.'

Gallow helped him onto his horse. That was the Screambreaker. He'd let the Marroc hold the walls of Andhun because he didn't trust them in the field, but give him a few thousand Lhosir and he'd face the Vathen in the open no matter how great their numbers. Five thousand Lhosir had beaten an army of Marroc said to be thirty thousand strong. That had been the height of the war before Sithhun fell, before Gallow had crossed the sea, and so all he'd heard were the stories. Corvin had earned his names that day. Widowmaker to the Marroc, Screambreaker to the Lhosir.

They reached the edges of the Crackmarsh. In the distance mountains darkened the southern horizon. Varyxhun nestled somewhere on their edges where the River Isset emerged into the hills. A canyon channelled the water, funnelling its energy, and then spat it into a great flat plain two score miles wide and circled by hills. The Crackmarsh, and here it was. Water everywhere.

It rained that night and they rose stiff and miserable in the morning. Corvin's face was glassy-pale. He didn't complain but then he wouldn't, not until he fell off his horse stone dead and probably not even then. As soon as they set off, Gallow steered their course deeper into the water meadows. The changes came slowly. The ground became wetter, the undergrowth darker and denser and more tangled. Their horses' hooves began to sink into the earth. By the middle of the day they were walking through ankle-deep water that stretched ahead as far as either of them could see. Islands hunched out of it – hundreds of them – some bare, most clustered with dense stands of trees. Here and there some grew out of the water itself. They stood on thick tangles of roots and their branches were twisted and ancient. They looked sickly.

'That Vathan who escaped, he'll have reached Fedderhun by now.' In the distance, away from the mountains, Gallow could see the hills on the far side of the marsh where the land rose and then sloped towards Andhun and the sea. 'With luck we'll be across the marsh before they get here.'

He tied Corvin to his saddle in the afternoon when the old warrior finally lost his battle with sleep and succumbed, and pushed them on hard and far. One night in the Crackmarsh would be more than enough. As the daylight began to fade he chose an island that looked big enough to shelter two men and their horses. He tried to light a fire, but between the rain and the marsh everything was too wet.

'The Marroc have a story about this marsh,' said Corvin. Gallow grunted. He'd thought the old general was asleep.

'They have several.'

'They used to tell me that the marsh was cursed and haunted. They told me there were hills here once long ago. The Aulians crossed the mountains and built a great city in the middle of it. They catacombed the hills with tunnels to bury their dead, just as the Marroc do now. They liked to dig, the Aulians. Then the city was struck by plague and there were so many dead that the living couldn't make new tunnels quickly enough, and so one night the dead got up and dug tunnels of their own. They dug an enormous labyrinth, huge and vast and so far and so deep that one day they reached the river. The water rushed under the hills and brought their tunnels down, and the hills and the city on top of them as well, but the dead didn't know any better and so they kept on digging. They're still there. Still digging. The ghosts and spirits that haunt this place are Aulians.'

'The Aulians never built a city here and there aren't any ghosts or spirits.' Gallow lay down and closed his eyes. 'The Marroc around Fedderhun say there used to be a fine valley here until a witch came to live in it. The witch was so wicked that the one day the river changed its course to wash her away and scour the land of every trace of her. That's why nothing good grows here. Witch's taint.'

'That's quite a witch then.'

'Oh, she was a very powerful witch and very wicked.' Gallow laughed. 'Aren't they all? And have you ever met a real one?'

'If a witch is an old crone then I've met many. But one who talks to the spirits of the Herenian Marches?' The Screambreaker spat. 'Witches or the dead of some ancient plague scratching away under our feet? Ghosts and goblins. Stories for frightening children.'

'The ghuldogs are real enough.'

'Then you watch for them, bare-beard.'

'I will.'

By the time he'd stripped the horses, the general was already snoring again.

12

IRON AND STEEL

For the third time in as many hours Sarvic's boot stuck in the mud of the Crackmarsh and he couldn't pull it out. The water on top was only ankle-deep, but the mud would swallow a man whole if he stood still for long enough.

'Shit on a stick, Sarvic!' hissed Valaric. 'You're worse than a forkbeard. Special shoes, is it?' He crouched low in the swamp, motionless amid the tree roots. Sarvic took the bow off his back and handed it to Angry Jonnic. Every movement had to be painstakingly slow. The Vathen on their horses were close. Trouble was, slow and careful wasn't going to get his boot out of the mud. Angry Jonnic wrinkled his nose.

'Swamp stink gets worse every time you move.'

Valaric was watching the Vathen. 'I wondered why that forkbeard saved your worthless hide back on Lostring Hill. Now I know. Make my life miserable, that's why.'

Angry Jonnic braced himself against a tree. He and Sarvic wrapped their arms around each other and heaved. The swamp let go of Sarvic's foot with a deep belch and a pungent stink of marsh gas. Valaric shook his head and winced at the splash. Jonnic settled himself against a tree. When Sarvic had done the same, Jonnic handed him his bow.

'Wait on me,' growled Valaric. 'And Sarvic, for the love of Modris, show me it was worth it.' It was already clear as the sky on a summer's day that the only reason Sarvic was riding with them at all was because the filthy bastard demon-beard who'd saved his skin when the line broke on

Lostring Hill hadn't left any of them with too much choice. But he was here *now*, soaking and mud-covered instead of still on the back of his nice new horse, because he'd said he could shoot a bow. And that, at least, he could.

Luck was a fickle thing in war. He'd been lucky to live through Lostring Hill. Lucky to find a dozen dead fork-beards and their horses – some good looting there. Not so lucky that twenty-odd Vathen had been following them for a day now. Valaric had ridden off the road and into the Crackmarsh to see if they'd go away but they hadn't. So now it came to this. Twenty Vathen probably thought they had the easy beating of a dozen Marroc, but that was because they hadn't met Valaric the Wolf until now. The Wolf made his own luck.

Valaric let fly when the nearest Vathen were some fifty paces away. He didn't shoot at the ones at the front. His first arrow flew wide, must have missed the Vathan at the back by a finger. The rider jerked, startled. Angry Jonnic put an arrow in his neck. Sarvic shot the lead rider's horse neatly through the ear.

'Rat's piss!' Valaric strung another arrow. The Vathen were confused but they wouldn't stay that way for long. One in the middle must have found his helmet uncomfortable and had taken it off. Sarvic cleaned out his ear with a shaft of wood and tickled his skull with a tip of iron. The Vathan was dead before he even started to fall.

Jonnic and Valaric went for the horses now. The Vathen had worked out where the arrows were coming from, but Torvic and Stannic and Silent Jonnic were leading the rest of the Marroc out from where they'd hidden behind the largest of the nearby islands, splashing their own horses out towards the Vathen while arrows tipped rider after rider off into the swamp. The Vathen had good armour and carried shields, so Valaric had said go for the horses as soon as the first volley was off – drop all that nice heavy armour into the water and the mud and watch it flounder. Now he cursed as each one fell. A fighting horse was worth a good purse.

One of the Vathen was looking right at him. Open helm. Sarvic shot him in the face. Down three men already, with five more thrashing in the water, the rest of the Vathen thought better of it, turned and fled.

'Save your arrows.' Valaric watched them go. He unwrapped himself from his tree and strode with slow deliberate steps out into the water. Stannic and the rest got there first. Sarvic was last but at least he didn't get stuck again. By the time he caught up, Valaric had taken his axe to two of the Vathen and Torvic was in the middle of riding down a third. A fourth was face down in the swamp and hadn't moved. Which left the fifth. The one who'd been at the front. Valaric picked him up right out of the water, armour and all. 'And who by the tears of the Weeping God are you?' He didn't wait for the Vathan to answer, just threw him back into the water and then went and pulled him out again. 'I'm Valaric. Every bit as mean and every bit as much of a bastard as any forkbeard. I piss on your name, horse-lover, and I wouldn't give the wrong half of a dead rat for you or anything about you. Why are you following us?'

Took a while and a good bit of beating, but it turned out the Vathen were looking for the Screambreaker. Sarvic stood in the water meadow, soaked and smelling of swamp-rot without the first idea what they were talking about, but once the Vathan came out with that, Valaric threw back his head and roared with laughter like he'd just been offered the throne of Aulia.

'Whey-faced weasel!' He gave the Vathan a kick. 'Does it look like he's here?'

'But you found him. Didn't you?'

A chill ran all over Sarvic as he remembered the dead Lhosir in the wood, and Valaric was still there, laughing away. 'Yes, horse-lover, we did. We certainly did.' And then

Valaric spun some wild-arsed story about the forkbeard who'd dragged Sarvic down the hill and the two of them finding the Widowmaker still alive and Valaric letting the forkbeard take him – didn't ask where and didn't care – but most likely they were nicely on their way to Andhun by now. And then after all that, after they'd stripped the Vathen of anything they might sell, Valaric kicked the last one up the arse and let him go, and they all watched and laughed as the skinny little viper splashed and ran and splashed and fell his way across the Crackmarsh, getting himself away from them as fast as he possibly could.

'They do look *different* when they're not on the back of their horses,' muttered one of the Jonnics.

'Was any of that true?' Stannic and Torvic didn't look too pleased at the thought. Valaric nodded and Stannic rolled his eyes. 'Sweet Modris. The *Widowmaker*? We had the Widowmaker and you let him go?'

Valaric shot a look at Sarvic. 'A life for a life,' he said. 'Now shut it!' He bared his teeth at them all and swung himself back onto his horse. 'If you're all done stripping the bodies, boys, we'd best be gone before it's dark and the ghuldogs come sniffing.' No one was going to argue with that.

When Sarvic tried to move, his foot was stuck again.

13

THE ROAD TO ANDHUN

It was a quiet splash at the edge of the water that woke him, but Gallow had his axe in his hand even before he'd finished opening his eyes. In the gloom a shape was crawling out of the Crackmarsh. It had arms and legs like a man, scrawny and thin, but it crawled out of the water on all fours and its head had a pointed snout like a dog. It crouched where Gallow had guided their horses onto the island and sniffed. Behind it another snouty head poked out of the water. A second creature emerged and then a third.

Ghuldogs. Gallow let out a shout, half fear, half fury, and charged through the trees. Three heads whipped round to stare at him. The nearest sprang, leaping straight at him, jaws wide to rip out his throat. Gallow smashed the beast with his shield and battered it away. The other two crouched and stared. Moonlight shone in their dead eyes; then one jumped for the arm that held his axe while the other snapped at his feet. He blocked low with his shield, twisted out of the way and brought his axe down on the creature's skull. Bone crunched and blood and brains spattered his arm.

The first ghuldog was up again; it threw itself at his throat; he dodged, but not enough and its teeth clamped down, tearing at his shoulder through his mail. The second one seized his shield; he dropped that and let out a gleeful howl and swung again, shearing the creature's spine between the shoulder blades before it thought to let go. It fell twitching at his feet.

The last one still had his shield arm. He bashed it with the haft of his axe, cracking its nose. It shrieked and let go, snarled, and before it could think to spring again Gallow split its head in two. He stood over the corpses, fighting for air, watching the light fade from their eyes and looking around for any more. His shield was at his feet, the hand that would have held it pressed to his chest, to the locket and the little piece of Arda he still carried with him.

'Stupid, stupid ...' Who or what, he didn't know. When no more ghuldogs came, he picked up the shield. His arm hurt, aching and throbbing. The bite of a ghuldog was poisonous and rumoured to be cursed, but he didn't dare take off his hauberk to see if its teeth had broken his skin, not now.

The Screambreaker was still snoring where Gallow had left him. Gallow sat beside him, rested his axe across his knees and leaned his shield against his arm. There'd be no more sleep tonight. He touched the locket again and looked at the old man sleeping. 'You'd never understand, old man. You just wouldn't. It was a convenience to start with, that's true. Nadric was growing too old to wield the hammer. Arda with a child by a man lost from the fighting. And I ... Well, I had my reasons for not sailing back across the sea with the rest of you. I was off to Aulia across the mountains, but truth was I just needed a place and a thing to be. We sheltered each other.'

The Screambreaker mumbled something and shifted in his sleep. Gallow pressed the locket hard against his skin. 'I wish you hadn't broken that, old man. I was happy with that life.'

He sat watch until dawn and then shook Corvin awake. 'Ghuldogs,' he said shortly. 'Guard yourself.' The bodies by the shore were gone when he looked. There must have been more then. They'd be out there in the water now, watching and waiting for the next twilight. He went back to Corvin once the old general was up and moving and took off his hauberk and the leather jerkin underneath. The mail had held. His shoulder was sore and scraped from the mauling but the ghuldog's teeth hadn't found a way through. There'd be bruises and some stiffness but nothing worse.

The Screambreaker glared at him. 'I'm hungry.'

'Good. You've hardly eaten for days.'

They shared the last of the food from the village and set off again through the marsh. In places the water was still ankle-deep but more often now it came to their horses' knees and sometimes they were almost swimming. Late spring – the Isset was in full flow and the marsh water was as deep as it would get. Ghuldog territory, although in daylight the ghuldogs wouldn't trouble them as long as they kept going. He stopped them once around midday to let the horses rest a while – Corvin was asleep again – and after that they pushed on until dusk. They were slow, though, and as the light began to fail they were still in the marsh. He'd hoped to be out by now – between the Ghuldogs and the Vathen they weren't short of reasons to press on hard – but it was what it was.

'You sleep; I'll watch. In the middle of the night we'll change.' He gave the Screambreaker the harder watch, the one through the small hours before dawn, but the Scream-breaker didn't complain, and he didn't mention it when Gallow didn't wake him up until the sky started to lighten again. There were no ghuldogs this time, at least. He slept for an hour while the Screambreaker sat beside the horses, grumbling on about being hungry.

They reached the edge of the Crackmarsh in the early afternoon, pushed on over the first brow of the wild grassy hills until they were out of sight of the wetland, and there they stopped. Gallow dismounted and fell into the grass with a smile and a sigh. 'The horses need to rest,' he said. 'They haven't eaten for two days either. They need to graze and so do I.'

Neither of them would say it but the Screambreaker

needed to rest too. He was already taking off his boots and rubbing his feet. 'So have you *got* any food?'

'No, and you know it.'

'Fat lot of use you are then.'

'How about *you* find us some.'

'*You're* the Marroc. Have you not got a bow? Didn't they teach you?'

He wasn't a Marroc and he hadn't learned much since he'd crossed the sea, except how, maybe, it didn't matter as much as he'd always thought whether you were Marroc, Vathan, Lhosir, Aulian or what. But the Screambreaker could barely move and so he took a Vathan bow and a quiver of arrows from one of the horses and lost nearly all of them shooting at rabbits until he got one. More a stroke of luck than skill, but he wasn't going to shake his fist at it. After the last few days he reckoned he was due a bit of luck. With the rabbit in his hands, he walked back up to the crest of the last hill and looked out across the Crackmarsh. Miles and miles of water glittering still in the sun, pockmarked by islands like boils on a pox victim's skin. The wind blew in his face, bringing the smell of rot. The Vathen, if they were following, would be on the other side of all this by now. From here that looked pleasingly distant. With a bit of luck they wouldn't be ready for the ghuldogs either.

He stretched his aching back. Eight years working in a forge and his muscles had forgotten all about riding a horse.

Corvin was asleep and the horses had strayed when he returned so he skinned the rabbit and let it hang for a while and dozed. As darkness fell he set a fire. The rabbit was cooked and eaten and he and the Screambreaker sat licking their fingers.

'I remember days like this,' Gallow said. 'Scouting these hills, looking for traces of the Marroc so you could fight them.'

'You were a scout?' Corvin snorted.

'Sometimes.'

'I do remember a Gallow,' he said after he'd stared at the flames a while. 'A good fighter.' He tugged the braids of his beard. 'Why did you shame yourself?'

'I chose to stay.' Gallow shrugged. 'I thought cutting my beard would make me more a part of them.'

'But in the name of the Maker-Devourer, why would you want that? They're sheep! The man I remember didn't belong here. I remember a warrior. Fierce. A whirlwind and a wolf. Men looked up to you. Or maybe I have some other Gallow in mind. Gallow Truesword, he used to be called. Killed a lot of Marroc. Never wavered.'

'I did kill a lot of Marroc.'

'How many?'

'More than I can remember.'

The Screambreaker lay back and stretched out his arms. 'So why *did* you stay, Truesword?'

'I told you – I didn't care for Twelvefingers and it looked like he was about to become our king.'

'You were wrong.'

'Yurlak was stronger than any of us thought.'

The Screambreaker stretched again and groaned. 'It did him good to be home. The air is different here. Stifling. The air across the sea is cold and crisp and smells of mountains and the ocean. It tastes of salt. Here it tastes of nothing. See?' He sniffed. 'Medrin made mistakes when he was young, that's true. Coming across the sea to fight the Marroc changed him. That wound he got. Everyone thought he was going to die, but he didn't. Made him stronger on the inside as well, when he finally got over it.'

Gallow sniffed. 'They'll need you in Andhun.'

'There are already two thousand of us in Andhun and more on the way.' Corvin laughed. 'They don't need me.'

'The Vathen still outnumber you ten to one. You saw how many there were.'

'It didn't help King Tane.'

'Perhaps not, but the Vathen aren't the Marroc either.'

They sat in silence for a while, watching the fire die. 'Grow back your beard, Gallow,' said Corvin. 'Stay in Andhun. Fight with us.'

'I have a wife and family who'll be waiting for me in Varyxhun.'

'You still have a wife?' The Screambreaker snorted. Gallow couldn't answer that, not easily. Yes. He did. But ...

He shook his head. 'I have sons, Screambreaker. I should abandon them?'

'Tell me, Gallow, would you see them grow up as Marroc or as Lhosir?'

He had no answer to that. Both.

'Go and fetch them. When the Vathen are broken, bring them back across the sea and raise them as they should be raised. *We're* your people, Gallow, not these sheep. You can't escape that. I saw you fight the Vathen outside your home. You made me proud. You were a warrior.' He laughed. 'I'll not quickly forget how we sat on our stolen horses, mailed and with sharp iron in our hands, the two of us and all those Marroc circled around, scared out of their wits. I could barely keep my head up. Sheep, Gallow. You live among sheep and yet you remain a wolf.'

'They do make a good ale though.'

'That they do.'

They slept under the stars. In the morning Gallow carefully lifted a sod of turf and buried the remains of their fire and the bones of the rabbit beneath it. He pushed them on as hard as he dared, stopping only for water and to hunt with the last of the Vathan arrows. Another day took them to the edge of the hills. The Screambreaker was getting stronger. Three or four more would see them to Andhun, and then ... And then to Varyxhun. To Arda. He'd have to face her and face what she'd done. He dreaded it.

At the top of the last rise before the plains he stopped. Andhun was out there somewhere, beyond the horizon haze. 'I tell you one thing, Screambreaker. There's simplicity to battle. Sometimes having a family feels like having to run kingdom in a court where no one listens to a word I say.'

The Screambreaker laughed. 'I can't offer you any kingdoms but I can find you a fight or two if that's what you're after.' He pointed out over the plain to a plume of smoke a few miles away, too large to be a campfire. 'What's that?'

Gallow squinted. 'There are Marroc farms and villages here. Nothing else. Andhun is that way.' He pointed off into the haze. 'Another three nights.'

'And will these Marroc farms and villages have food for us? My belly rumbles and you've used up all our arrows with your poor shooting.'

'The Screambreaker *I* remember could catch a rabbit with his bare hands.'

Corvin laughed. 'I could never do that. I did see a man kill a rabbit with his axe once. A fine throw.'

'A lucky one.'

'I thought so, but it was Jyrdas One-Eye back when he had two, and so I chose to hold my tongue.'

They sat on their horses, watching in silence as the smoke rose.

'That's too big for a campfire. That's a house burning, or else a barn,' said Corvin. 'That means Vathen. How many down there, do you think?'

'More than two.' Gallow wrinkled his nose. What were the Vathen doing this far from the coast?

'There might be some of your precious Marroc to save.'

'Doubt it. For all we know the whole Vathan army could be between us and Andhun by now. The wise thing would be to avoid them. Stick close to the edge of the hills and circle round. Come at Andhun along the valley of the Isset.'

Then again, the Isset valley itself could be crawling with Vathen looking for a place to cross the river.

The Screambreaker shrugged. 'There's only one way to know, Gallow, and I *am* hungry. When it's dark, we'll go and look.'

14

GOSOMON

Duvakh stepped over the body of the Marroc farmer who'd been stupid enough not to run away and looked the other man up and down. Shivering, starving, dull-eyed and with nothing to his name except a shirt. He couldn't have been in the hills for more than a few days, yet he was half-dead. Still, he was definitely Vathan. Duvakh even knew him. 'Gosomon? From Krenda's ride? Why, Gosomon of Krenda's Ride, are you hiding in a Marroc barn?'

Gosomon told him. By the time he was done they were inside the farmhouse, eating some of the dead Marroc's food and drinking his beer. Duvakh's head was buzzing. The rest of his ride sat around, scratching themselves and patting their bellies. Good food was to be cherished. There were only five of them – six if you threw in the ghost he'd found in the barn – and the Marroc here had a good larder.

'I reckon we'll stay here another day or two.' He pointed to Gosomon. 'You might want to stay here a bit longer. Get your strength up.'

Gosomon shook his head. 'Krenda Bashar and the ardshan are waiting on my news. I need one of your horses.'

The other riders laughed but Duvakh didn't. The sun was setting. The flames from the burned-out barn had largely died away. The glowing embers would keep his riders and his horses pleasantly warm through the night. He looked at the gash on the back of his hand and then sucked at it. The wound was still weeping. 'Krenda and the ardshan? I'd go right back to your swamp if I were you.' He shook his head. 'Hai Frika!'

The laughter died. Duvakh scowled. Gosomon's expression made him uneasy. He helped himself to some more of the dead farmer's ale and made a face. An unpleasant drink, but it did the job. 'We smashed those Marroc at Lostring Hill to pieces, eh?' he said. 'Broke their line and slaughtered them.' He'd killed three men by his own count, charging down from the crest of the hill, cutting them down before the Marroc managed to reach the woods. 'No one thought the forkbeards would be at Fedderhun, but they were and they broke like the rest. So you were one of the ones who went chasing off after the runners, eh?'

Gosomon looked up. His face was hollow and haunted. Even in front of the fire with a couple of blankets wrapped around him he was shivering. A sheen of sweat covered his brow.

'Scatter them far and wide,' Duvakh said. 'We learned that when we took gold from the forkbeards. The Marroc are good at running but not as good as our riders are at chasing, eh?' He poured himself another cup. '*While* you were off chasing, you might like to know that the ardshan and the Weeping Giant had a falling-out. Next thing we knew we were on the move again.' He puffed his cheeks, remembering the disappointment of Fedderhun, small and worthless, and how eager the bashars and their riders had been sink their teeth into something worth plundering. 'Someone put it in the ardshan's head that the forkbeards at Andhun weren't ready for us. We thought we'd get in quick and have the place to ourselves for a few days before the Weeping Giant and his foot-sloggers could catch up with us. Load of toss that was. Not ready? Forkbeards looked plenty ready to me.'

'Wasn't so bad, though,' chipped in another rider. 'At least we didn't have the Weeping Giant looming over us all the time telling us what we couldn't do ...'

Gosomon's head jerked sideways, staring at the wall as though if he looked hard enough, he might see right through it. A hand, sharply raised, drew silence. For a few long seconds they sat there frozen. Then Gosomon relaxed. 'Thought I heard a noise.'

Duvakh got up. 'I'll go and look. Need a piss anyway. Dansukh, tell him what happened at Andhun, eh? Let him know why he's just a little bit too late with that word he's carrying to Krenda and the ardshan.'

'You took it? You took Andhun?'

'Not exactly.' Duvakh laughed, shook his head and got up, leaving Dansukh to pick up the story. Outside, he walked around the farmhouse in case someone was out there but he couldn't see anything except the dying flames from the barn and the shadows they cast. He belched loudly and stamped away from the embers for a piss. The forkbeards had come out from behind Andhun's walls. Duvakh reckoned the ardshan had had the numbers by about two to one and everyone who'd fought with them said that the forkbeards knew squat about fighting against mounted soldiers; then again everyone who fought with them knew they were crazy too. Well, there wouldn't be any Vathen coming back from Andhun saying the forkbeards knew squat about fighting horsemen any more. Turned out they knew perfectly well with their wall of shields and their long spears and their Marroc archers. Still crazy, though.

He sighed as the pressure in his bladder eased. Say one thing for the Marroc – their beer tasted rotten but it did the trick. Oh, and say another thing for them – they could shoot. An arrow had torn through his gauntlet and ripped open the skin across the back of his hand. He counted himself lucky it hadn't been a lot worse. The forkbeards, when they'd charged, had hit the ardshan's lines like a battering ram. The ardshan's foot-sloggers had simply folded and crumbled. Duvakh wasn't sure the forkbeards had ever actually stopped moving.

He kicked the dead Marroc farmer one more time, wondering why this one hadn't run like the rest when he'd seen Vathen coming over the hill. Marroc always ran. That was the joy of them.

Quiet footsteps came up behind him.

'Suppose we'll have to cross the hills or make our way back to the coast and the Weeping Giant,' he muttered to whoever it was who'd come out to join him. He laughed. 'And then listen to the foot-sloggers' jibes and taunts.' He spat. 'Maybe we should stay out here on the edge of the wild, helping ourselves to whatever comes our way. Tempting thought, eh?'

Some sixth sense suddenly made him wonder if the footsteps behind him weren't another one of his ride out for a piss after all. His sixth sense was right too, just not quick enough. By the time he turned the axe was already coming down.

The Vathan turned at the last moment. His mouth fell open and he reeled back in surprise. Gallow's axe blade went straight through his face, opening him from cheek to cheek and smashing his jaw. He made a hooting noise and then the backswing caught him cleanly on the nape of his neck. Gallow caught him as he fell. He dragged the dead Vathan into the shadows and crouched beside him, listening. There were five horses tethered outside the farmhouse. Four more Vathen inside then. With luck the others were drunk too.

The house fell quiet. A voice called, 'Duvakh?' Gallow crept back around the walls, bent almost double as he passed each window, to where the Screambreaker stood with an ear pressed against the stone. He held up four fingers and pointed inside. Trying to get Corvin to stay a half-mile away with the horses was like talking to the tide, asking it not to ebb and flow. He'd given up.

The Screambreaker shook his head and held up another finger.

'They heard me,' Gallow whispered.

The Screambreaker yanked him close and hissed in his ear. 'Didn't they just. Clumsy oaf. Should have let him go back inside.'

'I want to take them where there's space.'

'And *I* wanted to hear what happened at Andhun.' He spat. 'Still, too late for that now. They heard something and now they're nervy as virgins in spring. Get on with it and call them out!'

'No.' He wished he'd kept some of the Vathan arrows now. When they were on their horses, the Vathen preferred bows or their javelots, spears light enough to throw but hefty enough to run a man through. The quivers on the horses here were empty. 'They'll come out soon enough, looking for their friend.' Gallow pointed to the edge of the shadows cast by the embers of the barn. 'I want you to stand there. They'll see you when they come out. Don't move when they challenge you. I'll take them from the side.' He'd have to be quick too, before they could get to the Screambreaker. The old man was getting stronger but he was in no shape to fight.

'That sounds like Marroc talk. We should stand together and call them out.'

'And if you were at your strength, Corvin Screambreaker, I would like nothing better. But you're not, and so a Marroc strategy must suffice if you want to eat bread and not steel tonight.'

The Screambreaker stiffened. A Lhosir was either fit to fight or useless.

'Oh, the wound to your head,' muttered Gallow. 'I dare say it impedes your sight. It's not a fair fight.' He looked at the old man, but all he got was that word on his lips. Silent but there. *Nioingr.* 'Fine then! Do it your way and die. In fact no, I'll not give you the pleasure of killing any of them.' He stalked back past the house, openly this time, shaking his axe arm loose and gripping his shield. 'Hoy!' he shouted. 'Vathen! Are you listening? There's more of us out here but none of the rest can be bothered with fighting you. They say it's too easy!' He reached the door and kicked it in. The farmhouse was a typical Marroc dwelling, one big space with a curtained-off night room. The Vathen were on their feet and ready for him with their heavy leather riding coats, long knives and axes. Not one of them had thought to put on his helm. And he was right – four not five, although there was an odd-looking Marroc cowering in a corner wearing nothing but a shirt. They had food too. It reminded Gallow how hungry he was.

Two of the Vathen rushed him together. The other two bolted for the back door. Gallow met the charge with his own, buffeting one away with a great blow from his shield. He caught the swinging axe from the other with his own weapon, barged on with his shoulder and head-butted the next Vathan in the face, cracking the man's nose. As he staggered back, Gallow turned and brought his axe down, shattering the first Vathan's collar and splitting him to his breastbone. A torrent of blood exploded over both of them and the man went down. Gallow turned. The Vathan with the broken nose dived through the curtain to the night room. Gallow ignored him, went for the two who'd run outside and caught them at their horses. The first was vaulting into the saddle – Gallow threw his axe, catching the man in the ribs and caving in his side. The horse bolted and vanished into the night, the Vathan lolling lifelessly on its back. The last one jumped at Gallow with his knife. He pulled Gallow's shield aside and stabbed. Gallow twisted sideways. The blade skittered off his mail, hard enough to spark; then he caught the man's arm with his own and gave a vicious twist. There was a crack of breaking bone and the Vathan screamed. Gallow twisted more. The man fell, writhing; before he could get back up, Gallow had his sword out and drove it through the back of the Vathan's neck.

He paused for an instant. Inside the house he saw movement – the Vathan with the broken nose bolting for the other door. He jumped up and gave chase but he needn't have bothered – the last Vathan ran straight into the Screambreaker's sword. The old man staggered. The Vathan stumbled on a few more paces and then toppled to his knees and fell to the dirt. Gallow made sure he was dead.

'That's a strong arm you have there, Screambreaker, to drive a sword through all that leather,' he said as he came back.

Corvin looked at him. He was breathing hard. 'You'll not give me the pleasure of killing any of them, eh?' He pointed. 'You missed one.'

Someone was bolting for the horses. It was the man Gallow had taken to be a Marroc. From the way he landed in the saddle and sped away, he was a Vathan after all. A Vathan with no weapon, no armour, nothing but a shirt. The Screambreaker had been right. Five, not four. Gallow reached for a stone to throw, but the old man held his arm back.

'Let him go,' he said. 'He saw my face and he knows who I am.' He bared his teeth. 'And that, Truesword, is a knife in every Vathan heart.'

15

ANDHUN

They ate what the Vathen had left and made themselves comfortable. In the morning when it was light Gallow found the first Vathan soldier who'd tried to flee lying on the ground with his horse standing beside him a hundred yards away from the farmhouse, Gallow's axe still stuck through his ribs. Gallow pulled the axe free and set about cleaning and sharpening it.

'We've missed the battle,' grumbled Corvin. 'You should have let me leave sooner.'

'You were welcome to leave whenever you wanted,' said Gallow. 'Debate that with whoever thumped you on the head after Lostring Hill. How do you know we missed it, anyway?'

'Listening to their talk before you made such a mule's arse of killing them. But look. Quivers on their saddles but no javelots, so they used them already. And the horses – they've been ridden hard. The first one you killed, he's got the sash of a ride leader. He should have sixteen men with him but he's got four. Got a fresh wound too, a cut on his hand. There's blood on one of the saddles that hasn't been cleaned. If they were scouts then their quivers would be full and they'd have bows. If they were foragers then they should have a cart or some mules. This lot were on the wrong end of a fight not long before we came. Look at the way they ran from us. No spirit left in them.'

Gallow shrugged. 'Doesn't mean they came from Andhun.'

'Well they did, no-beard. Where else?'

They took the Vathan horses and rode on towards the coast. The farms and hamlets they passed were deserted. A few were burned-out but most were intact. The Marroc had fled, fearing the coming of the Vathen, but the Vathen had followed the sea road and now the land was deserted. Even the fields were empty, the animals taken or gone.

'Twelvefingers must have sent them across the Isset.' Corvin nodded approvingly. 'Take away everything the Vathen can eat and Andhun is the only crossing.'

'Not so, old man. If you know the paths, a man – a whole army of men – could cross the Isset through the Crackmarsh. Still, I doubt the Vathen know that.'

The Screambreaker stopped and looked at him long and hard. 'They may not know it now, but sooner or later they'll find a Marroc to tell them.'

Gallow shrugged. 'Good luck to them if they try it. About time someone cleared out the ghuldogs.'

With each day the Screambreaker grew stronger. As they started at last into the line of hills before Andhun, a band of riders came over a crest heading the other way. Lhosir, eight of them. When they saw Gallow and Corvin they stopped and one rode forward apart from the rest.

'I'm Tolvis of the Black Mountain,' he called. 'Sworn blade to King Yurlak. Name yourselves.'

'I know him,' muttered Corvin.

'The man I ride with is Corvin Screambreaker,' cried Gallow. 'Known among the Marroc as the Widowmaker and the Nightmare of the North. He too is a sworn blade to King Yurlak. I am Gallow of Middislet, sworn to no one.'

'You're sworn to the king, bare-beard, whether you like it or not,' snapped Corvin.

'Corvin Screambreaker?' Tolvis of the Black Mountain took off his helm and cocked his head. 'Now there's a thing.

See, we'd heard the Nightmare of the North was dead. The Marroc have been quietly drinking to that for a week now. When they think we won't see and with one eye cast over their shoulder in case they're wrong of course.' He grinned.

'Someone at Lostring Hill was kind enough to land the Screambreaker a good blow to the head and render him senseless just long enough for me to drag him away. Come see him for yourself if you don't believe me.'

'I'll do that.' Tolvis of the Black Mountain rode closer. He was cautious, more so than Gallow would have expected, but as he came close enough to be sure of Corvin's face, a smile spread across his own. 'Maker-Devourer! It's true!'

The Screambreaker grunted. 'Tolvis of the Black Mountain is it now? You fought with me years ago but you weren't called that back then. It's a Tolvis Loudmouth that *I* seem to remember.'

The smile broadened. 'Pardon my caution, Screambreaker. You're on Vathan horses.'

'Their previous riders forgot their need of them. I'd hoped to aid you in the fight here but I hear the Vathen have already come.'

'They have, but not in all their numbers.' Tolvis turned his horse. 'Very obliging of them it was, and so we obliged them right back. I'll ride you to Andhun. We'll pass the field on the way. You'll know it when you see it – it'll be the one that's mostly the colour of Vathan blood. They were five or six thousand and a lot of them on horse, and we smashed them.'

The Screambreaker curled his nose. 'Five or six thousand? That all? There were five times that number at Fedderhun. Did they have the Sword of the Weeping God with them? The red sword Solace?'

Gallow looked at Corvin, curious. Fenaric had said something about the same thing, words he'd heard at Fedderhun, but Gallow had never repeated them to the Screambreaker.

Something he overheard from the Vathen at the farm, then?

Tolvis shrugged. 'The Comforter? They didn't have it here, no.'

'You haven't seen the main Vathan force yet.'

'Oh, we know *that*.' Tolvis laughed. 'But let them come in bits and pieces – we'll chew each one up and spit it back at the next.'

An hour later they began to see bodies. Dead Vathen, most of them speared from behind.

Corvin frowned as he passed them. 'They look like they were killed by their own horsemen.'

A black cloud of rooks or crows circled ahead of them past a stand of trees. Tolvis put on a face as though he'd eaten a mouthful of something rotten. 'Prince Medrin had those of us with horses mount up and ride them down, same as the Vathen used to do for us against the Marroc.' He laughed. 'I'll tell you, the Vathen are a lot better at it than we are. Spent more time collecting spears that had missed than we did riding.'

'*Medrin* had you do that?'

Tolvis wrinkled his nose. 'Can't say as any of us much liked it. Or were much good at it. But he *is* Yurlak's heir.'

Through the trees on the open ground Gallow could see the walls of Andhun and the valley of the Isset, which flowed through the middle of it to the sea beyond. He could smell the city in the air, the stink of human waste and fish. The battlefield was in front of them now. The bodies of the fallen had been cleared away but there were looters on the field still, nervous Marroc folk scouring the trampled grass for swords, shields, helms, anything that might have been dropped in the fight and somehow missed in the three days since. There couldn't be much left by now.

The Screambreaker rode a little further, then turned away from the walls of Andhun. He looked hard at the ground. 'The Vathen came from over there.' He pointed away from the city. 'They had horses.' He climbed down and picked up an arrow half buried in the mud. 'You had archers?'

Tolvis grunted. 'Marroc,' he said, disapproving. 'But then they came at us on horseback so they deserved that. We fought them properly after their riders fled.' He grinned. 'And we destroyed them. There were a thousand Vathan corpses here when we were done and a few hundred more scattered where they ran. Vris, Ironfoot and Igel lost a few dozen each and Jank took a thumping on the flank. Didn't get his spears and his shields sorted properly when the Vathen started throwing their javelots.'

'Vris is here?' For a moment the Screambreaker looked up and grinned. 'And Ironfoot? Jank was always a bit dim when it came to horses. Whoever put him in charge of anything, *he's* the one who needs to be thumped.'

Tolvis laughed. 'You can thump Twelvefingers then.'

'Oh, so he's here at last, is he? Then I will.'

They walked their horses slowly across the battlefield. There wasn't much left: the broken shaft of a javelot here, a few arrows in the ground, bloodstains in the mud and the grass. Three crows picked at the remains of a hand and half an arm already stripped to the bone. On the far side Gallow saw half a dozen corpses hanging from the trees. Closer and he could see what had been done to them. They hung, arms and legs dangling loose, each man drooping over a wheel with two stakes driven right through him and emerging from his back. A bolt fastened the stakes together. They were suspended like this from ropes. Below the stakes, ribs had been cleaved from spines, the lungs drawn out and with twine sewn into them and tied to the branches of the trees so the ragged sails of dead flesh seemed to rise like wings. Corvin wrinkled his nose. The men had been hanging there for days; birds had already pecked at them and strips of dried red skin and muscle dangled from gleaming bone.

Blood ravens. Gallow couldn't say whether they were

Vathen or Marroc, or Lhosir who'd first had their beards cut.

'Deserters?' Corvin frowned.

Tolvis shook his head. 'Vathen. The wounded horsemen. The ones who couldn't get away. Pretty, eh?'

'What did they do to deserve this?'

Tolvis shrugged carelessly. 'Lost.'

'Medrin ordered this, did he?' asked Gallow.

'Couldn't say. I was off discovering how hard it is to throw a spear into the back of a man who keeps dodging out of the way.'

They passed the hanging men and soon came to another cluster of corpses, this time bound upright to the trunks of trees. The bark around each one was scarred with the marks of spears and Gallow understood at once: the Lhosir had taken Vathan captives and used them for spear-throwing games. He'd seen it done with the Marroc once before, years ago, before the Screambreaker put a stop to it.

In the fields closer to Andhun small companies of Marroc were digging pits and erecting wooden poles. Dozens already stood surrounding the city. Each had a dead Vathan hanging from it. More blood ravens, like the ones around the battlefield.

'Something for the rest of the Vathen to think about when they get here, I suppose,' said Tolvis.

The Screambreaker frowned. 'This is for *nioingr*.'

'Apparently they're all *nioingr* for staying on their horses and throwing javelots at us instead of doing things properly and getting nice and close where we can chop them up with our axes and stab out their eyes with our spears.' Tolvis shrugged.

'No.' The Screambreaker's lips tightened. 'No. This isn't right.'

'Well you won't be the only one who doesn't think much of it, but Medrin wants it done and there's a lot of the younger ones who see it his way. Might be for the best. Maybe the Vathen are sheep like the Marroc, easily scared.' He laughed. 'Pity if they are though. Be a shame to come all this way only for them to go running back home again.'

They crossed another field, turned onto a road churned to mud and passed two open burial pits. The bodies, Gallow saw, were neither Vathan nor Lhosir. They were mostly Marroc.

'And this?' Corvin asked.

'Some trouble with the Marroc when we first came off the ships. Apparently a few of them weren't too pleased at having the son of their king come to visit. They learned to be happy about it soon enough.'

Close to the city walls black patches of earth and charred stumps of wood scarred the roadside. There had been huts outside Andhun's gates once but now they'd been burned. Gallow supposed it made sense. If it came to an assault on the walls then the slums here would give cover to the Vathen. Today, though, the gates stood open, inviting them in. Six bored and sour-looking Lhosir lounged around them, picking their noses and sharpening their axes. Over them a row of spikes stuck out from the stonework. The spikes looked new, the mortar around them fresh and lighter than the rest. Each spike had a head on it. The heads wore Vathan helms.

Tolvis rode up to the guards. 'Still scratching, Galdun? If it's a dried-up piece of turd you're looking for, you're poking at the wrong end.'

One of the guards looked up at him and rolled his eyes. 'Ha ha. At least you're not riding your horse backwards today, Loudmouth. You're not supposed to be here until dusk. What happened? Get lost again?'

'Oh, several times.' Tolvis jumped off his horse. 'Then I found the Screambreaker and he was kind enough to set me right. Thought I'd better come back with him in case he mistook you lot for a Marroc rabble.' He punched Galdun on the arm. Galdun puffed his cheeks and palmed Tolvis away.

'You're full of air, Loudmouth.' Galdun peered at Gallow and found nothing interesting, and then his eyes settled on Corvin. He frowned and took a step closer and then grinned. 'Maker-Devourer! Welcome to Andhun, Screambreaker. I knew you wouldn't be as easy to kill as they said.' He looked back to Tolvis. 'And Holy Eyes of Mother Fate, Loudmouth, you actually did something useful. You'd best run along now and make sure everyone gets to hear so it gets remembered. It'll be first on the list when someone finally has to speak you out. One of your greatest deeds, right up with that one bright day you managed to recognise your arse from your elbow. Pity it didn't last, eh? Off you go now. See if you can find the Fedderhun road this time.'

'Where's Twelvefingers?'

Galdun laughed. 'Do I look like a soothsayer? He's either somewhere in Andhun or else he's not. If he's not then he didn't leave this way. Probably he's in the keep like he always is, but I'd try the square first. I hear him and his Crimson Legion were hanging Marroc again this morning.'

They rode together through Andhun's gates. Gallow looked around him. After the Screambreaker had sailed back across the sea with King Yurlak, he'd wandered these streets and taverns, drinking his way through what he'd plundered from the Marroc in five years of fighting. He hadn't been the only one. Hundreds of Lhosir had stayed at first, helping themselves to whatever they wanted. Every day a few of them had turned up dead, stabbed during the night. The rest drifted away over time. Back across the sea mostly, or else across the Isset, until Gallow had been almost the only one left. When he'd turned his own back on the place at last, down to his last few scraps of silver, it was for the mountains. The Aulian Empire, or the shattered remains of what was left of it. He'd kept his mail and his axes and his sword, kept them all neat and clean and sharp, not traded them for ale like a lot of the others, and he'd never found a home for the hunger that five years of fighting had given him. Aulia. Plenty to do for a man like him, mired in blood, and the Marroc from around Varyxhun had said there was a pass that was mostly forgotten but still there, impossible when the winter snows closed in but not too bad in the summer.

His hand went to the locket under his mail. A tear stung his eye. The salt sea air, probably. Across the sea they'd flog Arda and hang her for what she'd done, but he wouldn't do that. Couldn't.

He'd never reached Aulia, nor the mountain pass, nor even got as far as Varyxhun. He'd managed as far as Middislet on the fringes of the wilderness and found his Arda instead, and it was all so unexpected and unlooked-for. He closed his eyes and squeezed them tight. Varyxhun. What would he do about her when he went back to Varyxhun? Couldn't do nothing. Did she hate him now? It had always been a fine line between them.

They crossed the open cobbled space beyond the gates. More of the wooden frames like the ones in the fields hung over the streets. Dead Marroc dangled from them like grotesque winged gargoyles. The corpses here were fresh, and there were more as they rode up the hill towards the keep and the town square. Marroc townsfolk scurried back and forth, keeping well out of the way of the mounted Lhosir. Their eyes, when they looked at Gallow, were filled with fear.

Halfway up he stopped. He took two of the riderless Vathan horses and left the other two for Corvin. He would have turned and simply ridden away but the Screambreaker stopped him.

'Two for you, two for me. I killed the man whose horse you're sitting on,' said Gallow. 'Seems fair. I've done what I said I'd do.'

'You killed six men. I killed one. You should have five of the horses, not three.'

Gallow thought about that for a moment. 'All right.'

'You should stay and fight the Vathen too.'

'I'd like that, and I envy you. But no.' Gallow looked around at the Marroc dangling from their gibbets. 'You'll do well enough without me.' He took the Vathan horses the Screambreaker had offered, turned and rode away.

Tolvis watched him go. He shook his head and spat. 'Barebeard.'

Beside him the Screambreaker shook his head. 'No,' he said. 'Not him. We called him Truesword once, and he was a terrible thing to see. He might have changed his face, but all the rest is as it always was.'

And he whispered something in Tolvis's ear.

16

MEDRIN

Prince Medrin Twelvefingers, first son of King Yurlak, Scourge of the Seas and Prince of the Marroc, stared out of a window high up in Andhun keep. The shutters were flung wide, letting in the crisp salt air of the sea. The smell of it soothed him when the wind blew right and wasn't tainted by the stench of death.

Below the window a few Marroc dangled in the wind, dead and ripped open, an example to the others. They were a drop in the ocean, but if the Marroc were so determined to hate him then they'd damn well fear him too. When the followers of the Weeping God came he would have the Marroc of Andhun up on its walls, fighting for their city, whether they wanted it or not. Yurlak and the Screambreaker had thought a few hundred Lhosir at Fedderhun would turn the horsemen back. Stupid pride and they'd paid dearly for it. The Vathen had seen a Lhosir army beaten for the first time in more than ten years. Worse still, the Marroc had seen it too, the ones who survived. Some of them had started on the idea that maybe the Vathen weren't such a bad thing. A chance to rid themselves of their unwanted king from over the sea. Medrin meant to crush that idea into dust.

A heavy fist banged on the door. Medrin stayed where he was, staring out at the sky. 'I told you to leave me be.'

'Loudmouth's here.' He'd picked Horsan to guard his door because Horsan was huge, about as big as a Lhosir ever got, tall enough to go nose to nose with even old Jyrdas

One-Eye, and he didn't think too much either, just did as he was told. Mostly.

'He's supposed to be sweeping the roads to the south for Vathan runaways. Tell him to get lost.'

He heard Horsan chuckle. 'Lost? He probably already is. Hey, what are you— Whoa!' The shuffle of feet at the doorway dragged Medrin away from his window. Horsan was backing in, all furrowed brows and confused, and there was Tolvis Loudmouth, a head shorter but shoving him on, poking him with the head of his axe.

'Is the castle on fire, Loudmouth?' Medrin shook his head. 'It had better be.'

A third man emerged from the shadows, stopped Medrin's ire and killed it dead. If anything he felt … he felt afraid. He stared at the old man with grey in his beard. Corvin the Screambreaker. Nodded, working out in his head all the things this might mean, and most of all whether the Screambreaker likely meant to kill him. Probably not, but with Yurlak getting older every year, he was never quite sure that the Screambreaker didn't mean to make himself the next king.

No. He hadn't come here with death in mind. Medrin relaxed a notch. 'I see you're not dead after all.' The Nightmare of the North. With the Screambreaker here the Marroc *would* be afraid, and they'd fight too – he'd managed to get a legion of them together at Fedderhun after all, for all the good it had done. *So it's good to have him back then. Isn't it?*

The Screambreaker glowered at him. 'No.'

Isn't it? He wasn't sure. Yurlak and the Screambreaker were of an age. They understood one another and saw things the same way, and neither was afraid to use blunt words with the other when what they saw didn't please them. Yes, he'd be useful for keeping Andhun and the Marroc in line, but in the larger scheme of things Medrin found he was happy enough for the Screambreaker to have been dead.

He paused for a moment and then marched to the door, punched the Screambreaker firmly on the shoulder and clasped his arm, welcoming him as a friend.

'Found him coming up the road from the south,' said Tolvis, 'so I brought him back here. The Vathen are long gone.'

'Thank you, Tolvis.' Medrin tried to smile. It was hard with Loudmouth. And there was another thing: the old ones who called the Screambreaker a friend and thought that made them special. Thought that meant they could say whatever they liked. 'Now go back and watch the roads, Loudmouth. I won't have the Vathen slipping through the hills and coming at me from the south.'

'No, you won't, because there aren't any of them there,' grumbled Tolvis.

Medrin glared. 'See it stays that way!'

Loudmouth left, sulking, down the stairs. Medrin was getting a lot of that. Stupid men who wanted nothing more than to fight and get drunk and gave no thought to where the Vathen would strike next.

'And they will, won't they,' he said as soon as Tolvis was gone.

The Screambreaker stared at him. 'Who will what?' Two months ago, when Medrin had seen him last, the Scream-breaker had been about to set sail in the vanguard of the Lhosir army. He'd been getting fat and had a sleepy look to him, but all that was gone now. *Now*, if anything he looked thin, as though he'd wasted away in this filthy Marroc air. He had a great gash on his head, terribly stitched and with a bruise that reached around his eye and down to the top of his cheek, all purples and yellows. His mouth twitched with impatience and he didn't look sleepy at all. Medrin stared at the bruise.

'And what happened to you?'

'A Vathan.' He stood there, still and at ease as if he was already bored.

'Well, that's who and what. You don't need to tell me it wasn't their full strength we faced.'

The Screambreaker shrugged. 'Tolvis said you faced five or six thousand so I'll assume it was more like four. They have another twenty or twenty-five thousand men and horse somewhere between here and Fedderhun. Unless they've had enough and gone home.'

Medrin clenched his teeth. *Unless they've had enough and gone home.* His father had had enough ten years ago. Yurlak and the Screambreaker had conquered a whole country and now, give it another few years, the Marroc would have it back. Not because they'd fought and pushed the Lhosir into the sea, but because his father and the Screambreaker and everyone like them simply couldn't be bothered with keeping the place in line. Medrin would have had them crossing mountains to Cimmer and the Aulian Empire and yes, the Vathen too, but Yurlak wanted none of it and the Screambreaker would be the same. He could already see it in the old man's face, the disapproval.

The frown flickered to half a smile. 'You bloodied them well, Twelvefingers. Better than I did.'

The compliment took him off guard. 'So did they have it with them at Fedderhun?' he snapped.

'Did they have what?'

'The sword. What do they call it? Peacebringer?' Although it had other names, as he'd come to learn not all that long ago. Much more important names.

'Solace. No, they're waiting for it. When it reaches them they'll come.'

'To Andhun?'

The Screambreaker gave him a hard look. 'Unless they mean to carry the Sword of the Weeping God all the way from where Tarris Starhelm buried it just to see how it looks in the sunset over the sea at Fedderhun instead then yes, of course to Andhun. Where else?' The old man sniffed. 'I see a lot of winged corpses hanging over the streets. Marroc giving you trouble?'

'No.' Medrin couldn't hide the sharpness in his words. 'Nor will they.' He clenched his teeth and pressed a hand to his chest, to the old Marroc spear wound.

The old man was smirking at him. 'I met another soldier after Lostring Hill. One who never came back from the last time. Gallow.'

'Gallow?'

'Gallow Truesword. I remembered him, eventually, from Varyxhun and other places. Fierce in his time but he's shaved his beard and lives with the sheep now. He seemed to think he knew you.' The hardness was still there in Corvin's eyes. 'I think perhaps he did.'

Gallow! Medrin pursed his lips, trying to keep his thoughts out of his face. 'Gallow? I thought he was dead. I thought he died in your war. But yes, I did know him, or *of* him at least.' He put on a grimace for the Screambreaker. 'Maker-Devourer, but that was a long time ago. Before either of us crossed the sea. You'd taken Sithhun.' His eyes narrowed. 'You'd taken King Tane's palace. You remember his shield?'

The Screambreaker nodded slowly. Medrin felt the old man's eyes watching him hard. 'They thought it made them invincible.' He laughed. 'Turned out it didn't. Don't think they ever got over that.'

'You remember what happened to it?'

The Screambreaker's eyes blazed. 'I know very well indeed what happened to it. My brother the Moontongue happened to it, and good riddance to both of them.'

'I mean before.'

'Before? You mean when the Fateguard sailed out of Nardjas for no discernible reason and demanded I hand it over. Yes, I remember that too.'

'And you gave it to them.'

The Screambreaker shrugged. 'A shield's a shield. I let them have it.'

Medrin grinned. 'I mean in between. You were still here, banging Marroc heads together.' His lips pinched to a smile as the old bitterness crept up inside for a moment and every word was a razor between them. He shook it away and looked hard at the Screambreaker. 'Everyone knows about what happened with Moontongue, but this was before. Before they sent it off to Brek. Beyard Ironshoe tried to steal it too, or so they said. I don't suppose the name means anything to you. The Fateguard always said he'd had an accomplice or two, but Ironshoe never told them who. There were whispers that Gallow was one of them. The two of them were friends.' He cocked his head. 'Whispers were enough to ruin his family though. The Fateguard took Ironshoe and no one ever saw him again. Killed him, I suppose. I wasn't pleased. Ironshoe was a friend, a good one.' He cocked his head. 'What was it like, the shield?'

He'd managed to take the Screambreaker off guard. Corvin frowned as if trying to remember. 'Big. Red. Heavy. Round.' He shrugged. 'The Marroc reckoned it was unbreakable so we had a go at it with some axes. Didn't scratch it. Wasn't too sorry to see it go after that, but in the end it was just a shield. A red one.'

'A shield that doesn't break. I was thinking we should try and get it back.'

The Screambreaker's face soured. 'Yes, I heard you've been looking. Ever since One-Eye came back with his daft stories. Why? Why not let it lie? It never did any good for anyone.'

'The Marroc still believe it's the shield of their god Modris, don't they? They'd follow it, Screambreaker.'

'It's just a shield, Medrin.' The Screambreaker snorted. 'The Fateguard weren't happy when I took it from Sithhun.

I doubt they'd look well on you following my example. Why in the name of the Maker-Devourer would you want to cross them?'

'Because the Marroc would *believe*. The Vathen have their sword. Let the sheep have their relic too.' For a moment the venom and the anger that Medrin Twelvefingers had spent the last dozen years trying to hide spilled through. He hissed, 'And if it's just a shield then why do the Fateguard care? I tell you, if they demand the Vathan sword, I'll give them the sharp end! 'He raised an eyebrow, catching himself. A moment to find his calm again. 'Just a shield that an axe can't mark, eh?' He smiled as the Screambreaker scowled. Lhosir were ferocious enough in battle, but wave a touch of supernatural under their noses and everything changed. 'At the least I was hoping it might give the Marroc some spirit.'

Corvin nodded slowly. 'It just might do that.'

'We'll take it away again after the Vathen are defeated. Let the Eyes of Time and the Fateguard have it back if they want it so much.' He bared his teeth. 'I'll take it to them myself.'

'So were One-Eye's stories true then? Does he know really where it is? I thought it went to the bottom of the sea and the Moontongue with it. A good place for both if you ask me.'

'It did.' Medrin laughed and shook his head. 'You know the story as well as anyone. Wouldn't surprise me if you'd even been there. Blood being thicker than water as it is.' He paused and waved a finger, revelling in the cloud of anger on Corvin's face. The Screambreaker looked ready to smash something. Then he let out a long breath.

'Tread carefully, Twelvefingers. I know the same as the rest of you. Moontongue stole it from the Fateguard on Brek. Some Marroc paid him to do it and then they killed him. The Moontongue's men got to hear of it, caught them and sent them to the bottom. Drowned the lot, shield and all. Years later, One-Eye comes back with his stories that the shield has washed up on one of the western isles. So what more do *you* know?'

'I know that One-Eye was right. It's spent the last years in a monastery on Gavis.'

'One-Eye!' The Screambreaker snorted a laugh and shook his head, and for a moment all the tension between them was gone. 'I suppose you want me to get it for you?' There was an eager gleam in the Screambreaker's eye. Up against the monks of Luonatta, relishing it already. Medrin shook his head.

'You're the Nightmare of the North. The Widowmaker. I want you here where the Marroc can see you. I know you don't like all my ravens – I saw *that* look on your face from the moment you came in. Well, deal with Andhun your way then. However suits you. It'll probably go down better than mine. I'll get the shield myself.'

'And if the Vathen come while you're gone?'

'You'll stay in Andhun behind the walls and wait for me.' He could see how much the Screambreaker didn't like *that*, even more than being left behind in the first place. 'We'll need some Marroc legions to fight beside us when the time comes. Archers to counter their riders. You won't have them ready before I get back with the shield.'

The Screambreaker growled. 'Two thousand Lhosir broke ten times that many Marroc. We'll break the Vathen too.'

Medrin smiled. 'You can go now, Screambreaker. It's good to have you back.' He paused as a last thought crossed his mind. 'Gallow. What's he like these days?'

'He's cut his beard off, but he's still one of us.'

'When you go down you'll find Loudmouth still skulking in the yard, I expect. Tell him to go after Gallow and get him back here. If the whispers about him and Beyard Ironshoe were true, perhaps he'd like to finally see it. Make sure they both understand their prince commands it.'

He watched the Screambreaker go. *Gallow*. Of course he remembered. How could he not?

THE TEMPLE OF LUONATTA

17

AN EXCHANGE OF GIFTS

Gallow rode slowly out through the gates of Andhun. The dead Vathan heads watched him go while the bored Lhosir guards gave him sour looks. A Lhosir with no beard, dressed as a Marroc, riding a Vathan horse and leading four others. He must look strange. He felt a freedom though, unexpected and unsought, and also a sadness. A part of him wanted to stay. He'd tasted what it felt like to be among his own people again and now he yearned for them, for their strength and their simplicity. The Vathen were coming. The surge of battle, the fire inside, yes, he remembered all that, all buried and half forgotten, boxed away because he had a new life now where such things had no value, but not gone, and now he wanted it back; and he might have stayed if it hadn't been for all the dead Vathen and Marroc, gazing down at him with their blind empty eyes. Another week, maybe two, maybe three before the Vathan host came. Varyxhun could have waited that long. Right now he still didn't want to go back. For nine years Arda had been a good wife, strong-boned and strong-willed, not like the other Marroc. Now she'd betrayed him to his enemies. There was no forgiveness for that. Across the sea he would have killed them both, would have had no choice about it. Fenaric with a sword, Arda by cutting off her hair and strangling her with it.

He laughed at himself. Strangle her? The idea was absurd. He patted the Vathan horse he rode on the neck. 'Maybe I should stay, eh, horse?' There were a hundred and one reasons why he shouldn't strangle her, but they were all by the by really, since he'd open his own throat first. Love didn't have much place in a marriage, Marroc, Lhosir or any other, but sometimes it came anyway in the most unlikely places. A mutual desire that sustained, never expected and never sought, but there nonetheless.

Stupid doubts – *they* had no place in a Lhosir. And he still didn't know what to do about her, because there really was no forgiveness for what she'd done. That lecherous *nioingr* of a carter, now *he* needed to be punished. Killing him would be too much for the Marroc. Send him away and take his wagon? Arda would shout and beat her fists but she'd see that he was right, wouldn't she?

Wouldn't she?

No, she probably wouldn't.

'Gallow! Gallow Truesword!'

Maker-Devourer! He hadn't been paying attention to where he was going, just aimlessly following the way he'd come. And *Truesword*? No one except the Screambreaker had called him that for years. He stopped and looked back, and there was Tolvis Loudmouth, slowing to a trot. He looked angry.

'Well then, bare-beard. Seems you're not going off to Varyxhun after all. Seems I'm to bring you back to Prince Medrin. So turn your horse around again, eh, clean-skin.'

There were ways of asking a man to do a thing, and then there were ways of asking a man to break your face for you. Gallow turned his horse. His hand fell off the reins. 'But Loudmouth, if I'd wanted to see Medrin, I'd have stayed in Andhun and seen him, wouldn't I?'

Tolvis bared his teeth. 'Well I certainly shan't be going back to Andhun on my own to tell him you said that. Our prince commands us. Both of us.'

Gallow shrugged. 'Not my prince. I turned my back on him years ago.'

'And took off your wolf pelt and dressed up as a sheep, but the Screambreaker says you're still a wolf underneath that fleece.' Tolvis grinned. 'Me? I'm not so sure. But either way, Yurlak is king of the Marroc too nowadays, or had you forgotten? So Medrin *is* your prince after all, and I don't give a goose whether you like that or not, and he wants you back in Andhun, and so now that's where you're going.'

'If that's what he wants then he can come and tell me himself.'

'Another thing I won't be going back to tell him. Are you coming with me freely, sheep-lover, or do I have to carry you over my shoulder like some old woman?'

With careful, almost bored movements, Gallow leaned forward. He swung his leg over the saddle and jumped to the ground. 'I was wondering which road to take. Me and my horse were having a good long talk about it, whether Varyxhun was the right place to be heading, back when the road was pleasant and peaceful. Now there's a bad smell in the air that seems to have set my mind for me. Can't put my finger on it but I think I'd like to be on my way. Since you ask so kindly, I'm going to Varyxhun, Tolvis Loudmouth. You have anything to say about that, I'll happily put you right.'

'Oh ho! I'm definitely sure you said Andhun.' Tolvis dismounted and pulled his axe from his belt. He gave it a few practice swings. 'This looks like it'll be some fun, eh? Twelvefingers wasn't clear about how many pieces he wanted, but I'll try not to break anything. I know how fragile you sheep lovers are.'

'Varyxhun.' Gallow drew his sword and settled his shield. It felt strange to face down another Lhosir again after so many years. But comfortable.

Tolvis glanced at the sword and shook his head. 'I'm not so sure the old Screambreaker's right about you at all.'

Gallow swung his arms back and forth, loosening his

shoulders. 'I use the axe for killing, Loudmouth. There's six Vathan corpses between here and Fedderhun can testify to that.' Now he gave the sword a few twirls. 'Mostly I use this for spanking my boys when they've been naughty. Mind you, they're only little. Shall we talk some more about kings and how little I care for them, or shall I spank you too?'

Tolvis let out a howl and ran at Gallow, shield first. Gallow met his charge, springing forward at the last moment before they collided. Both of them staggered away. Tolvis swung his axe at Gallow's head, the blade passing a few inches from his nose.

'You hit like my wife,' said Gallow. They circled each other now, half crouched and hidden behind their shields, eyes peering over the top.

'Yes, I've heard which one of you carries the axe in your house, Gallow Cripplecock.'

Tolvis danced closer and rained a flurry of blows on Gallow's shield, easily blocked. Gallow lunged once, poking Tolvis hard in the side. Tolvis's hauberk turned the point but Gallow saw him wince. 'Nasty bruise you'll have there.' They jumped apart. 'You can stop if it hurts too much. Take your time. Catch your breath if you need to.'

'Filthy Marroc!' Tolvis charged again, the way Lhosir often fought one another, trading shield blows until one of them was dazed enough for a swing of the axe to finish the fight. Gallow met him hard. The shock of the impact jolted his arm all the way to the shoulder and they stumbled apart. Gallow jumped right back at Tolvis, thumping shield against shield, pulled back and battered at him again. Tolvis took two steps back and now Gallow leaped once more, smashing the two of them together for a third time and pushing with all his strength, poking his sword over Tolvis's shield, stabbing at Loudmouth's face and driving him back. He gave one great heave and Tolvis staggered and almost lost his balance. For a moment his shield swung away from his body as he tried to catch himself. Gallow lunged again, a huge blow that caught Tolvis in the chest and knocked him down. He reversed his sword, ready to drive it down into Tolvis's face like a knife, and then stopped. The fire in his belly still burned but he didn't really want to kill this man.

'Fine,' he said. 'Andhun.' Varyxhun could wait. 'Was settling on staying to fight the Vathen anyway before you showed up. I make no promises when it comes to Medrin though.' He stabbed his sword back into its scabbard and offered Tolvis his hand. 'When I said you hit like my wife, I suppose I should tell you she's a giantess who fells trees with a flick of her fingers.'

Tolvis stayed where he was for a moment. The surprise on his face turned into a deep frown. He dropped his axe, took Gallow's hand and let Gallow haul him back to his feet. 'And when I said she carried your axe, I think I clearly meant she brings it for you when you go to fight your enemies.' He looked Gallow up and down. 'I may simply have been mistaken about you being filthy.'

'No, that was fair.' Gallow grinned. 'I've travelled a long way in these clothes. They *are* filthy.' He bent down and picked up Tolvis's axe and offered it back, haft first.

'Yours,' Tolvis wrinkled his nose. 'You won it fairly.' He was breathing hard, still bemused he was alive. Gallow looked at the axe. It was a decent piece, similar to his own and no small thing to give away.

'That's a fine axe and a fine gift then. I wish I had something that was its equal to give.' He pulled his own axe from its loop on his belt and slid Tolvis's in its place. Then he held out his own. 'Suppose I won't be needing this one any more. It's Marroc made but it has the blood of six Vathen on it.'

Tolvis stared at Gallow as if trying to read his mind. 'I can't take a gift from you, Truesword. I'd like to, but I can't.' He shook his head.

Gallow shrugged. 'I have enough things hanging off my

belt. Anything more would be uncomfortable. You can carry it for me, if you prefer.'

Tolvis took a deep breath and puffed his cheeks. He took the axe. 'All right then.'

'Do you know what Medrin wants?'

'Not really. The Screambreaker said I should bring you back. Said something about there being something you needed to hear.' He spat. 'I know Medrin wants to go off looking for the Crimson Shield of Modris. Maybe it's something to do with that.'

Gallow laughed. 'Well now, if you'd said all that at the start, we'd be halfway back by now.'

'Wouldn't have been half as much fun though, now would it?' Tolvis laughed too, then shook his head and looked Gallow over. 'Gallow Truesword eh? I remember him. You I'm not so sure. Are you one of us or not?'

Gallow shrugged. 'I suppose I'm a bit of both.'

18

THE OTHER JONNIC

Some days it seemed that every other Marroc in Andhun was called Jonnic. The harbour was full of them. There was Angry Jonnic and Laughing Jonnic and Fat Jonnic and Thin Jonnic and about a dozen others. Now and then Grumpy Jonnic wished he'd been bald or red-headed or something else more obvious, but fate had endowed him with a dour demeanour and an unremarkable unkempt appearance, and so Grumpy Jonnic he was, like it or not. It was little consolation that he was right about how often things turned out worse than they looked. The Vathan horde drawing the forkbeards back from across the sea, there was a thing. He'd seen *that* coming clear as the sun, and now here they were. He did his best to avoid them but it wasn't always so easy.

'Well?'

Valaric sat across the table. He had more scars than Jonnic remembered, most of them on the inside. The men with him were the Marroc soldiers from Lostring Hill. Years ago they'd all fought the forkbeards together and lost. Jonnic reckoned you got a sixth sense for that sort of thing. They ought to have been friends, but something about them unsettled him. And then the Vathen had come.

He took a deep swig of ale and glared at the other two Jonnics beside Valaric, Angry and Silent. 'There's a lot of them. Two thousand or so and more coming every day. They're eating everything and drinking the place dry.' He spat on the floor. 'This lot are demon-whores, that's for sure. With the demon himself living in our whore of a duke's keep.'

'Turns out the Widowmaker didn't die at Lostring Hill after all, and never mind what—'

'You think that's news here?' Jonnic hawked up a gob of phlegm. 'You're getting slow, Valaric. The Widowmaker came through the gates this afternoon.'

The look Valaric gave him after that was odd. Shifty, maybe. Troubled. 'The Vathen are looking for him,' he said after a bit. 'I was wondering whether to help them, or whether that was a bad idea. What's this Medrin like?'

Jonnic spat again. 'Twelvefingers the demon-prince? Worst of the lot.' He looked around, nervous. You never knew who was listening. There were good Marroc, the ones like Valaric that you could trust. Then there were the bad Marroc, the ones who'd sell you out for a handful of pennies. Most of the men sitting and drinking in the riverside tavern were men he knew, but there were always a few strangers. He leaned forward. 'He's the one who's been hanging people up in the square. So fond of his bloody ravens you'd think he was married to one. Even his own kinsmen don't seem to like him that much but they still do what he says. Don't know if the Widowmaker's any better but he can't be any worse. Funny, him showing up. Even the demon-beards thought he'd died at Fedderhun. Been drinking toasts to the end of his damned soul all week, we have.'

Valaric twitched. 'Turns out he didn't die after all. How many men here you trust?'

'In Andhun?' Jonnic shook his head. 'Fifty, maybe. Don't know they'd take up arms against the Widowmaker though. Don't know that I would either.'

'You've seen what they're doing to us,' snarled Valaric. 'You happy with that?'

''Course I'm not bloody happy!' Jonnic growled right

back at him. 'But what are you going to do with fifty swords, Valaric?'

'Make it two hundred.'

'And then what? Against two thousand forkbeards led by the Widowmaker?' He laughed. 'I don't mind swinging an axe for you, Valaric, but not when there's no point. You'll get us killed for nothing, and then this prick Twelvefingers, he'll decimate the city. He'll not baulk at murdering women and children, this one. You'll have the streets swimming red with his bloody ravens.'

'You get your men ready for the call, Jonnic, and then we'll see. There might be two thousand of them now but there won't be so many when the Vathen are done.'

Jonnic shook his head. 'They smashed the Vathen already, Valaric. You're too late.'

'No. I've seen their army and that was just the start.' Valaric got up. 'My money would be on the Vathen, if I had any. Doesn't really matter though, does it? Whoever wins, you don't suppose they're just going to wave and go home? That's not what they do. And this time it'll be worse, because if it's the forkbeards, we'll just let them shove sticks up our arses and then ask for more. Like we already do.'

Jonnic watched him go. *That's not what they do.* He was right about that. Valaric had had a family once. Wasn't the forkbeards that had killed them either. Just a winter that had been sharp and harsh, a wasting disease among the animals, and the whole village had simply frozen and starved to death, every last one of them. There were whispers of an Aulian shadewalker but Valaric blamed the demon-beards. If he hadn't been off fighting them, he'd have been in his home. He could have saved them or else died with them, one or the other.

Jonnic finished his drink and got up. When three forkbeards followed him out it didn't seem that strange, not with so many of them in the city these days. Not until he turned down an alley to the river and they still they followed him and then stopped to watch while he took a piss into the Isset. By then he knew he was going to die.

He turned. 'So what do you three ugly *nioingr* want then?'

They closed around him. All three had knives at their belts and Jonnic had nothing, so he lunged at the nearest, pushed him back and pulled out the man's knife for himself. The other two grabbed him as he did it, one from each side. He stabbed backwards with the knife and one of the forkbeards shouted and fell away. 'Maker-Devourer! He cut me!' The other pulled him hard, spinning him around, and head-butted him. Jonnic staggered. For a moment the night was filled with stars.

Arms tackled him from the side, lifting him up and throwing him down. He stabbed out with the knife again but this time they pinned his arm.

'Maker-Devourer! The little mare's killed me! Turn his face inside out!'

He caught sight of a flying boot in time to turn his face away. It smashed into the side of his head in an explosion of noise and light and pain. Someone stamped on his hand and he dropped the knife. He screamed as they broke his fingers. When he looked up he could see that one of the three demon-beards was clutching his side, blood seeping through his fingers. After that he lay curled in a ball while they kicked him and stamped on him and cursed. *Traitor! Bare-face! Nioingr! Feeble-finger! Mare!* Caught one last glimpse of the stars as one of the forkbeards lifted a lump of wood and brought it down, and then nothing until a shock of cold water roused him again.

They'd thrown him into the river. Into the Isset. He felt the pull of the water dragging him towards the sea, dragging him down and sucking him under.

And then the darkness again.

19

GIVEN TO THE RIVER

Tolvis and Gallow rode back to Andhun together. Gallow made sour faces at the burial pits and the Marroc hung up over the streets of their own city. Tolvis pursed his lips. 'We never used to do this,' he muttered. 'The Screambreaker would never have had it.'

Gallow snorted. There were ways of saying things without having to put them into words. The relief at having the Screambreaker back was a solid thing among the few Lhosir he'd seen in Andhun, real enough that Gallow could almost have reached out and grabbed hold and shaken it. Maybe that was why he hadn't left Tolvis on the road.

The blood-streaked corpses looked down, mocking. *Stupid, coming back here.* Stupid, thinking he could make some difference to the Marroc. Stupid to have left his old life at all. He almost turned right back round again. *Go home*, the bodies said. *Put things right with Arda. Go home and shout and scream and then hold each other tight and forget about us.*

Tolvis sniffed and stretched his arms, cracking his shoulders. 'I'm in your debt, Truesword. Don't particularly want to be but here we are. Stuff Twelvefingers – the Marroc make good beer. You want ...' He chuckled and shook his head. 'What am I saying? You already know that. Those Vathan horses – Medrin will take them if he sees them. He's seized almost every horse in the city. Don't see why he'd make yours an exception.'

'You tell me that now?'

'Well, I didn't think I'd mention it when you had me flat on my back in the road, no. Didn't seem the time, if you see what I mean. You want Medrin to have them or not? Because if you don't then now's the time to say.'

'Do I have a choice?'

Tolvis roared with laughter. 'With the Vathen coming, I'd have have a hard time showing you a man who wouldn't take them off you. It's finding someone who's still here but who has the coin, that's the trick.' He jumped out of his saddle and curled a beckoning finger, pointing off the wide Gateharbour road and into a side street so narrow that Gallow had to dismount and lead his horses in a line and Maker-Devourer help anyone who wanted to come the other way. 'Benelvic the Brewer. We drank him dry, but he's got a few carts he uses to bring in beer from wherever he can get it. Twelvefingers tried to take his horses and Benelvic made like he was happy enough to give them up. Just wouldn't be any more beer, that was all, and so we told Twelvefingers where to stick it right there and then.' He laughed. 'Benelvic does favours for some of the other Marroc. Sort of thing that would have him hanging from a wheel over the street if Medrin ever knew. Some of us do, but we don't tell Medrin because we like our beer. We have an, ah ... *understanding*. So he owes me a favour or two.'

'That sounds very Marroc of you.'

Tolvis didn't rise to that. He pushed open a gate and led the way into a big yard filled with barrels, most of them empty. There was another gate on the other side, wide enough to take a cart. As Gallow led his horses into the space, Tolvis pushed him gently back again. 'Go on down to the river. There's a tavern at the bottom of the street. I'll meet you there.'

'Why?'

Tolvis kept pushing. There was a pained look on his face.

'Because you look like a Marroc, and Marroc don't have any money, and if he sees you and thinks you're not one of us, I won't get as much for them, that's why. Grow a beard, Gallow.' He closed the gate with Gallow on the other side, left to the sounds of the Isset rippling its way to the sea at the far end of the alley.

Benelvic turned out to be more than happy to have a handful of Vathan horses come his way for a fraction of their worth. Tolvis finished their business and sauntered down the alley towards the river, leading his own horse and with a nice fat purse on his belt, smiling to himself but also a little wary. He found Gallow quickly enough, not in the tavern like he was supposed to be but outside, standing on the river path over a dead Marroc, both of them soaking wet.

'Can't leave you alone, eh?' Tolvis put a hand on his shoulder. 'I was wondering where you'd gone. I suppose I should have warned you. There's Marroc here who see a Lhosir alone at night and don't think too much about the consequences of a quick knife in the dark.'

'Can you blame them?' Gallow sounded bitter.

'You hurt?'

'Me?' Truesword laughed, full of scorn. 'I just caught the end of it. Three of our brothers from over the sea. They beat him half to death and then threw him in the river. No idea why.'

Tolvis shrugged. 'Marroc say stupid things to get themselves killed every day.'

'*I'm* Marroc now.' Gallow spun to face him.

'No, you're not.'

They stood by the water for a while, watching the Marroc, but he didn't move. Drowned, by the looks of him when Tolvis knelt down to see. 'You hauled him out again, did you?' Stupid question. Who else? 'Why? Thought you could save him?'

'One of ours went away with a hole in him.' Gallow was staring down the path as if he had half a mind to go after the three Lhosir, whoever they were. Tolvis caught his arm and pulled him towards the warmth of the tavern.

'Come and share a cup or two with me before we go up to the castle, Gallow. Medrin won't notice. Best you know how things are just now. Leave this be. Not your business.'

'Then what *is* my business? Why did we come across the sea?'

'To kick the sheep and make them bleed and take their women and their gold and drink their beer, that's why! Maker-Devourer, maybe you *are* one of them after all.'

'I thought we came because we were better.' Gallow spoke softly.

'We were!' Tolvis put a hand on his shoulder, steering him away. 'We were better than them every time apart from Selleuk's Bridge. But only because I wasn't well that day. Something I ate. If I'd been myself then it would have been a different story.' He rolled his eyes. 'Could have ended it all there and then, I reckon.'

Gallow spat. 'I should have kept on to Varyxhun. I don't belong in this war.'

'Don't belong in this war?' Tolvis shook his head and guided Gallow inside. 'Choice tavern this. Feel the air! Lhosir come here; Marroc come here. Both want the others gone. Good place for a fight later, if that's what you need, but I'd suggest you choose your side before you start laying about with those fists.' Tolvis tossed him the purse. 'For your horses. I sold them all. You didn't want to keep one, did you?'

Gallow weighed it in his hand and looked inside. He wrinkled his nose. 'Not really. No use for one in Varyxhun.'

'That's a lot of silver, that is. A good price in these times, I promise you.' Tolvis flicked some pennies at a Marroc, who ran away and came back a moment later with two foaming cups of beer.

'Mind you, I could have gotten twice this if I'd taken them with me.' Gallow tied the purse to a string and tucked it under his shirt. 'Ah well. Arda's not to know how many there were.'

'Arda your woman?'

Gallow nodded, although with a pause as though he somehow wasn't entirely sure. 'She looks after the money.'

Tolvis raised his cup and laughed. 'Don't they all. That should be enough to put a greedy smile on her face though.' He stopped. Gallow was staring over his shoulder through the open doorway at the riverside. When Tolvis looked, the drowned dead Marroc was hauling himself up off the dirt, not quite as drowned and dead as Tolvis had thought. He glanced back at Gallow but the big man made no move. Just watched, and so they watched together until the Marroc was gone. He didn't come inside. Tolvis shrugged and turned back. 'She's a Marroc then is she, your woman? She why you stayed?'

Gallow looked dour. 'With the Marroc, everything is coin.' He shook his head. 'That's one thing about them I'll never understand. There's a carter who comes through our village. Fenaric.' As he said the name a flash of something dark crossed his face. 'Sometimes he needs work done at the forge. I tell him he doesn't need to pay, that I can give him a list of things we need and he can bring them the next time he's passing through. Or else a keg of Fedderhun ale when the chance arises. But he never does. He smiles and nods and then he goes to see my wife and pays her his money anyway; and then when he comes through with a keg of ale or a new hammer for the forge, or whatever else we need, we pay it back to him. I ask Arda sometimes: if Fenaric came to us and he had no money and all he could offer were promises, would we send him away? She calls me a fool and says no, of course not, the carter is our friend. So I ask her are his promises worth more when he has no money? And if they aren't worth more, why are they not good enough when he has coins in his pocket? She tells me coins are better than promises, that coins can't be broken. But coins can be lost or stolen and the Marroc are as much people of their word as we are. I've lived among them for nine years but I don't think I'll ever understand their fascination with money.'

All the while he talked, Gallow stared at the table, at the floor, anywhere that was down. He held one hand pressed to his heart as if trying to keep something safe. Then he suddenly stood up. 'You know, I have half a mind to ask everyone here about that Marroc I pulled out of the river. Who he is. And why—'

Tolvis pushed Gallow gently back onto his stool and put his cup back in his hand. He raised his own. 'To the crazy Marroc. May they find the strength to defend their homes against the Vathen. Leave it, Gallow. You saved him, or maybe he would have lived anyway, but he's gone now, and, Marroc or Lhosir, no one here wants you to ask questions.' He steered the talk to the old days then, to the fights against the Marroc and the Screambreaker's campaigns. Turned out they'd both been at Vanhun and at Varyxhun and Andhun and half a dozen other places, even on the bridge together at Selleuk's Bridge. Then later Tolvis had gone back home like most of the other Lhosir when the fighting was done, and now he filled the evening with stories of all the other soldiers they'd known and what had happened to them. Grown fat on all the plunder they'd carried home and made lots of children, mostly. 'It's strange,' he said, 'to see this place again. It's not how I remember it. It was filthy back then and the Marroc were so terrified of us.'

'They're not now?'

'Not like they were. But then we never touched Andhun. They must have been waiting for the Screambreaker to turn his eyes on them for more than a year. They knew he'd come for them one day, sooner or later. And then Tane died out in the middle of nowhere and ...' He paused. 'What did happen at Varyxhun in the end? I heard all sorts at the time.'

'We found the castle empty, the gates open, the last of the Marroc huscarls already dead. They killed themselves rather than be taken.' As he spoke, Gallow touched a finger to his scar, to the small piece missing from his nose.

Tolvis shook his head and chuckled into his cup. 'That's so ... *Marroc*. No wonder they all looked so terrified when we got here at last. They must have thought we'd burn the place down around them.'

'It wouldn't have been the first time.'

'I remember all those stories about Varyxhun. The river flooding to wipe away anyone who attacked it and those other curses the Aulians left behind. How we laughed.'

'No curses. Just dead men.'

Tolvis stretched his neck and looked around the tavern. There were other Lhosir here but not so many Marroc to-night. Maybe they'd finally settled whose drinking place this was going to be. 'I always liked a good burning. Pretty stuff, fire. Twelvefingers would never hold with it though. Too much waste. Empty their houses and then burn them down, that's how it was at the start. Then the burnings stopped and we just emptied their houses. Now Twelvefingers acts like he wants to be some sort of king and we just empty their pockets instead. I suppose he *will* be king when old Yurlak goes, Maker-Devourer help us.' He looked Gallow up and down. His eyes narrowed. 'There's a lot of us are going to miss Yurlak. Some would say it's the Screambreaker who should follow him.'

Gallow met his eye. 'Do they say it to Medrin's face?'

Tolvis threw back his head and roared. 'Not unless they want to end up like those Marroc sheep strung up over the streets!'

'So who *do* they say it to, Loudmouth? I fought with the Screambreaker and so did you. He was never one to take cowards to his cause. Men spoke their minds freely in those days. Have things changed so much?'

Tolvis flushed. His brow furrowed and then he paused and looked confused for a moment. 'Strong words, Gallow Truesword. Be careful with them.'

'I ask if things across the sea have changed, Tolvis Loudmouth.' Gallow shrugged. 'The Screambreaker judged men by their hearts. Marroc or Lhosir, it never mattered. If you showed courage, he kept you. If you were weak then he threw you away. He was the finest we had, and that's why we followed him. Strong as an ox and sure as the sea, but the men around him weren't ever afraid to tell him when he was wrong. If men are scared to speak before their prince, the Screambreaker will have naught but scorn for them.'

'Would *you* tell the Screambreaker he was wrong?'

'I did so on the road to Andhun, and more than once. I don't say he listened, mind!'

They both laughed. Tolvis wiped the spit from his mouth. 'Did he ever go any way but his own?'

By the time they left the tavern, night had long settled over the streets. Clouds scudded across the moon like ghosts. A fresh wind blew in from the sea, warning of storms on the way. Tolvis was too drunk to even walk straight and Gallow was little better. They staggered up the steepness of the hill, holding on to one another, leaning on Tolvis's horse, both of them still dressed in their mail and carrying their shields and with their swords and axes at their belts. Here and there they had to walk up wide steps, or detour around sheer sides of rock that jutted out from among the houses.

'Need to keep your ears open down there,' muttered Tolvis. 'Docks aren't far. Marroc there aren't like the ones up near the castle. Got more balls.' He turned and roared into the night. 'More balls, I said! Eh?' He looked back at Gallow and laughed. 'Don't like our sort down in the docks, not at all.'

Gallow picked his way up the next flight of steps, weaving precariously from side to side. 'After Yurlak and the Screambreaker left, those of us who stayed started to show up in the river. Every day one or two more.' Gallow shook his head. 'Andhun and the Isset probably killed more of us than Tane did when we took Sithhun from him.'

'So what was it made you stay, eh? Why didn't you come home? Your Marroc woman?' Tolvis peered at him. 'No? Something else then.'

Gallow grunted. 'Is every bastard Lhosir I ever meet going to ask the same thing? Thought Yurlak was going to die. Didn't like Medrin. That's why. Good enough?'

Tolvis hooted with laughter. 'No one *likes* Twelvefingers.'

'Then perhaps I didn't like him more than the rest of you.' He stopped. 'He wants to go off chasing after the Crimson Shield, does he? You remember we had it once? It was in the Temple of Fates in Nardjas for a few days. Someone tried to steal it, or that was the story that went round.'

Tolvis nodded. 'I was with the Screambreaker, killing Marroc, but we heard eventually, yes. Don't remember the thief's name. Bard or something. I know the Moontongue did the job not long after. Always supposed they were together, somehow.'

'Beyard, not Bard. And Medrin was the king's son. He should have said why Beyard was really there. But he didn't, and Beyard died. He was my friend.'

Gallow fell quiet and they walked in silence up the last winding road to the castle. Tolvis led the way to the keep. The doors were open, warm stale air wafting out between them. A pair of Lhosir soldiers waved them inside, yawning.

'Who's the Marroc, Loudmouth?' one of them called. Tolvis ignored him.

'For the love of the Maker-Devourer, grow your beard, Gallow. Cut it off again when the Vathen are gone if you must go back to living with the sheep.' He took them into what had been the Marroc duke's feasting hall before Medrin had come and the Lhosir had filled it up with furs and straw and snores. He sat against a wall in the gloom, pulling off his mail, his head already spinning, his eyes starting to close. 'Sleep where you can,' he mumbled. 'Like being back home. One big longhouse.' He lay down on the first piece of floor he could find, a smile on his face. 'Why did we come across the sea, Truesword? Truly? Marroc beer, that's why. It's certainly why I came back.'

20

THE WEEPING GOD

Gallow lay down. Loudmouth was right: the smell of the air and the sounds of men breathing brought old memories out of hiding. This was how it was when he'd been a child out in a homestead somewhere on the coast. One longhouse and a dozen barns and sheds, and at night they'd all slept together. He'd never counted, but there must have been nearly thirty of them. One big extended family, and in winter they'd have the animals inside as well for their warmth. The Marroc did that too, but the Marroc didn't have winters like the ones Gallow remembered. He closed his eyes. The memories were strong, the smell of straw, of sheep and horses. He could see his father again, as he'd been when Gallow was young, before they'd gone to Nardjas. Yurlak had wanted smiths to hammer the swords and armour for his raids against the Marroc. It had seemed to Gallow that the Lhosir had always been at war, but for a moment he wasn't so sure.

His thoughts lost their focus. They wandered, drifting past the edges of the Herenian Marches and he found himself standing in a great stone hall, far larger than the one in Andhun where he slept. The hall was filled with soldiers, shouting, waving swords and burning brands, but their cries seemed small and helpless, and when he looked to see what it was that made their blood burn so fiercely, he saw another warrior had entered the hall, striding through great gates streaming with sunlight. The newcomer was a giant, head and shoulders above the rest. He strode through them, cleaving left and right with the great rust-red sword he carried. His mail dripped with the blood of those he slew. He carried no shield and yet no blade touched him, and where the red sword swung, shields and mail split and tore apart. He walked and slew with deadly purpose, yet slowly and sorrowfully too, and when the last of the warriors fell to his sword he lifted his helm and surveyed the bodies. Gallow knew him, for the giant's eyes wept tears of blood. He was the Weeping God, and the sword he carried was the blade the Marroc called Solace, the Vathen called the Comforter, and the Aulians had always named the Edge of Sorrows.

Gallow saw that the giant wasn't alone. Beside him was a boy clothed in a golden shift. Diaran the Lifegiver. The boy-god came to stand beside Gallow instead, unafraid as the giant stepped slowly forward.

I am sorry, the Weeping God seemed to say. *I am sorry but there is no other way. All life ends in slaughter. I see it always. Let it end.* He lifted his sword to strike the boy-god down. Gallow drew his own, but in his hand all he found was a sapling branch.

The boy-god beside him looked up and Gallow saw he was Tathic, his own son.

Don't be afraid. But how could he not be? He launched himself at the giant but the Weeping God swatted him aside. In his dreams Gallow watched, broken-boned and helpless, as the old-blood blade of Solace swept down, but the blow didn't land. At the last moment another god stood beside the boy, Modris the Protector with his Crimson Shield, and his shield caught the Edge of Sorrows and turned it away. The old story, as it had always been.

21

THE LEGION OF
THE CRIMSON SHIELD

On the next high tide two Lhosir ships eased their way out of Andhun harbour through the many that had come from across the sea and the more that were still coming with band after band of raucous Lhosir eager to fight the Vathen. Medrin had taken only a few dozen warriors in each ship, the rest left with the Screambreaker in case the Vathen marched before Medrin returned with his precious shield. The monastery where the shield was kept wasn't guarded by an army, just a few crazy monks.

Medrin captained his own ship, filled with young Lhosir who'd been children when Gallow had crossed the sea. Medrin's men they called themselves, young and full of vinegar and so desperate for a fight to show their strength Gallow wondered how many would survive. The prince had chosen them and they'd sworn themselves to him as his own Fateguard, the Legion of the Crimson Shield, with their shields painted red. Gallow's ship was much the same. He looked at the men around him and found few faces he knew. The old soldiers, the ones who'd fought with the Scream-breaker that last time round, they'd all stayed in Andhun. These were more of Medrin's men, all except for Tolvis and their captain, Jyrdas One-Eye, who'd been the one to find the shield in the first place. The young ones had an air to them, an arrogance. They looked at Gallow askance, wondering at his lack of a beard, their eyes filled with a cold disdain even as they pushed the ships into the water and set Andhun behind them. Gallow watched it diminishing, the two hills shrinking away, the castle on top of the taller, the sharp valley of the Isset between them and the line of Teenar's Bridge slanting over it. Most Lhosir thought the bridge had been built by the Aulians but Gallow knew better. The Aulians had never come this far. The Marroc, when they were left to get on with things, were good at building. The huge trees that made the bridge had come from Varyxhun less than a hundred years ago, floated down on the river. Maybe the library the Aulians had left behind there had told the Marroc how to do it, but the bridge was Marroc-made.

'Gallow, is it?' Jyrdas loomed over him as he pulled at the oar. Jyrdas was a hand taller than even he was, barrel-chested and, from the grey streaks through his beard, a good ten years older. His hands were scarred and his face looked as though it had been clawed by some beast long ago. A scar ran across one eye, which was now milky white. The two braids of his beard were long and there were blades woven into the ends. Gallow nodded.

'Jyrdas One-Eye. I remember you.' Someone like Jyrdas, once you saw him, you were hardly likely to forget.

Jyrdas spat on the deck. 'Well, I don't remember you. You Marroc all look the same to me.'

Beside Gallow, Tolvis looked up. 'He's one of us, Jyrdas. Gallow. Gallow Truesword.' He nudged Gallow. 'Jyrdas is rolling in Twelvefingers' favour right now on account of accidentally stumbling into some Marroc plot or other while he was bashing heads for the fun of it.'

'Huh.' Jyrdas laughed. 'You've got two eyes to my one, Loudmouth, but I say my one works better. I know a sheep when I see one. Gallow Truesword? *Him* I remember. *You* I'm not so sure.'

Tolvis shrugged and turned back to Gallow as Jyrdas left. 'See? Please the Maker-Devourer, Truesword. Grow your beard.'

They rowed hard, pushing against the wind, which kept everyone busy for a while, and then One-Eye held up a finger to test the air and scowled and waited a while longer than he really needed to before he called in the oars and raised his sails. As the wind caught them and Andhun drifted into a haze on the horizon, Gallow felt a hollowness inside him. He wandered to the stern, watching the land fade, and touched the locket around his neck.

'I will come back,' he whispered to the wind. 'On my word. On my life. Tell her that.'

'Missing the stink of your city already, Marroc?' A Lhosir whose name he didn't even know shoved into him. 'What's a sheep doing here, eh?'

Gallow couldn't pull his eyes off the horizon. 'You've chosen a bad time, friend. Go away.'

'Marroc *nioingr*.'

A savage fury stabbed him. At the word, yes, but more at being pulled away, at the shattering of his thoughts of home. He spun round and shoved the young Lhosir away and then looked him up and down. Painfully young, an untried blade full of bile and piss like most of the rest of them, but there wasn't really any going back from this. '*Nioingr?* Do any of you even understand what that means any more? Eat your words, boy, before I cut your beard and shove it down your throat.'

'Kyorgan!' One-Eye had spotted them. There was plenty enough warning in his voice, but the young Lhosir chose not to hear.

'You can try, *nioingr*.' Kyorgan snarled and laughed, but he glanced around too, looking for allies, checking to see who was with him and who wasn't. The other Lhosir had quietly stopped what they were doing. They'd watch but they all knew better than to intervene. Gallow felt sorry for him. He was barely a man. 'Kyorgan of Beltim,' he said loudly, as though it mattered. He looked around again. 'I've killed—'

Gallow split his skull with Tolvis's axe. Kyorgan stood looking stupid for a moment, then realised he was dead and fell over. Gallow looked down at him. Half the other Lhosir hadn't even seen him move. 'You've killed a few sheep in Andhun, is that it? Butchered a few who gave you sour looks in the street?' He shrugged and pulled his axe out of Kyorgan's head, then looked at Tolvis. 'Nice edge you put on that. Sorry if I've blunted it.'

Tolvis shrugged. 'A few scrapes with a whetstone and you'll have it back as good as ever. Keeps well that one.' He didn't even look at Kyorgan. Gallow took his time to look at the rest of the crew, to meet their eyes one after another. At least they didn't look away, but he knew now which ones were Kyorgan's friends. One in particular. When Gallow stared at him, he stared back. He had that blood feud look on his face. The rest ... most of them just looked shocked. As they should.

And then Jyrdas was standing next to Kyorgan's friend, bending down and whispering loudly in his ear. 'If you say anything, Latti Draketongue, if you even say a word, you'll answer to me.'

'I'll say—'

Jyrdas jabbed him in the face with the haft of his axe and cracked his jaw. He glared at Gallow. 'I'll be thinking I'm on a whole bloody ship full of *nioingr* soon. Waste of a good helmet that, bare-skin, and this is *my* ship and so you can clean up that bloody mess you made. Strip his stuff and hang him out. We'll burn him when we hit land. I'll even let Latti speak him out if he can make his mouth work with his head instead of his balls by then. And that's the end of it. The rest of you can watch your manners and save it for the Luonattans. All of you. Even you, Loudmouth.' He turned away, muttering to himself.

In the end Kyorgan started to stink before they reached land and so they sank him into the sea, offering him up to

136

the Maker-Devourer. He'd died a good death, after all, cut down in battle. The Maker-Devourer didn't care if you were stupid. If anything, Gallow thought, he preferred his soldiers that way. So he watched Kyorgan sink, dressed up in his mail and with his sword and his shield tied into his hands, and felt nothing very much at all about what he'd done. Latti's jaw was swollen up so bad he could barely say a word that anyone else could make any sense of, so One-Eye spoke Kyorgan out before they dropped him in the water. Recited his deeds, what he was known for, good and bad. Not that it added up to much. Years of living with the Marroc made Gallow feel a bit sorry for him by the end. But only a bit.

'Waste of good steel and a good shield,' muttered Tolvis. 'At least it made him sink quick. Did you have to kill him?'

Gallow looked out across the sea. The other ship had stopped to watch and Gallow thought he caught Medrin staring at him from across the water. He imagined a wry smile on the prince's face. As yet Twelvefingers had managed to avoid him, or else the fates had kept them apart. Probably for the best. 'Won't say I didn't want to. But if it wasn't him then it would have been one of the others, sooner or later. Best to get it over with quick, I thought.'

Tolvis shook his head. 'Grow your beard, Truesword.'

'What if I don't want to?'

'Then go back and be with your sheep.'

Gallow laughed. 'Remind me, Loudmouth, who it was who dragged me back to Andhun in the first place.'

One-Eye, it turned out, had been to Gavis a good few times and knew where there were beaches for landing. As they sliced through the surf, the monastery was visible in the distance. It sat on the top of a rauk, a pillar of rock cut off from the land by the sea and surrounded by crashing waves. The Lhosir were still drawing their ships up onto the shore when the first warning beacon lit up, perhaps only a mile away.

'Bollocks!' Jyrdas threw a stone across the beach as hard as he could in the direction of the smoke.

'Thought you'd have been glad,' said Tolvis. 'You'll have a fight now.'

'No, I won't. Problem wasn't ever going to be the killing. It's the getting inside in the first place. They'll all run back behind their walls and close the gates and that'll be that. We can stay outside and throw stones and call them cowards all we like, they won't come out. There's a bridge, but you won't like it when you see it.'

'We'll build a ram and smash the doors in.'

Jyrdas cocked his head in scorn. 'Been here before have you, Loudmouth? You do that. See how far it gets you.'

They left a party to watch the boats, Latti and a few others. That was Jyrdas keeping the two of them apart, and Gallow might have thanked him only One-Eye would probably have spat in his face.

'This would never have happened with the Screambreaker.' Tolvis ran with Gallow as they left. 'Would the Screambreaker need some old relic of a shield to beat the Vathen? No. He'd just go up and thump them and be done with it.'

'He already tried that once.'

Tolvis rolled his eyes in exasperation. 'Well, then maybe Twelvefingers has a point, eh? Maybe he's not stupid after all.'

Gallow looked away. 'I never said he was stupid.'

They ran at a steady pace along the coast towards the monastery, up the cliff paths and along their tops. For much of the time the headland was lost behind the ups and downs and the thick heathers that grew beside the sea. In the final cove the Lhosir reached a village in time to see the last stragglers desperately running ahead, carrying chickens and chasing pigs. Medrin let out a cry and raced after them, through the abandoned houses and on. As he closed, the last islander turned. He wasn't even armed but he threw himself at Medrin, crashing the two of them back into the others. He came up fighting, swinging his fist and landing a good blow before someone spitted him on the end of a sword and hurled him back down the path. Jyrdas took the lead and promptly took a stone to his face, splitting his cheek just beneath his helmet.

'Sheep buggerers!' he roared. 'I was only going to eat your women and rape your men until you did *that*!' The next man tried to break from the path into the heather and went down with a spear in his back. 'Fall on your knees and we'll let you live! A bit.' A pig came charging down the path into the middle of them, squealing in terror. Jyrdas brought his axe down on the back of its neck and kicked it into the heather. 'Roast hog tonight!'

They passed blankets, pots, pans, loaves of bread, squawking chickens, all thrown aside in desperation. But when Gallow ran past a small squalling bundle, he stopped. A Lhosir woman would have turned and fought them to the death for her children. Arda too.

He reached into the heather. The baby had been put there with hurried care, perhaps in the hope that the Lhosir wouldn't see; perhaps in the hope that it would somehow still be there and still be alive when the Lhosir were gone. He picked it up and unwrapped it. A girl. That made it easier. He wrapped her up again and tucked her under his arm and followed the others, past three more bodies, and then the path flattened out and widened into a field of long grass. He could see the monastery again now. Its walls weren't particularly high or thick or strong, but the twenty-odd feet of empty air that separated the rauk from the rest of the island cliffs might as well have been a steel curtain. The bridge, Gallow saw now, curved and then curved back, narrow enough that a horse would have trouble crossing it. A clever design. The gates were black and bound with iron – still open, but a man who tried to run at them risked falling over the edge and a ram would be almost impossible.

The gates closed as the Lhosir reached the bridge. Up on the walls the islanders jeered and hooted. The Lhosir stood and laughed and cursed back. They had a few men from the village, three or four run down in the chase but not killed yet. Medrin would have them beheaded one by one in sight of the walls, daring the islanders to come out and stop him. When that didn't work they'd put the heads on spikes. Or maybe he'd make some more blood ravens. Gallow winced at the thought. He pushed past Jyrdas and Medrin and walked onto the bridge. If the islanders had had bows then they'd have used them by now; still, they surely had javelins and stones, so as he crossed he held the baby up high. When he reached the gates, he put the child down. By now both the Lhosir and the islanders had fallen silent. He looked up at the men on the walls.

'Take her back!' he shouted to them. 'The Lhosir don't make war on children.' He walked back across the bridge, daring them to try and spear him.

When he got back, Medrin slapped him on the shoulder. 'Vicious, Gallow. I didn't think you had it in you.' They were the first words the prince had spoken to him.

'It's a child, Medrin,' Gallow said. 'Let them take it in.'

'It is, isn't it? And likely as not with the mother inside.' Medrin laughed. 'Gorrin, Durlak, come with me. Bring your hunting bows and show me a place where you'll see through the door when they open it. Gorrin, you shoot the first man you see. Durlak, you shoot the next.' Medrin turned to the rest of his men and raised his voice so they'd all hear. 'You all know how it is. If they were men then they'd come out and face us, sword and axe. A man who hides behind a wall and throws spears at you, he's man full of fear and not a man at all. The Maker-Devourer spits on them. They deserve any death they get. Don't think of these as men, think of them as sheep.' He grinned at Gallow then turned to the others again. 'Ferron, you've got fast legs. When Gorrin lets fly, you head the charge.' His eyes flicked back to Gallow. 'Very nice indeed.'

Gallow spat at his feet.

22

ENEMY AT THE GATES

The child screamed for hours but the gate didn't open. Eventually the cries fell silent. Gallow had no way of knowing if the girl had simply fallen asleep or if she was dead. The wind wasn't that cold, though, so probably not dead, not yet.

He hoped.

Late in the afternoon Medrin brought the islander men he'd caught up to the end of the bridge. He slit their throats one by one and held them up by their hair until they stopped jittering and jiggling and the blood turned from a river to a trickle. After that he had Horsan chop off their heads with his big axe. Jyrdas took each one by the hair and had a go at hurling them over the monastery walls. The first two bounced off the cliffs and down into the sea. The third one made it over. The Lhosir gave a cheer. Medrin walked out onto the bridge. The islanders watched him.

'I only want one thing!' he shouted up at them. 'That's all. It's not even yours. The Crimson Shield. I know it's here. Give it to me and I'll go.' He pointed to the baby at the gates. She was crying again. 'You can just take her back.' Now his arm swept towards the cove and the village they'd passed. 'And that. Your homes. Why should I burn your homes when I have what I want? Give me the shield and no one else need die.' He smiled. 'These monks who shelter you might not care about any of those things, but ask them: will they come out and build back your houses for you after we're gone? Will they make the tools you've lost? Will they replace the animals you need to live? You had lives. Simple, peaceful lives. Why should these mad fools take those away from you for some old shield? Does it help you? Does it catch fish for you? Does it grow your crops? Does it feed you and keep your children safe? No. It's brought us, and after us it will bring others. Give me the Crimson Shield and we'll go. Or open the gates to us, if these monks will not. Let us fight it out between us. If we die, so be it. If we do not, we'll take the shield and be gone. But all the time we're out here, we have nothing better to do than make fires from your homes and feast upon your animals. What's this shield to you? And as for you, soldiers of Luonatta – can you call yourselves soldiers? Are we so many? I'd heard you were fierce! Face us then, for we are not afraid of you!'

Silence met him. Medrin stood on the bridge, alone in the failing light and the quiet. The waves below hissed and splashed over the broken rocks at the foot of the cliffs. The tide was nearly out. Slabs of stone caked in barnacles and seaweed filled the space between the shore and the rauk. When no answer came, Medrin turned back. He surely couldn't be surprised, Gallow thought. Not after what he'd done to their men.

'The babe,' he said. 'When night falls they'll come for the babe and then we'll be inside. Keep your mail on and your eyes open.'

Which made for a lot of grumbling after Medrin went back to where Gorrin and Durlak were out on the cliff with their bows. Gallow dozed, and the moon was up high when Jyrdas nudged him. 'Very quiet and still now, lad,' he hissed. He nudged Tolvis too. Others were crouched on their haunches, staring at the monastery. 'They've opened the gate a crack and now they're waiting to see if we move. But we don't. Not until Medrin says.' He gave Gallow a hard look with his one eye. 'What is it between the two of you?'

'Our business, that's what. Old business.'

'Best forgotten then.' Jyrdas's good eye gleamed. 'If any of you think you can creep up closer without anyone noticing then go right ahead. But if they see you and slam the door, I'll throw you off the cliff and then come down to stamp on the bits.'

No one moved. Gallow watched the monastery gates. A crack of orange light from the fire inside split the door. As he waited, it slowly grew wider.

'Should have crept someone out on the bridge to cling on under it,' muttered Jyrdas.

'Rather you than me,' said Tolvis.

'Not up to it?'

'Do I have eight arms and legs? Or is there something else about me that makes you think I can hang upside down like a spider as the mood takes me?'

For a moment the crack went dark as someone stepped across the light. One of the islanders had come out onto the bridge. Jyrdas tensed. It had to be now.

'Go!' screamed a voice from off in the dark. The shape on the bridge bucked and stumbled, but didn't fall. Gallow was up on his feet, running. Tolvis and Jyrdas and Ferron and a dozen others charged beside him. The orange light darkened again.

'Take him now! While he's in the door!'

Another arrow flew. This time the figure fell. Gorrin and Durlak had shot perfectly. Whoever had come out for the babe, they'd brought him down between the two gates and Ferron was already on the bridge.

Shouts went up from the wall. A javelin flew square into Ferron's chest. He fell forward, skidded and tumbled off the edge of the bridge with a scream and a splash. 'On the walls!' Gallow lifted his shield, covering himself as best he could. Jyrdas reached the gates and shoved his sword through the gap; then suddenly the gates burst open and

Jyrdas flew back. He stumbled and fell and rolled and caught himself just before he went over the edge, but the fall saved him. A volley of javelins fizzed through the air. One hit Gallow's shield hard enough to spin him round. Clevis took another in the throat, hard enough to lift him off his feet and dump him off the bridge. Another Lhosir screamed and fell – Gallow didn't see who. Through the gates the javelin throwers dropped to their knees and there were more right behind them.

'Shields!' Half the Lhosir must have roared it all at once. Gallow dropped to a crouch. He was halfway across the bridge, in the open and with nowhere to run. Most of the others had done the same and this time the javelins flew over his head.

'On!' Medrin again, but now the islanders had pulled their fallen man in and the gates slammed closed.

'You've got axes!' screamed Medrin. 'Chop it down.'

Jyrdas was the first there again. He swung hard and the gates shuddered. Gallow saw movement on the walls above. 'Jyrdas! The sky!'

One-Eye dived sideways and away from the gate just in time as buckets of hot pitch rained down. The air stank of it. Medrin waved his sword. 'Smash it down! Smash it down!' He had Gorrin and Durlak with him. Gorrin ran past Gallow. He had his bow and shot up at the wall. There was a scream.

'Archer square!' shouted Tolvis. He crouched down on one side of Gorrin with his shield covering both of them. Gallow crouched on the other side. Two more quickly took up position behind them. For the men on the walls, all there was to see were four round shields with a small hole in the middle; from that hole Gorrin would pick them off one by one. Gallow had used the tactic before once or twice, when he'd had no other option, and it worked well enough when the enemy on the walls had Marroc hunting bows. Less well when they had crossbows or something as heavy as a Vathan javelot. Forming it twenty feet away from the walls, though, that was madness and desperation.

Jyrdas and two others were back to hewing at the gate with their axes. Jyrdas swore as he slipped and fell on the hot pitch. Gorrin loosed again. Another scream, but then two islanders appeared at the top of the walls, easy enough to see this time because of the torches they carried.

'Fire!' roared Medrin. 'Jyrdas! Fire!'

For the second time Jyrdas jumped out of the way. Both torches came down. For a moment they simply lay on the blackened stone, burning, and then something else came over the wall, a pot of hot fish-oil probably, and shattered between them, and the bridge in front of the gate erupted in flames. Jyrdas ran, another flailing silhouette beside him, flames rising off his back, straight at Gallow. There was nowhere for him to go – the bridge was already too narrow for the arrow square – but Jyrdas didn't stop. Gallow braced himself as the huge Lhosir, bellowing and howling, jumped straight onto his shield, onto the next and over the top of them. The other Lhosir followed the same way, knocking Gallow sideways so he almost fell off the bridge. His shield waved wildly as he fought to catch himself.

A javelin flew straight into the middle of them. It hit Gorrin and the archer let out a roar and cursed loud enough to shake the walls down.

'Back!' shouted Gallow. Picking men off the walls was pointless with the gates wrapped in flames and so they ran and limped off the bridge, out of range of the javelins, past Jyrdas rolling around in the grass to put out the last of the fire on his back, and nursed their wounds. Four men lost. Gorrin's mail had saved him from that last javelin but he had a broken arm which made him useless as an archer. Jyrdas's injuries seemed to be no more than a stink of burned pitch.

'Up up up!' Medrin was shouting at them. 'The fools have

set fire to their own gates! Get down to the village! Down the path! Come on, you dogs, get on your feet. Anything that will burn. Bring it up and fire the gates!'

The Lhosir pulled themselves back to their feet and started down the path to the cove, full of angry mutterings as they ran. Gallow found himself kicking in doors, tearing down piles of thatch, anything that would burn, and then as soon as he had an armful, running back up to the top. They took it in turns to run out onto the bridge, shields up, dodging the stones and javelins as best they could to throw armfuls of straw and sticks. Later they stood at the far end, running up and throwing pieces of wood across the gap and then running back again. They kept the fire going for an hour before the islanders came up to the walls with buckets of seawater and tipped them over the flames. When the fire was out, the gate was still there. Jyrdas ran across and chopped at it but it was as solid as ever. With that, the Lhosir turned their backs in disgust and went to their furs and their blankets, too exhausted now to listen to Medrin's pacing and cursing.

23

SARVIC

Sarvic watched from the darkness of the alley in Andhun as the two Lhosir rolled up Castle Hill. They were so drunk they could barely stand and they passed Sarvic's hiding place without the first idea he was there. Sarvic kissed his knife.

'Forkbeard bastards.'

He slipped out behind them, wrapped an arm around the first one's face and ran the knife across his neck. Blood fountained over the street and over the second forkbeard too, and by the time he'd turned to see what was happening, Sarvic's knife was buried in his belly. Sarvic yanked it free again. The Lhosir looked down and the knife came up into his face and straight into his open mouth. He gagged and staggered. Sarvic jerked the knife back and tried again.

'Hoy!'

He'd been seen. He took one last slash at the stumbling drunkard, who was too deep in his cups to notice he was dead yet, and bolted down the hill.

'Hey! Filthy Marroc! Murdering sheep!' Another forkbeard was coming after him at full pelt, sober and armed this one, one of the demon-prince's guards. Sarvic dropped the knife. Easier to run with empty hands. He looked up. Couldn't help it, because this was where they hung the Marroc they murdered. Men – sometimes women – who'd said the wrong thing, or who were in the wrong place. The forkbeards ripped open their backs and snapped their ribs and pulled out their lungs and hung them on wheels from gibbets over the street, and for that the forkbeards deserved to die, all of them.

Ahead four more burst out of a tavern. The Grey Man. They were drunk and had two giggling Marroc women with them – giggling, but their eyes were fearful and with good reason. Chosen by a forkbeard. Give them what they want, because if you don't they'll take it anyway and hang you from a gibbet afterwards; but if you do, you might just get a knife from a Marroc like Sarvic for your pains.

Whores and bastards. He raced towards them; the forkbeards looked up and saw the guard and heard his shouts and suddenly forgot about their women. They fanned out across the road and ran at him. Sarvic skidded sideways and dived into Leatherbottle Lane, narrow and lightless – maybe he could lose them here. With luck the Marroc women had had the sense to slip away, but the Grey Man? Tomorrow it could burn right down. The Marroc in there were no Marroc at all. Men who sold their own kind to these animals, and for gold the forkbeards had stolen from their own pockets in the first place.

He had five of them after him now, all shouting their lungs out and only a matter of time before another one showed up in front of him. Damn but they were fast. Even the one in mail was keeping up and showed no sign of tiring. For the first time since he'd turned and run, he started to wonder whether he'd really get away this time.

Marroc are good at running. That's what the forkbeards always said. *Good at running away. It's all they do.* A surge of anger pushed him faster. But even if he didn't pelt right into another one, there'd be a Marroc who'd sell him to them.

Ahead someone quickly got off the street at the sight of him, to skulk in an alley until the forkbeards were safely gone. That was how it was. What he really needed now were some Marroc with the spine to stand with him. Stand up to the bastards. He turned hard, crashed into a wall and dived into the same alley as the Marroc who'd skittered away. The alley was empty now, but he was only three paces into the darkness when an arm shot out of a doorway and grabbed him, pulling him into a tight space. A hand went over his mouth. 'Stay very, very quiet. And still.'

Sarvic froze. The forkbeards poured into the alley a moment later and ran straight past where he stood invisible in the darkness. A moment later and they vanished out into Sailmaker's Row at the far end.

'Move! Right now! Before they come back.' The arm around his face let go and pushed him out into the alley and back into Leatherbottle Lane, back the way he'd come.

'Valaric?'

'Yes, Valaric, you bloody idiot. Now shut your hole and move!' They ran back up Leatherbottle Lane and down another alley until Valaric stopped at a door and banged on it, three times and then another two. When it opened, the air inside smelled of food and beer, and a hum of loud voices and laughter crept through the walls. Another Marroc hurried them into the gloom of a kitchen, face lost in the shadows, but Sarvic knew him from how he moved. Silent Jonnic from the Crackmarsh.

The sound of voices rose and fell as a door opened and closed. Valaric looked Sarvic up and down. 'Squirrels' balls, but you're a dim one.'

'Valaric?' Obviously, but he couldn't think of anything else to say. He hadn't seen Valaric since they'd reached Andhun. 'I thought you were going home. Back to your family.'

Valaric pushed him away. 'Dumb Marroc. This *is* my family. Look at you!' He shook his head. 'Been watching you. A Marroc running about the streets with forkbeard blood all over him. How long did you think you were going to last?' His nose wrinkled in disdain. 'Where's your knife, Marroc? Drop it like you dropped your spear and your shield when the Vathen came over Lostring Hill?'

'I was—'

'Took a forkbeard to keep your blood on the right side of your skin back then. You remember that? How's that sit for you?'

Yes, he remembered right enough. He squared up to Valaric. '*Someone* has to do something. I see people hung up for the crows all over Castle Hill and Varyxhun Square. Mean nothing to you, does it? Might as well grow a fork-beard of your own then.'

Valaric hit him. Sarvic crashed into the wall, sending pots and pans flying as Valaric came after him, grabbing him by the shirt. 'And every time some knife-in-the-dark like you slits a throat, how many more hearts do you think the demon-prince tears out? I should turn you in. If he hasn't got you up on a gibbet by midday tomorrow, he'll take ten more of us. Doesn't bother *him* who they are. Your life to save ten? Yes, I *should* turn you in.' With a heavy sigh, Valaric let him go. 'You think about that when you see fresh blood dripping up on the square in the morning.'

'I killed two of them,' said Sarvic. 'Not one.' Ten Marroc put to death for every Lhosir murdered. The demon-prince had made sure everyone knew.

Valaric turned away. 'You want to fight them, you fight them my way.'

'And what way's that, Valaric? Sit around and wait for them to get old? They won't stop coming. It's like it was fifteen years ago, all over again.'

'Is it? And how would you know that?' Valaric turned back sharply. 'Fifteen years ago you were barely even a boy. You know nothing, Sarvic, and no, it's not like it was the last time. The last time they came we still had our pride. No, we don't wait for them to get old, we wait for the Vathen to come, you clod. The demon-prince has gone off looking for the Crimson Shield. The Widowmaker's setting his camp, and say what you will about him but the Nightmare of the North is far less fond of his ravens than that bastard Twelvefingers. Or he would be if people like you stopped to think for a bit.' Valaric's eyes glittered. 'My way is the way of letting the Vathen and the forkbeards kill each other. That's what they both want, after all. It doesn't matter to me who wins, because afterwards we finish them off, whoever they are. Vathen, Lhosir, we take our land back from both. That's my way, Sarvic, and I'll be needing an army to do it, not a handful of angry murderers. A *Marroc* army, you fool.' He pulled at Sarvic's shirt and then waved his hands in disgust. 'Look at you. Throw that away. Get the blood off you. And stay out of my sight. You'll know when it's time. Keep quiet, and if that's just too much for you, go and find others and tell them the same.' He gave Sarvic his own shirt and then looked down. 'New boots?' Sarvic nodded. 'Throw them in the river. You got blood on them.'

He pushed Sarvic back out into the alley. The forkbeards were probably long gone, but Sarvic stuck to the shadows as he made his way home. Just in case.

It was only later that he realised where Valaric had taken him. The back of the Grey Man.

24

SHADOWS UNDER STARS

The monastery gates stayed closed. In the morning light it was clear that the fire had hardly touched them. Medrin swore and cursed and had the Lhosir cutting down trees to make a ram for something to do, all of which seemed to Gallow a waste of time. Jyrdas simply shook his head, laughed and walked off while the others set to work. He didn't come back until the middle of the day.

'There's a rise a few miles back that way.' He pointed inland. 'You can see all the way to Pendrin castle.'

Medrin looked at him as though he was mad. Tolvis shook his head. 'Getting excited, One-Eye?'

Jyrdas cuffed him. 'Strawhead! There's two hundred men could come at us from Pendrin, and they saw that beacon lit as we came in, clear as I did. They know we're here. They won't know our strength and that'll make them cautious, but they'll come. Be quite a fight when they do. Glorious.' By which he meant they'd all die.

'Are they marching on us already?' snapped Medrin.

Jyrdas gave him a scornful look. 'Even with two eyes I could never see across twenty miles of hills and look inside a castle. If they're on the move, they're not close. Take them a day to sort their arses and their elbows from one another, but they'll be on the move before long, I'd reckon. Master of Pendrin castle was a fierce old sod last time I heard.'

'They'll be on us tomorrow then?' Medrin's jaw twitched. None of them liked the idea of trying to force a ram through the monastery gates, not with the bridge curved like it was and the islanders up above dropping rocks and javelins and burning pitch and Maker-Devourer knew what else on them. But the bridge was the only way in.

Jyrdas shrugged like he didn't much care either way. 'Might be. Might be they'll wait longer. Might be the old bastard's off elsewhere bashing some other heads and they won't come at all. If he *is* there, then sooner or later he'll come. I'll stake my eye on it.'

Medrin looked up at him askance. 'Which one?'

Jyrdas didn't answer. He towered and glared instead, letting his size speak for him. The two of them stood glowering at each other until Horsan, who was every bit as big as Jyrdas, came and stood beside his prince and Medrin turned away with a shake of his head.

They made their ram and carried it to the bridge anyway. Then they had a good long look at what they were about to try and even Medrin had to bow his head and agree that it wasn't going to work. With the curve of the bridge being what it was, they could get maybe six men to swing the ram, while the gates were solid wood and iron. Maybe, left to get on with it for a bit, the ram might have been enough, but six men left no one to hold shields over them and the bridge was too narrow for shield bearers to stand to either side. Whoever had built it had known what they were doing.

'Bugger to get stuff in and out,' muttered Tolvis, which didn't help.

Medrin sent them back to the woods with their axes. They'd build a cover for the ram, he told them. A wooden box on wheels with the ram hanging inside, thick and strong enough to keep out stones and javelins. Jyrdas just laughed. 'Over that bridge? I don't think so.' He watched them work, merrily telling them everything they were doing wrong without lifting a finger to help. 'It's not going to work,' he said. 'Nice as it is to get a bit of practice swinging my axe,

I'd rather it was at someone's head. Even if you get it to the gate, they'll just drop fire on you.'

As the sun started to fade, Gorrin came back all out of breath from the rise where Medrin had sent him to keep watch. Someone with two eyes that actually work, Medrin had said, and it wasn't like Gorrin was much use for anything else with his arm smashed up. 'There's a force on the way from the castle. A few miles away. Can't see how many.'

'Couple of hundred.' Jyrdas yawned.

'Could be that.'

'Or could be anything else!' snapped Medrin.

'Well that's how many men he has.' Jyrdas shrugged. 'Might have killed a dragon while no one was looking and grown a few more from its teeth, I suppose. Might have.' He shook his head and rolled his one eye.

Gorrin blinked, confused. 'They're setting a camp. I can't see all of it.'

'Was here a couple of years back,' said Jyrdas, stretching and stifling a yawn. 'That was when I first heard about the shield. Just a ship of us. Thought we'd have a fine old time sacking a few villages up and down the coast. Couple of hundred men came out of that castle right quick and they were a mean lot too.'

'You fought them?' Medrin frowned.

'Nope, we hopped back on our ship and buggered off sharp-like.' Jyrdas cricked his neck. 'Weren't here for a fight. Not that time.'

'How far to this camp?'

Gorrin winced and held his arm. 'Couple of hours if they march quick. Could have been here by nightfall if they'd kept on coming.'

Jyrdas shook his head. 'Worn down from a day's march and no idea how many we are? No, and they know that no one's getting into that monastery in any hurry. Could take the fight to them, I suppose. Wait until dark and then fall on them in their beds. Make a big noise. That way they won't see we're not so many after all. Might work. Probably would if they were Marroc. Not so sure about here – ferocious bunch, these sheep-shaggers. Could be they'll hold and then likely as not they'll kick us back into the sea, but it would make a good offering to the Maker-Devourer either way.'

'We're here to get the shield,' Medrin growled. 'Fine. Jyrdas, go back to the ship. Take the men we left there. Fall on them in their beds and send them running.'

Jyrdas looked at him like he was mad. 'What?'

'You heard. Take the men watching the ships and do it.'

'I see. Well, if that's what you want, then yes, I could do that. Don't see as how it would help you. Thirteen against a couple of hundred. We'd have to be mighty terrible indeed.'

'Aren't you?'

'There's me with my one eye. Still terrible, I reckon. Then there's Latti with that jaw I cracked for him. Maybe not quite as mighty as he was right now. And Yeshk with his foot. I mean, he'll fight well enough once he gets there, but that might not be until tomorrow morning. And Dvag's got three broken fingers on account of that punch he threw at Blue Forri, and Forri's shoulder hasn't been working right ever since. But, right enough, if you want some heads broken, we'll do that. Pity about none of us getting to see the Crimson Shield in the end, but when they burn our ships and pin you to the cliffs and send you off to visit us in the Maker-Devourer's cauldron on the morrow, you can tells us all what you *thought* it would look like, eh?'

For a moment Medrin stared at Jyrdas like he was a rabid animal needing to be put down. Whatever favour Jyrdas had had, Gallow reckoned he'd just lost it. But he'd said what he'd said, and so had Medrin, and neither of them would move an inch now, and so Jyrdas and the others would march off into the twilight and get themselves killed just to prove a point, and Medrin would let it happen, and when they sailed empty-handed back to Andhun, Jyrdas would take the blame.

'There might be another way,' Gallow said. Because there was, and he'd been thinking about it all through the day.

Medrin fixed an eye on him. 'You can go with Jyrdas too. The mighty Gallow Truesword. The Screambreaker seems to like you. You can show us you're not a sheep even if you look like one.'

'I'm here, aren't I? There was another time we went looking for the Crimson Shield, you and I. Don't think I've forgotten.'

'And don't think I have, either.' Medrin glowered, poised to go on, then bit back on whatever words were waiting. Instead he laughed. 'So, what is it, this other way? Going to take some nice Marroc words with you and ask these *nioingr* to open their gates for us?' He rolled his eyes. 'If it was that easy—'

'Go on,' butted in Jyrdas. 'What's this other way that none of the rest of us have thought of then, clean-skin?'

'We climb the cliff.'

Several of them laughed. 'And how do we get there? Got an Aulian witch squirrelled away to cast some spells so we can walk across the water?'

'When the tide's right out, you can see rocks down in the water almost right across the gap. That'll be about an hour after dark.' The look on them changed right there, Jyrdas and Tolvis and a few of the others who could see where he was going. Even Medrin, but then no one had ever said Medrin was stupid. 'Won't be easy, but there's rocks to hold right across to the bottom of the cliff.'

'And some right buggers of waves in between them,' grumbled Jyrdas. 'No place in the Maker-Devourer's cauldron for the drowned.'

Gallow shrugged. 'If you don't think you can do it ...'

'Don't *you* start.' Jyrdas's one good eye burned. 'So if you get across the water, then what, clean-skin?'

'Climb the cliff.'

'And then?'

'Climb the wall. Slip inside. Open the gate.'

Jyrdas was shaking his head. 'Might as well just get that Aulian witch of yours to grow us some wings – would be a mighty sight easier than making the sea be still and making the watchers on the wall go blind and stupid. I'll grant you might climb the cliff. Don't know how you're going to climb the wall on the top of it though. Get a cloud to carry you?' He laughed.

'They'll be watching the bridge. They won't be watching the other side.'

Medrin was looking at Gallow intently. 'O One-Eye, you don't know this man like I do. Gallow here could climb that wall right enough. Always was good for that sort of thing.' He smiled. 'Jyrdas, go and get the men from the ship and bring them anyway. Gallow opens the gates for us or else you can show the *nioingr* over the hill how terrible you are. One or the other.'

'I'll want two more men with me. Climbers who aren't afraid of the sea.'

'Loudmouth,' said Medrin at once. 'He'll have to be quiet for once. Be a new experience for him and he needs the practice.' He started looking among the others for a third.

'Me,' said Jyrdas. 'I'll go.'

For a long time Medrin held his eye. Then, very slowly, he nodded. 'The Screambreaker's men. All three of you. Fitting. Even here, with a hundred miles of sea between us, he has to make his point. Go on then, One-Eye. You do that.'

'And if we bugger it up and you have to go traipsing across the hills to bring down a few nightmares on Pendrin's sleeping army, you can do that yourself. Can't think of anyone better.'

Gallow hid a smile. Medrin wore his on his face but there

was no love in it, not one little bit. 'Nicely done, One-Eye. Nicely done.'

Jyrdas laughed and ran off to get the men from the ships. If someone came in the night and set fire to them both, well then that was just the Maker-Devourer's way of telling them that they weren't meant to have the shield – that or that they were meant to fight their way to the nearest fishing village and steal themselves a new boat. Gallow and Tolvis went and sat at the top of the cliff, looking at the monastery, far enough from the bridge so they didn't have to worry about the odd javelin. They watched while the islanders on the wall watched them back. Gallow's eyes traced the routes around the cliff.

'I was thinking,' Tolvis said quietly, 'that we could simply send half the men away on the ships while the rest of us hide nearby for a few days. They'd see our sails from up there. They'd think we were gone.'

'Take them a few days to feel safe enough to come out.'

'Are we in a hurry?'

'The Vathen will march on Andhun sooner or later. You have to wonder what's holding them up.'

'The sword,' said Tolvis. 'That's what the Screambreaker said. They were waiting for the sword. Their Sword of the Weeping God.'

'*I* think they're waiting for Medrin to come back with the shield. Maybe it's fate for the two to meet again.'

Tolvis puckered up his face. 'That some Marroc idea? In which case I think it might be fate that either you or Jyrdas are going to kill Medrin if we stay out here much longer. Which would be a pity, because then the rest of us would have to tear your lungs out and stick you on a pole for old Yurlak. Medrin and the Screambreaker I can understand – they can't stand each other, and there's the whole thing about what happened to Medrin when he came to join the Screambreaker's fight against the Marroc all those years ago, and then which one of them will stand in Yurlak's shoes when the Maker-Devourer finally takes him. But you two? What happened between you?'

Gallow shook his head. He stared out over the sea at the cliff beneath the monastery. A part of him was looking at the rocks, at the waves. They'd have to make their way around the base of the cliff with the sea crashing over them, right round to the other side. The waves would hide any noise. Good chance they'd smash them to bits as well. Stupid idea, except he really thought that perhaps it could be done.

Another part of him had got to thinking about fate. About Arda and Tathic and Feya and little Pursic, and even Jelira, whom he still loved even though she wasn't his. Wondering what *their* fate would be. Wondering where they were, whether they were in Varyxhun, whether they were safe. Whether he should have stayed on the road from Andhun and left Tolvis lying there in the dirt. Whether he'd see them again and whether he was meant to. Hadn't really thought about it back then. He'd still been too angry with Arda, too desperate to see a way out, too eager for anything to delay the words that would inevitably pass between them. Kyorgan had eaten that anger. Bad luck for him to be in the wrong place at the wrong time – or was that simply fate too?

'We did something stupid together once, that's all,' he said. 'A long time ago. Didn't end well.'

Jyrdas was back as the sun set. He'd brought a great pile of wood with him and a bundle of sacks. 'Still think we'll fall off and drown in the sea,' he said, 'but if we're going to do this, we're going to do this properly.'

25

SEA AND STONE

'But I like hearing about stupid things,' hissed Tolvis. 'Puts my own many foolish deeds into a more forgiving context.'

Jyrdas hit him. 'Shut it, Loudmouth.'

They stood at the bottom of the cliff a little way from the bridge, where it was easy enough to scramble down from the top even in mail and with swords and axes hanging from their belts. They'd left their shields and Jyrdas was still muttering about that. Making them wear sacks over their mail seemed like it was his revenge.

'When the Fateguard brought the shield back across the sea, they were going to take it to the Isle of Fates. Medrin wanted to see it before it went,' said Gallow.

'Yap, yap!' snapped Jyrdas. 'Everyone wanted a look at that damned shield. Now shall we all shout and wave at the islanders on the wall while we're at it?'

The other Lhosir were making a noise up on the cliff beside the bridge, jeering and shouting. They'd made the wood Jyrdas had brought into a bonfire and then gone to get more. It was burning nicely. Give the men on the walls something to look at. Take their minds off anything else. A fire made it harder to see a man hiding off in the shadows. Jyrdas's idea. The sacks were to stop the moonlight from glinting off their mail.

'A man might think you'd done this sort of thing before, One-Eye.' Tolvis grinned. 'Care to tell?'

'Nothing this stupid.'

They crept along the foot of the cliff. Low tide exposed a litter of rocks fallen from the cliffs long ago. The three of them picked their way slowly and carefully along the shore, hugging the shadows, down on their hands and knees where they had to. Spray from the breaking waves soaked them.

'Don't look at the light,' growled Jyrdas. When they reached the pool of black beneath the bridge, he pointed to where the shadows were deepest. 'That way. Keep in the darkness.'

A half-moon shone high up in the sky. A fresh wind chased heavy rags of black cloud across the stars. A good wind for blowing them back across the sea to Andhun. They paused, waiting for the next cloud to darken the sky. The men up on the cliff had taken to singing bawdy songs, the words changed a little to give some needle to the islanders. Gallow knew these songs, knew their words. Not long ago he'd almost have wept with joy to hear them. Now they only made him sad. Truth was, he didn't belong any more, not here, not anywhere.

He touched the locket at his breast. Crazy stupid woman, pig-headed and bloody-minded. But his, and he missed her.

The moon slid behind ragged black shadow. Gallow crept out among the waves, clinging to the rocks. When the moon came out again, they stopped where they were, hugging barnacles and seaweed, heads down, sackcloth wrapped over their helms and the surf breaking over their heads. The sea tossed and churned, clawing and tearing, did everything it could to rip Gallow away and suck him under. The water came suddenly up over his head and into his nose and his mouth to make him choke and then fell away again. Wave after wave, but they all three held fast, and at last a new cloud covered the moon once more. Beside him, One-Eye growled.

'Waves looked smaller from up top.'

'It's not deep, One-Eye. Calm day, even Loudmouth could walk straight across without getting his hair wet.'

'And if we had the time to wait for one of those then I'm sure that thought would cheer me greatly. First wave hits you, it's going to knock you flat and you'll sink like a stone. Keep your lungs full and your legs underneath you, and when you feel something hard under your feet, kick and kick hard. Bit a bit of luck it might be Loudmouth.' He bared his teeth and chuckled. 'True enough, it's not that deep and it's not that far. You keep telling yourself that. I'd have roped us up, but I reckon chances are good that one of you is going to drown and I don't want the dead weight tugging on me. Go on then, Gallow. Show us how it's done.'

Gallow waited for the ebb and launched himself into the foaming water for the next boulder to break the surface. He took one step and his ankle turned. The next wave came, smashing him back against the stone he'd let go. He kicked again, pushing against it, took two steps before another wave bowled him over. The weight of his mail sucked him down at once and he couldn't help but kick and thrash as the water covered him. Another wave sent him spinning. His feet touched stone; he pushed hard against it and broke the surface gasping. The ebb picked him up and threw him a yard further and then dashed him against the next slab of rock, thumping his head and shoulder against it, the barnacles shredding the sackcloth away from his helm. His fingers turned to claws, gripping at the stone, his feet scrabbling and slipping on seaweed then finally finding purchase, heaving him up until his head was out of the water and he could breathe again.

The next wave broke over him and almost knocked him loose. It smothered him. He felt his helm slip but he didn't dare let go with either hand. As it fell, he snapped his head around and caught the noseguard between his teeth, cracking one and slashing his lip. Blood and the sea mixed their salts in his mouth. He pulled himself tighter to the boulder and hauled himself round the other side where the crash of the waves kept him pressed in place and he could put his helm back where it belonged.

He looked up. The moon was still hidden behind her shrouds. He knew where Tolvis and Jyrdas had been but they were lost now, swallowed by the darkness and the battering of the waves and perhaps by the sea herself.

Maker-Devourer preserve us! Lhosir weren't much for prayers because the Maker-Devourer wasn't much for answering them. Another gulf that lay between him and the Marroc, what with Modris the Protector and all their other gods. They believed in guiding hands and greater purposes, but the Maker-Devourer offered none of that. Each man had his own fate and each man followed it to his doom, and that's all there was.

The next wave was a big one. He didn't see it coming until it broke over him hard enough to knock the air out of his lungs and shake him loose, and then the ebb came after and pulled him off and he was sinking, everything icy and black. He thrashed wildly but found no purchase. Tried to kick towards the next stone but the swirl of the water had turned him around and he had no idea where it was. Salt and icy cold crept into his nose, making him gag. He still had the taste of blood in his mouth, and then the next wave caught him and dashed his head against stone hard enough to make him see stars. He grabbed at it but the ebb pulled him away and sucked him under once more, bouncing him across the stones under the water. Try as he might, he couldn't get his feet underneath him. He envied the Marroc for a moment, for their gods. At least if he'd believed in Modris and Diaran and the Weeping God then he could have had a last moment of hope. Wouldn't have made any difference to him drowning, but he could have hoped.

His hand caught something. Too soft for a rock. It felt like …

Sacking. With mail underneath!

He clutched at it, swung his other hand towards it, all in the pitch-black heaving water, lungs burning now, and then another hand grasped his and was hauling him up, and at last he got his feet down to push against the bottom. He broke the surface and took a great gasp of air. Tolvis! He'd found Tolvis and they were right under the bridge, almost at the other side. They waited together for the next cloud and then launched themselves one after the other across the last foam-filled gap of water. It was easier with two. Tolvis went first and Gallow half threw him across; and then when he was on the other side, Gallow followed and Tolvis was waiting to pull him in. With a grinding effort they dragged themselves up the stones and out of the water and clung to the tumbled rocks at the foot of the rauk beneath the bridge, every limb as heavy as lead, slowly remembering how to breathe. Tolvis had somehow lost his sword. Gallow, when he thought to check, found he'd lost his helm again. At least they were under the bridge where the watchers on the wall couldn't see them.

'Right under the gate.' In the light of the stars Tolvis's eyes glittered. He patted Gallow's head. 'And you're right. Calm day, I could have walked right across without even getting my hair wet.'

They waited another minute and Gallow was beginning to think it would be just the two of them when Jyrdas finally clawed his way out of the water. His helmet was twisted around so he could barely see with his one eye.

'Maker-Devourer's bollocks!' he spat, sitting on the stone beside them. 'I've come out the wrong end of battles easier than that. Wish I'd gone with Medrin's plan now.' He looked up at the cliff above them. 'Ah crap!'

'You can always go back,' panted Tolvis.

'Only if I can make a boat out of your bones, both of you. Mostly yours, Truesword.' *Truesword.* First time Jyrdas had called him that.

'Can't have been that bad with so much talk still in you,' said Tolvis.

Jyrdas straightened his helm and bared his teeth at Gallow. 'Go on then. Show us the way up. I'll be as ready as it gets for splitting heads by the time we're up there.'

Gallow made his way along the side of the cliff. He went slowly, each movement as smooth as it could be. Peppered with ledges and crevices, it wasn't as hard as it had looked from across the water, even in mail and with a sword on his belt. Up by the bridge Medrin's men were still singing their songs and shouting their taunts and insults while their fire burned brightly, and no one saw the three Lhosir as they traversed the cliff to the far end of the rauk and began to climb. Once they were above the water the stone was dry, even if it crumbled in places under Gallow's fingers and clumps of grass came away in his hand.

The monastery wall rose straight up from the the cliff. It was an old wall, the stones large and ill-fitting, the mortar between them crumbling and badly eroded. Gallow pulled a dirk from his belt and held it between his teeth. Where the cracks were too narrow for his fingers, he took it and widened them; where he couldn't do that, he forced the dirk itself deep into the crack until it would take his weight. His feet found what purchase they could. The wall wasn't tall, and he thanked the Maker-Devourer for that.

There were no sentries on the back wall and he thanked the Maker-Devourer for that too. Once he was over he wrapped the end of his rope around his waist, braced himself and tugged. On the other end, Jyrdas tugged back. He came up fast, jumping over the top of the wall and landing with the grace of a man half his age, sword already out and gleaming in the moonlight. Tolvis followed, and there they were, the three of them in an empty darkness. The walls curved around to each side of them, following the shape of the rauk. From the outside they'd looked taller than they were. Two small towers rose from the walls, each with a sentry on top. The walls and the towers wrapped the space around the monastery itself, a stone longhouse with a steep leaded roof and that was all. Small and shabby. Gallow had expected something grander.

The sentries on the towers and on the walls were all looking towards the bridge. So far the three Lhosir hadn't been seen.

'Right then.' Tolvis squinted across the yard. 'That was so easy that One-Eye here might possibly still be asleep.' He frowned. Close by stood a pile of wood, a beacon carefully prepared and ready to be lit. 'So now what? One-Eye shakes the ground with one of his farts and then while the islanders are screaming in horror and choking to death, you and I see if we can hold our breath long enough to get the gates open? Either of you got any idea how many people are actually in this place? Not that I suppose you care, eh?'

Jyrdas grabbed him round the throat and snarled, 'The sentries, piss-pot boy. We cut their scrawny necks.'

'Really?' Tolvis blinked as Jyrdas let him go. 'Well, I suppose. If you say so, but I thought my way sounded easier. Painful as it is to say, One-Eye, but after sharing a ship with you, I think you underestimate your prowess.'

26

LOYALTY

Gallow pulled them apart. Jyrdas took his axe off his belt and hefted it. He aimed at the sentry on the closer tower. Gallow caught his wrist. 'Even the Screambreaker couldn't fell a man from this distance, One-Eye.'

'In my prime I would have split his skull.'

'In your prime you had more eyes!' hissed Tolvis.

Jyrdas glowered, but he lowered the axe and crept toward the tower instead. Gallow watched him go and then turned his eyes to the one on the other side of the rauk. With Tolvis close behind, he sidled along the wall until he could see the gates past the dark bulk of the monastery. Torches lit the yard around them and he could see men moving there, maybe a dozen or so split between the yard and the walls. The shouting had died down, as though the Lhosir outside had given up and gone to their beds.

When he pushed gently at the tower door it swung open onto a spiral stair. Gallow climbed in silence to a small round room, empty except for a handful of crossbows hung from pegs and a ladder to the roof. He put a finger to his lips and handed Tolvis the sword and axe from his belt, then inched up the ladder until the cool sea breeze touched his head and his eyes emerged back into the night. The sentry was looking the other way and Gallow didn't hesitate: he grabbed the islander's ankles and pulled hard, falling down the ladder and into the guardroom and taking the sentry with him. The islander let out a squawk. His arms flew out as the rest of him flew back, his face smacked into the stone roof, he fell down the ladder and the back of his head hit the floor below. He might have been dead from that, but in case he wasn't, Tolvis jumped on him and twisted his neck until it snapped.

Gallow climbed up again. From the tower roof he could see the gates clearly, the bridge and Medrin's bonfire dying slowly. There was no gatehouse, just the two squat stone columns that held the gates. The gates themselves were barred, the sort of bars that would take two men to lift. And he was right: there were a dozen or so men in the yard and on the battlements, too many for even Jyrdas to hold at bay while he and Tolvis opened the way for Medrin and the others.

He went back down and took a crossbow. 'What we need is Gorrin or Durlak.' They were a Marroc thing, crossbows, brought across the mountains by Aulian traders before they'd vanished when their empire collapsed. The Screambreaker had looked down his nose at anyone who tried to learn the use of one; Medrin doubtless saw them differently.

Tolvis spat. '*Nioingr* weapons.' Arrows were bad enough.

On the south side Jyrdas had silenced the other sentry. They watched across the darkness, waiting until they saw him slipping back along the wall. Tolvis's lips twitched. 'I hate to say this and he surely wouldn't thank me for mentioning it, but One-Eye was quite a good shot with one of these once. Back when he had both eyes.'

Jyrdas climbed up through the tower. His eye gleamed at Gallow in the starlight. 'Managed to keep Loudmouth quiet enough not to give yourselves away, eh? That must be a first. So, here's what I say: stuff Twelvefingers. Half the islanders are out at the gate and the other half must be asleep. I say we slip into the monastery and find their shield and slip out again and murder anyone who opens an eye to our passing.'

Gallow thrust a crossbow into One-Eye's hands and picked up the fallen sentry's shield and helm. They made him feel whole again. 'We open the gates,' he said. 'That's what we came to do.'

Jyrdas gave him a long hard look, then shrugged and nodded. He looked past Gallow at the crossbows still hanging on the wall. 'All right then. So we load them all up. You and I get as close as we can. Loudmouth stands at the top of the tower and starts shooting. When they all start running around like frightened chickens, we throw the gates open. Anyone comes after us, Loudmouth does for them.'

'Which is fine enough,' agreed Tolvis, 'except I can't hit a barn door with one of these things.' He winked at Gallow. 'Mind you, I have got two eyes, so at least when I shoot at something there's a chance of the arrow at least going in the right *sort* of direction. So yes, probably best I take them.'

'Give me those!' Jyrdas pushed past Gallow into the tower and started cocking the crossbows. Gallow and Tolvis slipped out into the darkness of the yard. They hugged the wall, keeping in its shadows. The half-moon was heading towards the horizon now but the clouds were breaking apart and the stars were many.

'Knowing that I'm about to trust my life to a one-eyed archer, I think I'd rather have gone with Twelvefingers' plan too.' Tolvis still had Gallow's sword. Gallow loosened his axe. A small bonfire burned in the middle of the yard behind the gates. A cauldron hung over it and Gallow caught a whiff of boiling pitch.

'A javelin or two would be nice.' Gallow counted the islanders again. Four down in the yard, two of them tending the fire, the other two by the gate pacing back and forth and looking bored. Eight or nine up on the battlements, but there were wooden steps down from either side of the gates and the men up there would be down them quick enough when the fighting started. He wondered whether he and

Tolvis could simply walk out into the yard and how far they'd get before anyone realised they were Lhosir. Gallow had a sentry's helm and shield. It was dark. They'd know Tolvis for what he was as soon as they saw his forked beard, but they wouldn't know *him*. Not until he spoke. Which just might be enough. He risked a glance back at Jyrdas's tower. 'Your one eye had better be a good one,' he muttered. And then to Tolvis, 'Stay here and follow my lead.'

He walked out into the open towards the flames in the middle of the yard and the two men beside the fire. They glanced at him as he came up to them, but it took a moment for the nearest to realise that under the helm was someone he didn't know.

'Reidas?'

Gallow picked up a burning brand from the fire. He nodded and grunted and shrugged.

'Reidas?' The islander was reaching for his sword. The other one had turned and cocked his head, trying to understand what was going on. Then a crossbow bolt hit him in the chest. He staggered back with a grunt and fell. 'Luonatta!' shouted the man in front of Gallow. 'They're inside!' He drew his sword but too late: Gallow gave the cauldron over the fire a mighty kick towards the nearer steps up to the battlements. The cauldron wobbled and toppled. Burning hot pitch spewed across the yard and he threw the burning brand into it. Flames jumped across the stones as he ran for the other stairs. The islander who'd sounded the alarm came after him with his sword and then stopped short and slumped, another crossbow bolt in his back. Gallow raced to the steps. He whipped his axe from his belt and swung at them. The two soldiers by the gates saw him too late. His axe split one of the wooden supports clean in two and a solid kick brought the whole lot crashing down.

'Maker-Devourer!' he yelled. Two on two in the yard, now *that* was better. The islanders on the battlements now either had to jump down with their mail and shields or walk through fire. Enough to slow them and Jyrdas would be shooting at them. He bellowed and ran at the nearest gate guard, hooking the man's shield with his axe and then slicing at his neck. The islander jumped out of the way and straight into his fellow, tripping him up, and then Tolvis was there to split the man's skull while Gallow stamped on the second soldier's arm, snapping it. His axe finished the job, smashed into the man's face.

Tolvis looked at the axe in his hand and held it up to the moonlight. 'Nice edge you keep on this,' he said. 'Six Vathen was it?' They ran to the gate. Someone on the battlement screamed and fell. Gallow remembered six crossbows hanging in the sentry tower. The first three had all counted and the other three had to count too. For a moment, though, they were the only ones alive beside the gate. The smoke from the burning pitch swirled around them, choking. Three bars held the gates closed. They reached for the top one.

'It would be helpful just about now,' roared Tolvis, 'if Medrin and the rest of them came hollering across the bridge.'

Two islanders ran down the burning steps, yelling and shouting through the flames, waving their swords. Gallow and Tolvis heaved the beam from the door at them, staggering one and pinning the other. The trapped islander screamed as the flames licked through his mail. The other one died with Jyrdas's next arrow in his back. Tolvis shook his fist at the tower. 'Don't waste them, you one-eyed clod!'

They lifted the second bar out. The men from the other battlement were jumping down now, the danger of a broken ankle less than the danger if the gates fell. Another islander howled as Jyrdas's fifth bolt took him in the leg. Two more came at Gallow. He turned to face them but Tolvis jumped in the way.

'You're the one with the arms of a smith! Get the last bar!' He launched himself at the two islanders with such savagery that for a moment they backed away. Gallow took a deep breath and grabbed the beam and heaved. Damn thing was as heavy as a man and it was stuck. Behind him Tolvis was howling away: 'Take your time, Truesword. These two aren't much sport but I'll have another couple in a moment and I'd hate for that opportunity to go to waste!'

With one last savage effort he lifted the beam away. He turned to drop it and stared straight at another islander who'd jumped through the flames on the stairs. A crossbow bolt flew between them, inches from Gallow's face and buried itself in the gate. For an instant they looked at each other, then the islander brought down his axe and Gallow did the only thing he could: he lifted the beam to put it in the way. The axe bit into the wood and stuck. Gallow dropped the beam on the islander's foot and kicked the gates open.

The bridge was empty. Medrin and the others who should have been hammering to get in weren't there. Gallow whipped out his axe and hacked the islander who'd come at him, severing his wrist. Tolvis was facing three now and there were more coming. Gallow ran to him. They stood back to back.

'Medrin!' he roared. 'Now or never, Twelvefingers!'

The three islanders circled them. Two more, the last from the battlements and the one with the arrow in his leg, came warily closer then stopped where they stood, looked at Gallow and Tolvis, and went for the gate instead. The monastery doors were open now and more islanders were running out from inside, half-mailed, helms askew, grim-faced.

'Medrin!' They'd never get it open again. But two men side by side could hold the gateway. For a while. If they could get to it. Gallow let out a cry and launched himself at the nearest islander, the one between him and the gate.

The islander met him, took Gallow's axe on his shield and stabbed back, forcing Gallow sideways. A second islander lunged, slicing across his mail, driving him even further away from the gate. The men from the monastery were flooding the yard now, surrounding him and Tolvis. The islanders by the gate had it closed and now they were trying to lift one of the beams back into place. Another, a huge brute of a man, was running along the battlements to help.

Back to back, he and Tolvis held their ground, a dozen men around them now. Here was where he was going to die. Medrin had betrayed them.

I'm sorry, Arda.

'Come on then!' The huge brute from the battlements jumped down to the gates, swinging steel and bellowing. Jyrdas!

The gates swung open again. Jyrdas stood between them, towering over everything, an axe in each hand and dead islanders all around him. And there, finally, at the other end of the bridge was Medrin, the other Lhosir yelling and waving their spears and their swords and their shields and charging across the bridge. The men around Gallow backed away, wavered, then as one turned and ran towards the monastery and its flimsy doors. Jyrdas came screaming past, chasing them, and then the yard was filled with Lhosir, all shouting in triumph, and Tolvis had Medrin by the throat.

27

JYRDAS

Jyrdas pulled Tolvis away before one of them did something stupid. 'Get your hands off your prince, Loudmouth.' That done, he gave Twelvefingers a good shove too, enough to make him stumble and almost fall. 'And where were you? Should have been at the gates the moment they opened. Fall asleep, did you?' He turned away, not wanting for a reply. 'Would never have happened with the Screambreaker.' Didn't need to even look to see how sharp *that* cut. It would have to do, though. Merited it might be, ripping Twelvefingers to pieces, but here wasn't the time or place. *Here* he had a yard full of battle-hungry Lhosir with no one to fight but each other. 'You lot!' He pointed to the nearest group of the them. 'Go back and get that ram we built. The rest of this is going to be easy.'

Twelvefingers looked murderous but he hadn't said anything yet. Jyrdas clapped him on the shoulder and got in quick before the prince could open his mouth. 'We'll be through that gate in no time. You'll have your shield and be back on the sea nicely before that lot from Pendrin fall on us. You can hold it up high in Andhun and watch the Marroc weep.' Weep with joy or weep with sorrow? Jyrdas wasn't sure and he certainly didn't care. Sheep were sheep.

He held Twelvefingers' eyes with his one good one for a moment longer. 'You and Gallow. Whatever it is, put it away until we get back.' Anyone could see the two of them had some old feud far from forgotten between them – the mystery was why they didn't just get on with it, fight each other and then one of them would be dead and that would be the end. Because Yurlak was king and that somehow made Twelvefingers special? But Yurlak himself would fall out of his shoes laughing at that.

Jyrdas shook his head. He let Twelvefingers go and went to help carry the ram to the monastery doors. The other Lhosir were already hacking at them with their axes. There was no stopping it. For better or worse, Twelvefingers would have his shield tonight.

'Hoy! Dog-buggerer!' He grabbed Tolvis. The two of them being the oldest, veterans of the Screambreaker's first war, as far as Jyrdas was concerned they were in charge of the fighting and never mind what Twelvefingers had to say about that. *Prince?* The Marroc were the ones impressed by titles, not Lhosir.

'What do you want, One-Eye? Did you wink at someone and think you'd gone blind and get confused?'

'Ha bloody ha. The beacon in the back yard. You think of that?'

'I did.' Loudmouth made a big show of shrugging his shoulders. 'Some fool lit it. Couldn't be bothered to put it out. Seemed like it might not be such a bad thing actually. Makes some good light and gives us plenty of burning brands for setting fire to things.'

'And if the soldiers out of Pendrin see it?'

Tolvis shrugged again. 'If they see it then they already saw the fire Medrin lit by the bridge. Otherwise they won't see the smoke until dawn. Either way it makes no difference.'

'They know we're inside, they'll come quick.'

'Well then I guess we're none of us clever enough to have thought of that until it was too late.' Loudmouth laughed. 'Although *now* a clever man would surely think that we'd have to get out of here sharp-like when we're done. No time for making any ravens. Shame, eh?'

Jyrdas considered that. He gritted his teeth. 'Likes his ravens, doesn't he?' Blood ravens were for *nioingr*. Doing it to any old Marroc who happened to look at you in a funny way made the whole thing a mockery. Man called you a pig, you ripped his lungs out. Man murdered your family in their sleep? Same thing. Might as well go ahead and do the murdering then. Someone crossed you, you had a fight about it, quick and simple. Nothing wrong with a fair fight. Even the Marroc understood that much. Maybe you killed them or maybe they killed you, or maybe one of you marked the other and then you were all friends again. Ravens though, that was for something else. The Maker-Devourer would frown on them if he cared about anything at all.

Sod it. He looked about for Gallow and saw the no-beard running past the monastery towards the back yard. Maybe he wasn't quite as clever as Loudmouth and had decided to go and put out the beacon. Jyrdas shrugged. There was killing to be done here and he was eager for it. He headed for the ram.

The monastery door splintered at the first blow and fell at the second. The Lhosir let out their battle cries and charged into a hail of rocks and javelins. A stone hit Jyrdas on the helm and a spear went straight through the man beside him. Stupid not to think of picking up a shield, but too late for that now. They swarmed through, swinging their axes and swords. Jyrdas charged the first islander he saw, shoulder dropped straight into the man's shield, knocking him down. He ducked the swing of a sword and stabbed at a face. The inside of the monastery was dark, so damn dark that everything was reduced to shapes and shadows, glimmers in the feeble starlight that came in through the windows and wild dancing shadows from the burning beacon, and in the middle of all that the men and the women from the village below the cliff, screaming and shrieking and running and falling over, desperate just to get away. The kind of fight where everything came to luck, where the fearless won out over the afraid, which was fine by him.

A blow from behind caught him on the shoulder, cracking a bone. He roared in pain and spun around, lashing with his axes. His left arm hung almost useless. He caught sight of a shape and screamed, jumping at it, bringing the other axe down. The shape threw up a shield.

'For Yurlak!' He swung again, battering the man back.

'For Medrin!' The islander lunged with his sword. In the dark Jyrdas didn't see it coming and it caught him hard in the ribs, snapping at least one. His mail held, though, and he had the bloodlust on him now. A dim thought wondered why the islander trying to kill him was shouting his own prince's name.

But the man *was* trying kill him. He ducked and lashed out with a foot at where the islander's legs ought to be. Caught something. The islander staggered and his shield dropped and that was enough. Jyrdas brought his axe down and felt the blade bite deep. The islander shrieked and Jyrdas swung again, a backhand swipe to the head that shattered the islander's cheek and tore most of his face off. Jyrdas stamped on him and looked for the next. His shoulder hurt and his ribs too and he couldn't breathe without stabbing pains, but he'd had worse and more than once.

The fight was ebbing now. Shapes in the dark, that was all he could see, curse his one good eye. The screams were mostly outside. The villagers either dead or they'd got away.

'The shield!' shouted Twelvefingers over the ruckus. 'Where's the shield? Bring it to me!'

Jyrdas pulled himself straight. 'Come on!' he roared. 'Which one of you *nioingr* wants to fight me?'

A silhouette appeared against the broken doors, darkening to the vague idea of a shape as it came inside. 'Jyrdas?'

'Who wants me?'

'Gallow. Maker-Devourer, this is madness!' Gallow ran

out and came back with a burning branch taken from the beacon. 'Someone lit it,' he said, not sounding much bothered. 'Didn't get there in time to stop them.'

'I think you might want to ask Loudmouth about that.' Jyrdas clenched his good fist. 'Seemed far too smug about it if you ask me.'

'Some of the women from the village got away. Some of the men too. There's quite a few of them dead out there though.'

'Ach, let the bastards from Pendrin come. Damn but I want to kill something.'

The light from Gallow's torch showed the fight was all but over. The last few islanders were surrounded and being cut down one by one. They didn't try to surrender even though they must have known there was no hope. Good for them. The Maker-Devourer liked that sort of spirit.

'Looks like you already did.' Gallow was looking at Jyrdas's axe, at the blood still dripping off it. And at the man lying on the floor with his jaw hanging off his face by a flap of skin. The dead man was a Lhosir. Mangled beyond recognition but he had the forked beard. Couldn't be anyone else.

'Stupid shit hit me in the back with an axe.' He couldn't move that arm at all now. 'Bugger couldn't tell the difference between friend and foe in the dark. Serves him right. What kind of *nioingr* takes a man from behind anyway?'

There was an odd look on Gallow's face. 'Where's Tolvis?'

'Do I care? Where are the bloody monks?' Jyrdas clenched his teeth and snarled. Damn but that shoulder hurt.

The other Lhosir were scaling the stairs and ladders to the upper floor of the monastery, or else running outside to smash in the doors of the little outbuildings that pressed against the walls. Jyrdas pushed past Gallow, looking for Twelvefingers. 'Where's the shield, boy? I want to see it!' Every breath hurt. Not coughing up a bloody froth though, so no need to go and pick a fight with someone just so he could go to the Maker-Devourer with a weapon in his hand. He found Twelvefingers and a few of his closer Lhosir clustered at the hearth. Someone had pulled back the furs that had been scattered there. There was a door in the floor. 'Is it down there?'

Twelvefingers looked at him and laughed. Little prick. 'It may be, old One-Eye. Do you want to go and look for it?'

'Do I? Out of the way, boy.' Jyrdas pushed at him with the one arm that still worked but this time Twelvefingers stood his ground. His eyes glittered in the firelight, a flash of hostility.

'Mind your mouth, One-Eye! Looks to me like you're down to one of almost everything. Not sure you could handle a few monks right now.'

'You little ...' He clenched his fist, but before he could punch Twelvefingers across the hall, Loudmouth was beside him and had a hold of his arm.

'If the shield's down there then Prince Medrin, may his glory shine like a thousand suns, should have the honours. This is his hunt, not yours.'

Jyrdas backed away. 'Half mine,' he muttered. Loudmouth being right didn't make it any better. 'Little prick,' he muttered again. 'If Yurlak was here or even the Screambreaker, they'd put him over their knee and spank him. May his glory shine like a thousand suns? Head gone as soft as the rest of you, has it, Loudmouth?'

Tolvis laughed. 'You need to sit down, old man. Take some air.'

'No, I bloody don't. I need to stand up so I don't shove the broken end of some rib or other through a lung and bleed to death on the inside.'

'Then lie down.'

'*Lie down?* Have you lost your balls? Anyway, some shit stain smashed my shoulder. Can't lie down.' His head was spinning a little.

'Battle's over, Jyrdas. Here. Have a spear to lean on.'

'Daft bugger! Shoulder and ribs, I said! Nothing wrong with my legs!' He gripped his axe. Might be that Loudmouth had a point, though. 'Who are *you* calling old, anyway?'

Tolvis smiled. 'You got me there, One-Eye.' Medrin's men were vanishing down the hole in the floor, big Horsan at the front. Jyrdas felt a surge of envy. That was where *he* should be. Would have been too, in the old days. Wouldn't have been stupid enough to get thumped. Wouldn't have been stupid enough to fight a man in the pitch dark. Axed in the back by one of his own? Maker-Devourer! Still, no accounting for idiots. 'Children. Half of them should be back across the sea still sucking at their mothers' tits by the look of them.'

'They have their beards, One-eye. How old were you on your first raid?'

Twelvefingers and his men had all gone down to the cellars now. With a bit of luck someone would knife a few of them in the dark. Learn them a thing or two about a bit of common sense. Jyrdas sank to his knees and clutched at the spear. His head was buzzing and all the pain made it hard to breathe. 'Don't let those little shits see me like this, Loudmouth.' He could smell smoke, little wafts of it creeping in from outside where others were setting fire to the outbuildings. Like the old times. He smiled.

'Lean on me if you want.'

'Lean on *you*, Loudmouth? I'd snap you like a dead twig.' He bared his teeth and growled. 'Ah but it hurts, damn it.'

'Pain, Jyrdas? A Lhosir doesn't feel pain. You told me that. I had a Marroc arrow in my leg at the time, but I'm sure you were right.'

'Time I lost my eye? Hurt like being taken up the arse by the Maker-Devourer himself. Worse than this. I'll live.' He spat back at the dead Lhosir on the floor. 'Stupid *nioingr* crap stain piece of shit!'

One of Medrin's men poked his face up out of the floor. 'It's here! The shield! It's here!'

Jyrdas tried to get up. If there was one thing he was going to do now he was here, he was going to see the damn thing with his own eyes. The Crimson Shield, holy relic of the Marroc and their gods. The shield the Fateguard had said was too dangerous for the Screambreaker to take. Why? Because he'd have made himself king? Probably, but he could have done that anyway if he'd wanted to.

Instead of getting up, he seemed to be sliding closer to the ground, hands slipping down the shaft of Tolvis's spear.

'Loudmouth! Your spear's not working properly!'

'It's a lump of wood, you daft half-blind ...'

He caught sight of a strange look on Tolvis's face and then his one good eye wouldn't stay open and all he could hear were the monks singing from down in the cellar while a pleasant warmth spread through him.

28

THE CRIMSON SHIELD

'Since we both know you're as keen as I am, you might as well lead the way.' Medrin slapped Gallow on the shoulder and pushed him towards the ladder leading under the monastery hall. Gallow climbed down, the rest of the Lhosir pressing after him. The ladder led them into a narrow tunnel, a dank and winding thing so low that he had to stoop. He passed niches in the walls, crudely cut from the raw stone, dozens of them, in each a desiccated body wrapped in bandages. The smoke from the Lhosir torches quickly filled the air, choking him, making his eyes water so he could hardly see.

The tunnel led lower, deeper, past pits filled with skulls and bones. The passage grew narrower and uneven, steeper, until it was little more than a fissure in the rock crudely etched with steps that wound down from the crypts sunk deep in the rauk. Gallow heard the Lhosir behind him muttering, wondering where he was leading them. They were men of the sea and the mountains and wide-open spaces. Cramped dark places deep under the earth brought out the superstitious in them. Monsters dwelt in the darkness deep beneath the earth – they all knew that.

The fissure widened, spilling them out into a slanting cave that ran deep to the bottom of the rauk. He could smell the seawater at the bottom, rank and salty. The Lhosir torches barely touched the darkness of it, but it was easy to see where the cave ended and the water began because that was where the monks of Luonatta were waiting for them, fifty feet below. They stood in a circle on a tiny island surrounded by rings and rings of candles and black glittering water. A narrow wooden stair, steep and creaking, wound down the side of the rift, little more than a string of wooden pegs hammered into holes in the rock. Now and then, as Gallow shifted his weight from one to the next, he felt them flex and bend, heard them creak. There was nothing to hold on to except the damp wall of stone, pressed so close beside him that it seemed to want to push him over, down into the depths below.

As the Lhosir entered the cave the monks began chanting. Something lay in the middle of their circle, large and round. The cave was too dark to make out what it was, but there was only one thing it could be: the shield. Gallow shook his head. Monks were the same everywhere – he'd seen it enough times among the Marroc. When terror came to call they made a circle and prayed to their gods, and from when he'd followed the Screambreaker he couldn't think of a single time those prayers had been answered. What were they praying for? That Medrin and all his men would slip on the narrow steps and break their necks? Lhosir didn't pray. The best they could hope for was for the Maker-Devourer to ignore them. The closest thing the Lhosir had to people like these monks were the iron devils of the Fateguard, the soldiers of the Eyes of Time, and *they* certainly wouldn't meekly close their eyes and pray and die.

A man swore behind him and then another screamed as he slipped and plunged into the darkness below. Gallow didn't dare turn to look. A deep unease washed over him here in this dark place under the earth with strange men and their strange gods waiting for him. Maybe there *was* something to those prayers after all. Prayers to what?

The steps brought him down to a shelf of rock almost level with the water and slippery with black seaweed. A small wooden bridge led to the island. After the crudeness of the steps, it was strangely ornate, narrow but with a rail on either side and carved with fish-like figures. Water monsters. Serpents. Women who were half beast. The other men stopped behind him, waiting, none of them sure what to do until Medrin pushed past them all and came to stand beside Gallow at the bridge.

'Hey there!' He waved his sword across the narrow waters. 'We've come for your shield. It belongs to the Marroc. If you'd be so kind as to pass it over, we can be on our way. I also have some swords here that you can fall on, if you're feeling accommodating.' The shadows of the flickering torchlight had changed his face. He looked somehow monstrous. Eyes agleam, teeth bared in a hungry grimace.

The monks didn't even look at him. Their faces were glassy, chanting the same words over and over: Modris, Modris, Protector! Modris, Modris, Builder! Modris, Modris, Maker! Modris Modris …

Modris? Gallow started as though he'd been stung. Wasn't this supposed to be a temple to Luonatta the battle god? Why were the monks chanting the name of Modris?

'Oh never mind.' Medrin stepped back from the bridge. 'Gallow, since you were clever enough to get us through the gates, I give you the honour. Kill them for me.'

Gallow's feet wouldn't move at first. He touched the locket around his neck and felt it urge him to turn and leave and go home and never look back. There was something wrong with this place; but maybe that was only his old Lhosir blood and all its wariness of what lurked in the deeper places of the world where the shadewalkers were born. And then his Lhosir pride had him too, refusing to let him show his fear, and so he stepped onto the bridge, tense as a drawn knife. When nothing happened he began to walk across. His hand felt tight on the hilt of his sword, restless and twitchy, screaming at him for release. He pushed the hunger aside and merely shoved the first two monks out of his way and pushed them into the water. The others didn't move. He reached for the shield. His arm tingled as he did and his heart beat a little faster. A dozen years ago Medrin and Beyard had been transfixed by this god-forged shield and what it meant, and he'd been no better. Now he told himself what the Screambreaker had told him after he'd crossed the sea and found the courage to ask: it was just a shield and nothing more, one that happened to be red. And yet the hairs on his arm prickled as he touched it. The Crimson Shield. The invincible shield of Modris the Protector.

Not that it had saved the Marroc. Just a shield, that's all.

He pushed another monk away, set his own shield down and took the Crimson Shield instead. It was heavy. Instinct demanded that he put it on his arm but that would be to claim it for himself, so he carried it carefully back across the bridge, hairs still prickling all over his skin. The monks continued their chanting as though nothing had happened. Even the ones he'd pushed into the sea were climbing back out of the water, shaking their robes and retaking their places back in the circle. Gallow took a long look at the shield as he held it out in front of him. The darkness and the torchlight hid its colour. It looked like a simple round shield, thick wood reinforced and studded with metal. A single colour, dark grey in the cave but surely crimson in the sunlight. No design. He offered it up to Medrin. 'Here you go then.'

'Funny,' said the prince as he took it, 'to hold it after all these years. Don't you think?'

'It's just a shield.' Gallow let it go. His fingers didn't believe him and his guts didn't either, but how could it be anything else?

'You seem to have left yours behind.'

'That was some islander piece of rot. I left *mine* back on the cliff.' He shrugged and walked away.

'Gallow!' Medrin called him back.

'Twelvefingers?'

'I told you to kill them.'

'And I didn't. I got you the shield. That's what you wanted.'

'No, I wanted you to kill these thieves who took what was ours and claimed it for themselves.'

'King Tane's heir are you now?'

'My father is king of the Marroc.'

'Then kill them yourself. There's no honour in slaughter.' Where was Jyrdas when he was needed? Even bloodthirsty old One-Eye would say the same.

'There's honour in serving your prince, clean-skin.'

'Then I'm sure you'll find someone to do it for you.'

Medrin looked past Gallow to the other men. 'A village full of Marroc to whoever kills a monk. Go. Have yourselves some fun.'

No one moved, not straight away. 'Lord of a village full of sheep?' called a voice from the back. 'What would I do with them?' *Tolvis. Damn it, where was Jyrdas?*

'Probably something unnatural, Loudmouth.' The big man Horsan stepped forward, gripping his giant axe. Gorrin, the archer with the broken arm, pushed his way to the bridge too.

'If I kill two, do I get two?'

'Kill six, you get six,' said Medrin with a shrug, and with that half the Lhosir swarmed over the bridge, howling and swinging their swords. The other half stood and looked at one another, muttering uneasily. It was over in a moment and then the Lhosir fell silent and stopped to look at what they'd done: a dozen unarmed monks crumpled in a ring around the stone where the shield had been. A dark tension swirled around them.

'I don't know about the rest of you,' said Tolvis from the back, 'but I think I've had about enough of this place. I think

I shall be off a-looking to see if these monks had themselves a wine cellar anywhere. Those who fancy a swill, Gallow, are very welcome to join me.'

Tolvis began to climb the steps. He wasn't the only one, but in the gloom Gallow couldn't see who else went with him. And he ought to go too, he knew it, but he couldn't quite bring himself to move. Medrin ignored them all. 'It's called what it's called for a reason,' he said, and he walked across the bridge and put the shield back where Gallow had found it. He knelt beside a dead monk and began to cut out the man's heart.

'No.' Gallow pushed his way back towards Medrin. 'No, Medrin, we do not do this.'

'Stop him.' Medrin didn't look up. 'Kill him if you have to.'

Twelvefingers took out a knife, felt for the bottom of the dead man's ribs, then drove the blade in deep and slit the monk open. He reached in, struggling for a moment before he tore out the dead monk's heart, bloody strands of flesh trailing behind it, and squeezed it over the shield. Gallow drew his sword. Three men seized him. He tried to shake them off. 'Blood rites, Medrin!'

'Let it go, Gallow,' warned Horsan. 'There's no good end to this. Our prince knows what he's doing.' He didn't even seem surprised.

Gallow broke free and readied his sword again. He surged towards the bridge, the other Lhosir moving uncertainly out of his path. 'Innocent blood, Medrin!'

'Innocent?' Medrin lifted the shield and held it high. 'These monks?' he cried. 'Innocent? Maker-Devourer, they're dead! And maybe these monks *were* innocent, but what of all the Marroc that you and the Screambreaker and all the rest put to the sword?' He bared his teeth. 'You've forgotten what you are, Gallow. You're no *nioingr* but you're no Lhosir either. You're nothing but a Marroc like any other.' He kicked the nearest dead monk, slapped the iron rim of the shield down on the stone and pointed at Gallow with his sword. 'You have no idea what this is, no-beard. You have no idea what it can do, what it means. If you did, you wouldn't ride your sanctimony so sweetly. A little ritual of thanks to the Maker-Devourer and you draw steel on me? You forget where this came from and you forget what you are! Yes, Gorrin, please.'

Gallow blinked, realised that Medrin was no longer looking at him but past him instead, and that was when someone hit him round the back of the head with the butt of an axe.

Light and noise and then quiet and dark. He was standing on a hilltop in the twilight, a steady wind blowing around him. He knew the place at once. His old home, where he'd grown up before his father had taken them to Yurlak's Nardjas to make armour for the Screambreaker. He remembered the hill. A favourite place, especially when the sun was setting. He used to go there with Kyerla, the sweetheart of his childhood. He hadn't thought about Kyerla in ten years, but he remembered now how much he'd missed her when his father had taken them away. In a different world, one where they'd stayed in their forge and their farm by the sea, he and Kyerla would have been married, younger even than when Gallow had crossed the sea. He could be there now, curled up with her softness under a pile of furs with six or seven fine sons ...

He sensed movement and turned, expecting to see her, but the woman waiting for him was Arda, arms outstretched. 'Remember us, Gallow.' He couldn't see his children, but they were there too. He felt them. Kyerla was forgotten as quickly as she'd filled him. He tried to walk towards Arda but something caught his eye to make him look away. When he looked back she was gone and all he saw standing at the top of the hill was a long sword, dark red, stuck fast, point down in the chalky earth.

'No, don't kill him ...' Words drifted in and out. Light flickered and came and went.

'We could just leave him.'

'Any of you want a fight about it?'

'What about him?' The pain was huge. Even blinking hurt.

'One-Eye?' The back of his head. 'Is he still alive then?' He couldn't touch it. His hands were tied. When he moved he felt a sharp tug on the skin at the back of his neck. Dried blood.

'He's made of granite, that one. He's bound to live.' His blood.

'Bring them both.' Deep breaths. Fighting back the waves of nausea. 'The dead too.' One after the other. 'Put a torch to the rest.' Too much effort. His eyes wanted to close again. To let it all pass.

Another voice, hurried. 'Get back to the ships!' He forced his eyes open. Took deep breaths, one after the other. He slipped in and out of darkness a while, but by the time the Lhosir were ready to leave, his senses were back enough that he could stand. His hands were tied behind his back. Gorrin and two men who'd sailed with Medrin were standing guard. A few bodies lay around him. Off across the yard Tolvis was shouting at someone about an axe. He had Jyrdas slumped against him, leaning hard on his shoulder. The big man looked ready to collapse.

They'd taken his weapons. The worst humiliation. 'Gorrin!' It had to have been the archer. 'You hit me. You took me from behind.'

Gorrin gave him a look of disdain. 'You were heading sword drawn towards our prince, Marroc.'

'A good blow for a man with a broken arm, I'll give you that. You don't need me to say what sort of man takes another from behind. You know the answer.'

Gorrin leaned into him. 'When I have my arm back, Marroc, I'll be happy to talk about the answer to all sorts of things. Prince Twelvefingers killed a few monks? So? You're on your own if you think anyone gives a pot of piss about that.'

Medrin got them back on the move quickly. The Lhosir were surly now. The fighting was done, the battle madness sated, the fires were lit and buildings blazed all around them. They had little to show for their fight; they were hungry and tired and they wanted to go to sleep, and now Twelvefingers was going to make them walk back across the cliffs to the ships in the dark and row out to sea. Gorrin turned to Gallow. 'If the soldiers from that castle catch us out in the open, I'll cut you free, but only for that.'

The moon had sunk below the horizon. Clouds hid half the stars, making every stone and every divot a hazard in the dark. They stumbled across the fields and cliff-tops in moody silence, carrying what they could, shields thrown over their backs, plunder on their shoulders, the fires of the burning monastery lighting their way. Medrin would expect them to sail as soon as they reached the ships and work the oars until the morning. As far as Gallow could see, the monks of Luonatta had hardly been rich. The spoils were meagre. A few barrels and casks stolen from the pantry but no gold, no treasures, no women, nothing worth taking home, nothing even making it worth leaving Andhun in the first place except for the Crimson Shield.

Tolvis and Gallow took turns to prop up Jyrdas. They reached the beach. No one had burned their ships, and before dawn broke the sky they were riding the sea again. A melancholy settled around them despite their victory. A sadness for the men who were dead and an uneasy sense of something changed and thus something lost. Maybe on the other ship, with Medrin and with the Crimson Shield there for all to see, things were different, but on the second boat Gallow thought he felt a creeping edge of doubt. Jyrdas hobbled around, screaming murder at anyone in his way, face screwed up in permanent pain. Wind and wave fought against them as if trying to turn them back, making them slow. With the madness of the fight cleared from their heads, the Lhosir around him remembered what they and Medrin had done. Gallow made sure to remind them.

They kept him bound, tied to the mast through wind and rain even when they could have used another strong pair of arms on the oars. 'I can row,' he told them. 'Where am I going to go?' He saw them waver but that was all. Even Jyrdas looked at him with a face full of rage. Maybe they were afraid he'd throw them all over the side and sail to Andhun single-handed.

On their third day at sea a storm hit. They took in water and almost foundered. Oars broke, snapped by the strength of the waves. The Marroc in Gallow would have said it was a miracle they didn't sink and drown, but Lhosir didn't believe in miracles. Fate, perhaps, had spared them, or perhaps they were merely lucky: Jyrdas and the others who'd been to sea before certainly thought so. When the winds passed and the waves fell, they lay about the deck and slept and broke open a cask of mead taken from the monastery and drank toasts to the Maker-Devourer, and Gallow thought nothing of it until Tivik, who might have been the youngest of them, raised a drunken horn to the clouds.

'To Medrin! It was the Crimson Shield that guided us! The shield of the Protector!'

Jyrdas, on another day, might have thrown Tivik into the sea for being an idiot, but Jyrdas was fast asleep and half dead. The other Lhosir gave Tivik queer looks and muttered to themselves, but he wasn't alone. It spread among them like some disease, slow but lethal.

'It's just a shield,' Gallow tried to tell them, but by the time they reached Andhun none of them wanted to know.

29

THE MARROC

After the storm, the wind and the waves favoured them to Andhun. The castle still sat on the cliffs overlooking the harbour. Teenar's Bridge still lay strung across the Isset. Nothing, as far as Gallow could see, had burned down, although the blood ravens hung across the docks had been cut down and the gibbets were gone. The town felt quiet and peaceful. The Vathen, then, hadn't yet come.

The Lhosir made good their ships and unloaded what was left of their plunder from the monastery. Their melancholy had gone after the storm, replaced by a strange fervour for the shield. They bound Gallow and manhandled him to the shore and then when they were standing on the beach together, they crowded Medrin, trying to see the shield more closely. Touching it. And yes, in the light of the day it was as crimson as fresh blood, and either Medrin had spent a great deal of time cleaning and polishing it, or perhaps it did have a magic to it after all.

The shield took their eyes, and that was why they didn't see the Marroc at first. Not too many, just a dozen men gradually gathering together, keeping their distance but watching from the top of the shingle beach with the air of those waiting for something to happen. As Gallow eyed them they were joined by more, and then more still, until the first dozen had become two and more were coming all the time. He saw Valaric among them, and was that Sarvic too?

Soldiers. Marroc soldiers. A cry of alarm caught in Gallow's throat. The Lhosir were still hauling their swords and their armour and everything else out of the boats, or were clustered around Medrin. Elsewhere the docks were falling still, Marroc workmen scurrying to safety or else joining Valaric and his band. Something was coming and they knew it.

'Loudmouth!' Gallow shouted. But Tolvis was still on the ship, and the devil inside Gallow wanted to wait, wait for the Marroc numbers to swell a bit. A good charge now and they'd break and scatter and that would be that, but if more came … He wondered what Valaric was thinking, yet still the Lhosir didn't see, not until Tolvis finally started climbing out of the boat, helping Jyrdas, who kept trying to push him away, the last ones ashore.

'Get off me, you sheep!'

From across the beach a Marroc let fly an arrow. It hit Jyrdas and staggered Tolvis enough to make him jump down from the boat. He half caught One-Eye as he fell and they both stared at the arrow sticking out of One-Eye's side. Jyrdas bellowed in pain. He stumbled back to his feet and picked up the first axe he saw and looked, wild-eyed, for someone to hit. He stared at the Marroc mob and held the axe high. '*Nioingr*! Come on then, if you think you can take me!'

There were forty or fifty of them now, the same sort of numbers as the Lhosir, and the arrow must have been a sign, because even as Jyrdas raised his axe, they howled and ran down the beach, waving clubs and spears. They had shields and helms and some even had armour and swords. The Lhosir drew back around Medrin.

'Loudmouth! Cut me loose!' Gallow looked about for anyone to help him, but all the Lhosir eyes were on the Marroc now. Valaric at their van slowed and raised a hand. The Marroc stopped around him, an angry line facing the Lhosir.

'What you have there belongs to the Marroc, Twelve-fingers,' he cried. 'Give it here and go back where you belong before I cut you down to six.'

Medrin burst out laughing. 'How many are you? Fifty? Sixty? And you think to throw me out of my own city.' He shook his head. With deliberate care he buckled the Crimson Shield to his arm and bent to pick up a seagull feather from the ground. He held it high. 'When this touches the ground, I'll have every Marroc still standing in front of me hung by his own spine.'

'How many are we?' Valaric laughed right back in Medrin's face. 'How many Marroc in Andhun? And how many demon-beards? Take a look around you. The Vathen are coming. Your army has moved outside the walls to face the enemy and we've closed the gates behind them. There's not one of you left inside the walls to save you. So drop your feather and let me kill you or just give me the shield and slink away like a fox before a bear. I'll have it from you either way.'

Medrin cocked his head. He let the feather slip from his fingers. The Marroc and the Lhosir watched each other as it fell. Nobody moved. Gallow howled again for Tolvis to cut him free but no one was listening. More Marroc had stopped to watch. Valaric's fifty would become a hundred the moment it seemed as though they might win. And if they did, that one hundred would become five, and then a thousand, and with the Crimson Shield Valaric would turn the whole of Andhun, and its gates would stay closed to both Vathen and Lhosir alike.

And Gallow wondered: *Would that be so bad?* 'Cut me free!' He couldn't have said, even to himself, whose side his sword would have taken. For Medrin? The thought was bitter. Turn against his own kin? More bitter still. But worst of all was to stand idly by and do nothing, to be cut down by some Marroc who saw only another forkbeard, easy and helpless.

The feather touched the beach. The stillness remained, and then Valaric howled and Medrin screamed and drew his sword, and the Marroc and the Lhosir threw themselves at one another. There was no shield wall, no tight press of men pushed together. They flew at each other, spears and swords and axes fired by fury. Gallow watched, helpless. Valaric and Medrin were trying to reach each other while the other Marroc and the Lhosir tried to protect them. He watched a score of men die on either side, then the Marroc suddenly scattered and ran back across the beach, even Valaric, and Medrin stood by his ships, blood dripping from his sword in one hand, the Crimson Shield in the other, the Lhosir jeering and waving their spears. Bodies lay scattered around them, the dead and the dying. Dozens of them. Half the Lhosir to come back from the monastery were down and no more had appeared. Valaric's words were true then: the Screambreaker had left the city.

Jyrdas broke away from Medrin's men and staggered up to Gallow, walking like he was steaming drunk. He still had the Marroc arrow sticking out of his side. His beard and his shirt were soaked in blood. He sat beside Gallow.

'I lost my sword,' he said. 'I killed two of the faithless *nioingr* and then I dropped it.' For a moment he looked scared. 'I can't pick it up again, Truesword.' Frothy blood bubbled from the corners of his mouth when he spoke.

'Cut me loose! I'll find it for you.'

Jyrdas shrugged. 'I don't have the strength. Don't have a blade. I can see the Marches, Gallow. Don't let me die without my sword.'

The Lhosir survivors were pushing Medrin's ship back into the sea now. At the top of the beach Valaric and his Marroc were gathering again. They'd run but they weren't broken, and Valaric was screaming and pointing. In a few minutes Medrin would have his ship back in the water. He'd sail away and the shield would go with him. If Valaric couldn't get enough men together with the courage to fight this last handful of Lhosir then perhaps the Marroc didn't deserve to have it. Gallow hobbled, bent almost double by the ropes that tied his ankles to his wrists, to where the dead lay. With his hands tied behind his back he groped for a sword and hobbled back to Jyrdas. Valaric and a dozen Marroc were starting back down the beach again now, but he didn't have enough and Medrin's ship was almost in the water.

'That's right!' shouted Valaric. 'Run! What's your word for it? *Nioingr!* Faithless worthless cowards, that's what you are!'

Trying to goad Medrin into another fight. Gallow managed to drop the sword into Jyrdas's lap. 'If it was you and not Medrin, you'd stop and turn and fight him for that, never mind how many Marroc there were behind him.'

'He wouldn't have to call me names. I'd do it anyway.' Jyrdas groped for the sword. The ship was in the water now, the Lhosir ignoring Valaric. 'If it was me or Yurlak or the Screambreaker, or any one of us who fought them the first time, we'd never have thought about leaving. Twenty of us, a whole city of them, so what? We fought, they ran, the city was ours. We'd have taken it. Hindhun was taken from a thousand Marroc by fifty of us. We'd win or we died trying, and either way served a purpose.' Jyrdas closed his eyes. 'Maker-Devourer take me quickly, before I see a prince of the sea driven from these shores by a rabble of Marroc.' His brow furrowed and then he stood up and turned. 'No. I'll not watch this in silence.' Up on the beach the Marroc were finding their numbers and their nerve, spurred by Valaric's taunts. 'Hoy! Twelvefingers!' Jyrdas roared. 'The Marroc's right. You're *nioingr*! You hear me? Running like a sheep? *Nioingr!*' He shouted it until the Lhosir couldn't pretend not to hear. It must have taken the last strength he had; he sat heavily down and the sword fell from his hand again.

Medrin walked quickly over, two men at his back, all of them glancing up the beach towards the approaching Marroc as the ship ground out into the surf. 'Eat your words and beg for forgiveness, One-Eye,' hissed Medrin. 'These men will witness it.'

'*Nioingr*,' whispered Jyrdas again. Medrin whipped out a thin dagger and stabbed him through his good eye. Jyrdas slumped sideways and fell without another sound.

'Was it really an accident that one of your men took Jyrdas from behind in the monastery?' Gallow asked him.

Medrin bared his teeth. He backed away, shouting as he ran into the breaking waves and to his ship, 'The Marroc can have you! Back to your own kind, clean-skin!'

Gallow watched him go. He watched Valaric and the Marroc on the beach do the same and pitied them for how it must feel, seeing Medrin get away when they had so nearly stopped him. When the only thing that stood in their way was their own fear. How it must feel for Valaric, who had the courage in himself but couldn't find it in the men around him. Or for the Marroc who were afraid, who knew it was their own weakness that brought their defeat. Terrible to be either. One day the Marroc would find their hearts. One day the sheep would become wolves.

He bent down and fumbled Jyrdas's sword off the beach and dropped it beside him. It was the best he could do, but the Maker-Devourer would understand.

31

THE PYRE

The Marroc didn't know what to make of him. The first ones looked at his face, saw no beard, took him to be a Marroc prisoner and cut him loose. When they kicked and spat on Jyrdas's corpse and Gallow knocked them both to the floor, they wondered what they'd done.

'Valaric knows me,' he said, 'and any who fought at Lostring Hill. They'll vouch for who I am. One way or the other.'

'Lock him up. We'll deal with him later,' said Valaric when they brought him to Gallow. 'He's not one of us and he's not one of them. He's half and half and you never really know which half it's going to be.' He looked Gallow up and down and stared hard at the sword Gallow held – Jyrdas's sword. 'You coming nicely or do we have to have a fight at last, you and I?'

Gallow glanced at the bodies on the beach. 'Is Marroc justice to a Lhosir any better then Medrin's was to you?'

'Maybe. Maybe not.' Valaric stared out at the sea, at Medrin's ship ploughing through the waves. 'He won't go far. And he'll be back, and it won't be long either.' He nodded to himself and then his eyes came back to Gallow.

Gallow looked down to Jyrdas. 'I'll ask one thing of you, if you want my surrender.'

Valaric laughed. 'You don't get to ask for anything, forkbeard, you get to thank me for not killing you.' But he followed Gallow's gaze.

'Give him a proper Lhosir pyre. Burn him.'

Valaric prodded Jyrdas with his boot and rolled him onto his back. 'I know him. Jyrdas One-Eye. A right bastard. I should hang him up over the gates like he did to us.'

'A proper Lhosir pyre or I'll kill every man who comes near him until you take me down, Valaric.'

'So be it.' Valaric drew his sword. There was no anger in his eyes, no glee, no joy, only a cold sadness. 'I wasn't going to kill you, Gallow, but it does make everything that bit easier.'

'Jyrdas didn't hang your people, Valaric. He hated it. But if you want a reason, I'll give you one. After Medrin broke you and he was about to sail away and you and your Marroc were standing at the top of the beach not finding the courage to do anything more than bawl names at him, did you not hear him? He called Medrin out for running away. He had an arrow in him; he could barely stand, and he shouted and shouted it for everyone to hear.'

Valaric's lips tightened. A slight nod. '*Nioingr*. Yes, I heard. What of it?'

'Until even Medrin couldn't ignore him and came and stuck a knife in his eye to shut him up. You all saw *that*.' He looked up at the houses and streets of Andhun. 'And if you'd had even one man like him in this city then Medrin would be dead and you'd be standing in front of me holding your precious shield. You know you've just brought doom on the whole of Andhun, don't you?'

Valaric glowered. 'Shut your hole, forkbeard.' He snarled, looked away and took a deep breath as though struggling with something. 'Go on, burn him then,' he said at last. 'You do it. You can make his pyre and you can light it and watch him burn and not one Marroc will lift a finger to help you. Then you can go. Get out of my city and get out of my sight. Go and fight the Vathen. I never want to see you again. If I do, you're just another forkbeard to me and that's all. Now give me your sword.'

Gallow blinked. He reversed the sword and held it out. 'It's not mine, Valaric. It's just a blade I found and it belongs to Jyrdas now. But I think he'd be happy for me to give it to you. Please take this sword, the sword that Jyrdas held in his hand as he died, as his thanks for honouring him as a valiant foe.'

Valaric took the hilt and lifted the sword. He shook his head. 'You Lhosir are demented.' He left and the Marroc moved around Gallow, collecting the weapons and armour and the food and plunder that Medrin's men had unloaded from their ships and then abandoned on the beach. Gallow took an axe to the ship that had been left behind, Jyrdas's ship. It seemed only fitting that it should make his pyre. He took its oars and chopped out its rowing benches and collected pieces broken by the storm, but he left its hull and mast alone. It was still a good ship. He worked into the night and then slept on the beach in the shelter of its hull, and in the morning, when the rising sun woke him, he took the time to carve a name onto the ship's prow: *The One-Eyed Hunter of the Sea*. He carved it deep and large. If ever it sailed again then it would take Jyrdas's memory with it.

Afterwards, as he began to build his pyre, a Marroc came down onto the beach. Sarvic. He didn't say anything, just started to help pile the wood. They worked until the middle of the day and the pyre was done.

'For what you did on Lostring Hill and the debt I owe you,' said Sarvic when it was finished. 'Not for him. *He* was a bastard.'

There were still helms and hauberks and shields. Gallow took one of each for Jyrdas and carried them to the pyre. The rest he piled beside the ship for Valaric to take away. The Marroc of Andhun would need them, one way or the other. After that he carried and dragged Jyrdas across the beach and lifted him up onto the pile of wood, then looked at the sky. Clear and bright with no sign of rain, and so he sat waiting for twilight. Jyrdas would burn as the sun went down, dressed in mail, carrying a shield. Pity about his sword, but he could take an axe with him, the one Gallow had used to chop the wood.

The sun crept lower, the day wore on and a small crowd of Marroc began to gather. They didn't do much except stand and stare but Gallow felt their hostility. Once or twice he saw Valaric moving among them, pushing and shoving and snapping at them. As the sun reddened and sank and its light began to fail, Gallow took the last mail hauberk he'd left hidden on the ship. He polished up his helm and his shield, and walked up the beach. The Marroc shouted and jeered at him, but they parted as he came.

A rock pinged off his helm. Not a big one, but he stopped and turned and stared at them anyway. Sheep, Jyrdas called them, but that was hardly fair. They were fishermen and weavers and bakers and housewives. People content to spend their time building a life for themselves, laughing and singing and making more happy Marroc. He stared at them and saw the same thing he saw in Middislet, in the eyes of the villagers. Muted after all these years but it was still there. They were afraid. Afraid of him because of what he was. Because men like Jyrdas would have tried to take an entire city from them with just a few dozen warriors and wouldn't have given a fig of a thought for how it might end.

He snatched a torch from one and walked back down the beach to the pyre and stood before it, the brand held over his head. They could shoot him if they wanted too. They'd shot Jyrdas, after all, but it didn't bother him. If that's what they did, then that was his fate. A sadness settled over him. To the Marroc he was always a forkbeard, to the Lhosir always a sheep. To Arda, he'd just been Gallow, and that had been enough and right, but she'd betrayed him and now it was gone. *Choose one or the other*, said the voices in his head, but in the final reckoning he'd always chosen her and never mind the rest. Without her he didn't know who to be any more.

Most songs for the fallen that he knew were rowdy bawdy things because that was how the Lhosir dealt with death. The Maker-Devourer cast them out of his cauldron to live a life however they saw fit to live it, and when they died the Maker-Devourer took them back again and he only ever asked one question: Did you live it well? And he'd look into the eyes of the newly dead and see into their souls and know the truth of their answer, and if they answered yes and they believed it in their hearts, he'd take them back no matter what they'd done; and if they answered no then they were cast straight back to live a new life again, one that would be harder and more testing than the last, over and over until they found their courage. The ones who answered yes but knew in their hearts that it was a lie, best not to dwell on those. *Nioingr*. The true meaning of the word. Liars of the worst sort. Self-deceivers. They were ones who were devoured, their bones and shredded ghosts left to roam the Herenian Marches. Thus was the Maker-Devourer's brew made ever richer and stronger.

He held the torch high and began to speak out the deeds of Jyrdas One-Eye, both the good and the bad as far as he knew them. He spoke them loud and clear, straight to the pyre, with the thought that they would find Jyrdas as he waited for the Maker-Devourer's question, and remind him of anything he might forget. Everything that had made him. Everything that would be remembered.

'Jyrdas will make your cauldron.' He threw back his head to the dying sun and began to sing, the 'Last Lament of Pennas Tar', until something jabbed him in the side.

'For the love of Modris, stop howling!'

He turned, ready to tear apart whoever had interrupted this moment, and there was Valaric, holding a sword. The one he'd just poked into Gallow's mail. Gallow turned back to the pyre. 'Go away, Marroc.'

'The Vathen will be here tomorrow or the day after. The Widowmaker took his men out of the city. Every single one. To save Andhun from the Vathen. They can hardly launch an assault or dig in for a siege with the Nightmare of the North and four thousand Lhosir at their backs. The duke has his castle again and he'll open the gates for whoever wins. If it was me, I'd keep them closed. I'd fight either of you. Both of you if I had to.'

'Spoken like a forkbeard, Valaric. Now go away.'

'The Widowmaker took my land from my people. Thousands of us died on the ends of his spears. Yet he came to Fedderhun and he fought at Lostring Hill. He's my enemy and I'll kill him if I can, but if he falls, I'll let you honour his corpse too.' He thumped Gallow with the sword again and then held it out, hilt first. 'You want to give him this or not?' Then he took the sword back. 'No, *I'll* do it. He really did call Twelvefingers a *nioingr* to his face, didn't he?'

'He did.'

'And you?'

Gallow shrugged. 'The Screambreaker said that Medrin had changed. He was wrong.'

Valaric walked to the pyre. He put the sword across Jyrdas's chest beside the axe. When he stepped back, Gallow touched the torch to the kindling. As the flames leaped up, he stood away.

'I'm not staying here on some all-night vigil to honour him, though.' Valaric turned to leave. 'That's what you do, isn't it?'

'It is.' Gallow stared at the flames.

'Then I'll come for you in the morning. I meant what I said. You can go and you can fight the Vathen or sail across the sea or find your Marroc wife and grow beans and cabbages for the rest of your life. I don't care. Just get out of my city and get out of my sight. If I see you again and it's not to get my horse shod or a new blade for my scythe, I'll kill you.'

Valaric left him. The sun slowly set and Gallow watched Jyrdas One-Eye burn.

32

THE SCREAMBREAKER

The Screambreaker looked out over the fires that sprang up in the fields outside Andhun's walls. His father had called him Corvin after a rock at the end of one of his fields. Corvin's Rock. He'd thought it was a strong name, hard and weathering like the stone. Turned out it had been called Corvin's Rock after an old crow that had taken to making the rock its place to watch the world back a generation, but his father hadn't known that. Corvin the crow. Mostly Corvin preferred the idea of being a rock, but there were days when he knew, in secret, that he was really the crow. Crows were drawn to battlefields, after all.

They called him Screambreaker after he shattered King Tane's army. They said his battle cry as the two sides had met had broken the Marroc. It wasn't true but it was a good story and so they called him that anyway. The other names, the ones the Marroc had given him, he supposed he'd earned them. He might, on another day, have claimed that they'd fallen on him unsought, that he'd never gone looking for them, but on nights like tonight he knew better. Battles made for widows. Wars made for nightmares. Death had danced with him with such an easy grace and for so long now that they might as well be wed. Together, the two of them in a longhouse somewhere growing old, Death and the Widowmaker. But they weren't. They were looking for each other still, finding each other now and then, and yet somehow one of them had always had another lover at the time, and so they were never joined. *Next year, when this one is gone. We both know we were meant to be.* Twenty years of it. He looked out over the fires. Would they find each other tomorrow?

The Vathen wouldn't reach Andhun until the afternoon. They wouldn't want a fight after a day of marching, and so he'd see that they got one. Tomorrow. One way or the other, his last great battle.

'General, the prince wants to see you.'

The Screambreaker didn't move. *General?* When had he become that? A long time ago, and another thing he'd never sought. A firebrand even in his own land, just like his brother, and so Yurlak had sent him across the sea. *Go and do something useful. If you have to stir up trouble, stir it with the Marroc not with me.* Yurlak had been afraid of him … no, *afraid* wasn't the right word, because he and Yurlak were two of a kind and neither had ever been afraid of anything. But Yurlak had known well enough that Corvin, left to his own ends, was bound to break something. Better if what he broke was somewhere far away.

'I came here to be less trouble for my kin.' He was talking to the stars.

'General?'

Bring me back something pretty, and what he'd brought back was a crunching great war and a kingdom three times the size of the one Yurlak already had, and he'd given it away without a thought. There had been moments when he'd wondered about that. Set himself up as king of the Marroc? But a throne and a crown, what did he want with either of those? What use were they to a man?

He'd never married. Never raised a son. Rarely even taken a lover for long because he'd always known that death would be his bride. A tragic romance drawn out over the years, but they were bound together by fate, and every Lhosir knew better than to flout his destiny.

'General, the prince requires your ear.'

Corvin got to his feet. His knees ached from sitting still for too long. His bones creaked and groaned. He was getting old. He could have lived out his days back across the sea and taken his pick of what he wanted. Could have had Yurlak's own throne if he'd fancied it, pickling himself in mead and women until he was too fat to put on his armour, until horses screamed and bolted rather than carry him. The thought had filled him with daily horror as he'd seen the torpor of a quiet life slowly overtake him. Only a fool prayed to the Maker-Devourer, so he'd prayed to his mistress, to death. And death had answered and had sent the Vathen for him.

'What does he want, our great prince?' The words dripped out of him. Twelvefingers had been so like the young Corvin that Yurlak had sent away. But the fates were fickle and Medrin had almost died in his first battle at Corvin's side, and the wound had taken years to truly heal, and by the time he was strong again, the war was all but done. Now look at him.

'That's for him to say, General.'

It hardly mattered. Tomorrow he'd either smash the Vathen or the Vathen would break him at last, and it would be what it would be. He followed the young soldier who'd been sent for him, a man too young to even have a full beard yet. Medrin's men they called themselves, the young ones who'd grown up seeing their fathers and their uncles sailing across the sea to fight. Who were used to tales of war and battles, used to hearing of nothing but victory, even if maybe their fathers and half their uncles never came back again. They were hungry for it, feeling they'd missed something, yet they had no idea of what war truly was. Tomorrow they'd know better.

Medrin had taken his tent. The Screambreaker supposed he was entitled. Yurlak's son, after all, but didn't he have his own?

'Screambreaker.' Medrin sat on a stool. He had a thin

knife in his hand and he was using it to pick at the dirt under his fingernails.

'Medrin.' Corvin didn't bow. Medrin might expect it but that was a Marroc thing. Lhosir faced one another as equals. Always.

'You left Andhun to the Marroc.'

'Yes.'

'When I returned they tried to take the shield from me.'

'Did they succeed?'

Medrin stopped his picking and looked up. 'Clearly not, Screambreaker, otherwise I would not be here. Would you like to see it?'

'I've seen it before.' He nodded. 'It's a good thing. People will sing your saga for this. Your men will fight harder when they face the Vathen.'

'Why did you leave Andhun, Screambreaker?'

'To face the Vathen in the field.'

'But Andhun has walls.'

'It does. And a Lhosir doesn't hide behind walls.'

'And what's a row of shields then, if not a wall, Scream-breaker? Indeed, do we not call it a wall? A wall of shields?'

'A wall held by men.' Corvin closed his eyes for a moment. A headache. Yes, he had a headache coming. Now *there* was a thing that never used to trouble him on the night before a battle. Slept like a newborn, he used to. 'Do you mean to order us back through the gates, Medrin?'

'I strongly doubt the Marroc will open them for you. If the reception they gave their prince is anything to go by, I imagine they'd welcome us with arrows and javelins and anything else they can lift and throw.'

'They gave their word they wouldn't close their gates until the Vathen were in sight of the walls.'

'Have you looked, Screambreaker? Don't bother, because *I* have and they're firmly shut. I had to beach my ship a mile down the coast to get here at all.' Twelvefingers got up and walked to the back of the tent. He picked something out of the shadows, something dark and round. The shield. In the gloom it had lost its colour. 'Are we going to win, Screambreaker? Are *you* going to win?'

'Yes.' Strange to have no doubts about such a thing.

'They are ten times our number.'

'More like five.'

'They beat you outside Fedderhun.'

'Fedderhun was lost before the first blow.'

'Yet you fought it anyway?'

'Yes.' Hoping some good might come of it. Or that he might finally die.

'Me, I would have stayed behind the walls – as I was told by my prince until my prince came back and said otherwise.' He lifted the shield. 'You'll face the Vathen in the vanguard?'

'A man who claims leadership can do no less.'

Medrin put a hand over his heart, over the wound he'd taken half a lifetime ago when he'd first crossed the sea. 'Harder for some than others.'

'Yes. But still true.'

'Should I give you this shield then, since you say you lead my army?'

'I lead those who will follow, no more. You took the shield. It's yours by right.'

Twelvefingers smiled for a moment. '*You* took it first.'

'And I lost it, and now you have it. It's a shield and I already have one.'

'I might give it to you as a gift.'

'And I will accept any gift given with a good heart, Twelvefingers. But there's no need.'

'I'm displeased with you about Andhun, so you'll get no gifts from me today. Win this battle and the shield is yours, Screambreaker. Now tell me how you'll do it.'

So Corvin told him. It wasn't any work of genius. Only the plan of a man who'd seen more of war than any other.

33

THE ROAD TO VARYXHUN

Gallow watched Jyrdas burn through the night. As the flames died, he went back to the beached ship and slept. In the morning Valaric was waiting for him. 'Give me your axe. No Lhosir carries arms in the streets of Andhun now.'

'My axe went to Jyrdas. If you want it, pick over his ashes.'

They walked side by side in silence up the beach, along the bank of the Isset and up the hill, past the castle towards the Castle Gate. The gibbets were all gone. Valaric followed his eyes. 'What, did you think we'd leave them?' Marroc soldiers fell in behind them. They jeered and threw insults, and if Valaric hadn't been there, Gallow knew they would have set upon him. They knew who he was. *What* he was.

The gates opened to let him through. Valaric turned his back.

'I fought among you against the Vathen,' Gallow said. 'I don't regret that. As for the rest, all I wanted was my family and my forge, making a life for us all. Watching my sons grow up happy and strong.'

Valaric turned his head and spat. 'Isn't that what we all wanted? A lot more of us would have had it if you forkbeards had stayed across the sea where you belong.' He walked away. The gates closed and Gallow was alone. The stumps of the gibbets remained beside the road where they'd been cut down. He stopped beside them and took the locket out from under his shirt, closing his fist around it. The Vathen had come. How could he not fight them? *Our land, yours and mine. I didn't ask for it. I didn't ask to find the Screambreaker half dead after we fled, but how could I leave him when he'd stood and fought as I had, with no reason save the doing of what was right? I didn't ask you to bring the Vathen to our home, and when you did, how could I send him away alone, barely alive? O Arda, why did you have to do that?* His grip on the locket was so tight it hurt. His vision was swimming, tears on his cheeks. He still had the money Tolvis had given him for the horses. A little to get him home and plenty left to put a smile on Arda's face. If that was what he wanted.

Fate. He walked past the ruins of homes that had once crowded in the shadows of Andhun's walls. Was he sorry for what he was? No. But no one had made him sail with Medrin, chasing after the Crimson Shield. No one had made him offer Tolvis Loudmouth his axe instead of leaving him in the road and heading for Varyxhun with a string of Vathan horses. He could have been beside a warm fire, listening to Arda shout and rave at him for what had happened to their home, knowing all the while that she loved him despite herself. He could have been holding his children in his arms, watching them sleep. All he had to do was forgive her for the one terrible thing she'd done. Say it was a mistake, a moment of madness, though they both knew it had been neither of those things.

The gibbets, the blood ravens, Medrin's murderous hunger, Jyrdas's pyre: none of that would have been any different, but he wouldn't have seen it. Yet now he had. And Arda would be a lie too, however easy it might feel, and when the Maker-Devourer whispered in his head at the end of his days, *Have you led a good life?* what could he say? Not *Yes, yes, I have*, not any more.

He could feel Jyrdas's ghost laughing at him. *You've turned into one of them. A sheep.* And perhaps it was true and perhaps he was, and perhaps that wasn't so bad after all.

He looked at the locket one last time and then squeezed his eyes tightly shut as he put it back inside his shirt.

The road towards the mountains was the one that he and the Screambreaker had travelled after the hills around the Crackmarsh. If he followed it far enough, it would take him to Tarkhun, squeezed between the Isset and the Shadowwood and the Ironwood. A boat across the water and he'd be on the Aulian Way, past the Crackmarsh and then winding up the mountains to the Aulian Bridge and the old fortress of Witches' Reach guarding the entrance to the valley. And, past that, Varyxhun. He wasn't sure how long it would take. Ten days? Twelve? Something like that. Plenty of time to think about what to say when he got there.

Away from the city gates the gibbets were still up. The bodies were little more than skeletons now, pecked clean by the birds. Further still and he passed small knots of men on the road. Lhosir. They looked him over.

'Another Marroc who wants to fight,' said one. 'Good for you. That way.' They pointed across the fields to where a haze of smoke hung over a low rise.

'What's that way?' he asked.

'The Vathen!' They laughed. 'Any more of you in there?'

Gallow shrugged. 'I'd keep out of the city for a bit if I were you, after the battle's done. Be safer out here.'

'Oh, I wouldn't worry about that. Best if *you* keep away, more likely.' They laughed again and rode on towards the gates.

'And what does that mean?' he called after them. They didn't answer but they didn't need to. If Medrin won, his anger with the Marroc for what Valaric had done on the beach would be unquenchable. Andhun would burn.

He walked on, talking to himself, muttering under his breath. Varyxhun, that was where he should be going. To Arda. To his family. To what *mattered*. And if Medrin happened to beat the Vathen and turned on Andhun and then burned it to the ground and slaughtered and raped every man and woman within its walls, was that his business? Arda would tell him no, it wasn't. And she was right, wasn't she?

Was that how to say he'd led a good life? Just let that be?

He didn't even notice that his feet had left the road until he reached the rise and saw the Lhosir army spread out on the other side of it. They'd taken him that way instead of towards his home, quietly and without a fuss, as though they knew perfectly well where he needed to go. *A fat lot of good that pledge was then.* Arda was laughing at him, mocking and scornful. *Lasted what? A few minutes?*

He pushed his hand to his chest. 'Sorry.'

Was that how to say he'd led a good life? No, it wasn't.

Can't eat sorry. But she'd betrayed him. She'd betrayed all of them. And she had no answer to that.

Smoke from the campfires – he could smell it, could see its dirty stain in the air. It was hardly suffocating, but for some reason it was making his eyes water again. He saw Arda behind him, clear as the sun, waving him away as he'd gone to fight the Vathen at Lostring Hill, shaking her head. *Stupid men. Always think they have to fight. Can't you just stay here and look after the people who matter? What about us, Gallow? What do we do when you get yourself stuck on the end of a spear?* She too had had tears in her eyes. *Going to have to find myself a Vathan now, am I?* The more she shouted and raved at him not to go, the more she gave herself away.

'I will come back,' he'd murmured, 'I swear it.'

That's what Merethin said. She turned her back on him and disappeared.

No one challenged him as he walked through the Lhosir army. He found the Screambreaker at his breakfast at the far edge of the camp, looking out towards where the Vathen would come.

'Truesword.' He didn't look up. 'When Medrin came back with the shield, I wondered what happened to you. And to Loudmouth and to Jyrdas.'

Gallow looked around him. The soldiers nearby were old ones. The Screambreaker's men, the ones who'd fought the Marroc years ago. Men he trusted. 'Jyrdas? A Marroc put an arrow in him. Jyrdas killed a couple of them anyway, just to make a point. Then he called Medrin *nioingr* until Medrin stuck a knife through his good eye to shut him up.'

'Sounds like Jyrdas.'

'The Marroc let me built him a pyre and speak him out and then they let me go.'

'Good of them.' The Screambreaker was still staring out across the fields as though none of what Gallow was telling him particularly mattered. He pointed. 'The Vathen will come from there. They won't want to fight today, so we'll take it to them.' He beckoned an old Lhosir closer and whispered in his ear. The soldier nodded and trotted away.

'I feel the Maker-Devourer more closely these days,' said Gallow. 'You and I have a grudge between us. I would have it ended before I meet him. You spoke words not fitting for a guest in my house. Or were you too gone with fever to remember?'

'I've not forgotten, Gallow. We'll settle it after the Vathen are defeated.'

'And if I want to settle it now?'

'I'll say no and remind you that you're a Marroc and have no voice here. If I call you *nioingr*, so what?' He turned sharply, before Gallow could reach for a blade. 'Hold your hand, Truesword. Fight the Vathen. Fight beside me as I know you can and I'll concede that the words I spoke were wrong.'

'Concede it now!'

'No.'

'Why?'

215

The Screambreaker stood up and faced Gallow squarely. 'I remember you from the old days, Truesword. You were fierce and terrible, without mercy or remorse, and I was proud to have you fight among my men. I saw you fight the Vathen on the way to Andhun and I saw the man I remembered. But you've changed. Your beard is gone. You're either more or less than the man I once knew and I don't know which it is. Do you, Gallow?'

Maker-Devourer! But this was the Screambreaker, who never gave ground, not to anyone and not for anything. Half a smile crept onto Gallow's face. 'I'm me, old man. Born every part a Lhosir but Marroc too. So yes, I'll fight beside you if that's what it takes, and if I have to kill three Vathen for every one of yours to prove what I say then so be it. But when you take back your words, you'll owe me a boon.'

'True enough.'

'Then I'll ask you for it now, so that if I die you'll know what to do. When the battle is won, Medrin will call for Andhun to be sacked. Deny him.'

'This isn't my army, Truesword. Twelvefingers can do what he wants.'

Gallow laughed in his face. 'It's every bit your army, Screambreaker, and if you give them victory today, they'd follow you even if old Yurlak himself was here to tell them otherwise.'

'Twelvefingers is Yurlak's son. You're asking me to defy my king and my friend.' The Screambreaker sniffed. 'The Marroc of Andhun gave their word that they would open the gates to us if the Vathen are defeated. If they honour that, I see no reason for any reprisal. But the Marroc who attacked Medrin and killed One-Eye, I'll not spare them. They made their fate and they'll be punished for that without mercy. They'll hang in the streets. For once I agree with Twelvefingers. I'll not move on that, Truesword.'

Gallow met his eye. 'Then if the gates open, let the

punishment be theirs and theirs alone. That's the boon I ask.'

'Done.' The Screambreaker scowled and flipped a knife from his belt. He made a shallow cut in his arm a little above the wrist and offered the blade to Gallow, who took it and did the same. They clasped their arms together so their blood would mingle. The Screambreaker looked at the men around him. 'Witness this, my friends. This man Gallow Truesword claims I have slandered him. If he fights well today, he will have proved he is right and I will have spoken poorly of him and unjustly so. *If* he is right, there shall be no plundering of Andhun after the Vathen are broken, and if others say otherwise, I stand against them.' He let Gallow go. 'I'm only one man, Truesword.'

Gallow snorted. 'No, you're not, Widowmaker. You've not been that for a long time.'

'Either way, you have to prove me wrong first.'

'That I can do.'

For a moment the Screambreaker smiled. 'Yes. The man I remember could do that.'

'I have another boon to ask.'

The general laughed. 'Against what debt?'

'None.' He took the purse of silver off his belt and held it out. 'But if I die, I'd have this taken to my family. To my wife Arda in Varyxhun.'

The Screambreaker shook his head and waved him away. 'And what if *I* die, Truesword? Who will take it then?'

'You'll never die.'

A dark look crossed the Screambreaker's face. He turned away. 'Don't be so sure, Truesword, not today.' He snatched the purse. 'But very well. I'll find a way. If you die and I live, I will have it done. If I die and *you* live, it will find its way back to you.' He sighed and leaned forward. 'The truth is, Truesword, that perhaps I do owe you a boon. Do you want a reason to live through his battle? Perhaps I have one for you. It was not your wife who betrayed me to the Vathen. It was the old man.'

For a moment Gallow stared into nothing. 'What? *What?*'

'It was the old man who told the carter that I was in your house. The old smith. Nadric? Was that his name?'

'Nadric, yes. But . . .' All the feeling drained out of Gallow's face and his fingers, as though his heart had stopped pumping blood and was keeping it all to itself. 'How do . . .' He shook his head.

'How do I know?' The Screambreaker's lips twitched into a thin smile. 'Because when you dragged the carter and your wife out of the barn, every man and woman there, me included, was quite certain you were going to kill them. The old man blabbed then. Said it was him. Wailed and howled and kept clutching at my foot until I had to kick him in the face to shut him up. Wasn't at my best then, if you remember. I've seen a lot of begging and wailing in my time, Truesword. I know the ones who are telling the truth. He meant it. It was him, Truesword. Not your wife.'

Gallow couldn't move. 'And you thought I was going to kill her, and you didn't stop me?'

'No.'

'And you didn't tell me. All the way to Andhun and you *never thought to tell me.*'

Rage was boiling up inside him. The Screambreaker looked him in the eye. 'For a while I thought you *had* killed her and the carter. It's what I would have done, and if you had, I didn't think you'd want to hear. After that, I wanted you back in Andhun.'

'You *what?*'

'I wanted you here, Truesword. I wanted you at my side against the Vathen. And against Twelvefingers, if it comes to it. So live through this day, Truesword, and then go back to your Marroc wife and your sons when it's done. And ask, if you must, why *she* didn't tell you either. But I think we both know the answer. Now go away. Eat and rest. We have a hard day before us. Find yourself a spear and a sword and an axe to go with that shield. We have plenty.'

The Screambreaker turned away. Gallow watched him go. *Why? Why didn't you tell me?* But the Screambreaker was right, the answer obvious: because in his anger he would have murdered Nadric there and then, and there would have been no going back from that. And so she'd lied to him and trusted to the truth that she was the one person he could never hurt.

He closed his eyes and thought of her. Arda. She hadn't betrayed him after all and everything would be as it was.

The two of you are the same, she seemed to whisper. *You dress it up in valour and glory, but really you just like fighting.* He thought that if he listened hard enough, there might have been a smile somewhere in there.

He settled himself among the Screambreaker's men, keeping among them and away from others who might recognise him. He filled his belly and armed himself as he was told, and then he sat, quietly waiting for the Vathen to come, touching the locket under his shirt.

I have to make my life a good one, he told her.

You might find it easier if you didn't try so bloody hard, she answered, and he smiled and sat easily, waiting for the Vathen to come, full of all his memories of her, of all the scoldings and the rolling eyes and the rare twinkle that now and then lay behind them.

34

THE VANGUARD

Gallow stood shoulder to shoulder with men he barely knew. The Screambreaker faced them from the back of his horse, proud and noble and fierce. He was the best. The Lhosir knew that. He was invincible, *they* were invincible, and the Vathan numbers would be no use to them. They'd stumble over their own dead as they ran and the slaughter would be terrible.

'For Andhun,' Gallow whispered to himself. 'For all the Marroc. And for you, Arda. Please understand why I must do this.' He held his shield firmly in one hand, a spear in the other. At his belt he carried an axe and a sword. He stood loose, not tense like the younger men. His mail felt old and comfortable like a long-missed friend and his helm seemed to whisper words of calm into his ear. The mail at least was still his own, good solid metal plundered from a dead Marroc a decade ago, and he trusted it now as he'd trusted it then. He'd been here before, more times than he cared to count. He remembered how it felt, the tension, the blood running fast and hot.

'Look at them!' the Screambreaker shouted. 'Look at them! See how many they are and rejoice, my warriors! Feel how it will be, for they will break upon your shields like water on the rocks and die writhing upon your spears like fish caught helpless in a net. You will stand fast and they will see you there, waiting for them with your shields held strong and your spears held high, helms bright, and they will come up this hill and every step will sap their strength. Their legs will ache and their souls will quiver. You will scream Yurlak's name in their faces and fall upon them, and they will quiver like women and they will break! And as each slaughtered rank turns and flees they will spread your terror and their numbers will count for nothing! We are Lhosir! We have the strength of the bear, the fangs of the wolf and the speed of the hawk!'

The Vathen were crossing the bottom of the valley, the first rank now marching steadily up the hill. So many, but they'd been marching all day, and now it was the middle of the afternoon and they'd be tired while the Screambreaker's army was fresh.

The Screambreaker turned his horse and cantered away. He'd be back. Back to the centre where his own small band of Lhosir stood waiting for him, Gallow among them. The men he'd brought back across the sea with him for one more fight. *They* wouldn't break. They were soldiers who'd seen ten years of war, who'd fought in a dozen battles like this and won all but one.

Either side of the advancing Vathan centre black swarms of horse scattered towards the flanks, ready to envelop the Lhosir and come at them from the side and the rear. Pits filled with spikes waited for them, and hidden clusters of spearmen with shields and javelin throwers lurked at the edge of the trees. Archers, even a few hundred of those, from the few Marroc who'd come out to fight. There were more than Gallow had thought and Valaric would be fuming if he knew, but this was right, wasn't it? Lhosir and Marroc together, fighting for their land.

The Vathen were a hundred yards away when the Scream-breaker returned. He walked slowly between the two armies as though the enemy was barely worth his notice and took his place in the front line in the middle of his men. They made space for him with an easy movement practised for years.

Fifty yards and the Marroc archers behind the Lhosir line let fly. They were shooting long, Gallow saw, over the top of the Vathan shield wall, raining their havoc on the lines behind where men couldn't see what was happening around them. The arrows would bring confusion and despair. Men would raise their shields over their heads so as not to be scythed down, and then they wouldn't see anything except the man standing in front of them. This was how the Screambreaker fought his wars, with fear and panic as his sword and shield.

Thirty yards and the black-painted Vathen let out a roar and charged. The sky grew dark as the ranks behind both lines of shields hurled javelins, clubs, sticks, stones, anything they'd been able to carry into battle. Men screamed and fell. Gallow raised his shield, hiding his face, shielding the man on his left as well. A javelin almost split the wood right in front of his eyes. A stone glanced off his helm. The Lhosir on his right howled as blood fountained from his ripped-open neck.

'Get him out! Get him out!' Gallow smashed the javelin out of his shield and then the Vathen and the Lhosir crashed together. A spear came at his face. He ducked and jabbed his own point at a Vathan, caving in the man's teeth, slicing open his cheek and ripping the back of his throat.

The Lhosir beside him finished dying. He sank slowly down with another spear through his face, pointlessly killed for a second time. Another stepped up from behind. They'd be standing on each others' corpses soon, but better that than fall. Anyone who fell was dead. Men screamed as they tried to kill each other and men screamed as they died, and soon the screams all sounded the same. A Vathan swung an axe. It turned off the mail on Gallow's shoulder and then hooked his shield, tugging it away. Gallow stabbed the man with his spear. The crush was suffocating. He ducked another thrust. Ribs cracked from the sheer press of men. His shield was pressed hard into the Vathan in front of him, so close he could see the whites of his eyes, but the crush made them both almost powerless.

Another spear point glanced off his helm. He pushed his shield forward, hard and sudden, made a momentary inch of space and lunged his spear straight down into the foot of the Vathan in front of him. The Vathan screamed and dropped his guard and the Lhosir behind Gallow jabbed a spear into his face. Gallow watched the Vathan die, a terrible glee inside him. A dead man trapped in front of him meant he could strike more freely, and so he did, thrust after thrust. Most of the Vathen were down to knives and axes now, but the Lhosir had learned to keep their spears. The battle turned slowly to slaughter.

A horn sounded. The Vathen broke off and stumbled away. The Lhosir line took two paces forward, unable to help themselves. A few cheered, the young ones who didn't know any better. For a moment Gallow had to brace himself against his own men so as not to be pushed forward down the hill. He was breathing hard and the battle had barely started.

A cloud moved across the sun, stealing its light and its heat. He was grateful for that. He sucked in the spring air, the smell of grass and flowers and trees now tainted by the sweat of men and the tang of steel and blood. The sun was too hot for a heavy leather coat and mail but he held back the urge to take off his helm and cool his head. That was how men died. He'd seen it.

The black-painted Vathen front line melted away down the hill. The next line waited just out of javelin range, shields raised against the Marroc archers. He could see the enemy – from the brow of the hill they all could. The last ranks of the Vathen were at the bottom of the valley now, still crossing the stream there. The rest were massing on the lower slope, taking their time.

So many.

It started to rain. An hour earlier and that might have changed the battle, made the hill into a sea of mud and crippled the Vathan advance. Too late now, but the cold water was still delicious. It wouldn't last. Five minutes, maybe ten, and then the cloud would pass and he'd have the sun on his back again.

'For Yurlak!' shouted the man beside him. 'For the Screambreaker!' The Lhosir was quivering. He still had his shield, but his spear was gone and all he had now was an axe. Gallow watched the Vathen. The next line of them was painted bloody red. They didn't move. Very slowly, without taking his eyes off them, Gallow moved his spear to his shield hand. He carefully crouched and leaned forward, reaching for a spear that hung from the belly of a dead Vathan. The rain was coming down hard now, dripping into his eyes. His fingers closed around the haft of the spear. He pulled it slowly towards him and then jerked it free and passed it to the soldier beside him.

'They bleed like any others,' he said. The rain was already easing.

'Don't they just.'

The Vathen lowered their spears, pointing them straight at the faces of the Lhosir. Gallow felt the soldiers around him tense, bracing for another fight, but the Vathen held their ground, and then through the midst of them came a giant in blood-red mail. His shield was black, but when the giant drew out his sword, the blade was a deep red like his mail, with an edge as long as a man's leg. The air fell still, the voices of the Lhosir and the Vathen alike quiet. The giant held out his sword and swung it this way and that. As he cut the air, the sound it made was like the shivering moans of lost souls.

'The Sword of the Weeping God!' The Lhosir beside him raised an eye. 'So they really have it then.'

'And we have the shield,' said Gallow. He stared. The sword he'd seen in his dream of the Weeping God, before he'd left Andhun, and again after Gorrin had hit him on the back of his head under the monastery. 'It's just a sword, no better or worse than the man who wields it.' Today he said it as much for himself as for anyone else.

The soldier grinned. 'Aye. And that man is no Lhosir!'

The giant walked up to the Lhosir line, batting aside a hail of missiles with his shield or simply letting them bounce off his armour. When he reached them and the first Lhosir tried to stab him, he caught the spear in the sword's guard and wrenched it away. He took another blow to his shield, this time from a sword, and then Gallow couldn't see anything, but there were screams and the giant was bellowing something; and then there was the Screambreaker, out in front of the Lhosir.

'Here!' he cried. 'Here I am! Corvin the Screambreaker. Widowmaker! Nightmare of the North!' He threw down his spear, jamming the point into the ground, and drew his sword. 'I have no god-touched blade or shield, but I will still bleed you. So face me if you dare, Vathan!'

The giant turned. He pointed the red sword at the Screambreaker and roared. The second Vathan line raised their spears and charged, the hail of stones and javelins began again and the giant and the Screambreaker vanished into the swirl of swords and spears. At the front of the shield wall, crushed by friends from behind and the enemy in front, barely able to move, Gallow had no eyes for either. The flash of swords and spear points became all that mattered. He stabbed the Vathan in front of him in the foot, same as he had the last, and the man behind Gallow, a stranger, finished the job just as he had before with a sure understanding for him even though they'd met only minutes ago. Blood flecked Gallow's face and spattered his helm. His arm screamed with the effort of holding up his spear but he shut out the pain and stabbed and stabbed until this line of Vathen fell back like the last, leaving their own new litter of corpses behind.

The giant with the red sword was still standing. He prowled between the lines, bellowing challenges. The Lhosir answered him again with stones and javelins, and the giant shrugged them aside in disdain. Again the Screambreaker stepped out to face him and again the giant ignored him. The Lhosir jeered. Another line of Vathen assembled down the slope.

'Where are their horse?' muttered Gallow. The longer they took about this next attack the better. His arm was killing him. They'd all tire soon. Whatever stamina advantage they'd had taking the battle to the Vathen today, that was surely gone now.

'Not here,' said the Lhosir beside him. 'That's all that matters. I don't know your face, but you must be Gallow Truesword since you're the only man without a beard. They say you've taken to living among the Marroc.'

'So I did.'

'Well you don't fight like them.' The soldier nudged him, the closest they could get to clasping arms with their shields still held up in front of them. 'Nodas of Houndfell. I've heard of you. Some things good, some things bad. The good came from men I know and trust, the bad I'm less keen to believe now I've stood beside you.'

'Well, Nodas of Houndfell, if we live through this, you can tell me all of both over a keg of Marroc beer.'

Nodas laughed. 'More likely I'll tell it to you in the Maker-Devourer's cauldron.'

Here and there, up and down the line as the giant walked, other Lhosir stepped forward, throwing down their own challenges and laughing as they were ignored. 'What's he doing?'

'Making a fool of himself.'

And the Vathen came again.

35

GIANT

Wave after wave came, and each time the Lhosir line threw them back and held its ground. Then finally the Vathen sent their horsemen, who threw a hail of javelots and withdrew, and when they did, the Lhosir plucked the javelots from the ground and out of their shields and passed them back to those behind them, so that the next ranks of advancing Vathen felt them too.

After each wave the giant was still there. The hill was awash with the dead now, piled up to make each Vathan advance harder than the last, but the Vathen weren't the only ones dying and there were still thousands upon thousands of them on the lower slopes. Taking their time. Waiting. Slowly wearing the Lhosir down until they didn't have the strength to hold their shields tight and their spears high. When Gallow looked over his shoulder, the Lhosir line looked thin. He couldn't see much past the helms and the angry faces, but there, right at the brow of the hill, Medrin's standard still flew. Five hundred men, the Screambreaker had said, to throw into the fight wherever they were needed.

'Let them miss it all,' said Nodas. 'All the glory for us.' He was breathing heavily and bleeding from a savage cut across his cheek that must have gone right through the skin, judging from the blood dripping from the corner of his mouth.

'Medrin needs to do something with those.'

'He does. Imagine if they miss it all. They'll kill him.'

The next wave came. A moment before it broke, the

Vathan in front of Gallow hooked Nodas's shield with an axe and pulled it down, and the next Vathan along stabbed Nodas squarely with a long knife. The blade skittered off Nodas's mail, straight up his chest and buried itself in his throat. Nodas looked surprised, then angry, and then nothing much at all. When the Vathen withdrew once more, he toppled forward onto the mound of bodies that lay in front of the Lhosir line. Gallow looked at the sky. A warm spring evening, the sun sinking low but not yet starting to tinge with orange. Another two hours maybe before dark. Two hours? He didn't have the strength for that.

'Twelvefingers!' The Screambreaker stepped out from the line again. He looked exhausted. 'Call our prince to the centre before we win the battle without him! Medrin! Medrin!' The shout went up, but when Gallow looked to the brow of the hill, the prince's standard never moved.

It started to rain again, a longer shower and heavier than the last. The Vathen didn't wait this time but came again, though they weren't happy about it. They slipped and stumbled among the bodies of their own fallen and this time broke quickly. On the slopes across the valley Gallow saw more movement. Men running away perhaps, chased down by Vathan riders? Or something else. But either way the battle was close to its end. The Lhosir were losing their strength and the Vathen were losing their stomach for it.

The giant was roaming in front of the next line of Vathen again. No one threw anything at him any more because no one had anything left to throw. Even the Marroc archers had fallen silent.

'Face me!' bellowed the Screambreaker. He looked as though he could barely stand. His shield sagged and he couldn't keep the point of his spear up. And now, at last, the giant stopped and turned. He faced the Screambreaker and twirled his sword. Around him the air moaned, and if the giant was worn down at all by two hours of fighting, he didn't show it. He came at the Screambreaker slowly, cautiously, while the Screambreaker circled away from his own men, inviting the giant in closer.

The giant closed the gap between them with a charge and swung the red sword. The Screambreaker didn't even try to strike back but threw himself out of the way, stumbling and barely keeping his feet. The giant whirled and swung again – this time the Screambreaker slipped as he ducked out of the way. He rolled and dropped his shield as he scrabbled back. Gallow frowned. The Screambreaker? Dropping his shield?

The giant roared. He came on slowly.

'He's playing with him,' Gallow whispered in disgust.

'Yes,' said the man beside him, a greybeard Lhosir who'd come up to stand in Nodas's place. 'But then he's only fighting a Vathan, and the Vathan has refused him a half a dozen times already. Give the old sword his sport.'

It took Gallow a moment to understand. The greybeard thought he'd meant the Screambreaker?

The Vathan took another swing. As the Screambreaker launched himself out of the way, the giant lunged with his shield, battering the Screambreaker back and knocking him down. The Screambreaker dropped his spear now too. He rolled and barely got out of the way as the giant struck out yet again. He hauled himself to his feet and stumbled away, then staggered and tripped over a body with a spear sticking out of it and fell. The Vathan laughed. As the Screambreaker pulled himself to his feet, the giant roared and drew back the red sword for the killing blow.

The Screambreaker drew his own sword in the middle of the giant's backswing and threw it. The Vathan swatted it away with his shield but just for a moment he blocked his own sight of the Screambreaker, and that was when Corvin moved with a sudden surge of speed, rolled and snatched his spear from the ground where he'd dropped it. The Vathan took a moment to see where the Screambreaker had gone and by then it was too late. The Nightmare of the North came up into a crouch to one side of him and thrust the spear sideways into the giant's knee. The Vathan screamed. Now the Screambreaker didn't look tired at all. He picked up an axe and a shield from the battlefield and marched straight forward, whirling the axe over his head as if to finish the fight, and then dropped suddenly to one knee and let the axe fly. It caught the giant just above the ankle of his other leg; the Vathan roared and down he went, both legs ruined. The Screambreaker picked up another spear. The giant tried to protect himself with his shield as Corvin walked in circles around him, out of reach of the red sword, jabbing with his spear, but it was hardly any time at all before the Screambreaker found a way through and touched the spear point to the giant's throat. He held it there lightly.

'Yield!' he cried, loud enough for both the Vathen and the Lhosir to hear.

The giant's answer, if he gave one, was lost to the wind, but it was clear what it must have been, for the Screambreaker suddenly leaned hard into his spear and drove it through the giant's neck. Then he took another axe, cut off the giant's hand, unpeeled his dead fingers from the red sword and held it high where everyone could to see. 'Solace!' He cried. 'The Peacebringer! The Comforter! The Sword of the Weeping God! Sorrow's Edge! See! Just a sword! That's all it is! There is no god here guiding any hand to victory. There are only men.'

Cries went up from the Lhosir lines, jeering and cheering and laughing at their enemy, but if the Screambreaker was hoping for the Vathen to break and flee, what he got was the opposite. Instead of coming up the hill at a steady pace, the next wave broke into a run, howling in rage and fury, surging forward at such a fierce pace that the Screambreaker had to run to make it back to his own line. He pushed into the shield wall beside Gallow.

'Look at it,' he hissed. 'It's just a sword. Give me a spear any day.' Gallow offered his own, but the Screambreaker shook his head. 'I left the scabbard for this on the giant's body.'

'Then throw it away, if it's just a sword.'

'I'll see how it swings first.' The Vathen smashed into the Lhosir line and their first ranks were slaughtered, undone by their own fury, but more and more and more of them came, rank after rank running up the hill to pile into the back of the heaving melee, pushing and pushing. Gallow stabbed with his spear over and over. Beside him the Sword of the Weeping God sang as it cut the air. And it *wasn't* just a sword, whatever the Screambreaker said, for the red steel cut through mail and man as nothing Gallow had ever seen. From behind his shield the Screambreaker lunged and the sword point seemed to seek out the Vathen with a will of its own over and over, throats and necks and faces. And the Vathen were afraid of it, Gallow saw that too. Within the Screambreaker's reach they whimpered, eyes wild, and dropped their swords and axes and clutched at their shields, eyes on nothing else.

But beyond the circle of fear that reached to the tip of the red sword, the Vathen had become a raging horde. They pressed and howled and died at the points of the Lhosir spears but still they came on, and the push of them forced the Lhosir slowly back up the hill, a litter of dead in their wake for the Vathen to climb.

'Medrin!' roared the Screambreaker. 'Twelvefingers! We need his five hundred! We need them here! To the centre! Now!'

Gallow lost his spear, lodged in some Vathan helmet and torn out of his hand. A brief rain of arrows fell, loosed by the Vathen but falling on Vathen and Lhosir alike. He hacked and slashed with his axe, tearing at the men either side of him. His face was covered with blood, his helm, his mail; Vathan gore spattered across his shield. And always beside him the red sword lunged and lunged as if the Screambreaker's arm was made of iron and never tired. The Lhosir beside Gallow on the other side fell and another pushed up to take his place and fell in turn to be replaced by yet another.

'Where's Twelvefingers?' the Screambreaker shouted again.

The man on the other side of Gallow staggered, his helm knocked sideways by a javelin from among the Vathen. Before he could recover, an axe hooked his shield, a sword lunged and he was falling backwards. This time no one stepped forward. Gallow snatched a glance behind him. There was no one there. No Lhosir left, only fifty yards of open grass to the top of the hill. And Medrin with his five hundred. Standing fast and doing nothing.

The Vathen swarmed around him. He took a step back – had no choice or they'd be round his shield. Took another, back among those few Lhosir that were left. For a moment the Screambreaker was open. Unguarded where Gallow's shield should have been. Gallow watched helplessly as the onslaught battered him back. They were all over Corvin. A Vathan clawed at the Screambreaker's shield, pulling it away with his fingers. The red sword rose and fell, driven with such force it burst clear through the Vathan's head. Another swung an axe and the arc of the red sword cut both axe and man in two; yet as that Vathan fell, another lunged with his sword and another leaped at the Screambreaker, and then another and another and they bore him staggering to the ground. Gallow screamed and swung his own axe in great circles around him, but there was no getting through. The Vathen were everywhere now. The centre of the Lhosir line had gone. There simply weren't any of them left.

Then finally Medrin came.

36

THE SWORD OF
THE WEEPING GOD

Medrin and his five hundred swept down the hillside, spears held high, Medrin in the middle of them, the Crimson Shield gleaming in the evening sun. A minute sooner and the Screambreaker would still have stood. A minute later and Gallow would have fallen too. The Vathen around him faltered and wavered. He swung wildly, not caring whether or what he struck, thinking of nothing except to drive them away from the fallen Screambreaker. He smashed this way and that and then Medrin's Lhosir swept into the swirling melee and at last the Vathen broke and ran, colliding with their own men still marching up the hill. Gallow curled up as the Lhosir hit, and when they were past he staggered to where the Screambreaker lay still, surrounded by a ring of corpses, his face in a pool of blood. His grey beard was black, matted with it. There was no way to know *whose* blood, but he wasn't moving. Gallow crouched beside him, cradling the old warrior. The roar of the battle died away, the shouts of victory mingling with the wails of the dying. Corvin looked old now, so frail and fragile and nothing like the Screambreaker who'd stood before them at the start of the battle, telling them how the Vathen would be smashed. There was so much blood that Gallow couldn't see the wound that had finally brought him down. The Screambreaker was still breathing, though fast and shallow. Gallow had seen it a hundred times before: the last ragged breaths of a man as he set his sails and packed his axe for the Maker-Devourer's cauldron.

'He let this happen,' Gallow whispered. 'Medrin. He stood and watched with his men all around him, doing nothing, waiting for you to fall. And you very nearly didn't.'

A coldness washed through him as the frenzy of battle slowly drained. He hadn't really thought about what he was saying, but now the words were spoken he saw they had a truth to them. Medrin *had* waited, and now there was no one left to stand up to him. No one left to keep him from crashing into Andhun, from slaughtering every Marroc inside, man, woman and child.

He let the Screambreaker slide back into the bloody mud. The dead littered the hillside like autumn leaves after a storm. The sun hung low and bloated and orange. It shimmered on burnished helms, broken swords and blood-drenched mail. Solace slipped out of the old man's fingers, almost as if he was making one last wish. *You* stop him.

Gallow looked at the red sword. His hand closed around the hilt. Medrin wanted that sword, he wanted it badly. Maybe Gallow could bargain with it. The sword for Andhun? But Medrin was the worst *nioingr*, a liar and not to be trusted. Gallow stood with the Sword of the Weeping God in his hand, looking down the hill. The Vathen were streaming away down the hillside. Bodies lay scattered everywhere, trampled. In the dying light of the day the valley was stained by a tide of red. Like a beach at low tide after a storm, littered with debris, only here the sea had been a sea of blood.

A last few Lhosir were standing around him, dazed and confused and wondering what to do. The Screambreaker's men, the handful who'd survived. Old soldiers all, most of them bloody and broken from Vathan swords and spears, staggering and close to collapse. They'd fought for hours, watched the battle slowly slip away and then watched Medrin steal it back at the last. Gallow raised the red sword.

'Men of the sea! You fought for the Screambreaker. Here

he lies!' He began to walk among them, pointing to the Screambreaker's body, still surrounded by Vathan dead. 'It was no Vathan who killed him. Twelvefingers did this. Your prince. He waited for us to die.'

'He gave us glory,' said one whose arm hung uselessly at his side.

'No. We took our own glory. Twelvefingers wants us gone. We who remember the old ways, who honour the Maker-Devourer.' He picked a face he knew. 'I knew you once, Thanni Ironfoot. Jyrdas was your friend. Medrin poked out his other eye.' Another. 'Galdun. You too. At Selleuk's Bridge we turned and ran, but never again. And Twelve-fingers has you guarding gates?'

But they wouldn't listen. They were too hurt, too dimmed by their wounds and dazzled by victory. He'd end it himself then. The Red Sword raised once more against the Crimson Shield. The Weeping God come at last to face his old brother and foe, Modris the Protector. He left the Screambreaker where he'd fallen to finish his dying among the men who remembered him best and started off down the hill, picking his way through the dead. There were so many, Lhosir and Vathen all jumbled together, lying on top of one another; and then further on there were only Vathen. He reached the black-armoured giant and stopped to take the belt and the scabbard of the Weeping God. On the ground the giant didn't seem so large after all.

So many dead. Did any of them even know why the Vathen had come? Did the Vathen know themselves? He saw a few of them still alive, the injured, the crippled, the ones too frightened or damaged to move. They watched him fearfully but he let them be. There was only one man left on this battlefield he wanted to add to the tally of the dead.

He began to pass Lhosir moving among the bodies, loot-ing them while it was still light. Men who'd lost their spears and their axes, their helms, searching among the dead for weapons, stripping boots and hauberks, plucking out arrows, collecting javelins before night fell and the battle-field belonged to the wolves. The sun had touched the hills now. It would be too dark to chase the Vathen down before long, and so the Screambreaker's design had a flaw after all. The Vathen wouldn't be scattered. They'd come again in the morning, if they had the will for it.

'Medrin?' The Lhosir he passed pointed down into the valley where the last shouts of fighting still echoed; and as the sun sank behind the hills he found the prince marching back up the slope of the battlefield with Horsan and a dozen more of his men around him. They stopped when they saw Gallow. Medrin spread his arms wide.

'Truesword! Look at us! Victorious once again.' He squinted at Gallow. 'How many Vathen came to this field today? My men say thirty thousand marched through Fedderhun. The Screambreaker said it was more like twenty-five and my own eyes say more like twenty. But still, four or five times our numbers, and look at them, Gallow. Look! When word of this crosses the sea, more will come. We'll march across their nation as the Screambreaker marched across the Marroc!'

All the while his eyes were locked on the sword. Gallow held it up in the orange light of the dying sun. 'Is this what you're looking for?'

'We saw the Screambreaker take down the Vathan giant and take his sword, every one of us. His legend is complete. But ... how is that *you* carry it now, Gallow?'

'The Screambreaker fell while you stood at the top of the hill and did nothing.'

'He's gone?' Medrin didn't even bother trying to sound troubled or surprised.

'He is.'

'Give me the sword, Gallow.' Medrin held out his hand. 'Give me the sword. I will carry it in his name, for his memory, and you will march beside me. The sword and the shield together. No one will stand before the Lhosir.'

'*You?*' Gallow spat at his feet. 'Carry it in *his* memory?' He pointed the sword at Medrin. 'And when your father dies, shall we build his pyre from a pile of turds too? Do you imagine I've forgotten the temple of the Fates, Medrin? You and Beyard and I? The Screambreaker told me you'd changed, you were now a man whose beard was fine and strong, but I've watched you and I do not believe that to be so. Where were you when Jyrdas and Tolvis and I opened the gates of the monastery for you? How was it that one of your men struck Jyrdas in the back? And when he *still* wouldn't die, you finished the work yourself!'

'Jyrdas spoke words that could not be left unanswered!' Medrin's face darkened.

'You let the Screambreaker die. You waited for him to fall.'

'No, Gallow. I waited for the moment when the Vathen would break. And they did.'

'This victory is his. It could not have been without him.'

Medrin nodded. 'True enough.' He held out his hand again. 'Now give me the sword, Gallow.' For a moment his face changed. He looked sad, almost pained. 'I need it to put something right.' He nodded at Gallow. 'All those years ago.'

'I will not give it to a *nioingr*!'

A stillness swept over the Lhosir. They stopped whispering to each other and stared.

'*Nioingr!*' declared Gallow again. 'You're not fit to crawl across the mud he walked, Twelvefingers. You're a coward and a liar. I call you again. *Nioingr!*'

Called three times. There was no turning back from that, and now Medrin had to answer with steel, and then Gallow would kill him no matter what shield he carried.

But Medrin only laughed. Not just laughed, but threw

back his head and howled while his men looked uncertainly at one another. 'And who are you, Gallow? Or what? Here are my words, then, to answer your slur, for *I* have not forgotten that day in the Temple of Fates either. Yes, I ran, that's true and shameful. But what fate befell *you*, Gallow? Nothing, though it was *your* foolishness that betrayed us. Never caught? Never punished? I've long held that against you, Gallow, for it was you I thought of as I watched a man I called a friend cast away by my own father and taken across the cold seas to the icy castle of the Eyes of Time. How was it that *you*, Gallow, didn't suffer the same fate? Yet you brought the Screambreaker to Andhun and he spoke for you. "Pay no heed to his clean chin," he told me. "This is Gallow Truesword who fought with me against the Marroc. A fine man worthy of his beard and he has not changed, not in his heart. Grown strong now by the forge of war." And so I offered you a place at my side again to see the shield we sought once before. An effort to look past the friend I lost, yet my reward for such trust? You turn my men against me. Tolvis, Jyrdas, how many minds did you poison with your lies? And when that wasn't enough, when the shield was mine for the taking, finally we all saw the truth of Gallow Truesword, the bitterness and the envy. I take your name and give you another: Gallow Foxbeard. From this time hence that is how you shall be known and remembered by those who care to remember you at all. And how is it, Gallow Foxbeard, that I left you bound among the Marroc and yet here you are? How is it that you escaped Andhun when the streets ran with traitors baying for Lhosir blood? Did you not walk openly to the gates? Did they not throw them wide for you? Why weren't you killed, clean-skin? Because you're one of them and you've turned against your own kind, that's why.'

Gallow hurled himself forward, howling. '*Nioingr!* Kin-traitor!' He swung the sword as he ran and the air seemed to moan like ghosts around him, but Medrin didn't step forward and the Lhosir around him moved to block Gallow's path. 'You let the Screambreaker die! Him and all those like him. The ones who would have stood up to you for the old ways. You let them all die.' He hacked at the first man to stand in his way; Solace struck the other man's blade and shattered it, sending shards of steel flying. The Lhosir lurched back as the red sword clove the air an inch from his face, but another one stepped in and lunged at Gallow.

'Let him die? And what could you see from where you stood, pressed hard up against the Vathen? What did you see of my men on the hill? Nothing! And yes, I dare say you fought with courage and strength, all the easier when you're watching your enemies butcher one another. Do you want to know what I did while you fought so hard? I sat on my horse and did nothing but watch! No, no honour or glory for Medrin Twelvefingers.' He was snarling now, his fist clenched on the hilt of the ornate Marroc sword he carried. Gallow lunged at another of the Lhosir standing in his way and drove them back, but only for a moment before they pressed around him again. 'And when my warriors wavered, I rode my men to rally the left and then to the right, because the centre held firm, always, even though that was where the Vathen pressed the hardest. And why? Because the Screambreaker was there and he had no need of this Crimson Shield or that sword you carry.' His eyes narrowed. 'I saw who was beside him at the end, Foxbeard. Whose sword was it that dealt him that fatal blow? Was it Vathan or was it yours?'

Gallow howled with rage and swung at the Lhosir around him. They kept their distance, still uncertain and wary of the red sword but not afraid of him either. Waiting for Medrin's order.

'You would have me spare Andhun for their treachery,' said Medrin mildly. 'I know the bargain you struck with the

Screambreaker.' Six of Medrin's men were around him, and now Horsan stepped in front of him while the others moved to encircle him. Gallow backed away. He slashed at the haft of one man's spear, cutting it in two; the man threw it at him, catching him in the chest and winding him, then drew an axe. Gallow staggered back. They were all advancing on him now. 'But Andhun was not his to give you, Foxbeard; Andhun is mine. The Marroc who came out to fight the Vathen, they'll be honoured as they deserve. The rest? The rest burn!' He slammed the Crimson Shield into the ground and the earth shook. Gallow almost fell, while the soldiers around him paused, awed and stunned by the power of the shield. 'Kill this sheep, Horsan. I'll not dirty myself with him.'

He couldn't face this many. Couldn't and he knew it. And Medrin knew it and the other Lhosir knew it too. If he stood his ground there was only one way for this to end and, sword or no sword, he'd fought for hours against the Vathen while these men were still fresh. He turned while Horsan and the Lhosir stood there with their eyes wide, threw down his shield and ran into the twilight.

'Stop him!' roared Medrin. 'Bring me back the sword!' He heard them running after him, felt their feet shake the ground but he didn't look back, didn't dare.

'Everyone knows Lhosir don't run, Gallow Foxbeard!' Medrin again, and there was nothing else that Gallow could do.

ANDHUN

37

TOLVIS

On the day that Jyrdas died, the day before the battle with the Vathen, Tolvis stood on the beach in Andhun with a handful of dead Marroc and a few dead Lhosir in front of him, breathing hard in the moment of calm after the Marroc had run. He'd killed one of the Marroc himself. It hadn't much bothered him. Which, he mused, meant that whatever it was that *was* troubling him, it must be something else.

Not that he had much time to think about it as they pushed Medrin's ship back into the sea before the Marroc found some more courage from somewhere, but it niggled at him anyway, itching like an old scab. He watched Medrin stab Jyrdas in the eye and come and climb into his ship and push away from the shores of Andhun. As he pulled at his oar he watched Gallow too, standing on the beach over Jyrdas and a pile of Marroc bodies. He watched the crowd waving angry fists and knives, and then he looked around him at the men in the ship and realised they were all Medrin's men, every one of them, and that was the moment he understood what troubled him. The young ones Medrin had brought with him from across the sea, they knew the Screambreaker by his name but they'd never fought with him, never fought a real battle at all. Medrin had sailed for the monastery of Luonatta with sixty men. Maybe they'd only had a handful of old soldiers to start with, but now not one of that handful was left except him. Not that Medrin had done away with them, except for Jyrdas in the end, and that had just been old One-Eye looking for a clean way to die, but still, it was the sort of thing that set a man to thinking. And after that, now and then as they sailed along the coast, he caught Medrin looking at him. Looks that made him uneasy.

Damn the man! If he'd *seen* the prince do anything wrong then he could have called him out on it, but Medrin hadn't, not really. *Really* all he'd done was honour the old ones. He'd let the Screambreaker's men stand at the front of his lines where they were proud to fight. He'd let them have the glorious deaths they wanted.

But not me. Not that he was shy of a fight if a fight had to be had, but mostly what he liked was the swapping of stories afterwards over a good bottle of mead or a cask of Marroc beer.

No, he didn't like the way Medrin was looking at him at all. Couldn't have said why but it set the hairs on his back all on edge; so when they beached the boat a few miles out of Andhun, where the cliffs parted to make a little cove, Tolvis made sure he was first over the side and into the waves. He made sure he had his shield and his sword and his axe and he didn't look back, just set off along the beach away from Andhun. He didn't turn to see if anyone followed. There were a few shouts, but over the breaking waves he couldn't hear what they said, and it might just have been the others shouting at each other about making the ship safe on the beach.

He reached a headland where he had to climb over broken rocks that had fallen from the cliffs to get past. When he'd done that and the ship was out of sight, he collected a few good-sized stones from the litter on the beach, throwing stones that fitted nicely in the palm of his hand, and then he sat down to wait and to see what would happen.

He didn't have to wait long before two more Lhosir came

picking their way carefully through the rocks. Treacherous out on those rocks. The broken remains of waves still reached far enough to lap at a man's feet here and there, and the lower parts were slimy with seaweed. He let them come closer, close enough that he could see who they were. Latti with his jaw all wrapped up tight and Dvag with his broken fingers. Two of Medrin's closest, shields over their shoulders, helms and hauberks and all dressed up for a fight. Tolvis sighed and wearily got to his feet, a stone in his hand. He waited on the edge of the shambles of rocks until they were a few dozen paces away.

'So this is what it comes to, is it? Twelvefingers couldn't think of a way to do it properly, so he sends you two?'

The two Lhosir on the rocks stopped. Dvag opened his arms. 'Loudmouth! Friend! We wanted to know where you were going, that's all. In case you were lost. That's the way to the Vathen.'

'You might at least try and pretend there's a good reason. I don't know, maybe say I'm in league with them or something equally stupid.'

Dvag tried to smile. 'Reason for what, Loudmouth?'

Tolvis threw his stone. It probably surprised them both when it flew straight and true and smacked Dvag in the face. He staggered on the top of his rock, lost his footing and fell out of sight between the boulders. After a moment, when he didn't get back up again, Latti cocked his head. 'Reckon that's a reason enough right there.'

The words were mashed by his broken mouth, but the meaning was clear enough. Tolvis backed away into the shingle of the beach. 'Reckon it is.'

'You going to throw rocks at me too?' Latti screwed up his face in pain.

'Only if you pretend you didn't come because Twelvefingers sent you to kill me. And if it hurts to talk, do feel free to spare us both.'

Latti shook his head. 'Not Medrin. Came ourselves.'

'Then you should have brought some men with you who can actually fight.' Tolvis backed away some more and yawned, waiting for Latti to make his way through the boulders. 'Take your time. Don't want you to slip and hurt yourself and spoil the fun of killing you.'

'*Nioingr!*'

Tolvis shrugged. 'I hear that word so much that I'm beginning to think it doesn't mean what I thought it meant. Seems to me it just means someone who doesn't do what Twelvefingers says.'

'Medrin ... our prince.' Latti jumped onto the shingle. He took the shield off his back and drew his sword, swinging it from side to side, warming up his arms.

Tolvis began to pace back and forth. 'For a man with a broken jaw you talk far too much. That bandage round your face isn't tight enough. Now learn something before you die, boy: a *nioingr* is someone who is a traitor to himself, not to anyone else. I see I'll have to teach you that.' He ran at Latti and clattered into him, shield against shield, knocking him back, then brought his axe down at his head. Latti lurched sideways. Tolvis came at him again, before Latti could find his balance, battering him a second time. This time his axe slipped around Latti's shield and Latti didn't have a hand any more. He shrieked and stumbled back, falling on the stones. Tolvis jumped on him, crushing a foot hard into his throat.

'Anything to say? No? At least you died well. No begging and pleading for mercy. Good for you.' Tolvis leaned down, pushing all his weight into Latti's throat, crushing until the light went out of his eyes. Then he went back to look at Dvag. Not much hope that a simple rock on the head had killed him, and when he found the bastard he was stuck between two boulders, eyes rolled back, muttering nonsense to himself. One of his ankles was twisted all wrong. He could add that to his mangled fingers. 'I'd wake up before the tide comes in if I were you,' Tolvis said, and left him there.

He walked a little way further along the beach until he found a way up the cliff and headed inland, looking for the Lhosir camp. Tricky, figuring out a way to get close that wouldn't lead him into more of Medrin's men or a band of Vathan scouts, and so he crept to the tops of ridges to survey the land ahead before retreating to make his way on beside hedges, along streams and ditches and, where he could, through woods. Twelvefingers would get to the Screambreaker first but that was by the way. Didn't matter much either way as long as the Screambreaker got to hear what needed to be said.

The campfires in the evening darkness were what finally led him to the Lhosir camp – not that he knew which army it was until he got close and heard the swearing and the songs. Even then he walked among the soldiers with his head down, hiding his face as best he could, keeping his shield by his side. *Medrin didn't send anyone. We sent ourselves.* Maybe that was even true. Twelvefingers had the knack of letting people know what he wanted done without ever saying, and once it was all too late he could put on that well practised look of horror he had and throw up his hands in despair and shake his head.

He reached the Screambreaker's tent only to find Twelvefingers already in it and it was only sheer luck that no one happened to look up and see his face before he turned away and moved on. When he eventually found the Screambreaker's standard, the old man was sitting on a stool, dressed in his mail, staring out across the fields.

'Screambreaker!'

The old man didn't move. Just sat and stared. 'Maker-Devourer watch over you, Loudmouth. Medrin said you'd wandered off.'

'That's about right. Say anything else much?'

'Lots of things, but none that particularly matter save that he has the Crimson Shield. There's at least some Marroc that will fight with us now.'

'The Marroc aren't our enemy, Screambreaker.'

The Screambreaker turned and looked up at him. 'It's a wonder you need to say such a thing.' He stared at Tolvis long and hard, and it seemed the old man was looking right through him at something far away. The Screambreaker looked … lost. Then the moment broke and the Screambreaker cocked his head. 'Whatever you have on your mind, Loudmouth, you'd best shed it. It's a stone around your shoulders as clear as the sun. Draw up a stool.'

So he did, and he told the Screambreaker about everything that had happened since Medrin had left Andhun, about Gallow and Jyrdas and Latti and Dvag, and how it was that Twelvefingers wasn't to be trusted any more. The Screambreaker listened patiently, and when Tolvis was done, he offered him a horn of mead. 'We'll fight the Vathen tomorrow, Loudmouth,' he said. 'For now that's all that matters.'

And that was all he would say while they drank together, and Tolvis talked and talked and finally walked away filled with anger and frustration, but in the middle of the next day, as the Lhosir army formed its lines, the Screambreaker called him one last time and told him how Gallow Truesword had come out of Andhun and how things were between the two of them, and how, if he wasn't alive by the end of the day, it would fall to Tolvis and to the dozen Lhosir beside him who'd fought in the last war from the beginning. He told Tolvis one other thing and then he laughed and told Tolvis what he had to do before any of that could happen. 'The woods on our seaward flank. Take ropes and shovels and fill it with traps for their horsemen. Let none of the Vathen pass.'

Tolvis looked at the men he'd been given. 'A dozen of us

and you want us to hold off a thousand Vathan horsemen?'

'But you're more than a dozen. You have the trees, Loudmouth, and there are more trees than there are Vathen. And you're Lhosir so it shouldn't be too hard for you.'

He never stopped smiling and somehow he was right, and by the end of the day as the sun sank and the Vathen fled, Tolvis was still alive and he hadn't had to kill quite as many as a thousand Vathan horsemen after all.

38

THE ARDSHAN

Gulsukh Ardshan watched the disaster unfold from the top of a hill of his own. Two defeats in a row now, and the best that could said of this one was that it wasn't *his* defeat. He'd taken four thousand men to fight two thousand Lhosir and lost nearly half of them. Now the Weeping Giant had taken twenty thousand, but he'd also taken his time, and the Lhosir had kept on coming from across the sea while he'd sat in Fedderhun, waiting for the sword to tell him it was the right day to march.

'It was the right day to march when I said it was,' Gulsukh muttered to himself.

'There are more of them now?' Moonjal Bashar hadn't seen the first battle. A part of Gulsukh was disappointed – it would have been a good lesson for a young bashar to see an ardshan beaten. A larger part was relieved that a son hadn't seen his own father humiliated. 'Twice as many. Perhaps more. If we'd all marched on Andhun a month ago, we'd have destroyed the Lhosir and taken it. We'd be in Sithhun by now.'

Still, twenty thousand men should have been enough. The bashars of the Weeping Giant had conducted themselves well, sending each of the clans into battle one after the other and withdrawing each one before they turned to rout. Wearing the supposedly invincible forkbeards down, because no one, in the end, was truly unbeatable. The horsemasters were wary this time too, racing their men in to hurl their javelots and racing out again before the Marroc archers could wreak the havoc they had before. The forkbeards had chosen their field well, pitched between a steep gully lined with stakes and a light wood. From his hill Gulsukh hadn't been able to see what had happened to the horsemasters and their efforts to flank the Lhosir line and take it from behind, but they'd clearly failed.

The Weeping Giant had fallen, but even then the day hadn't been lost. The enraged Vathen fell on the forkbeards, heedless of their bashars. They pushed and pushed them back, slowly breaking them down until finally, *finally*, they broke the Lhosir line. Gulsukh had to admire whoever had held the top of that hill for the forkbeards. However many men he had there, he'd waited and he'd waited. A lesser mind might have thrown them into the fight sooner, but no, this one waited until the very last possible moment, for when the battle hung in the balance and the Vathen had taken beating after beating and yet found themselves on the point of victory, and *then* he threw them in, snatching it away again. Five hundred men, give or take, while the Vathen were still thousands upon thousands, but in that one moment he broke their spirit. The Vathan soldiers crumbled, their bashars failed, they broke and they ran, and the Lhosir cut them down. The best that could be said for what happened next was that the forkbeards themselves were too bloodied and spent to turn the rout into a proper slaughter.

He raised an eyebrow to Moonjal Bashar. 'My advice would be to have the horsemasters supply cover to our retreat.' Not that anyone listened to him any more. An ardshan in disgrace. Disobedient to the Weeping Giant, and then he'd gone and lost as well.

'I'll send a messenger.'

'Will you? I'm not sure who you're going to send it to.' He watched Moonjal send a runner anyway.

'You don't seem disturbed, Ardshan. Is there some finer point I'm missing?'

'Not really. The setting sun means the forkbeards won't be able to make the most of what they've done to us. Other than that, no.' There was a little consolation to be taken there, but the smile on his face that he couldn't quite hide was because the Weeping Giant was dead. The Sword Brothers would be in disarray and a good few of those dead too. They needed an ardshan again. There was still a horde here, if he could keep it together.

'Should we join the retreat, Ardshan?'

Gulsukh shook his head. 'Let the Sword Brothers deal with it. Let them be seen and let them take the blame. Let them cherish their defeat. An ardshan knows that defeat comes as well as victory. Time they learned it too. We'll find them later. I want to see our prisoner.' He turned his horse and rode down the back of the hill and left the fleeing Vathan army that was no longer his to whatever fate the Lhosir would find for it. He rode to his own camp in the woods, away from the main Vathan force and the onrushing forkbeards. He had a few score men now, no more. Kinsmen mostly, who still took his orders over anyone else's. The last vestiges of his old clan, before the Sword Brothers had swept through the steppes. A meagre handful, but among the Vathen the right man with the right words could make a handful into a horde with a snap of his fingers.

The forkbeard was waiting for him inside his tent, still bloody from the beating he'd taken the night before. Gulsukh's men had found this one on his own, creeping about down by the sea. He was bound so tightly that his hands had gone blue. Gulsukh cut him loose. He sat down beside the Lhosir and offered him a cup of Aulian wine. The Lhosir batted it away.

'When my men found you, they swear to me that someone had done this to you already. They tell me they were gentle and that you didn't put up much resistance for a forkbeard. So what were you doing down by the sea at the dead of night? Did you come on that ship out of Andhun? The one drawn up and abandoned on the shore?'

The Lhosir shrugged but the pinch of his lips gave him away.

'After you beat me the first time, I haven't had much else to do except stay out here watching who comes and who goes. Your prince has taken the Crimson Shield of the Marroc and that ship on the beach is his. So why weren't you with him?'

The Lhosir spat at him. Gulsukh poured another cup of wine, for himself this time, and supped it. 'In the old Aulian Empire it was understood that men might divulge their secrets and retain their honour after they were taken. Any prisoner was permitted to remain silent for one day and one night. When that time was done, it was assumed that a torturer of any skill would have reduced him to the point of revealing whatever he knew. So instead of the torturer, there was only ever the *idea* of a torturer, and of the pain and everything else that comes with such people. At the end of one day and one night, a man like me would come to a man like you. I would offer you a fine wine and a pleasant meal and we would discuss matters. It was understood to be honourable, then, for the captive to reveal everything he knew, and in return he was spared any unkindness. That's not to say that he would keep his life, but often that was the case; and even when it wasn't, death would be swift and clean and proud. I think you'd understand *that*, at least.' He poured a second cup of wine for the Lhosir. 'That was the Aulian way, but the Aulians are gone now. I simply stake my enemies to the ground, cut strips of skin from their flesh and sprinkle them with salt until they tell me what I want and then let the ants eat them. I don't know how it is among you forkbeards, but I've seen the men your prince hung up from his poles after you beat us. They were my men. I knew them. Their families. Their wives, their sons, their brothers. I was the one who led them to defeat. It doesn't make me think well of you, what your prince did to them.' He offered the cup of wine. 'I fought for your king once, so I know you well enough to suppose you'll opt for pain and heroic resistance, but I'll offer you the Aulian way anyway in case you'd prefer it.' Gulsukh moved in closer to the Lhosir. 'I won't tell if you won't. What do you say, forkbeard?'

'I say you talk too much.' The Lhosir slapped the cup across the tent.

Gulsukh nodded. 'I do. Perhaps that's why I prefer the Aulian way to this.' He rose and whistled for his torturer, the best he had among the men left to him. When the torturer had dragged the Lhosir away, he called in Moonjal. There was no reason why a father and son shouldn't share what was left of what was a rather fine old Aulian vintage.

Moonjal Bashar bowed low as he came in. Gulsukh picked up the cup that the forkbeard had refused and refilled it. 'Did he say what he was doing?' asked his son.

Gulsukh shook his head but smiled as he did. 'He thought not. He was very brave. But let us suppose that Twelvefingers left his ship where he did because he was unable to enter Andhun. Why would that be?' He didn't wait for an answer. 'How far away are the nearest bashars of the Weeping Giant?'

'A few miles, no more.'

'What would *you* do, Moonjal?'

Moonjal Bashar stiffened. 'The Lhosir have beaten us soundly but are unable to press their advantage. Many of our clans remain strong. I would rally the bashars and attack again at dawn, pressing them as hard as possible and keeping them away from the city if I could. They committed all of their men while half of ours barely fought at all. They will be tired. I would continue as we planned and wear them down.'

'Exactly right. Exactly what I'd have done if we hadn't found this Lhosir on the beach.'

'But will the forkbeards not withdraw behind their walls?'

Gulsukh smiled. 'What if they can't, Moonjal?' He laughed. 'We shall see to it that the forkbeard scouts find camps abandoned in the night. That they see us scattering and fleeing along the coast road and into the hills. We watch them and we watch Andhun and we see what will happen; and we keep all our riders close, each with a fresh fast horse to hand.' Gulsukh leaned forward. 'I also mean to send a young bashar out into the night with a few good men at his side to go looking for the forkbeards. In case they need some encouragement to see us running away.'

39

THE WOODS AT NIGHT

Horsan and his men chased the bastard *nioingr* Gallow Foxbeard right across the battlefield, hurdling the bodies of a thousand broken men, into the trees where the shadows were black and welcoming, and in the dark they lost him. Horsan supposed he must have slipped away out the other side. The Marroc were good at running. It only went to show that Medrin was right: a Lhosir didn't run and a Lhosir didn't hide. A Lhosir stood, one against one or one against a hundred. Maybe a Lhosir died, but so what?

Now they'd lost him they'd have to go back to Medrin and tell them that both the *nioingr* and the Vathan sword had slipped away in the twilight, and Medrin would have a belly full of rage when he heard and Horsan didn't want to be the one who had to tell him.

Halfway back through the trees, Durlak pointed and yelled and started to run. 'He's there! I see him!' A shape broke cover right where Horsan was looking and bolted through the bracken. The woods were full of shadows and not much else, but it wasn't the Foxbeard. Horsan wasn't sure he remembered Gallow having a helm, but it certainly hadn't had a Vathan plume on the top.

'Wait!' But Durlak was jumping and shouting and whoever had been hiding in the woods was running and plain for all to see. They chased the darting shape right through the wood and out the other end. The sky was a dim grey now, streaked with a long bruise of purple over the horizon, the last dying light of day. Enough to show Horsan that he was right.

'It's a Vathan!' And now they really had missed the Foxbeard and he'd be halfway to Andhun. Horsan pulled up. 'Leave him! It's the *nioingr* we're after.'

The others ignored him and ran on and after a moment Horsan followed too, because what else was there to do except go back to Medrin with their heads hanging to tell him they'd failed? And maybe Gallow hadn't gone to Andhun and his precious Marroc but had taken the sword back to the Vathen instead. It was a *nioingr* sort of thing to do. Maybe these Vathen would lead him right where he wanted to go.

For all his running and darting through shadows, the Vathan never quite managed to get away. It seemed ... *odd* ... and for a moment Horsan was almost inclined to stop and let him go.

'Forkbeards! Forkbeards!' the Vathan cried out to the night, sharp with fear. 'Hundreds of them! Run!'

Hundreds? Horsan laughed and forgot about stopping and ambushes and caution. *Hundreds? There's a dozen of us, you fool!*

But the Vathan kept shouting and running, and now Horsan could see fires in the woods ahead, quickly being stamped out, sparks shooting into the air like Aulian rockets. Shapes and shadows of more men moved ahead of them, and once more the cries went up: *Forkbeards! Flee!*

Gallow crouched in the dark beside the road. The moon was up and the gates of Andhun lay in sight. A handful of Lhosir stood clustered around a small fire, far enough away to be out of range of any arrows. Medrin's men. Watchers. Watching for *him* perhaps, and Andhun's gates were firmly closed. No fires burned up on the walls, no stars of torches moved back and forth. And even if he found a Marroc and called out, why would they let him in?

I have Solace. I have the holy sword of the Vathen, the Sword of the Weeping God. But the Marroc god was Modris, and Modris and the Weeping God fought their eternal battle, the Protector and the Peacebringer, the Crimson Shield and Solace. They'd never allow the red sword through their gates. More likely they'd kill the man who carried it and hurl it from their cliffs far out to sea. It was cursed. He could feel it. There was a burden that came with bearing such a sword.

Arda! He touched the locket, but he knew what Arda's words would be. He could hear them, clear as a bell. *Sell it, you oaf! Sell it and come home. Must be worth a fortune and more than we've any need for. So get what you can and think of your sons. Or throw it into the sea if you must, but whatever you do, don't you be sneaking around the bottom of the cliffs, finding your way past those walls! Just don't!*

Just don't! In the darkness Gallow laughed. That was how she did it. She went by what she knew of him, guessed what he was most likely to do and then told him to do something else. The opposite if she could find one, just so she could shake her head and wag her finger and tell him how wrong he was. It was never about what she wanted, it was about being able to scold him afterwards. Eight years of being married to the woman and he'd never seen through her until now, carrying a cursed sword and trapped between the Marroc on one side and Medrin on the other, probably with some Vathen still around for good measure and all of them wanting to kill him; and now he had to clamp a hand over his mouth to stop himself laughing aloud. He could see her, eyes rolling, shaking her head in disbelief. *And there you go, keeping on wondering why it is you can't leave me be, you great lump of wood. Now get yourself home. You can give Nadric a good shouting at for being such a thistlefinger if you need something to look forward to.*

He didn't, but there was something else to done before

he could leave. 'I have to get into Andhun. I have to warn them. Medrin will slaughter them.'

Naturally I disagree, but I suppose you do. If she'd been there he would have kissed her, and if she'd shaken her head and told him that no, really, he *did* have to go with her instead, he would have gone.

Only a fool would climb the cliffs in the dark wearing mail and gauntlets, but then again, a Lhosir never abandoned his shield or his weapon, not if he could help it, and the Maker-Devourer preferred fools armed and ready for battle over wise men who came to him old and empty-handed, and Gallow had always been a good climber. It was part of what had started all this in the first place.

Once he was inside, he set about looking for Valaric.

The Vathan camp wasn't a big one, only a few dozen soldiers and their horses, and Horsan ran right into the middle of it and roared and swung his sword at the first shape he saw, and the Vathen panicked and fled. After they were gone he searched the camp, and that was when they found Dvag, or what was left of him, still alive if only barely. Dvag Bloodbeard they'd call him now, by the looks of him. As names went it wasn't so bad. Horsan and the others hoisted Dvag between them and limped him home. By the time they got back, the sun was rising and Medrin was up again. He listened to Dvag's tale as he broke his fast. To the things Dvag had heard around him while the Vathen had flayed his face. It wasn't much. Something about the sword and a Marroc in Andhun.

Medrin's eyes gleamed.

40

THE WALLS OF ANDHUN

Valaric watched the battle from a hill beside the sea. He watched the Vathen break like waves on the wall of forkbeard shields. He watched the wall waver and almost crumble, and then hold and the last forkbeards surge down the hill, and he watched the Vathen turn and flee. He didn't stay to see what happened after that but walked quickly back to the sea cliffs and down a path that ran to the shore and to the little boat that waited there. A tiny thing, hardly big enough to fit the half a dozen men it had carried out of Andhun. The others looked at him expectantly.

'Close, but the forkbeards broke them.'

The other Marroc fell to cursing as they pushed the boat out into the waves. Valaric said nothing. What difference did it make whether the invaders were Vathen or forkbeards? Both sides smashed to pieces, that was the best he could hope for. 'The Vathen are still out there.' When the waves were breaking around his chest, he hauled himself aboard. 'We keep the gates closed and the forkbeards have nowhere to go. And they can't do anything about it while the Vathen are still there.'

'And if the duke keeps his word and opens them?'

Valaric looked away. He'd felt the change in the city as soon as the demon-prince Twelvefingers had gone off looking for the Crimson Shield and the Nightmare of the North had cut down the gibbets. A few more Marroc had been hung and then the Widowmaker had moved his army out of the city. The killing had stopped. Better for the forkbeards perhaps, not to have their numbers whittled slowly down, but better for the Marroc too. It had taken Valaric a while to see that. And then the Vathen had come, and the puppet Marroc duke who ruled Andhun with Yurlak's hand shoved up his arse had promised, sworn on everything holy, that Andhun would open its gates to the Screambreaker when the battle was done.

It occurred to Valaric, as they sailed their little boat through the twilight sea and back into the harbour of Andhun, that the Nightmare of the North might be kinder to his people than some Vathan ardshan. Yet he'd take a Vathan anything over the demon-prince. Anything was better than that.

'We have to make sure he doesn't,' he said, after such a long pause that no one knew what he was talking about any more.

'We make our stand now,' said Sarvic. 'Doesn't matter who won. Never did. We keep them out until they go home.'

It wasn't a stupid idea either. When the forkbeards had first come across the sea there were good reasons why Andhun had been the last city to fall. 'Good luck telling that to the duke.'

Sarvic gave him a look as though he was mad. 'Me? *You* have to tell him! You have to make him keep them closed!'

'I'm an old soldier who fought the forkbeards and lost his family to old man winter for his pains.' Valaric spat into the sea. 'He's not going to listen to me.'

'If he won't, others will. People know you! They *will* listen to you.'

'And what would you have us do, Sarvic? Seize the gates and hold them closed? Fight among ourselves while the forkbeards laugh at us? I'll not do that. I'll not lift a blade against another Marroc. Might as well throw myself in the sea.'

'So you're just going to do nothing?'

No. Couldn't do that either, but what else was there but to take the gates and hold them shut? Words, maybe? A silver tongue might caress the duke around to his way of thinking, but Valaric was never that. Hard rusty old iron, more like, and besides, he'd never get close enough to even try.

He didn't sleep well that night. Every time he closed his eyes the shadows filled with old faces. Men he'd fought beside in the early days. Friends, killed, one after the other by the faceless forkbeard terror. And then forkbeards too, the ones he'd killed in the later days when he'd turned from battlefields and taken to hunting them in ones and twos, any who strayed from the pack and Wolf of the Wild Woods had been his name for a time. And when he finally pushed all the faces away, what he saw was the slight hump of broken earth, already covered with grass, where his family had been buried. All of them together, because the savagery of that winter hadn't left those who'd survived with enough strength to dig separate graves for so many dead.

Forkbeard bastards.

Snow and starvation and the curse of an Aulian shade-walker, but he could have done something about any and all of those things if he'd been there. Could have hunted for them. Could have found more food. Could have taken them away to another place. Somehow. Something. He didn't know what but he would never have let them die.

The forkbeards hadn't killed them though. It was his fault and his alone. His choice. No getting away from it.

Sarvic was right. The gates should stay closed. The duke was right too. He'd made a promise to open them and promises should be honoured. Who was wrong then? Who'd be wrong when the forkbeards came back inside the walls and wreaked their revenge for what he'd done when the demon-prince had come with the Crimson Shield in his hand? Him, that was who. He'd tried to take the shield and he'd failed, and now it didn't matter who led the forkbeards when they came, they'd want blood for that.

Stupid. Stupid to fail. Stupid to even try, and Gallow's words chased him like hounds after a fox. *If you'd had even one man like him in this city, Medrin would be dead and you'd be standing in front of me holding your precious shield. You know you've just brought doom on the whole of Andhun, don't you?* And he had, and Gallow was right, and all the other forkbeards too, and the Marroc were just frightened sheep and you couldn't rouse a sheep to be a wolf, whatever you said to him.

He gave up on sleeping and wandered the streets for a while in the dark, until he came to the city gates and stopped where the rows of gibbets had been.

Maybe there was a way after all.

And Tolvis Loudmouth watched the battle at its end too, when the Vathen had finally hurled themselves in one last madness at the Screambreaker's line. The fighting was over for him by then. Of the dozen men he'd taken into the woods, four were dead. Too few to stand in a wall of shields and spears against the Vathan horsemen who tried to come around the edge of the battle, they'd strung ropes between trees, dug trenches and set spikes in the ground. They'd thrown javelins and led the horsemen into one trap or another and then fallen upon them. A tiny skirmish when set against the battle as a whole, a hundred or so Vathen held and turned away, maybe a dozen killed and as many again wounded. A small victory. Perhaps it played some part in the greater one or perhaps not, but it would be quickly forgotten either way. But then the Screambreaker hadn't sent them to that wood to turn the battle, he'd sent them there for what would come after and they all knew that too. In the darkness of the Lhosir victory they slipped back into the camp, in among the tents, looking for the men they knew, faces they called friends. The old soldiers who'd fought at the Screambreaker's side long ago. The Screambreaker's men. They took the words he'd whispered to them and passed them along to any who would listen and quietly they gathered themselves. In the morning they spoke out his deeds, one after the other for the wind and the sun to carry away across the land and his name passed among the Lhosir like fire across a stubble field. A thousand men had seen him fell the Vathan giant. They'd seen the Screambreaker take the unholy sword and hold it high, and when they couldn't find his body in the breaking dawn light it was because the Maker-Devourer himself had come to take it, and so they made another pyre, a dozen men at once, all brothers-in-arms since that first crossing of the sea. The Screambreaker was gone but he'd left them his legend, and they took their time to honour him, even Twelvefingers. When they were done, the Screambreaker's men turned their faces to Andhun.

41

THE OFFERING

'I'm not a fool.' Medrin stared at the little statue of the Maker-Devourer he'd brought with him from across the sea. Outside his tent the sun was rising. 'I am *not* a fool,' he said again. 'We both know there can be no turning away from this. The Screambreaker would have known though, somehow he would have known which way to face. The Vathen or the Marroc? Which is it to be? I need a sign.' And for a moment he felt himself missing the old man who just might have been planning to steal his birthright. Missing his certainty, his presence, his assurance.

And then, waiting for him outside his tent, were Horsan and the others to tell him how the Vathen were fleeing in terror, witless and lost without their precious sword, and what was that if it wasn't a sign? 'Which isn't to say they'll stay that way,' he said to the statue of the god, 'but when they turn, we'll be ready. We'll destroy them for a second time.'

There were a few Vathan wounded who weren't dead yet. He saw to it that they were kept alive and set men to cutting wood for gibbets. Scouts rode off through the hills to keep an eye on the Vathan retreat. While they were away the Lhosir stopped what they were doing and honoured the Screambreaker and the dead who'd fallen beside him. He let the old ones do that, Tolvis Loudmouth and the rest. Let them start the pyre and, when the pyre was built, put the bodies of those they most wanted to honour on top and set it alight. He said a few words himself, because he was their prince after all, then let the old ones who'd fought with the Screambreaker against the Marroc finish speaking him out. The pyre was huge and there probably wasn't a single Lhosir who hadn't put a piece of something on it. It troubled him a little that they actually couldn't find the Screambreaker's body and the foolish whispers that spread like fire when that got out. More than likely the Screambreaker hadn't been quite dead, had crawled off to breathe his last alone in the night and didn't want to be spoken out because no one had spoken out his brother the Moontongue down at the bottom of the sea and he'd be damned if he didn't find his way to the Maker-Devourer's cauldron on his own too. But Medrin let it pass, let the old ones who'd known him stay staring at the flames until his scouts came back to tell him what he already knew: camps abandoned, Vathen flooding away, a disordered rabble, thousands and thousands of them. Oh, they'd come together again in time – they were too many to be truly broken – but not today. Today he could let them go.

He turned his army to Andhun then, to the city the Screambreaker had abandoned. The Marroc would keep their gates closed but he was ready for that. He would array his men outside, build his gibbets, hang Vathan after Vathan outside the walls to remind the Marroc who they were dealing with until they finally cracked and let him in. And then ...

And then? He wasn't sure. Burn the city down for trying to take the shield from him? Or let them live? What would the Screambreaker do? Both. Somehow he'd find a way to do both.

He'd barely even started, though, when the gates creaked open and a dozen Marroc soldiers carrying the shield of their puppet duke lined the entrance to honour him. A herald cried out from the walls, 'Duke Zardic of Andhun welcomes Prince Medrin, son of Yurlak, king of the Marroc!'

They weren't going to keep him out after all.

Fools.

Valaric stood in an alley, hidden in its shadows from the afternoon sun, watching the gates as they opened to let in the demon from over the sea. He wore his sword and his mail and carried a spear in his hand. His shield was propped against the wall beside him. The gates hung open, and for a while Medrin waited where he was, outside the walls, more and more men gathering around him.

Close the gates! Modris, let them see him for what he is! Don't let him in!

But the gates stayed as they were, and when Medrin at last advanced across the cobbles it was with a hundred men around him and more behind to keep the gateway clear. He entered the city slowly, the Crimson Shield carried close in his hand, tense, held high for all to see. No stones fell from above, no javelins, no arrows. Not yet.

Pity.

Valaric had thought about that. Thought about what one well aimed spear or arrow could do. But if a lone killer struck down the forkbeards' prince, the reprisals would be terrible. Andhun would burn.

Medrin stopped. He stood in the middle of the square. Marroc watched from the edges, from windows and alleys and side streets. Scores of them. Watching and waiting to see what would happen and doing nothing. *And what do I expect of them?* They were ordinary folk with no swords, no mail, no weapons to speak of. The only soldiers here were the ones who'd honoured Medrin's entrance and the duke's herald who stood on the walls above, head bowed. *So where are the rest of you? Kept in your barracks to keep the demon at his ease? Or waiting around the first corner?*

A murmur rose from the far side of the square. Valaric stepped out of his alley to see what it was, but it was only the arse-licker pretend-duke Zardic, come with a bare handful of men to fawn over Medrin and hand over his castle again. The demon-prince smirked and raised the Crimson Shield high over his head, turning it slowly so that every Marroc could see. 'The Shield of Modris the Protector!' he cried. 'Returned to you! I, Medrin, have brought it back to the land where it belongs! I, Medrin, have carried it into battle to face your enemies and I, Medrin, have defeated them! The Vathen! Tens of thousands of them! An army so great their numbers would have filled every street in this great city and still spilled through the gates and into the fields beyond! I, Medrin, son of Yurlak, have defeated them and I have done this for you.' Medrin cast his eyes around the square looking for the challenge, for anyone who would meet his gaze, but no, they all looked away. Even Valaric. *Not yet. Not while there's still a flicker of hope.*

The prince laughed. 'See,' he said to the man beside him, quite loud enough for even Valaric to hear. 'They really are sheep.'

The forkbeards laughed. The pretend-duke walked slowly towards the demon-prince, head bowed. The square fell silent. 'Prince Medrin, son of Yurlak, king of the Marroc, the people of Andhun greet and welc—'

Medrin cut him off. 'When I came to this city two days ago, the people of Andhun set upon me. A goodly number of bodies attest to this. Marroc mostly, but not all. I'm not interested in your welcome.' The duke opened his mouth but Twelvefingers waved him away. He pointed into the crowd and singled out two men. 'Bring those two to me, Duke of Andhun.'

Why are we such cowards? Valaric looked away. He knew what came next. The men would be dragged from the crowd by Marroc soldiers. They'd be flogged, and it would be Marroc hands holding the whips. Marroc arms and Marroc tools would build gibbets and these two men would be torn open and staked to wheels like the Vathen outside the city, hung beside the gates as a lesson to others and not a single forkbeard would even have to raise a hand to do it.

All of a sudden Medrin was shouting into the face of the duke: ' . . . until their leaders are found, and I expect you and your soldiers to deal with them as I require! Those soldiers who should have been out on the battlefield, fighting the Vathen!' he thundered. 'Now bring those men to me!'

Valaric picked up his spear and shield and stepped out of the shadows. He pushed his way through the few Marroc who stood around the edges of the square. 'Oi! Prince Forkbeard. Twelvefingers. Demon-spawn.'

The closest forkbeards turned and readied their weapons. Valaric stopped. Medrin was still shouting.

'Medrin! Demon-beard! Prince *nioingr.*'

Now Medrin stopped.

'I'm the one you want, you pox-scarred prince of filth. Twelve-fingered son of the mother of monsters. I'm the one who stood before you on the beach and I stand before you now. I, Valaric of Witterslet. I, Valaric of the Marroc. I'm the one you want and here I am. You wouldn't face me then; do you dare to face me now, or are you the coward that even your own men know you to be?'

Medrin turned. He faced Valaric with the Crimson Shield held high. 'A Marroc crippled me some fifteen years ago, Valaric of Witterslet. Men die from such wounds as I took that day, and so they should, for it left me as weak as a child and what place is there in this world for a weakling warrior? Yet I didn't die. I fought for my life and I clawed it back again. I've taken this shield and I defeated an army that would have swept across your land. I will face you, Valaric of the Marroc, but only if you will face me as I am.' His words changed for the duke, but his eyes stayed on Valaric. 'Have your soldiers take this man and run a spear through his chest. Close the wound with hot pitch. Then we'll duel.

If he fights well, we'll say no more of this. If he fights poorly, I'll have one man in every twenty taken from your city and sent back across the sea to live as slaves.'

Valaric clenched his hand around his spear. 'I came here to die so others might live,' he hissed. 'I'll take your challenge, prince of oafs.'

He felt a movement in the Marroc behind him, and then a man come to stand at his side.

'You try to take this man, Medrin, you come through me first.'

Gallow.

42

DEFIANCE

Gallow raised the Sword of the Weeping God high. He'd come to the square behind Andhun's gates to see what Medrin would do. To stand against him, to fight and die if he had to. And seen that he wasn't alone.

'You're neither shoeing my horse nor blading my scythe,' muttered Valaric.

'Settle that later?'

Valaric nodded. 'It can wait.'

'Horsan!' Gallow called him out. Medrin's sword-hand. 'The servant of a man with no honour shares in his shame. The servant of a man with no courage shares in his cowardice. The servant of a man with no heart shares in his disgrace. You bring shame and dishonour to your kin. You're a coward.'

Horsan pushed his way out from among the Lhosir, shaking his head, face set hard. 'I'll rip you apart, *nioingr*.'

Gallow ran at him. Horsan met him head on. The two crashed into each other and careened sideways. The lunge of Horsan's spear pierced the air an inch from Gallow's ear while Solace skittered off Horsan's shield.

'I knew your family from before I crossed the sea,' said Gallow grimly. 'Your father always thought you were carrying a bit too much fat on you. Lazy, he said.'

Horsan snarled. He circled more cautiously this time, crouched behind his shield, spear held in one fist over the top, point remorselessly aimed at Gallow's eyes.

'I was on the same battlefield as him when he died.' Gallow circled the other way, careful not to get too close to Medrin's Lhosir.

'Spit him, Horsan!' The Lhosir were cheering and jeering. Gallow glanced around the crowd. The Marroc hadn't moved but there was a change to them. They were restless. One bent down. When he stood up again he was holding a stone.

'I didn't see him fall. Barely knew him. But we recited the names of the dead that day and everyone who fell was spoken out, their words and their deeds offered up to the Maker-Devourer. I've heard a thousand men spoken out like that, Horsan. Spoken out a good few myself. Last man I spoke for was Jyrdas One-Eye. How many men have you spoken out, Horsan? Any at all?'

No. He could see that. They probably hadn't honoured the dead yet. Too busy with Andhun and whether the Vathen would return. Times like this the fallen just had to stay where they fell for a day or two before they could be properly burned and honoured, but it made the Lhosir uncomfortable to think about it, that was the thing. Made them wonder, for a moment, if they were right. What if they were all somehow struck down? What if the fallen were never spoken out? What if they were lost, abandoned, alone after all they'd done. Unthinkable. Horrible.

A grim smile set on Gallow's face. 'No matter. The Maker-Devourer himself will speak for the Screambreaker and those who stood with him, and there were men there for your father. Who's going to speak for you, Horsan? When you stand beside the Maker-Devourer's cauldron and he turns up his ear to listen, what's he going to hear? Nothing.'

'We spoke out the Screambreaker. Every one of us. The rest have to wait.' Horsan's mouth twitched; as it did, Gallow leaped. The red sword smashed down onto Horsan's shield and split it in two. Horsan jabbed his spear at Gallow's neck, but Gallow simply lifted his own shield and turned the spear over his head. He kicked at Horsan's knees and staggered him. The air hissed as he lunged with Solace. The sword caught Horsan neatly between his hauberk and his helm, driving through the naked flesh of his throat. A great spurt of blood sprayed across the cobbles. Horsan opened his mouth to say something more but all that came out was a river of red. He fell to his knees and toppled over. Gallow turned to face the rest of them.

'So that was the best of you, was it?' yelled Valaric. 'You've forgotten who you are. Go back where you came from, forkbeards. Go back across the sea and stay there!'

One or two Marroc among the crowd shouted as well. 'Go home!'

'So who fights for Medrin now?' Gallow lowered Solace and pointed its bloody blade at the Lhosir one by one. They each met his eye but none of them moved.

Medrin's lips pursed as though he tasted something sour. He cocked his head and turned to the Marroc duke. 'You're sheltering a *nioingr* and a traitor. Hang him.'

'He's from across the sea, my lord.' The duke didn't move. Neither did any of the Marroc soldiers. 'My men can't touch him. A Marroc who lifts a hand against a Lhosir shall have that hand cut off, as you have commanded.'

'Gallow? He might have come from across the sea but he stayed and he took one of your women. He's a Marroc now. Hang him.'

The duke still didn't move.

'Hang him, or I will hang you.'

'No, my lord, I will not.'

Medrin took a spear from the Lhosir beside him, drove it into the duke's belly and kicked him over. He looked around the crowd and at the Marroc soldiers. 'So who else wants to be duke, then? I'll give it to whichever one of you brings me the head of that man there.' He pointed at Gallow.

None of the Marroc moved. Gallow felt the tension in the air, unbearable. They were on the brink of turning.

'Marroc! Be free!' Valaric hurled his spear at Medrin. The prince lifted the Crimson Shield, instinct saving him. Valaric's spear struck the wood hard, but when Medrin lowered the shield, it wasn't even scratched.

A Marroc raised his arm and threw a stone. Then another and another did the same. Medrin howled and the Lhosir burst out of their circle around him. Valaric and Gallow launched themselves forward. The Marroc soldiers lifted their shields and their spears to face the Lhosir, the men and women around the square throwing stones and whatever else they could find. The first Lhosir hit Valaric head on, shield on shield, spear points lunging. Everything narrowed to sharpened points of steel. And over it all he heard Medrin roaring, 'Kill them all! Burn their city! Leave nothing standing but bare stone walls!'

43

OUTSIDE

L hosir poured through the gates of Andhun. The Marroc who'd thrown stones lay dead now, broken dolls, limp and ragged, trampled underfoot when Medrin's men let loose their charge. The rest had fled after the initial surge, and now Gallow and Valaric were side by side, pinned into an alley narrow enough for them to block with just the two of their shields, a dozen Lhosir pressing them.

'What happened to …' Valaric twisted as the Lhosir in front of him hooked his shield with an axe while the next one back jabbed with his spear. '… going to Varyxhun?' He ducked another swing. The man in front of him howled as Valaric stamped on his foot.

Gallow barely heard. He could see Arda's face. She was smiling but she looked sad. *Pig-headed forkbeard.* In his hand Solace felt as light as a feather and the air hummed as the sword cut through it. In Marroc stories the red sword cut through shield and mail like an axe through cheese. The Lhosir still standing in front of him proved the lie of that, but it still moved with a life of its own, as though it was a part of him, and it had already split a couple of badly made shields. He lunged over a shield now, the sword biting at the neck of the Lhosir in front of him. It had a knack, it seemed, for finding the gaps in a man's armour. The Lhosir lurched away and then came back at him, forced by the press of men behind.

'You know what us forkbeards are like: can't resist a good fight.' Gallow stepped back. The Lhosir in front of him stumbled forward, lowered his shield for a moment to support himself and died as the red sword tore out his throat. 'I came to tell you to run away.' He lunged as the next Lhosir came, reached over the man's shield and stabbed, slicing his cheek.

Valaric ducked and stabbed beneath the next man's shield. He sheathed his own sword and snatched the dead man's spear as he fell. 'They'll get behind us soon.'

The next Lhosir didn't have a helm. Stupid, and Solace quickly split his skull. 'Then this will become a very bloody alleyway.'

'Hold them for a moment.' Valaric lunged and then leaped back and ran down the alley, leaving Gallow facing two at once. They pressed in on him hard then, swords stabbing around his shield while the men behind lunged with spears. A Lhosir learned to fight as soon as he was old enough to stand and hold a weapon. They learned to guard one another, how one man could hook away a shield and make an opening for another to lunge at unguarded skin, sometimes the man beside them with a sword or an axe, but more often the man pressed up close behind with a short spear. They learned how three or four together, if they worked as one, could kill almost any number of enemies until they tired, and now they turned that knowledge against Gallow. His own childhood had been the same: after the hook came the lunge, after the jab the thrust and then the swing. He knew where the spear thrusts and sword cuts would come, had honed all these in five years of war with the Marroc, but against four Lhosir, even ones who'd never faced a real enemy before the Vathen, he could barely keep them at bay. He retreated back down the alley, one step at a time, one lunge after another.

'Valaric!'

No answer and he couldn't look back. Didn't dare.

'Valaric?' A spear point sliced the skin of his neck. 'Valaric!'

Then he heard a roar behind him. For a moment the

Lhosir faltered and then Valaric barged into the back of Gallow and splashes of something hot spattered his arms. 'You bastards like what comes out of the Grey Man's kitchens so much?' yelled Valaric 'Have some!' He hurled a cauldron past Gallow's head. The Lhosir bellowed and recoiled and the air filled with steam and the smell of boiled cabbage. For a moment Gallow was free.

'Run!' Valaric pulled his arm. Gallow bolted down the alley on Valaric's heels as he raced for an open door. Valaric's spear was propped beside it; Valaric snatched it up, turned and hurled it. The first Lhosir dived sideways and the spear hit the one behind him, clattering off the side of the man's helm, the shaft spinning through the air. The last two Lhosir batted it aside but by then Gallow was through the door and Valaric was closing it behind them.

'The table!' Valaric rammed his shoulder to the door. They were in a kitchen. Gallow dragged the table from the middle of the room. The door shuddered as the first Lhosir outside kicked at it. Valaric let them force it open a hand's width and then stabbed his sword through the gap. The Lhosir backed away a moment, long enough for the two of them to push the table against the door and wedge it against a wall. 'Come on!' Valaric ran for a different door.

'What were you doing out there?' They ran out into an empty tavern hall.

'What do you mean?' Valaric stopped and shouted, 'Hoy! Any Marroc still here hiding away! Now's the time, lads! The forkbeards are here and they're burning our homes. Take up your arms!' The tavern remained empty and still. Valaric shrugged and ran to the far door. 'Good enough. The docks, Gallow. That's where we'll be. That's where we make our stand. We knew this was coming. We're as ready as we could ever be.' He pushed open the door and ran almost straight into another band of Lhosir.

'Maker-Devourer!' roared Gallow, raising his shield. The

Lhosir ran at them, but as Valaric and Gallow turned their backs and fled, the Lhosir stopped, laughed and turned into the Grey Man instead.

'They'll regret that later when we rip their drunken bellies open,' snarled Valaric.

'What were you doing at the gates? Did you think Medrin was going to fight you?'

'No.' Valaric darted into an alley that ran steep down the hill towards the Isset, so narrow they had to squeeze along it with their armour and their shields scraping the walls. The buildings either side blotted out the sun, casting them into gloomy shadow.

'Well? Then what?'

'I thought I was going to die.' Valaric's words came out through clenched teeth. 'If your prince was the sort of man to stand up and fight for himself when another man called him out ... But he isn't and he never was, and I knew that. I went there to give myself up to him. Take as many of you with me as I could but let him have the nasty Marroc who'd stood up to him on the beach. You were right, what you said there. I thought if he had me then he might not burn the whole city. So much for that.' The alley opened into another street. It was empty: no Marroc, no Lhosir. Shouting came from further down the hill, the sounds of men fighting. The tang of smoke tainted the air.

'I fought the Vathen at the Screambreaker's side. I saw him fight their champion. I saw him take the Sword of the Weeping God.' He held the blade up so Valaric could see it clearly. 'I was beside him when the Vathen broke our line and he fell. Medrin let it happen. He turned the tide of the battle with his men but he waited for the Screambreaker to fall before he did.'

Valaric stared. 'The red sword? *That* is the Comforter?' His face went tight, almost as though he was afraid of it. 'Modris preserve us!'

'Solace. The Peacebringer.'

Valaric took a step away. 'Oh, I know its names. The Edge of Sorrows. The Unholy Comforter. The blade of the Weeping God that struck at Diaran the Lifegiver and would have killed all men had not Modris the Protector taken the blow on his shield.' He shook his head and backed further away. 'That's a cursed blade, Gallow, and it brings death wherever it goes. You should never have brought it into my city!'

'It's just a sword, Valaric.' Gallow frowned but Valaric was still shaking his head, fists clenched.

'No. You know the tale of the Weeping God. You know how he became what he is but it comes from that sword. It's a pitiless thing. It serves no one, or perhaps everyone with an even-handed faithlessness. Blood follows that blade, Gallow. And now you've brought it here, and look around you.'

'The Vathen brought it here, Valaric, not me.'

Valaric seized Gallow by the shoulders. 'But *you* brought it into Andhun. Take it *away*! Ah. Modris preserve us! Forkbeards again!' He let go of Gallow and ran down the street towards the harbour. The Lhosir who'd gone into the Grey Man were coming out again. Gallow ran after Valaric for a few paces and then stopped and turned another way. He didn't believe in cursed swords just as he didn't believe in Modris and Diaran and the Weeping God and the rest of them. Stories, that's all they were. Some swords were better than others, no more. The skill of the smith and the quality of the metal he worked saw to that, but in the end they were all made from the Maker-Devourer's cauldron just like everything else.

But Valaric was right – there was a better place for this sword to be.

He turned his back on the docks where Valaric's men were waiting, and headed towards the keep on the top of the cliffs.

Medrin.

44

THE SCREAMBREAKER'S MEN

By the time Tolvis and the Screambreaker's men reached Andhun's gates, whatever had kicked off the fighting was done and over. Lhosir still trickled into the city, chasing with eager feet and hungry eyes after the scent of plunder and blood. A few of them loitered sulking around the gates, ordered to keep them open.

'And where are the Vathen?' Tolvis asked them but they only shrugged.

'Fled in the night,' they said. 'It's the Marroc against whom we hold the gates.' They weren't happy about it either, denied their share of plunder. Men who'd done something to earn Twelvefingers' disfavour. Tolvis passed on into the city. The cobbles were littered with bodies. Marroc mostly, from the looks of them, but there were Lhosir here too. A few of the bodies were soldiers, freshly dead in their mail, even with their swords and spears still lying beside them. Most of the Marroc wore simple clothes, the ordinary folk of the city in the wrong place at the wrong time. Many had been cut down from behind, stabbed in the back. Only a few had found the courage to die facing their fate.

He found the Marroc duke. When he turned over the bodies of the dead Lhosir to see their faces, he found Horsan. He laughed. *So much for you.*

Smoke wafted in wisps from the streets that led down towards the harbour. The Lhosir who came in after Tolvis and the Screambreaker's men headed that way. A few stopped among the dead, taking a spear if they didn't have one, or a sword or a helm. A couple were crouched down, stripping bodies of their mail. The stragglers weren't Medrin's men or anyone else's so Tolvis paid them no mind. They could head off down the hill towards the harbour – so much the better if they did – but *he* was aiming for the castle. Twelvefingers wasn't stupid. You couldn't come into Andhun and murder their duke and burn the place down without making sure you had the castle first, not if you were planning to stay. The plunder would be down in the harbour, but Medrin would be up there.

There were going to be some problems later, when it came to explaining to King Yurlak why he'd taken it on himself to hunt down the king's only son and stick his head on a spike. *The Screambreaker told me to* probably wasn't going to be good enough. Ah well. He could think of an excuse later.

Valaric ran through the streets to the first barricade. The Lhosir thought the Marroc were sheep and maybe they were; maybe they didn't have the madness in their blood that the men from over the sea called courage and bravery and honour. Didn't make them stupid, though.

'Valaric!' Sarvic was there keeping watch, ready for the forkbeards to sweep down the street.

'You heard then.' Valaric stopped in front of the barricade. Sarvic nodded. 'How many men have we got down here?'

'Hard to say. We had two hundred this morning before you left. When word came of what you did and how it went with the forkbeards ...' Sarvic shook his head. 'It's gone through the docks like fire. Most people are running for the sea. There's boats already leaving.'

Valaric winced. 'I'd hoped ...' But what had he hoped? That thousands of men and women who'd never raised a hand to another soul in their life would suddenly take up arms against an army of rampaging armoured monsters? Of course they were running for the boats.

'A few are staying. Hard to know how many.'

'You told them what they have to do?' Sarvic nodded. Valaric looked around. Enough men to hold the barricade for a few minutes. He looked at Sarvic long and hard, remembering Lostring Hill and the scared man he'd seen there. He nodded. 'Go to the harbour.' He pointed to three more of them, men he didn't know, but all soldiers in mail with shields and axes. 'Go to the boats. If there are men down there who think they can take everything a family has to let them onto a ship, show them your steel and explain to them why they're wrong. Give them a choice: They can keep their weapons and use them on the forkbeards or they can give them to someone else who will. I'll not have Marroc turning against Marroc.'

The other three turned and left without hesitation, glad to be let go and not to face the forkbeards. Sarvic didn't move.

'Well, go on then.'

'No.' Sarvic shook his head. 'I don't want to run.'

'Everyone who stays is going to die. Our lives buy time for the others, that's all.'

'I said I don't want to run.' When Sarvic's eyes didn't falter, Valaric clapped him on the shoulder.

'You want to kill forkbeards? Then come with me. Not long now.'

Tolvis looked over the litter of bodies in Castle Square. Marroc mostly. They'd put up some sort of fight in the end. Too little too late though, because there were hardly any Lhosir among the dead and the men at the castle gates had forked beards and waved at Tolvis as he came forward. Half a dozen of them. They looked tense, stamping their feet, eyes constantly roving. Tolvis grinned at them. He recognised this lot. Medrin's men, every one of them.

'A fine morning for sacking a city!' He waved back as he got up close. 'Wish you were down there, eh?'

The gate guards snorted. Who wouldn't really? Nothing to do up here. They'd had a great big fight yesterday and they'd won, but they'd all lost friends and half of them had lost family, some cousin or other at the very least, and what came after a big fight was a couple of days plundering to make up for it. And here they were, missing it. Tolvis nodded. He understood perfectly.

'The Maker-Devourer sends you some luck then.' He nodded back at the men he had behind him. Fifty or so Lhosir. The Screambreaker's men, what was left of them. Men who'd fought a dozen battles and lived through them all. 'We're here to relieve you. Go and have some fun. Kill some Marroc and get drunk.'

He had their attention now. He could see the thoughts running through their minds. *That would be nice, but Twelvefingers told us to guard the gate.* 'Prince Medrin ordered us to stay,' said the first man doubtfully.

Tolvis shrugged. 'Stay then. When the other guards on the inside come out to go off a-looting don't take it too personal if they laugh at you.'

The man shook his head. 'That won't happen. You can't go inside.'

Tolvis took his time over his next words. 'Thing is, you see, that *is* where we're going. Sure you don't want us to take over at the gate here? It was the Screambreaker himself said we should. *You've seen enough over the years. Let the young ones have their share of the plunder.* Or something a bit like that anyway.' Tolvis laughed. 'Me? I'm so old and bashed around the head, I can't remember *exactly* what he said. I probably couldn't remember how to plunder a Marroc city either. Best you lot get on and do it. Make a proper job of it.'

Medrin's men shuffled their feet. 'And you'd give us your word over the Maker-Devourer's cauldron that you'd all just stand here and not let anyone into the castle, eh? You included. You'd have to share blood with us about that.'

Tolvis shrugged. 'Not sure I could do *that*.'

The man let out a great sigh. 'Thought not.' He drew his sword and shook his head. 'Can't let you in, Loudmouth.'

Tolvis raised his shield and his spear. 'Ah well. Pity. I salute you. I'll speak you out to the Maker-Devourer myself when the time comes. Anything you want me to mention?'

'How about you just shut up and we get on with it?'

Tolvis took a deep breath. 'Fine, fine. I'm just trying to make it a bit easier for everyone.' He lunged with his spear, quick as a snake. The man caught the point on his shield and stepped back. In half a blink the six of them were in a circle, shields locked together. Tolvis left a dozen of the Screambreaker's Men to deal with them and moved on into the castle yard. Another handful of Medrin's men were lounging there, bored and not sure what to do with themselves. They found an answer to that quickly enough. After the gate guards, Tolvis didn't bother trying to talk his way past the rest.

They fought well. He'd give them that as he stepped over the bodies. They even managed to take a few of his men with them. Not many, but what did you expect when you put boys against men? Still, he'd speak out their names if he had the chance when all this was done. Brave men, all of them. Foolish, perhaps, but then the Maker-Devourer had never cared about *that*. Just as well really.

On a hill not far from the battlefield where the Scream-breaker had killed the Weeping Giant and set his fellow Vathen to flight, Gulsukh Ardshan watched from the back of his horse.

'Bashar,' he said without taking his eyes from the city.

'Ardshan?' Behind him, hidden by the bulk of the hill from the Lhosir who'd stayed outside Andhun's walls, two thousand Vathen were waiting for his order. A pitiful fraction of the army that had marched to sweep the Marroc aside, but here and now it would do.

'Now, Bashar.'

45

DARE TO DARE

Gallow ran up an alley, turned into a yard, found himself in a dead end and turned back. He tried to remember how Tolvis had led him to the castle from the river on the night they'd sold his Vathan horses, but they'd been deeper inside the city that night. There were the roads he used to follow when he'd been in Andhun before, but Lhosir in Andhun then had known better than to stray into dark and narrow alleys, especially after the Screambreaker crossed back over the sea. They'd walked in groups in the wider streets, always watchful and wary, and Gallow couldn't use these now.

He saw Lhosir here and there, groups of them, mostly running toward the sounds of fighting or screaming or the smell of burning. They too kept out of the alleys. The Marroc didn't, but they were all just desperate to get away. Whenever they saw Gallow coming, they fled.

But all he had to do was keep going uphill and so he did, keeping away from the main streets and the gangs of Medrin's Lhosir until he reached the Castle Square. The gates hung open. No one stood guard but there were bodies outside, a lot of them. Gallow picked his way through, casting his eyes around for anyone who was still alive. The bodies were Marroc at first. A few ordinary folk and a few dozen Marroc soldiers who'd made a stand and been over-whelmed with a handful of Lhosir around them. Inside in the castle yard there were plenty more dead, now all Lhosir. He found two locked together. One had his axe stuck through the other's collarbone, half into his neck, wedged fast. The second man's sword had been driven right through the first man's face, pinning him to the stones.

Fighting among themselves? He ran past them, across the castle yard and into the open doors of the keep.

The forkbeards came down the street at a slow run, shouting throat-cutting threats and battle whoops. Valaric watched from a window overlooking the barricade. They slowed as they reached it, forming a shield wall and levelling their spears as they advanced. He waited. The Marroc behind the barricade threw stones and pieces of wood and burning torches. The forkbeards batted them away, laughing. The Marroc were ordinary men from the harbour – fishermen and boatmen and oarsmen and sailors – not soldiers. They had no mail, few of them even had helms, and their weapons were boathooks and clubs and axes, whatever they'd been able to find. The barricade was a cart on its side and piles of crates. But they didn't run. Valaric felt a warmth course through him. Pride, that's what that was. *We don't have to be sheep. We don't.*

The forkbeards reached the barricade and started stabbing over the top of it with their spears, round the sides of it, anywhere there was a gap. At the edges they started to pull at the crates and boxes, tearing them down. Valaric's men shouted back, swinging their clubs and hooks, but the forkbeards were clearly going to pull the barricade down and sweep them away.

Or so they thought. Valaric lifted the first crossbow and cocked it. He looked at the handful of men around him and then through the window at the Marroc up on the other side of the street. He nodded, then leaned out and fired the crossbow down into the forkbeards. Picked his shot carefully, straight into the back of the neck of one at the front. He watched the man go down.

'Next.' He backed away from the window letting someone he didn't know, a fisherman, take the next shot. They
had five weapons, three windows, seven men. On the other
side of the street he had much the same. He left them to it,
ran down the stairs and into the alley round the back where
a dozen Marroc waited for him. These were soldiers, the few
that he had, and Sarvic was with them. He nodded grimly
and with a roar they ran out into the street, plunging into
the rear of the forkbeards, who were trapped by the barricade and just waking up to the death coming down on them
from above. From behind the barricade, bottles of burning
fish oil began to fly and suddenly the forkbeards were the
ones dying.

His spear sang in his hand. *Three years in the forests,
hunting you down. Picking you off one by one. Taking you as
I could. You trained me well, you bastards.*

Gulsukh Ardshan and his horsemen came over the hill, a
solid wall of horse and men and steel. The ground trembled
under the pounding of thousands of galloping hooves.
He felt a terrible elation as the Lhosir still outside the city
looked up and saw what was coming and snatched up their
shields and spears and formed into circles but the Vathen
didn't bother with them – they were too few to be any
trouble later. Instead, the Vathen swept through the Lhosir
camp like a storm. Spears struck men down, javelots arced
out from the riders, a steel rain that scythed down those
who stood to fight and those who turned and fled alike. The
camp was trampled into mud and ruin, the wounded and
the stricken crushed underhoof. In a blink the Lhosir were
scattered – as easy as that – and as they passed on towards
the gates of Andhun, Gulsukh was gritting his teeth. *Why
couldn't it have been that easy before?*

*

The open doors to Andhun keep beckoned Gallow inside. He ran up the steps and into the huge gloomy hall where the Screambreaker had once held his feasts. He paused for a moment there, uncertain which way to go. There were no dead men here – the fighting had been out in the yard. Whoever had come this way must have swept on inside. Somewhere.

He listened, hoping to hear sounds of a fight or cries of victory. *Medrin, where would you go? Where would you hide?*

A scream, long and thin, echoed down the far stairs. *Good enough.* Gallow ran through the hall, past the high table with its finery and its silver and leaped up the stairs behind it.

They killed perhaps half the Lhosir before the forkbeards pushed their way through the barricade. The Marroc behind it emptied the last of their oil over the wagon, set it alight and ran. The ones at the windows with their crossbows melted away. Valaric and Sarvic and the other soldiers turned and fled, not up the street but away into the maze of alleys. More forkbeards were coming down from the castle anyway. Time to go. Valaric made sure he was the last, backing down an alley too narrow for the forkbeards to get past him without killing him first. They howled and swore and yelled, but he kept his shield high and backed quickly away, and with his spear jabbing out they couldn't touch him. He stopped a few feet from the next street.

And now I have you trapped again. 'Burn, demon-beards!' he screamed, and shutters opened above and oil and fire rained on the forkbeards.

Tolvis found Medrin where he knew the prince would be. Hiding up in the rooms of the dead duke. He had a good few men with him too, a couple of dozen maybe. A few were faces Tolvis remembered from the monastery and old One-Eye's ship. They were waiting for him at the top of the spiralling stairs in the doorway, clustered around it so that he couldn't get through without killing them. Which was fine and fair enough – they couldn't get down the stairs and go anywhere else after all, not unless they fought their way through every man Tolvis had with him. Still he stopped. Gave them a chance, that was only fair.

'Fine men of the sea.' He held his ground carefully out of reach of a spear thrust. Maybe they had a bow of some sort and some arrows up here and maybe they didn't, but even men like these wouldn't stoop that low. 'May I offer you a parley?'

'Dog's piss on your parley, *nioingr*!' Ah. Durlak.

'Did I hear they're calling you Durlak Trueshaft now? Horsan was your brother, wasn't he? Fought well too, what I saw of him. Strong like an ox and he knew how to use a spear and a blade as well as any. So who laid him out? Wasn't me or any of mine but I'd like to know.'

'The Foxbeard.' When Tolvis cocked his head, Durlak added, 'Gallow.'

'Ah.' Tolvis smiled. So Gallow was still in Andhun, was he? That would make one of the many things the Screambreaker had asked of him a little easier.

'The *nioingr* turned on our prince as you've done. There's a blood feud between us now.'

'Really?' Tolvis raised an eyebrow. 'You might want to be careful with that if he killed Horsan. Still.' He opened his shield a fraction, exposing himself momentarily. A small gesture of peace perhaps, or one to invite a speculative thrust. 'If it's a feud you want, don't let me spoil it. I'm sure he's not far away. Go and fight him if you like. I'll not stop you. I've no grievance with any man here save one.' He frowned. 'No, actually, two. Which one of you was it struck Jyrdas in the back when we were fighting in that dingy little monastery?'

'Giedac. And Jyrdas killed him right there and then.'

'Did he? Good for One-Eye. Well that only leaves the coward who told him to do it then. So if you don't mind letting us pass, we'll deal with him as is right and proper and leave you to your looting. Must be plenty to be had from a place like this. If you were *permitted*, of course.'

A flash of greed crossed Durlak's face but his jaw tightened. 'No, Loudmouth. I already know you killed Latti. How you tried to kill Dvag.'

'Latti made his own choice. Was a fair fight that. Dvag played me false. *He* was a liar. Did I kill him? He was alive when I left him.'

'The Vathen found him. And then Horsan and I found the Vathen. And you'll not pass this door, Loudmouth.'

There didn't seem to be much to be said after that. Tolvis rolled his eyes. 'Bloody forkbeards eh?' he said. 'All the same. Never know when to give up.'

For a moment Durlak grinned. 'Secret of who we are, Loudmouth.'

Tolvis nodded. He eased up the last few steps and the two of them set about killing each another.

46

DARK ENTREATIES

Gallow ran up the stairs and stopped halfway. A Lhosir faced him, ugly and angry, shield close and spear held out. He kept his distance though, unsure of whom he faced. 'Who goes there?'

Valaric sprinted down the next street, on towards the harbour. Three forkbeards from the alley were chasing him. They were actually on fire but they were still coming. *Modris!* Were they simply too stupid? He rounded a corner and there was the next barricade waiting for them. And Sarvic.

'Get down, get down!' Grumpy Jonnic too. Valaric threw himself to the cobbles, skittering across them, his mail throwing up a shower of sparks. From behind the barricade a dozen men rose and fired a ragged volley of crossbow bolts. The men he'd had beside him overlooking the first barricade. Two of the three burning forkbeards fell and stayed still. The third jerked but stayed on his feet, even with two bolts sticking out of him. Valaric jumped up and stuck him with his spear.

'You people *really* don't know when to stop!' he screamed. He looked back up the street. More forkbeards were coming, dozens of them. Further up the Isset smoke rose over the water and drifted down towards the sea. They were burning things again. He jumped over the barricade and readied his spear for the next fight. Marroc ran screaming through the streets behind him, heading for the sea. A few picked up sticks or knives and joined the barricade. Valaric watched them from the corner of his eye as the forkbeards stormed towards them. Saw their courage fade to fear and watched them melt away. A handful stayed. He admired them, and he pitied them too. They weren't soldiers and the forkbeards would slaughter them. He shouted at them, waving them away.

'Go! Go to the ships. Help others get away from here. Live!' They stared at him, holding their ground. He took a step forward, waving his shield. 'Go, you stupid Marroc!' This was the last barricade before the docks. There weren't any more. He'd stand and fight here until there weren't any forkbeards left or until they killed him. Or until they found some other way round through the alleys and came at him from behind.

The Marroc, with their leather aprons and padded jackets for armour, with their clubs and knives for weapons, simply stared back at him. A few shook their heads. Stupid fools were going to die.

'Valaric!' Jonnic. The forkbeards howled and whooped as they ran down the street towards the barricade, spears high, shields tight. Valaric bared his teeth. There were no bowmen waiting to shoot down from above this time, no men waiting to stab them from behind. He'd make his stand here with whatever men were left who would fight beside him. Behind their barricade they'd hold this street as long as they could. And that was that.

'Crossbows!' The Marroc with crossbows rose again from behind the barricade and let loose. Most of the bolts hit the forkbeards' shields but a couple went down, and then the forkbeards were on the barricade, howling and swinging their axes. Valaric snarled something even he didn't understand and met them shield to shield, blade to blade, whispering prayers to Modris and Diaran as he did that the fight would be long and hard and he'd at least take a few of the enemy with him before he fell.

Tolvis was breathing heavily and bleeding from where one of Durlak's lunges had ripped open his face before Tolvis's sword had skewered him. A flap of skin hung off his cheek. The hole went right through; he could touch his tongue with his finger. If he'd had any looks before, they were gone now. The whole side of his head felt as if it was on fire.

He stepped over Durlak's body and the handful of Medrin's men who'd stayed to hold the doorway. In the small space of the spiral stairs and the tiny room beyond, spears and axes had no space to move. It came down to thrusting swords. They didn't like that. Tolvis didn't like it either and he was glad when Medrin's last few guards retreated into the space of the old duke's chamber. He stopped for a moment, turned back and rolled Durlak over. The dead man's eyes were still open. Sign of a good spirit. Tolvis dragged him away. 'I want to speak this one out,' he said to the Lhosir coming up from the stairs. 'They fought well. Brave. I owe it to him. Go and find Medrin.'

The Screambreaker's men nodded grimly. Most of them had blood on their swords and on their mail now. Lhosir blood. Medrin might rail at them for killing their own kin, but these were men who remembered how it was when Yurlak had first taken the throne, before the Screambreaker and the Marroc and crossing the sea. *How we used to fight and feud among ourselves. Like it was. The old way.* Maybe they'd wait or maybe they'd just kill Medrin without him. Most of them had known the Screambreaker better than he had. Some of them had been in the wood with him but there were some too who had fought beside the Screambreaker against the Vathen and watched him fall. Men who hadn't died while Twelvefingers had stayed on the top of his hill, watching and doing nothing – they had a grudge of their own to feed. Maybe they had spirited the Screambreaker's body away. It felt right that someone had done that. A dozen men had seen him fall and no one ever said he wasn't dead, but this way it was the Maker-Devourer himself who'd come away from his cauldron for the old Nightmare of the North. Made for a good story. A legend, even.

When he had Durlak in a corner out of the way, he crouched beside the dead man. 'Durlak. Don't know his father, don't know his family, don't have their roll of deeds to lay out beside him. I don't know what else he did in his life, fair or foul, but I was the one who fought him and I was the one who killed him, and I'll say to any who'll listen that he faced me without fear, that he fought fiercely and that he died bravely. Maker-Devourer, I offer you this man for your cauldron for he will enrich it with his spirit.' He screwed up his eyes, growling at the pain from his cheek.

'Tolvis?'

He looked up. A last pair of soldiers had come up the stairs. Stragglers from the fighting outside in the yard or at the gates perhaps. For a moment his eyes wouldn't focus in the gloom. He recognised the voice, though.

'Gallow?'

Gallow looked down at Tolvis crouching over a dead Lhosir wearing a bracer that marked him as one of Medrin's men. Loudmouth had blood all down the side of his face and over his neck and shoulder. 'You look a mess.'

Tolvis snorted then winced in pain. He stood. 'Nothing that won't heal, Truesword.'

'What are you doing?'

'And it's good to see you too. And how was the battle for you and so on and so on? Finishing Medrin, that's what.'

'Where is he?'

Tolvis nodded towards the door that led to the duke's

chamber. 'Hear all that ruckus? Take a guess. He's got no-where left to run.'

Gallow frowned, struggling to understand the mangled words that came out of Tolvis's mouth. 'I'd see someone about that mess of a face,' he said and turned towards the sounds of fighting.

'Nothing like a good scar to add to my fine looks, eh?'

Tolvis stayed where he was. Gallow couldn't make himself look any more. Wound like that didn't kill you straight away, but more often than not it went bad and green and oozed pus and rotted and then there was nothing to do but cut out whatever had gone bad. Not much to be done when it was a man's face. *Maker-Devourer spare him that. Let it heal clean or give him a good death first.*

The old Marroc duke's room wasn't anything more than a big open space with a bed and a few hangings, a place for dressing, a hole in the corner for shitting and pissing, a table by the window with a quill and ink, a chest and a few piles of furs on the floor. Medrin and the last of his Lhosir were backed into a corner. Three of them and the prince himself, though they were far from finished. Medrin still had the Crimson Shield strapped to his arm, a short stabbing blade held high and ready over the top of it. A dozen or more Lhosir penned him in, holding him at bay. They shouted at him while Medrin and his three bared their teeth and hurled back taunts and insults, challenging the Screambreaker's men to come forward and finish what they'd started.

'Turn on your king? You're outcasts already! *Nioingr,* all of you.'

'Yield, traitor!'

'You'll be hunted to the end of the world. Kill me and my father will do it. Let me live and I'll hunt you myself!'

'You betrayed the Screambreaker!'

'He fell in battle! He got what he wanted!'

Gallow pushed past them. As he did, he drew Solace from

its sheath. 'Yield, Medrin. End this. Go back across the sea and stay there. Say what you like about what happened here, just don't come back.'

'Never, Foxbeard!'

'Then go back in pieces.' Gallow shrugged. 'It's all the same to me.'

He closed on the prince and Medrin backed away behind his men. Gallow smiled. 'See. In the end you always were a coward.'

'*Nioingr!*' With sudden fury, Medrin leaped forward again, slamming the Crimson Shield into Gallow and lunging with his blade. The shock staggered Gallow, knocking him back as though the shield had a strength of its own beyond Medrin's arm. The prince's blade eased past his guard and skimmed off his mail. 'Die!' Twelvefingers lunged again, high this time at Gallow's collar, their shields still pressed together. Gallow barely dodged aside while Medrin kept pushing forward. 'You always had poison in your blood for me, you sheep-loving clean-skin no-beard! Now I'll let that poison out!'

With their shields locked together Medrin's short thrusting blade had the advantage over the long edge of the red sword. Gallow raised Solace over his head and brought it down but Medrin parried the blow with his own steel, keeping so close that Gallow could smell his breath. 'Yes,' said Gallow, 'I have.' With a mighty heave he threw Medrin back and for a moment they stood apart, circling each other. 'You led us to the Temple of Fates, Medrin, and you left us to the Fateguard.'

'And were you any better?' snarled Medrin. 'You let Beyard die!'

'*You* let us both die, you snivelling shit! "Hold them! I cannot be found here!" Do you remember those words as you ran? And we did hold them, Beyard and I, and at the last he threw himself into them and screamed at me to run too and there was nothing else I could do! But I held your words in my heart and I've carried them with me for fourteen years, and you haven't changed at all.'

'*Nioingr!*' Medrin charged again. Gallow brought the red sword down. Medrin caught it on the Crimson Shield, and a shock ran through Gallow as though he'd been stung by a spark from his father's forge. His arm fell limp and the red sword hung from his fingers. For a moment his grip on his shield loosened.

Medrin's blade lunged past, catching him on the shoulder, digging into the mail with enough force to split open its links. Gallow felt its point bite into him, scraping against bone. He jerked away, stumbling back. The pain was staggering. Medrin bared his teeth and came at him again, slamming the Crimson Shield into him and lunging at Gallow's face this time. Gallow could barely hold his sword. His shield arm felt as weak as a child's. He jumped back as Medrin's edge sliced past his nose.

'You wanted to fight me, clean-skin? You always did. So fight me!' Gallow tried to grip Solace but his fingers were still numb. It was all he could do not to drop the sword. Medrin slammed into him again and again, a lunge each time, pushing him back and back while Gallow's shield arm grew weaker with every blow.

They parted for a moment. Medrin wore a vicious smile. 'Now you know better than to strike this shield, but I'll take that Vathan sword too. Yield, clean-skin. Yield and give me the Edge of Sorrows and I'll put it to fine use. Beyard was your friend? He was mine too and I've not forgotten his fate. Give me that sword and I'll have revenge for both of us.' He took another step back. 'We'll do it together. I'll even spare the rest of these men. They'll be outcasts but I'll let them run a few days before I hang them as ravens over their own houses. Yield, clean-skin!'

Gallow shook his head. He let go of his shield and let it

slip off his arm and crash to the floor. 'No.' When he tried to lift the red sword, his arm twitched and refused.

Medrin shrugged. 'Look at you. Raise your blade at least before I finish you!'

'Take me if you can, demon-prince.'

'So be it. And then the rest of you will follow, and then I will take that sword you carry and settle what we started all those years ago.' He launched himself again, as he had before, each time always the same, the shield to batter his enemy down and the stabbing lunge over the top. Gallow pulled the red sword out of his one hand and into the other, threw himself sideways and swung as Medrin passed. The prince screamed. Something clattered on the floor. When Gallow staggered back to look at what he'd done, Medrin was hugging his arm to his side. Blood ran down his mail. His sword lay on the floor and the hand that had held it still gripped its hilt.

'No! No!' he screamed at Gallow. '*No!* What have you done to me?'

Gallow turned to face him. He held the Sword of the Weeping God out straight before him. 'The sword against the shield, Medrin? Or do you yield?'

'Kill him,' shouted Loudmouth from behind the rest of his men. 'Finish him properly. Let him end well at least.'

Medrin lowered the Crimson Shield. His face was filled with murder and hate. 'Yes, Foxbeard. Give me that at least. Let me die as a Lhosir should die. It's what your precious Screambreaker would have done.' He had his own blood all over him. He was already pale.

Gallow nodded. He lowered Solace. 'He would. But I'm wondering, Prince Sixfingers, what *you* would have done.'

47

JUSTICE FOR ALL

The Vathen reached Andhun and attacked. The Lhosir saw them coming and tried to close the gates but they were too late and Gulsukh and his horsemen were too quick. A hundred were inside before the Lhosir could form a wall of shields. It hung in the balance for a minute but that was all, and then Gulsukh and his riders broke the Lhosir. He called his bashars to him as they came through the gates and gave them their orders. Two hundred to stay here, to hold the gates and tear them down so they couldn't be closed again. Another hundred to ride back out after the Vathan clans retreating across the countryside, to tell them they didn't need the Weeping Giant and his god-touched sword, that Gulsukh had broken the Lhosir without either and that Andhun lay helpless and waiting for them. Others he sent down towards the Isset to take the bridge and hold it against any who would try to destroy it, and to the docks and to the harbour to find the Lhosir soldiers and the Marroc and kill them, but above all to stop them from leaving in their ships.

Some he took himself, up the hill from the gate towards the castle, where surely whoever commanded this city would be waiting for him.

Valaric's spear point rammed into a Lhosir collarbone and stuck tight. The forkbeard snatched at it and roared, pulling it with such force that Valaric had to let go or be pulled off the barricade. He switched to his axe until that stuck in a shield and was wrenched out of his hand. He drew his sword and fought on, kept hitting them but achieving nothing much, while all around him the Marroc were dying. *Damn them – why did they all wear armour? Where did they get such mail, so many swords?* But he knew the answer to that. They'd taken it from all the Marroc they'd killed for the last fifteen years. Iron and steel were cheap to the forkbeards, they had so much.

A Marroc fell at the far end of the barricade, blood gushing from an arm severed at the elbow. A forkbeard pulled himself up before anyone could take the dead man's place. Valaric swore and shouted and then realised there wasn't anyone left. The forkbeard swung his axe and caved in the skull of another Marroc and then jumped down, howling and chopping left and right. Valaric swung down behind him and stabbed him in the back of the head. He tried to climb back up before another forkbeard could get over the barricade but his legs failed him. There was no strength there any more. His arms could barely hold his sword and shield. He gritted his teeth and hauled himself back up anyway. Most of the Marroc he'd led here were dead. Sarvic was still up, Jonnic too. And the rest ... the rest were ordinary men who just didn't want to see their homes go up in flames.

'Enough!' he shouted. He looked at Sarvic and Jonnic. *We're the ones with mail. We hold them long enough for the others to get away.* He simply didn't have the energy to say that but he didn't need to. A look was enough.

Jonnic nodded. Sarvic looked at him too but his was a different look. His was *Look, Valaric, look!*

Behind the forkbeards at the end of the street, men on horseback were coming. Soldiers. A mass of them. Valaric had no idea who they were but they didn't look like forkbeards and they weren't dismounting as Marroc soldiers would. The forkbeards had noticed too and had started to turn.

Vathen!

The Vathen drew back their arms. Javelots rained on Lhosir and Marroc alike.

'What would you have done?' Gallow said again.

'Put an end to it,' slurred Tolvis. He sounded as though he was talking with his mouth stuffed full of food.

'No.' As Medrin slumped against a wall and the Crimson Shield fell from his other arm, Gallow stood over him. He closed his eyes for a moment at another wave of pain from his shoulder. The feeling in his sword arm was coming back and it was like being stabbed by a thousand needles. He sat Medrin up, lifted his arm, wrapped a belt around his severed wrist and squeezed it tighter and tighter until the bleeding stopped. 'Pitch?' he asked. 'Is there any?'

The last three of Medrin's men looked uneasily from one to the other. The others shook their heads.

'Fire? Torches?'

The prince was breathing too quickly. He was pale as death now, his eyes barely open. Tolvis stood watching. 'First you try to kill him, now you're trying to save him. Why, Truesword? So you can hang him beside the gates for the Marroc to see, the way he used to do to them? I'll not have that. I might turn my back if anyone speaks him out but I'll not have a prince of the sea strung up like that. Yurlak's son? No. Put an axe in his hand and kill him properly.' Behind him Medrin's men were surrendering their swords.

Gallow stood. 'It's not for me to decide, nor for you either. I mean to give him to the Marroc. Let them choose what to do with him.'

Tolvis shook his head. He tried to smile but the ruined side of his face was too swollen. 'Truesword, you know perfectly well what the Marroc will do. Hanging him won't be enough. They'll rip him to pieces and feed his parts to their dogs, and when word of that comes back across the sea to Yurlak, he'll shout for every man who can so much as hold a stick. He'll rouse them out of their homes and into a ship within a week. They'll sweep across this land in a tide of blood and slaughter that'll make the Screambreaker's campaigns look like a wedding feast. It won't be conquest and plunder this time. He'll be coming to wipe away the stain of the Marroc who'd killed his son. Is that what you want?'

Gallow shrugged. 'We stand on Marroc stone. They should be the ones to choose.'

Loudmouth turned away. A Lhosir came with a torch. 'Put his sword in his lap, Gallow. Finish it here. He died in battle after his first great victory against the Vathen. Give that to Yurlak. The Maker-Devourer will know the truth. Let that be enough.'

Gallow ignored his words but took the torch and held the blade of the red sword in the flame. Fire from burning wood should never have been enough to make a piece of iron even start to change its colour, but the sword seemed to glow with an an inner light in the flames.

'You might kill him doing that,' said Tolvis.

'I might. Hold him down and put some leather in his mouth.'

The Lhosir held Medrin down. Gallow gripped the prince's arm between his knees and pressed the hot steel into the wound. Blood sizzled and flesh cooked. Medrin's eyes flew wide open, his back arched. He screamed and bucked but the Lhosir held him fast, and after a moment he fell still again. His eyes rolled back into his head. Gallow took the sword away and loosened the belt around Medrin's arm. The bleeding had stopped.

'Is he alive?'

Gallow pressed his ear against Medrin's chest. 'His heart is faint but it still beats.'

'You'll not give him to the Marroc, Gallow,' said Tolvis.

'Do I have to fight you too?'

'No.' Tolvis pulled his axe from his belt – Gallow's axe

– and handed it back, haft first. 'Not if you just let it go. Best you have this back, I think.'

Gallow took the axe. He looked at the Lhosir around him, a dozen and then some. They were with Tolvis, all of them, and he couldn't fight that many even if he hadn't been stabbed in the shoulder. And he didn't want to.

'Do what you want.' He turned his back on them and walked away.

'Run! Run for the ships!' Valaric waved the rest of the Marroc away from the barricade. 'You too, Sarvic.' He stood and jabbed his sword at the forkbeards climbing the barricade. 'No reason to stay now. Let them fight among themselves. Leave them to it.'

Still alive. Well that's a surprise. He ran down the street, left into an alley and across to the Riverway. People streamed past him, running, screaming, heading helter-skelter for the docks. He looked up the river towards the bridge. There had been another barricade there but it was smashed now, bodies littered around it. His eyes hunted for forkbeards to kill, but he didn't see any.

Why are you all screaming?

A Vathan jumped his horse over the disintegrating barricade and hurled a javelot into the back of a fleeing Marroc. A dozen more followed him.

Oh. That's why. Modris! He gripped his shield and stepped out into the street.

Gulsukh Ardshan slowed as he reached the square outside the castle. *No one to greet us?* Just a lot of bodies and open gates with no one guarding them. He urged his horsemen on, riding with them, seizing this second set of gates before anyone could close them. There were more bodies in the yard beyond. And in the middle of it two handfuls of forkbeards, standing and staring at him as though he was the

Weeping Giant himself risen back from the dead.

One carried the Crimson Shield of the Marroc. Another had the red sword, Solace.

Mine!

He pointed his spear at them and screamed.

48

HOLDING THE DOORS

Valaric took the first Vathan rider down, rising out of the crowd of fleeing Marroc with his sword and sticking it straight through the rider's leather jerkin and between the ribs underneath. The rider tipped back. First thing Valaric did was grab his spear. Against a man on a horse a spear did a lot better than a sword.

He snatched it in time to turn it round and skewer the next Vathan. The spear flew up out of his hands, gone as quickly as it had come. The next rider slashed with a sword. Valaric leaped out of the way then turned the tip of a spear with his shield. The riders were simply hacking at him as they passed, moving straight on through the screaming Marroc beyond. There were more and more of them, a trickle turning to a flood. And here he was, standing around waiting to be trampled. Useless. He darted into an alley. At least the horsemen wouldn't trouble him there – wouldn't even fit.

'Why are there so many of them by the river?' he hissed into the air.

'The bridge, Marroc,' said the shadows behind him. Valaric almost jumped out of his mail. He spun round, lunging with his sword, and the steel skittered off a shield. He'd had a forkbeard standing right there, still and quiet in the shadows of a doorway, and he hadn't even seen him.

'We can fight if you want, Marroc,' said the forkbeard.

'Do I know you?' Valaric peered. Behind their helms it

was hard to tell one forkbeard from another. This one's beard was grey. He looked a bit like the Widowmaker, except Gallow had said the Widowmaker was dead.

'Not that I know, Marroc. So is it to be fighting or not?'

'Five fingers of the sun ago I'd have said yes.'

'I know you would. So would I. But the Vathen have the day now. Andhun will be theirs by sunset.'

The forkbeard had no sword. Slowly Valaric put his own back in his belt. 'Who are you?'

'The bridge, Marroc. Take down the bridge and the Vathen can't cross the Isset. Nowhere else for a hundred miles and then you're at the Crackmarsh. I'm told they could cross the Crackmarsh if someone showed them the way, but then again a clever man might make a whole army vanish in that swamp. Take down that bridge and by the time the Vathen have built it again, Yurlak himself will be here with the whole horde of the sea.'

Or I'll have time to raise an army of Marroc to fight both of you. Valaric looked the forkbeard up and down. 'And how would you take down the bridge, old man?'

The forkbeard laughed. 'Was always a chance it would come to this.'

'I can't trust you.' Valaric shook his head.

'And I can't trust *you*, Marroc.' The forkbeard pulled a knife from his belt and made a shallow cut on the flesh of his forearm. 'May the Maker-Devourer spit me into the Marches if I raise a hand against you while that bridge still stands. And take a look, Marroc. I have no sword. No spear. No axe.'

Valaric looked him over. He was old and battered. His mail was ripped in places and there was dried blood all over it. Some of it, he was sure, was the forkbeard's own.

'Well?' The forkbeard offered Valaric his knife.

'While that bridge still stands.' Valaric took the knife and cut himself. They clasped arms, blood to blood, and it felt the strangest thing in the world to Valaric in the burning ruin of a town that this forkbeard's kinsmen had set out to destroy.

Tolvis gave Medrin to the three Lhosir who'd stood with their prince. Let him be carried by his own soldiers. Gallow picked up one of their shields. He looked at it and his lip curled. Medrin's men. The Legion of the Crimson Shield. They'd had them painted so they all looked the same, like Medrin's god-borne shield itself.

'And what are *you* going to do with him?' he asked Tolvis, since Loudmouth hadn't yet stuck a sword in Medrin's hand and then finished him as he'd said.

'Wait for him to wake up, if he does. If he doesn't I'll build him a pyre and one of these three can speak him out and Yurlak can at least know that his son died well enough, even if he didn't live as he should.'

'And if he lives?'

Tolvis shrugged. 'Go home, Gallow. Go back to that Marroc woman of yours.' They trailed down the spiral stairs and into the Marroc duke's hall. Gallow's fingers felt for the locket under his mail. *Go home.* He could do that now. He'd only stayed to try and save the Marroc of Andhun from Medrin, and he'd largely failed at that.

'What *are* you going to do with Medrin?'

Tolvis shrugged. He opened the doors to the castle yard and strode out towards the open gates. 'I don't know, Truesword, I simply don't. Lost at sea, perhaps. We'll have to talk, all of us.' In the middle of the yard he stopped and turned. 'Truesword, before you and I part, the Scream-breaker gave—'

A column of riders trotted through the castle gates. Vathen. Dozens of them. They paused, as surprised as the Lhosir, and then one of them lowered his spear and pointed it straight at Gallow and howled.

'Feyrk's balls! Back to the keep!' Tolvis bolted back the way they'd come and the other Lhosir scrambled after him. Didn't matter how fierce a man was; caught in the open and surrounded by horsemen he died and died quickly. The last of the Lhosir fell across the threshold with a javelot in his back.

'Go!' shouted Tolvis. 'Take the cave path. I'll hold the door.'

'No, you won't.' Gallow helped him close it and then shoved his shoulder against it. 'You go. *I'll* hold them.'

Tolvis snorted. 'You can hardly hold your own shield.' They pressed themselves against the door.

'Half your face is missing.'

'Don't need a face to fight!'

The door jerked ajar as the Vathen threw themselves against it. Gallow shoved back, forcing it closed. 'You'd think there'd be a bar or something.'

The door shuddered again. Tolvis hissed. 'Well then, Truesword, shall we stand and face them like men?'

Gallow tossed him his axe – the one he'd given to Tolvis on the road away from Andhun and Tolvis had just returned. 'You'll be needing this.'

The door shuddered again. 'Is that it?' Tolvis yelled. 'My dead grandmother could push harder.'

Gallow blinked. Looked at him hard. Even with both of them putting their whole weight against it, the Vathen were coming through the door at any moment. 'One stays, one runs.' Gallow gritted his teeth. 'They're your men. You go.' When Tolvis didn't move, Gallow laughed. 'If you like, Loudmouth, I'll fight you for it. Besides, it's my turn.'

'What?' Loudmouth stared at him as though he was mad but he must have seen the certainty in Gallow's face, the simple resolve not to move.

'In the Temple of Fates. We had the ironskins on us, on the other side of a door just like this. One of us could run but not both. Almost came to blows about who got to hold them. That time it was Beyard. This time it's me. Now take the bloody axe and run before I hit you with it!'

As the door shook again Tolvis turned and looked at Gallow one last time. 'A hundred men will speak you out, Truesword,' he cried, and was gone.

No, Gallow thought, *they probably won't*. For a moment as he held fast, he touched a finger to the amulet around his neck. 'Sorry, but that's a debt I carried before you ever knew me.'

Tolvis sprinted after his men and caught them down in the kitchens, wrestling their way into the pantries, hurling kegs and crates out of the way. He tipped a huge barrel of pickles on its side, spilling salted water all over the floor. The trapdoor was still there, same door as had been there years ago when the Screambreaker had made this castle his and they'd all been waiting for Yurlak to die. He pulled it open.

'Come on then!' He sent two of his own men first and then the three of Medrin's, still carrying their prince. With a bit of luck they'd get to the bottom and find Twelvefingers was dead. Would save a lot of trouble.

'You two!' He picked men with good legs. 'You stay up here. You hold the path for Truesword if he gets this far! You understand?'

The door flew open. Gallow bolted across the hall as the first Vathen tumbled in behind him, stumbling over one another. Voices sang in his head, calling him, telling him to turn and face them and cut them down, as many as he could. Telling him to die in the middle of a mound of Vathan corpses as the Screambreaker had done, to be sent on his way to the Maker-Devourer covered in the blood of his enemies, cup filled with glory. But there were other voices now, ones that hadn't been born in those long years of war at the Screambreaker's side. Arda. His sons and his daughter calling him to come home. And so he raced after Loudmouth and his Lhosir, across the hall and down the stairs behind it which would take him to the kitchens and the secret pathway through the caves and the tunnels to the beach. To run across the stones and the debris fallen from the cliffs and to the harbour and to the Marroc and Valaric and be rid of the red sword. Give it to some Marroc hero and jump into a boat and sail away up the coast and finally go home.

The stairs spat him out into a hall lined with doors, with an iron gate at the end through which streamed light. Sunlight. He'd gone the wrong way.

Back in the day he'd been in this castle long enough not to make that sort of stupid mistake, and so he wondered how he could have been so cursed until he realised that the old Lhosir songs were still singing in his head while those of the Marroc he'd come to love had fallen quiet. And for some daft reason he could hear the Screambreaker talking to him too: *So, Truesword. Does that answer your question? Do you know who you are now?*

Tolvis ran as best he could through the tunnels and passages to the shore, hustling Medrin's men as fast as they could go. The tide was high, waves breaking into the throat of the caves, and the beach path was drowned so they'd have to make their way over the rocks with the sea crashing around their knees, but it was that or stay and fight the Vathen, and the Vathen were far too many for that. Find a way back to the rest of the army, that was the thing.

'Go!' Tolvis shouted. 'Go ahead!'

He waited for a few minutes but Truesword didn't come and neither did the two men he'd left. He waited longer than he should have. By then he knew they wouldn't be coming.

*

The gate opened onto the cliffs. Gallow knew this piece of the castle. A narrow strip of grass between the keep and the sea where the Marroc dukes once flew their sea eagles for sport. There was just the one gate, some walls, a strip of land a dozen yards wide and then the cliffs and the sea. He ran to the edge and looked down. Fifty feet below him the waves crashed against the bottom of the cliff.

A strong man, skilled and daring, might have climbed it, and he was all of those things and yet he paused.

Boats were flooding out of the harbour, big and small: Marroc fleeing the Lhosir and now the Vathen. There was a small one at the bottom of the cliff almost beneath him, barely past the breaking surf. Behind him the Vathen poured out into the sunlight. They fanned out around him, suddenly cautious. Gallow looked from them to the sea. And then he looked back again.

Gulsukh held up his hand, commanding his men to stop. One Lhosir. Wounded by the way he held his shield, but he had Solace the Comforter in his hand, and he'd turned to face them all. Gulsukh stepped forward. He took a deep breath and bowed his head. This beardless Lhosir would give him the sword in front of all his men. *Give* it, not have it taken, and then they'd all see that Gulsukh was the heir to the Weeping Giant and everything would change. They could go back to their homes or they could continue their conquest, one or the other, but it would be his to decide and even the priests of the Weeping God would have to bow to that.

He paused a little longer, letting the Lhosir see how hopeless his situation was. Gulsukh kept his head bowed. The Lhosir seemed to understand: he took off his helm and placed it on the grass by his feet. Then he sheathed the sword.

'I honour your courage,' said the ardshan as quietly as

the rush of the wind and the hiss of the waves below would allow. 'Your skill. Few men could do what you have done.'

'Why?' The ardshan's eyes twitched as the Lhosir unbuckled his belt but held on to the Comforter, still in its scabbard. 'Why? What have I done?'

'You're the warrior who killed the Weeping Giant.' Gulsukh frowned at the expression on the man's face. 'Are you not?'

'No. That man was the Screambreaker.' The Lhosir shook off his gauntlets. 'He fell beside me. I'm just a man who took up his sword.'

The ardshan raised his head and looked this *just-a-man* in the eye. He felt a quiver in his heart as the Lhosir met his gaze.

49

THE SEA

The old forkbeard knew his way around the city, no doubt about that. Knew it better than Valaric did, as though it was his home. He led Valaric through the maze of alleys down by the river to a place where a boat lay tied to a post and together they rowed across. There were Vathen already on the other bank but they weren't rampaging through the streets, not yet.

'Keeping the bridge,' said the forkbeard. He rowed them to the massive tree-trunk piles that rose from the base of the cliff on the western bank of the Isset and supported that end of the bridge, monstrous pines from far away in the Varyxhun valley, floated down the river. No one lived down at the foot of these cliffs. There were no houses, no roads, no paths. Just sheer rock.

'What's your plan, old man? Cut it down with an axe?'

'Something like that.'

'But I don't have an axe and nor do you.'

The old forkbeard drew the boat up against the cliff and tied it fast to an outcrop of stone. He hauled himself onto a narrow ledge and sat down beside one of the great trunks. The air stank of fish. The forkbeard produced an axe from among the stones and tossed it to Valaric. 'Now you do, Marroc.'

Valaric stared at him. He was hurt. You could see that. The way he moved gave him away. Either that or he was even older than he looked. Every movement was pain to him. And yet ... 'Who are you?'

'Care to cast your eyes upward, Marroc?' asked the old man. Now he had a flint and tinder. Underneath the western edge of the bridge a dozen kegs had been tied to the piles. Slick wet stains spread over the wood beneath them, all the way down to the sea. Fish oil. 'Never could make a keg that sealed properly in this town, you lot.' The old forkbeard shook his head, idly striking the flint until the tinder caught and he had a small smouldering pile of grass. Next thing he pulled out from behind the piles was a small stick wrapped in cloth. The stick stank of fish too. He offered it to Valaric. 'Yours if you want it.'

'What?'

'Seems to me it should be a Marroc who sets the bridge ablaze.' He tossed the stick to Valaric, who caught it without thinking. 'Come on, quick now, before this goes out.'

Valaric scrambled out of the boat. He shuffled past the old man to sit on the ledge. The forkbeard carefully lit the torch.

'Set it as you like. I'd watch out for bits of blazing wood and oil falling on your head though, so don't stay to admire your handiwork too long.'

The old forkbeard jumped into the boat. The next thing Valaric knew he'd cast off and was drifting away on the current and Valaric was stuck there on the ledge alone. He looked up. Yes, a man could climb the cliff easily enough. Maybe not if it was on fire though. 'Hey! What are you doing?'

'I have somewhere else to be. You can swim can't you, Valaric of Witterslet? Don't wait too long before you use that. It won't burn for ever.'

'Who are you? What's your name?'

The old forkbeard waved. 'Don't think I want any of those any more. Take care of your city, Marroc. Look after it. What we've left of it.'

Valaric watched him go then yelped and almost dropped

the torch as it burned his fingers. He touched the torch to the stream of oil dripping down from above. It lit very nicely, as if it had been mixed with something else. He stayed for bit and watched the flame climb steadily towards the leaking kegs under the upper beams of the bridge. As it reached the top, the fire began to burn more brightly.

It occurred to him then that maybe he *should* start swimming.

The Vathan with the crested helm held out his hand. 'The sword, Lhosir. The Sword of the Weeping God. Give it to me. No need for more to die. Give it to me and go in peace. This battle is lost to you.'

Gallow levelled the sword at the Vathan. 'Come and take it.'

The Vathan took a pace towards him. For one long moment Gallow thought he might even do it, that he might just hand this cursed sword over if the Vathan had the courage to lower his weapons and come close enough to simply take it from his hand. Maybe that was the sign of someone who'd earned it. What had *he* done, after all? Taken it from a dead man.

The Vathan took his step but then stopped. 'I am the ardshan of my people. Give me the sword!'

'Not if you can't take it. If you can't take it then you haven't earned it.'

The ardshan turned his back. 'Kill him. But do *not* touch the sword.'

The other Vathen hesitated. Gallow had seen it enough times before. The mustering of courage to charge enemy shields, knowing that some of you must die but that if you don't then death would come for all. The red sword held them at bay but they'd find their courage in a moment.

'*Arda!*'

He turned and flung the sword over the cliff, as far out

to sea as he could. The ardshan watched the Sword of the Weeping God arc out into the sky, eyes wide in horror. Before he could speak, Gallow was already running along the edge of the cliff – one step, two, three – and then the Vathen launched themselves towards him. Before they could reach him, he turned and leaped as mightily as he could, following the sword out over the cliffs and past the breaking waves to the sea.

'Arda!' Tolvis heard the shout above the crash of the waves. From the top of the cliff men were suddenly peering down at him. Vathen, and the way they looked and pointed was quite enough. By the time they were firing their arrows and throwing their javelots he was already running.

'This way. There's a ship.' Medrin's ship. The one he'd used to sail out of Andhun, assuming it hadn't been washed away or found and burned, or taken already by some other band of fleeing Lhosir. But a couple of miles of running along beaches and climbing cliffs and racing through woods and climbing down to the sea again later, the ship was still there. There were even a few dozen Lhosir standing around it. Keeping guard for some reason. Tolvis couldn't imagine what they were doing there but now wasn't the time to be thinking about that. As he and the others approached they waved and shouted and he waved and shouted back, 'Get the ship in the sea! Get the ship in the sea! The Vathen are coming!'

By the time he got to the bottom of the cliff the ship was already out in the surf, the sail rising. That was when he realised these Lhosir were more of Medrin's men, quite sharp enough to see what was coming towards them. Next thing Tolvis knew there were a dozen men on his side and twice that on the other, all with swords drawn and facing each other, with the Vathen coming over the hill in about one minute and the barely living body of Medrin Twelvefingers on the beach between them.

The Lhosir glared at each other. Tolvis closed his eyes. 'Really? Do we have to? I mean, right here and right now?' Medrin Twelvefingers? He'd be Medrin Sixfingers now.

No one moved.

'Well I don't know about you lot, but I've got an errand to run before we all kill each other. Let me know how it ends.' He turned his back on the lot of them and walked away. Then he remembered the Vathen and ran instead. He didn't look back.

EPILOGUE
VARYXHUN

Arda's hand still smarted from where she'd slapped Fenaric. She'd slapped him two days ago. Quite a slap then.

She sighed. More of a punch really.

He wasn't going to come back. Not this time. He'd still got half the money she'd made from selling the horses. *Her* money but she couldn't quite make herself get worked up about it the way she ought to. *Scheming little thief.* But Fenaric was only trying to do what he thought was right for her. Just couldn't get it into his thick head that she didn't want what anyone else thought was right for her. She wanted ...

She wanted *him*. Stupid pig-headed bloody-minded selfish forkbeard Gallow. She wanted him. And she was slowly realising that she wasn't going to get him.

Word of the battle of Andhun made its way up the river in bits and fragments: the Lhosir had been wiped out. They'd beaten the Vathen. Sometimes both, sometimes neither, and all said with gleeful joy. Andhun had fallen and then it hadn't. Stories were like that. Rubbish mostly, but if she was putting all the stories together right, whatever had happened had been bloody.

Stupid man hadn't been supposed to do anything except take his stupid vicious bastard Widowmaker half-friend or whatever he was back to his own kind. Half-friend? Hadn't even looked like *that* most of the time.

Stupid man. Stupid.

She had to stop for a moment to wipe her eyes. Stupid smoke from the stupid forge that Nadric could barely use any more making her eyes water all the time. At least he had that set up now. Maybe they had some chance of making a little money again and not starving when it came to winter.

Stupid men. Both of them. Leaving her with their children to look after and not coming back again. Something in the air up here near the mountains. Must be. Eyes seemed to water a lot since they'd come here.

'Arda Smithswife?'

She jumped and looked up at the ugliest forkbeard she'd ever seen. One side of his face was a mass of scarring, red and fresh.

'Who wants her?' He wasn't the first to have made his way this far south.

The forkbeard held out a purse. 'My name is Tolvis.'

The name meant nothing but the purse had her eyes. 'And what do you want, Tolvis from across the sea?'

He tossed the purse to her. 'I came here to give you this. A debt owed to Gallow Truesword.' He might have turned and gone after that and she might have let him too, since if Gallow had been alive he'd have delivered the purse himself; and then she could have beaten him around the head and cursed him roundly for taking so long and leaving her in the hands of that miserable carter who'd turned out to be far less of a man than she'd thought. But there was a hesitation to him, and to her too, as if there was more to this story than a bag of silver.

So she brought him inside and offered him goat's milk and cheese, both of which he took with unusual grace for a forkbeard. In his turn he gave her an axe. Gallow's axe, and she knew for sure then that Gallow wasn't coming back.

'You were a friend, were you?' she asked. 'Or did you loot his body?' But not that, or why come all this way to hand her a bag of silver? Yes, and she could see she'd insulted him. 'I'm sorry,' she said. Probably the first time she'd ever said sorry to a forkbeard.

He told her about Gallow and how it was his fault that Gallow hadn't come home, and of the crossing of the sea and the Crimson Shield and the fight with the Vathen and then in Andhun and what he'd done and how he'd finally come to his end.

'You were in his thoughts.' Tolvis had a distant look in his eyes. 'Always. That was always what he wanted just as soon as he'd made everything right. To come back to you.'

'Bloody idiot didn't though, did he?' Stupid eyes watering again. Stupid mountain air. 'So he died thinking it was me then, did he? Who gave him away to the Vathen?' Almost more than anything else, that was what she couldn't bear.

'The Screambreaker told him otherwise.' Tolvis smiled. Or tried to, as best his ruined face would let him. 'And Gallow believed him. And I'll not ask.'

She couldn't stop the tears. Had to look away. 'Bloody idiot,' she said again.

'Not the only idiot either.' Tolvis laughed and shook his head. 'Well I didn't have anything better to do, what with Medrin's men taking the only ship we had and leaving us on the beach and the Vathen hunting all over for us. So I went back. Last place they'd look. They were all a bit mad, mind you, on account of some crazy Marroc managing to fire the bridge across the Isset. The air stank of fish oil for days, but I think it was the bridge collapsing into the river that upset them rather than the smell.' He sighed and a perplexed look furrowed his face. 'They searched the beach for Gallow's body, you know, and for the sword too. I watched while they waited for the tide to go right out. They searched and searched, then and every low tide since, and for all I know they're searching still.' He grinned. 'Man jumps off a fifty-foot cliff into the sea in mail, he generally sinks right quick to the bottom by my reckoning. Same goes for swords. But they never found him and they never found Solace. The sea took them. Took him away and maybe washed him up somewhere and maybe didn't.'

He got up and she let him go, but when he was at the door and the wretched mountain air had stopped blurring everything for a moment she told him he could stay if he wanted. It was a long journey he'd come, and Varyxhun was a bit full of Marroc running from the Vathen just now, and he'd pay far more than he ought for a place to sleep, if a forkbeard could find a place at all, and that was hardly fair considering why he'd come. And the Lhosir Tolvis, he said well maybe, because he could do with a couple of days without there being Vathen in the morning and Marroc in the afternoon and brigands in between and all of them trying to kill him.

'Forkbeard wants it easy?' she mocked.

'Yes,' said Tolvis without any bitterness but maybe a touch of the wistful. 'Sometimes a forkbeard does.'

Pug-ugly scar though she thought to herself when he went to get his horse. But she was smiling as she thought it, and that was good, because there hadn't been any smiles for a while.

And Tolvis Loudmouth stayed, for a while at least. After all, the Vathen still hadn't crossed the Isset and likely wouldn't for a while now, so he was hardly going to miss anything. But mostly he stayed because he could have sworn that the very last time he'd looked back as he'd run from the hail of Vathan spears and arrows, he'd caught a glimpse of a boat amid the waves and some old Lhosir soldier hauling something big and heavy out of the water.

Or maybe that had just been wishful thinking, because the next time he looked the boat had been gone. But yes, he stayed a while in Varyxhun just in case, because if Gallow Truesword wasn't drowned after all then sooner or later this was where he'd show his face.

PROLOGUE
THE RAKSHASA

The gods had sent Oribas away from his home, out to the edge of this ocean of sand where it met the sea at the far fringes of what the Aulians had once called their own. They were mocking him for the audacity of asking for their help but he'd come anyway because he had nowhere else to go. He'd not expected to find anything except perhaps a snake with a novel poison or else a slow death from thirst and hunger.

He stared along the beach. An hour ago he could have looked either way for miles along the flat sands and the barely restless waters and seen nothing, not a single thing. It had been like that for days.

But now it wasn't. He quickened his pace. Something was on the sand. Something large. A chest, perhaps, washed up by the sea and wrapped in seaweed. *Filled with the treasure of the gods?* He laughed at himself. More likely it was the half-eaten corpse of some giant sea creature or a piece of a wrecked galley.

But it wasn't either of these things. When he came closer it was a man. Two arms, two legs. Surely dead so not much use, but wrapped in armour of metal rings. Maybe he had a use for that? The man was clinging to the remains of a mast or tree trunk, his arms still wrapped tight around it. He was lying on a shield and his hand was clenched tight around something that hung from his neck.

Oribas rolled the man over and his eyes grew wide. As

well as his shield the man was clutching a sword. A strange dark reddish steel, unusual but a fine weapon. Oribas reached down to take it.

Under the bright desert sun the man's eyes flicked open.

ACKNOWLEDGEMENTS

When Simon Spanton, who commissioned this and with whom I war perpetually on the subject of prologues, called me up to ask if I could do it, he didn't know I was surrounded by Vikings at the time. If there are a lot of axes in this, that's probably why. So thanks to Simon for his endless faith, sometimes rewarded and sometimes not, and to Marcus Gipps for his editorial work, and thanks to all the crazy people who thought the best way to spend a week in February was to strut though York in mail carrying an axe.

Thank you too for reading this. As always, if you liked this story, please tell others who might like it too.

ACKNOWLEDGEMENTS